"I left minutes before the hellhounds caught my scent," Nero said, with a starry look in his eyes. I would bet his heart was going pitter patter and butterflies were fluttering in his stomach. "I met with her since only briefly."

"You love her," I said.

"Yes," Nero answered with a combination of shame and delight. Makes sense. Grace would be his only forbidden fruit.

"So to sum up, despite being born of Hell and raised to destroy the world, ye find ye have no desire to actually hurt anyone," said Paddy.

"Sort of ruins both heredity and environment arguments," I said.

"To top it off, you are in love with your sworn enemy and the end of the world is scheduled to begin in three days."

"That's about it."

"Now let's see what we can do to change all that," Paddy said.

"It cannot be changed. Destiny is immutable."

"I do so love a challenge," said Paddy. At that moment Rainbow escaped Demeter again, leaping upon the bartop before he realized its lack of friction. Plopping on his bottom with his front legs outstretched the goat slid the entire length of the bar, scattering glasses in his wake before plunging to the floor with a crash.

"If you want a challenge, how about keeping that goat under control?" asked Dion.

"I do have my limits you know," he answered with a chuckle.

"You have just learned the world as you know it is about to cease and you are worried about a goat?" asked Nero incredulously.

"Which is the more immediate threat?"

"The goat, I guess."

"Exactly. It is all a matter of priorities. How does it begin?" Paddy asked Nero.

"Well, a nanny goat is standing in a field, then the billy goat comes along," Nero explained, grinning.

"No. Not the goat. The Apocalypse."

"Not much that will be seen by the general public. Grace opens the first seal of the Book of Seven and it begins."

MURPHY'S LORE:™

TALES FROM BULFINCHE'S PUB

PATRICK THOMAS

PADWOLF
PUBLISHING

PADWOLF PUBLISHING INC.
457 Main Street, #384
Farmingdale, NY 11735

www.padwolf.com

Padwolf Publishing & logo are registered trademarks of Padwolf Publishing Inc.

Cover art Burt Wood

Book Edited by Diane Raetz and Ann Herndon.
Copy Edited/Proofread by Ian Randal Strock

ISBN: 1-890096-07-5

Printed in the USA. Second printing.

FOR NANA AND SHORTIE

THE PUB LIST

RAINBOW'S END

My target was in sight. For three days I searched, fearing I had lost both him and all hope in the teeming masses of Manhattan. Today, the fates decide to smile on me. Now I almost had him. In other words, I got lucky.

Better late than never.

The old gentleman's height made him hard to track through the crowds. Everyone else, except the children, towered above him. As I strained to keep up, I was occasionally rewarded with a glimpse of white hair or a thick mustache. He might not have known I was following him, but he acted as if he was trying to elude somebody. He wove in and out of crowds with the ease of a master. How, I wondered, was I going to capture, let alone hold onto him? I questioned myself, "Is what I am doing even right? Do I still give a damn about right and wrong after what happened to Elsie?" My questions gave me one answer: I had to capture him or Louis Dent and his boys would make sure I saw my dead wife again. Soon.

He made a sharp turn and hopped over a baby stroller as he headed down into Penn Station. I saw signs for the LIRR and Amtrak tracks. For a moment, I hoped he was leaving the city. It would make what I had to do that much easier. No crowds. Of course I had no such luck. The fates were fickle that way. He passed the outbound trains and went toward the Jamaica–bound E line of the subway.

With a speed that belittled his years, he hustled through the turnstile and I almost lost him as I had to stop to buy a token. No train came before I found him again, so we hurried up and waited as time trickled by. The moment wasn't right yet. I had waited this long; a little longer wouldn't hurt. As I hid my face behind a newspaper, I casually observed him. I was so preoccupied that I didn't notice I had the paper upside down until a train arrived. Once it stopped we and scores of others boarded the rush hour train. People were packed in so tightly that I should have been engaged to the women on either side of me. I wondered how old the tall one's appendix scar was.

Instinctively, I grabbed hold of the pole in the middle of the car. Not that I needed to, mind you. Even if I passed out my body would be held upright until at least the next stop.

The feeling of pressure on my chest lessened when I timed my inhaling with my neighbor's exhaling. It also prevented me from crushing anyone.

Casually, I glanced over at the old man. He was very old, if the legends are to be believed. My gaze was met by a steely one. He intimidated me far too easily. Seeing this, his stone face lit up with a smile. He knew! The game was afoot and the level had just gotten more difficult. He'd been playing his entire life, while I was still new, so he had the advantage. But I was still going to give him a run for his money.

I expected him to bolt at the next stop. He didn't. Instead, more people packed in, moving him away from the door. He knew enough to stay out of my reach. I tried to get in range, but he melted through the crowds to reposition himself an equal distance away. I was no better off than when I started.

The train sped through the underground tunnels, the walls whipping by. All the old man did was smile and whistle a happy tune. He was trying to show me that he didn't take me seriously. I realized that he wanted to make me angry so I'd mess up. I vowed that it wouldn't work.

Suddenly the world went black. The lights in the car had all gone out. Typical NYC Transit Authority. There was nothing to worry about. Then I noticed the whistling had stopped. My pulse began pounding as I waited for the lights to come back on. "Come on," I thought. "Somebody fix them already." He and his kind are famous for stunts like this.

After what seemed to be an eternity, illumination was restored. It was just as I had feared, the old man vanished. I searched frantically, to no avail. The train was slowing. We were coming up to the next stop. I watched as people exited the train. I didn't see him. Out of the corner of my eye, I caught a glimpse of him in the next car over, waving to me mockingly as he stepped out on to the platform. I pressed my way toward the exit but the doors began to close. Luckily, another commuter on the outside grabbed hold of the doors. He wanted in. Good. I wanted out. With as much grace as I could muster, I plowed my way though everyone between me and the door.

"Getting off," I explained to nobody in particular. I almost knocked two people down but, other than a few curses, my actions went unnoticed.

Adding my efforts to those of the gentleman on the platform we managed to keep the door from fully closing. There was barely enough room to slide a newspaper through. The doors opened and we switched places, each passing the other a smile, a rarity in a sea of unfriendly faces. It's sad, but sometimes the city can really wear you down.

My legs carried me as fast as they could in the direction the old man had headed. The path led me to the uptown and downtown 6 subway. I heard a train in the distance. I had to choose which way to go. I picked, and as I reached the platform, the train doors began to shut. Accelerating, I threw myself through them, barely making it in time. I took a moment to catch my breath.

My search was fruitful. I found the old man three cars down from where I got on. I hid one car away. Best to let him think he had given me the slip. I stayed close to the door so that when he got out I was able to follow. The platform was practically deserted. I slowly inched up behind him. The old man had grown careless. He was totally unaware. It was now or never. I grabbed him in a head lock.

"Got you!" I cried in triumph.

"So you have, laddie. But can ye be keepin' me?" he questioned, a big smile wrapped around his face. In response, I tightened my grip. His struggling availed him naught, which I guess answered his question. He tried an elbow to the groin but I side–stepped it. I had enough of his foolishness; it was time to get down to business.

"I guess you know what I want," I said.

"Of course. It's in me back pocket," the old man informed me.

"What?" I exclaimed, very confused.

"Me wallet of course. Isn't that what all muggers want?" he asked. "Help, police," he added as an afterthought.

"No, it isn't your wallet I'm after and you may as well save your breath. Calling for a cop in New York is like asking for a snowball in the Sahara."

"Oh really?" answered an amused voice from behind me. A nightstick tapped me on the shoulder. My stomach began doing twists and turns as I attempted to come up with a reasonable excuse for my actions.

"I think you are being a bit too harsh on New York's Finest, not to mention that gentleman's windpipe," stated the police officer behind me. "Now, how about doing this the easy way and letting him go."

Damn. Where was he the two times I was mugged? I slowly turned around and when I saw the cop I received my answer. His head was haloed by the bright lights of a food shop. Of all the stupid moves I could have made; I grabbed him in front of a doughnut store.

Had to think fast.

"My friend here was choking..."

"And you decided to close his windpipe the rest of the way. Let go, now," he demanded. He couldn't understand what was involved. This was probably my last chance. I had come too far to turn back.

"No," I said.

"Okay, the hard way it is," he said. Before I could react, he had my arms behind my back. As he pushed me down to the platform floor, the cold steel of handcuffs closed around my wrists. The little man laughingly made for the station exit.

"You'll never be getting it now," he yelled mockingly as he ran up the stairs.

He made his way out onto the streets of the East side. A song was on his lips, a smile was in his heart and every few feet he would stop to dance a little jig as he made his way through the city streets.

"I haven't lost it. That one thinks he can be catchin' me? Better men have tried," he said as he slowed to perform a few dance steps. That's when I jumped him.

"Oh, I don't know about that," I added as I handcuffed his hands behind him, demonstrating a move I had learned just minutes before. I dragged him off into a nearby alley. This time there was no doughnut shop in sight.

"What? You! How did you get away from the officer?" he stammered. I noticed his brogue was suddenly not as thick.

"Wasn't that hard. I said you lost a bet with me and refused to pay up. I was just trying to get my money. Your behavior as you made your exit helped my credibility. If you wanted to get rid of me, you should have stuck around to press charges. He had to let me go. He had no case." And he didn't notice me keeping his handcuffs. Made me feel real safe.

"Now you and I have some unfinished business. No games this time."

"Perhaps if you be tellin' me what ye be wantin'?" The brogue was back.

"What else, leprechaun?"

"Me pot o' gold."

"You got it, me bucko."

"Ye caught me fair and square. By the rules I have to give ye what ye be wantin' if it is in my power to do so."

Unbelievable! It was true! My troubles are almost over. I can pay off Dent and my kneecaps will sleep easy again.

My kneecaps will sleep okay, but what about the rest of me? Can I live with myself after stealing from a man who has never done me any harm to pay off a man who has made my life a living nightmare?

For several seconds a wrestling match ensued between my conscience and my survival instinct. The stronger of the two soon pinned the other for the count. I did the only thing I could. I uncuffed him.

"What are ye doing?" he asked, as a look of shock spread across his freckled face.

"Letting you go. I can't go through with it. I'm sorry for putting you through all this. Keep your gold. I wouldn't feel right taking it. Elsie wouldn't have wanted it this way."

"My thanks for your mercy. You played the game well," said the little man. "Who is this Elsie you speak of?"

"She is, was, my wife. "

And where be she now?" he asked.

"She passed away two months ago from leukemia," I sadly replied.

"You loved her very much." He didn't ask it as a question but instead stated it as a fact. I nodded my head. He continued.

"Is your name John Murphy?"

"Yes," I said, it suddenly being my turn to be shocked. "How did you know that?"

"Allow me to maintain some mystery. Forgive my poor manners. My name is Padriac Moran—Paddy to my friends," he said as he debated whether or not to trust me enough to offer me his hand. He decided to and we shook. I quickly let go so as not to make him nervous.

"Well, Paddy, it's nice to meet you. My friends call me Murphy or Murph. Only people who ever called me John were Elsie and my parents."

"Glad to know you, Murph," he said. He then did the strangest thing. Licking the index finger of his left hand, he held it above his head for about thirty seconds. He muttered something about the barometric pressure being just about right, smiled and looked me right in the eyes. A good trick considering I was more than a foot taller than he was.

"John Murphy, I think I may be able to help you. Be out on that corner in exactly one hour. I'll send one of my people with a message for you."

"You want to help me? I don't know what to say."

"Then shut up. Hey, look up there!" he said as he pointed toward the sky. "A flock of turtles."

Like a fool, I looked. I knew it wasn't the right time of year for turtles to migrate, but I looked anyway. When I turned back around, he was gone. Disappeared into thick air—the smog was bad that day. I wondered why hadn't he done that when I was chasing him?

A drop fell on my nose. One fell on my ear, another on my chin. Soon whole groups were bombarding me. The sky opened and it began to pour.

I spent the better part of the next hour sitting in a coffee shop watching the street outside. Every cab became full as wet people scurried into them. Five minutes before the hour was up I stepped back onto the corner. The deluge was letting up. I stood alone one moment, trying to look inconspicuous. The next, a voice from behind let me know I was no longer the only fool standing in the rain.

"Greetings, John Murphy." I turned to greet him. I was expecting one of the little people, or the gentry, as my grandfather used to call them, but this man was six foot two, draped in a gray trenchcoat, and wearing a baseball cap. Brown, curly hair flowed from beneath the cap, ending just above his shoulders. On his feet were red high–top sneakers and before the trenchcoat wrapped itself around him, I swore the shoes sported wings.

"Greetings yourself. And who might you be?" I asked.

"I might be anyone. At the moment I am acting as messenger for my employer. Paddy Moran asks you to look towards the heavens for your salvation."

"Huh?" I said eloquently. Did he want me to convert to some religion?

"Which word didn't you understand?"

"You want me to look at the sky?" I asked. He nodded, vaguely bored.

Looking up, I did as he asked. There was nothing different about the skyline, save a stunning rainbow that stretched across it.

"I don't see anything."

"Yes, you do," he told me. Apparently he knew what I was seeing better than I did. Maybe he moonlighted as an optometrist.

"You mean the rainbow?" I guessed.

"Bingo. And you did it with no help."

I looked at the rainbow. I waited for something to happen. Nothing did. Maybe I needed to click my heels three times, but I don't look good in red pumps; makes my ankles look fat.

"Now what?" I questioned. My companion rolled his eyes back in exasperation.

"Follow it."

"Sure, no problem," I answered sarcastically. Ever try to follow a rainbow? Great way to kill an afternoon.

Seems easy enough in theory but I have tried to follow rainbows in the past, back when I was a kid, and I could never find the end.

"How?"

"Take a cab."

"Not only do you want me to follow a rainbow, but you expect me to find a cab in New York City after a major downpour?"

With a look of exasperation on his face, he stepped out into the middle of traffic, holding a hand out like one of the Supremes, his body immobile. I gritted my teeth and averted my eyes, expecting him to become roadkill. Instead, a taxi stopped. On top of that, it was empty; probably the last unoccupied cab in Manhattan. Opening the door, he gestured me inside.

"There is one other thing," I whispered in a confidential tone, embarrassed by the lint filling my pockets, "I don't have enough money to pay for a taxi."

"I know," he said as he handed me a wallet. Opening it, I saw my own face staring back at me from my driver's license photo.

"Hey! This is mine," I screamed as I checked my pockets for anything else that might be missing. When had he had taken it?

"Consider the extra fifty dollars a loan from Paddy. Make sure you get him a receipt for the cab ride. He is very particular where money is concerned."

I opened the worn leather wallet and, sure enough, inside were five tens next to the four dollars that were there earlier. I turned to say thanks but all I saw were two red high top sneakers and the bottom of a gray trenchcoat fly up past the taxi window. Jumping out of the cab, I looked up but he was gone. I got back into the cab a very confused man. None of what happened fazed the cabbie in the least.

"Where to, Mac?" he asked. What do I tell him? What the hell.

"Follow that rainbow."

"Okay, but you pay gas and tolls."

Fifteen minutes and three near death experiences later (those who have ridden in a New York City cab will understand what I mean), we found the end of the rainbow. . . and its name was Bulfinche's Pub. A small rainbow which ended in a pot of gold that looked remarkably like a full shot glass was painted over the front window.

"That'll be $17.20," said the cabbie. I gave him two tens and told him to keep the change. I also got a receipt.

To the naked eye (mine never did dress) it looked like an ordinary bar. My first clue something was different was a red sign in the window that said "Sorry, We're Open". I walked in and crossed the hardwood floor. Hey, if nothing else I could get a beer. The difference between being inside and outside was tremendous and instantaneous. As soon as I set foot inside the door all sound from outside ceased. No traffic, horns, or sirens. I thought I had gone deaf. I also was overwhelmed by feelings of warmth and comfort. It felt warm and fuzzy, like home. No place had done that for me since Elsie passed on.

The bar stood in front of a middle–aged man with dark hair and a beard. The man, not the bar. He was a bit large around the middle. I guessed he was the bartender. The fact that he was giving out drinks helped me more than a little in my deduction. As I approached, his face grew even more jovial, as if I were an old friend he hadn't seen in years.

"What will you have?" he asked.

"How about a beer?"

"No thanks, don't touch the stuff. Besides, I'm working," he joked. "May I suggest the house brand? We make it here."

"Sure." No sooner had I spoken than a mug appeared beneath the tap. It was soon filled and slid across the bar to stop in front of me.

"Thanks. How much do I owe you?"

"Nothing. Tradition at Bulfinche's. First drink's on the house."

"What's to stop someone from coming in at different times and saying it was their first visit?"

"Nothing except pain of death or being stripped down to the bare necessities and being left in the South Bronx. But I'd know. I didn't need to ask you, did I?"

"No I guess you didn't," I said.

"By the by, my name is Dionysus."

"Like the Greek god of wine? Great name for a bartender. My name's Murph."

"Glad to know you, Murph. What brings you to Bulfinche's?"

"Oddly enough, a rainbow."

"Let me guess, for some reason or another, you decided to follow a rainbow and it ended here."

"Yup. How'd you know?"

"Happens all the time. Usually to someone who needs help. Now all we do is find out what your problem is and what we can do to fix it. A favorite pastime of ours."

"Never mind, Dion. This one is mine," said a familiar Irish voice behind me. Paddy walked around to the other side. He appeared only a few inches shorter than Dionysus. Looking over the top, I saw the reason. He stood on a platform that ran around the inside of the bar.

"So you're the one who caught Paddy. Good job Murph. You are the first to catch him in about thirty years. The old boy from Erin has been getting sloppy."

"Sloppy? What do you mean sloppy?" Paddy questioned indignantly.

"Do you need details? You have been going out and taking the same path two, maybe three times a month. Besides, the fact that he nailed you speaks for itself."

"Bah," spat the Irish one.

"That you let him go impressed us all," said Dionysus as he halted his teasing of Paddy.

"When it came right down to it, I couldn't," I admitted.

"Wouldn't have done you any good if you could," said Paddy. "My pot of gold is safe from the hands of thieves. Protected by law, now, it is."

"I thought you had to give it to whoever caught you."

"True, but they might find it a bit too heavy to carry."

"What do you mean?"

"You're sitting in it," grinned Dionysus. "Paddy invested his pot of gold in the bar years ago. The rules say he has to bring you to his gold, not that he has to give it to you. And the law protects him from you trying to take his bar. Besides, no one would believe you. If you pushed it you'd end up in a padded room at Ringvue Hospital. Paddy could always pass it off as a publicity stunt for the bar."

"Sounds like you got it all worked out."

"It took the better part of a few centuries, but I can rest easier now. That is, if I could find some decent help to run the place," Paddy said, smiling at Dionysus.

"Oh dear me. No one seems to have come in the bar for me to serve in the last five minutes. Perhaps I should run out into the street and drag some passersby in. Would that please you, oh mighty one?"

"Give it a try. If it works, I'll get back to you," Paddy replied. Dionysus laughed, and walked down to the end of the bar, where a customer had come in and sat down. He was a priest dressed, all in black with the traditional white collar. He looked familiar.

"At least he's finally doing some work," quipped Paddy.

"If he is such a goldbrick, why do you keep him on?"

"Are you kidding? I make the beer and whiskey, but he makes the most incredible wine and ambrosia this side of the Styx."

"Is he a leprechaun like you?"

"Weren't you listening? He told you who he was."

"You mean he's a god?" I asked in disbelief.

"Of course. I hire only the best. And you already met Hermes."

Greek gods working for a leprechaun? The messenger of Zeus running errands for a bartender? Only in New York.

"Hello, Mr. Murphy," said the priest who had slid down the bar to sit next to me.

"Does everybody here know my name?" I asked, reminded of a song about a TV bar.

"You don't remember me, do you?" he asked. I knew I had seen him before, but I just couldn't place where. It wasn't from church. I was a lapsed Catholic and hadn't been to mass in years.

"Should I? No wait, let me guess. You are Saint Peter and you just popped down for a drink."

"Ha. No, I couldn't be St. Peter. He never comes in on Thursdays," he said. I couldn't tell if he was serious or not.

"I'm Father Mike Ryann. I visited you and your wife about two months ago."

I remembered. He was the priest who gave Elsie her Last Rites about a week before she died.

"I'm sorry, Father. I had forgotten."

"No reason to apologize. You were going though a rough period. I'm sure you still are. If you ever want to talk, I'm available, day or night."

"We all are," added Paddy.

"Part of both our job descriptions," added the good Father.

I thought about it. I hadn't talked to anyone about Elsie's death. Keeping everything inside was definitely becoming unhealthy. I needed to spill my guts, and I got the definite feeling these guys wouldn't complain about the mess. Trust and caring emanated from every face I saw.

I thought, *just tell them about Elsie. It should be so easy. But it's not. The memories are still painful.* Somehow I just couldn't pass up the opportunity to talk about the woman who was my life. Maybe it was just that I was in a room filled with friendly strangers that made it a little bit easier. They say sometimes it's easier to talk to strangers. Or maybe it was the beer. Didn't really matter. Everything inside came pouring out of my tap into their pitcher.

"No words could do Elsie justice. She was the most incredible woman I have ever known or will ever know. Elsie's smile could light up a room. Her eyes sparkled, and they had the power to see deep into people's souls. Somehow, she always found good in everyone; even me. Painting was her calling. Her portraits captured the very essence of her subjects. They are incredible," I said proudly.

"We met here in New York. I was a struggling writer, she a starving artist. The first time we saw each other was magic. Something clicked. It was like we had always known each other. It was love at first sight. We married so we could travel toward forever together. But our journey was interrupted by that damn disease. She fought the good fight against her leukemia for over four years. When she went into remission for awhile, we foolishly thought we had won. It was a fleeting victory. She soon grew worse than ever and had to return to the battle."

"We had no insurance. We lived hand to mouth, spending all we had on her medicines and treatments. During her last stay in the hospital our savings ran out. I was working two jobs and I still wasn't making enough. Despite what is said to the contrary, the ones who get quality care are those with money. With no money, nobody wanted to do more than they had to for her. The thought of her getting anything less than the best made me crazy. So crazy, in fact, that I borrowed ten thousand dollars from a loan shark named Louis Dent to pay for her last round of chemotherapy."

"She never faltered, cheerful even when all her hair fell out and her face swelled up. She joked that she looked like a chipmunk after a bizarre electrolysis accident. Elsie comforted me more than I her, I'm sad to say." I paused a moment to regain my crumbling composure. I had some more beer. It was the best brew I had ever tasted and it helped some, but not enough. My eyes were becoming misty.

"When we realized she wasn't going to get better, she decided she wanted to die at home with me. And that was what she did," I said, tears running freely down my cheeks. Dionysus handed me a handkerchief. Father Mike patted me on the shoulder. In their silence they shared my pain and comforted me.

Paddy raised his glass. A tear fell from each eye.

"To love," he said, breaking the silence. "And to Elsie. We hardly knew ye." The bar as one repeated his toast, raised their glasses and drained them to the last. We sat, again surrounded by the silence which had somehow repaired itself in the interim.

Paddy spoke up again, "Murph, you have the pleasure of sitting around with a bunch of busybodies who have nothing better to do than butt into other people's lives and try to help make things a little bit better than how we found them. It's what gods and the Gentry do, or at least what they should. But yours is a special case, because we all knew and loved Elsie, too. She was a regular here for many months before she left us," Paddy said.

I remember her telling me about a very special bar she often went to while I was working. She said the people there had helped her get though some rough times. She had tried to get me to go with her on a few occasions, but I always had an excuse. The truth is that for the little time we had together, I had no desire to share her with anyone else.

"Her own rainbow had led her to us; we all mourn her passing. Her courage and compassion touched each of us. Bulfinche's was a haven where she could spend time when she needed to not be alone. Elsie would sit in here for hours drawing, relaxing, helping others. She spoke often of you. She loved you very much," Paddy said. Elsie's love was something I never doubted, even in my darkest hours, but to hear someone else tell me of it was strangely comforting.

"But if you people are gods, why couldn't you make her better?" I challenged, hoping beyond hope that maybe they could bring her back. Sometimes in myth gods could do that.

"We're gods with a small not a capital g. We are not as powerful or as strong as we once were," said Hermes.

"The gods derive much of their powers from worship and belief. Without a place like Bulfinche's, many of the gods that are out there could not remain on the mortal plane long," explained Paddy.

"I'm the god of physicians, among other things, and if it was within my power to save her I would have," said Hermes. Hanging his head low, he seemed ashamed that he didn't do any better than he did.

"You did your best, my friend," comforted Paddy trying to console Hermes. "You helped her stay in remission as long as she did. I wish she had told me about all her bills. I would have helped out."

"That's something, coming from Paddy. He makes Scrooge look generous," said Hermes.

"Elsie would never burden someone else with her problems, although she would be the first one to take on someone else's. She was forever taking in strays, myself notwithstanding," I said. As I looked at everyone around the bar, I got a feeling of déjà vu. Then the memory struck me. As I was the only witness, I decided not to press charges.

"Holy!" I almost said "Oh my God," but was afraid I might get an answer. "I didn't make the connection before... this is 'Rainbow's End'!"

"Excuse me?" asked Paddy.

"'Rainbow's End'. It was Elsie's last and greatest painting, what she felt to be her masterpiece. I agreed. It was this bar in the painting."

"Elsie painted us? She said she had something special to show us but then she..." The silence hung awkwardly in the air for several moments. Paddy patted the back of my hand and refilled my glass. He tugged at his mustache while staring out the bar's window. His face was saddened.

When Paddy turned back he was all smiles again.

"I have a favor to ask of you, Murphy."

"What?"

"Would you mind bringing the painting here?"

"I don't see why not."

"Good. Any objections to me sending Hermes for it?" he asked. I nodded no. "Give him directions to your apartment and the key." I did as he requested, and the messenger of the gods and a bartender walked out the front door. I turned back to my beer, and before I had finished two fingers worth, Hermes had returned and laid the painting on the bar.

"What took you so long?" I asked sarcastically.

"Had to stop a mugging in Central Park and help out a cat burglar over on Park Avenue," he said. Seeing my confusion over the conflicting nature of his actions, he added, "It's a fine line being the god of thieves and the protector of travelers. I have a tough time deciding which side to help. I stop the thieves who prey on the innocent and help the ones whose plans and schemes impress me."

Without saying a word, Paddy began unwrapping the brown paper from around the painting. He treated it as if it were fine crystal; I appreciated the care he took in its handling. I had wrapped up many of my wife's paintings weeks ago to help preserve my sanity. The memories they invoked were too painful. Having them around made it seem like she wasn't really gone, that she would walk though the door any minute. Hope is wonderful, except when what you hope for is never going to happen.

Everyone gathered around him as he held it up. "Rainbow's End" was as beautiful as I remembered. It depicted a bar with quite unusual patrons, a mixture of men, women, gods and other beings. Behind the bar was Dionysus in a Roman red and white toga, with gold trim. Next to him stood Paddy in traditional green leprechaun garb, cleaning a beer mug with a dish rag. Father Mike sat at the end of the bar sipping a drink, the faintest luminescence around his head. Hermes was there, wearing his winged helmet. What looked like a Norse god, complete with horned helm, was on the stool next to Father Mike. At the door, club in hand, stood a man whose physique put body builders to shame. He had a lion's skin tied around his neck. There were more than a dozen other people in the picture. A large glass window decorated the right hand side of the picture. The lettering on the glass was reversed, but if read through a mirror it said "Bulfinche's". Through the yonder window broke the most glorious, dazzling, Technicolor rainbow ever to grace the sky: it seemed to shimmer. The painting seemed almost alive.

"Incredible. Never have I seen its like," said Dion.

"Nor I. Not even in ancient Athens or in Italy during the Renaissance," said Hermes. Everyone nodded agreement.

"Murphy, I have a proposition for you. I want to buy "Rainbow's End"," said Paddy.

"I'm flattered, but sell Elsie's painting? I don't know if I could."

"I'll give you ten thousand dollars," As one, Bulfinche's patrons turned toward him and gave him a dirty look. "Okay, twenty thousand," he said reluctantly.

Twenty thousand! I could pay off Dent and have extra besides. My worries would be over.

"Paddy, what would you do with the painting if I sold it to you?"

"Hang it over the bar," he said as he cleared away three pictures hanging there. One showed him with the Pope, another with the Dalai Lama, and the third with the present mayor of New York.

"I don't know why, but I get the feeling that this is where Elsie would have wanted the painting to be. Mr. Moran, you have yourself a deal, as long as I can have visitation rights."

"Deal."

"Do you want to draw up a contract or a bill of sale?"

"Nope. In this case a handshake will do. Now unless I miss my guess the first thing you are going to want to do is pay off this loan shark."

"True." I wanted to stop looking over my shoulder for a pin–striped dorsal fin.

"I would like to offer you the services of my bouncer," he said. "Hermes, go wake him up," Hermes nodded and went though a door behind the bar. I heard him going up stairs. "Now how much did you originally borrow."

"Ten thousand."

"And how much have you paid him so far?"

"Three thousand plus he took a watch my wife had given me on our wedding night instead of a payment one week. It had belonged to her grandfather."

"So you owe him seven thousand."

"Not exactly. That was just the interest payments."

"Just pay him seven thousand."

"Paddy, I appreciate you helping me, but if I try to pull that stunt, he'll still cause me some serious pain."

"No, he won't. We'll see to that," said Paddy. As we spoke I could hear large, thundering footsteps above us. They continued on down the stairs. The door behind the bar swung open and out stepped the most muscular man I have ever seen. He was wearing blue sweat pants and a white tank top. I recognized him as the man with the club and lion skin in the picture.

"Urgh," he mumbled.

"He's not a morning person," Paddy explained.

"Morning? It's seven o'clock at night," I said.

"Coffee," the big man stated. Paddy handed him a pot. Before I could say a word the big man had lifted it to his lips and chugged down the entire steaming, hot pot of java without flinching. He then opened his eyes, smiled and said "Ah."

"Glad to see you up and about," said Paddy.

"Why did you wake me at such an unreasonable hour, Paddy? My shift doesn't start until nine."

"I have a job for you to do. Let me introduce you to John Murphy. Murph meet Hercules."

The big man shook my hand firmly. He could have just as easily crushed my metacarpals to powder. I was completely overwhelmed. There was no doubt in my mind that I was shaking hands with the Hercules of legend. As a kid I had read the myths and imagined what it would be like to be him. Somehow the thought of him being a bouncer had never crossed my mind.

Paddy explained the situation. Hercules took everything in.

"Murphy, these gentlemen are prone to violence, carry guns, threaten old women, kick dogs, that sort of thing?" he asked. I answered affirmatively.

"Good," he said with a smile. "Let me go get my working clothes," he said as he went back upstairs. This time I couldn't hear a single footstep. Paddy followed him up. I finished my beer and talked with Dionysus and Father Mike for a while.

When they both returned, Paddy was carrying a briefcase and Hercules was wearing jeans and the lion hide but it looked different. Someone had tailored it into a trenchcoat.

Paddy popped open the briefcase and there was money staring back at me.

"There is seven thousand cash in here. Let Hercules carry it. I'll write you a check for the difference, less the fifty dollars I loaned you, when you get back. I'll also pay the cab fare. You did get a receipt, didn't you?" he asked. I handed it to him and he placed it in a ledger he had brought with him. "Hermes, go with them. Try to keep Herc out of trouble."

So there I stood, a Greek deity standing on either side of me, on my way to confront a mobster who had threatened to do me bodily harm on numerous occasions, and I could only think of one thing.

"Guys, shouldn't we stop somewhere and pick me up a trenchcoat, too?" They did not see the humor.

All too quickly we reached our destination. It was a seedy little dive with not much in the way of ambiance. The drinks were priced three times higher than the rest of the neighborhood and the only way in was with an invitation. Or having business to take care of. We fell in the latter category.

"Johnny, what a pleasure to see you. And early yet. You have my money already. That makes me very happy," said Louis, as he sat puffing on a cigar. He was wearing a shirt and tie. The underarms of the shirt were covered with sweat stains. His belly hung over his belt. If he was a woman, people would be asking him when he was due. He was flanked on either side by two large men in suits. I didn't know their names. He always referred to them as his "boys". The bar we all stood in was known as his "club". It was where he took care of his private business. It decreased the chance of an ambush or a police sting. The metal detector didn't hurt either.

"Yes, Mr. Dent. I have your money. All of it."

"All ten grand? Very good, Johnny. I guess your wife had some life insurance after all," he spoke. Only fear kept me from lashing out at the scum.

"Well, actually not ten..."

"Murph, let me handle this. Louie, I can call you Louie can't I?" asked Hercules. I flinched. The last person who had called him Louie in public had disappeared the next day without a trace. And that was his brother. "I'm here to negotiate on behalf of Mr. Murphy. Perhaps you should take Mr. Murphy outside Hermes, while Louie and I do business," Dent laughed.

"Hermes. Ha! Where'd you get a fag name like that?" Dent taunted.

"From my father," Hermes replied through clenched teeth, obviously not pleased by the mocking of his name. He then went up and shook Dent's hand. "Nice knowing you. The pleasure was all yours."

"Funny guy. Nobody leaves. I don't know who you think you are, wise ass, coming in here and trying to tell me what to do. Johnny, I expected more from you. I thought you was smarter than this. It's time my boys taught you a lesson." I backed away slowly, wondering if apples for his teacher "boys" would make the lesson less painful.

"C'mon, Murphy. It's about to get ugly in here. If it's possible to get any uglier," Hermes said directing his comments at Dent as he led me out the door. I heard two gunshots and turned to rush back in. Hermes stopped me.

"Don't worry. He's been doing this for centuries. Besides, the coat is bullet proof."

Five minutes later it was all over. We went back in to survey the damage. Not a single stick of furniture was left intact. One of the "boys" had been flung across the room, though the wall, and into the next room. The other was hanging from a light fixture on the ceiling. Louie was unconscious, the lower half of his body inserted into a newly formed hole in the floor.

"Wow," seemed the only appropriate thing to say.

"Louie and I were able to reach an agreement before he ... fainted. He agreed to my terms. He won't bother you any more."

"Thank you."

"You're welcome, Murph. Now how about a relaxing stroll through the park on our way back to Bulfinche's?"

I momentarily thought about objecting on the grounds that there were less dangerous ways of committing suicide than going into Central Park after dark. After looking at the remains of Louie's club, that thought quickly left my mind.

"By the way, I believe this belongs to you," Hermes said as he handed me the watch Louie had taken from me in lieu of a payment. He must have lifted it when he shook hands with Dent. I thanked him, but at the same time my hand was checking to make sure my wallet was still in my pocket.

Back at the bar Hercules told everyone the tale, although I personally didn't remember the twenty–five men armed with machine guns who surrounded and threatened to kill us if we so much as breathed. I enjoyed it. He gave Hermes the credit for taking out ten of the bad guys and I supposedly took out four of them myself with my bare hands. By the time he was done, he almost had me believing his version.

Paddy called me aside. He had something on his mind.

"Murphy, I have a proposition for you. Come work for me. From what I've heard from Elsie you're a pretty good bartender."

True enough. My night time job was that of a mixologist.

"Now before you say anything, the job pays well and includes free room and board upstairs," explained Paddy. Bulfinche's was a small building for New York, only fifteen stories, but it gave Paddy a lot of room to put folks up. "You also get health and dental benefits."

"How about profit sharing?"

"Fat chance. There is one other benefit that I think will appeal to you more than the others: being a writer, I think you'll find Bulfinche's a wealth of material. I even have a title for a collection of your work."

"Let me guess. *Bulfinche's Mythology*."

"Nope. Been done already. A couple of fine books, although not entirely accurate. The spelling is different anyhow. How does *Murphy's Lore* strike you?"

I liked it. Paddy also explained that the stories might foster belief, although not worship, in his patrons. Most of them didn't want to be worshiped, anyhow. It was too great a responsibility. If belief increased, so would their power levels. He made only one stipulation: I was not to disclose the exact address.

"They'll find us if they need us," he said.

There was no way I could turn down an offer like that, so I agreed. Paddy poured me a beer to celebrate.

"Next one goes on your tab and will be docked against your salary," he told me with a grin. I got behind the bar. Paddy had hung "Rainbow's End" over it like he said he would. I stopped for a minute to drink in the beer and the art. What I saw in the painting almost knocked me over. It had changed. My gaze caught that of Paddy's. His eyes told me he had seen it, too. There behind the bar, next to Paddy and Dionysus, was me! The rainbow almost seemed to glimmer, and for an instant I thought I saw Elsie's smiling face look down on me. I had no time to ponder because a customer had just sat down in front of me. As I poured him his drink, I knew I had come home.

CLOWN TEARS

I was standing among the little people and they were hiding from me. So were most of the big people. Not that we were doing anything wrong. Just the opposite in fact. The game was hide and seek and I was it. The playing field was the entire bar and restaurant area of Bulfinche's Pub, my place of employ. Yes, I actually get paid to play games and tend bar. A great way to make a living. My name is Murphy. Among the wee folk I was searching for were four children.

The two ladies in the group were Nellie and Shellie, five and nine years old respectively. They were sisters with rich black skin and braided pig tails. Calling them adorable did not do them justice. A ten year old, carrot topped boy named Brian was doing his level best to prove to the rest of us how mature he was. He had me convinced, at least compared to the adult company he was presently keeping. Next was the sweetest kid you ever could meet, name of Peter. Peter had Asian features that were drawn out to almost a caricature by a condition he had called Down's Syndrome. The last of the little people was my boss, Paddy Moran. Paddy, with his white hair, mustache and side burns, clocked in at just under five feet despite his claims to the contrary. The games and the children's presence were in large part due to him. The man loves children, and despite the extremes of his age, acts like a big kid himself. Dionysus, or Dion, as he prefers, was tending bar with Paddy and myself. He claims the main reason Paddy has the children hanging around is that they are the only ones in the bar shorter than Paddy is. Not true. Brian was the same height.

Each of the kids were street children, with nowhere else to go. The girls were left to fend for themselves when their mama, already having relocated her family to a staircase leading from the street outside Bloomingdales to the Fifty Ninth Street number six subway station, died of a drug overdose. Another resident of that stairwell sold them to a flesh broker for two bottles of gin and one vial of crack. Nice guy. Brian was a runaway, fleeing a step father who molested him, a mother who did not believe him, and a system who insisted he stay there because that was where he belonged.

Lastly there was Peter. His father was never home. His mother could not be bothered to look after him. Peter's a relatively bright kid, but because of the Down's, has some lapses in judgment and needs constant supervision. One night after being told to cook his own dinner– a lapse in their judgment–Peter left the stove on. His parents freaked. Rather than being responsible parents, they decided they needed to get rid of Peter. In their culture it was not uncommon to kill newborns who were ill or not male. Peter was too old to harm without involving the law. They couldn't ask for public assistance because they were illegal aliens, so instead they did what is commonly called granny, dumping except Peter was about seventy years younger than the average victim. What happens is a family who cannot or will not take care of a sick, old, or disabled member takes them to a hospital emergency room and dumps them. The hospital then is legally bound to care for that person and find them a place to be discharged to. It is not supposed to be the street, but it often is.

In Peter's case, the hospital couldn't do anything because he was a minor, and therefore a ward of the city. They had him sit in that waiting room for ten hours before someone from social services showed up. No one even watched him. It seems the poor kid slipped between the bureaucratic cracks in the system. By the time the proper authorities arrived he was gone, lured in by the same flesh broker that had snared the girls and Brian. Sometimes the system just doesn't work.

All would have been lost for these kids if not for the force of nature currently sitting at our center table, stubbornly refusing to be drawn into our game. "Utter foolishness," she said, but if one looked closely under the dirt and grime that covered her face, one could see her eyes light up as the children, both young and old, played.

The woman was dressed in rags. They were the finest rags available, mind you. On her they looked natural, down to the kerchief wrapped around her graying brown hair. The woman's name was Rebecca. Never used a last name, but neither do many of our patrons. Rebecca has lived on the streets for decades, despite attempts and offers by Paddy and the rest of the gang here at Bulfinche's. The woman has helped get dozens, maybe hundreds, off the streets in her lifetime. Brought many of them here to Bulfinche's so they could get the help they need. It is that kind of bar with that kind of people. Rebecca has done more good than a dozen social workers. Still she refuses to help herself. The woman is more stubborn than a mule.

"The streets are my home now. They know me and I am their Mama. They are all that is left to me now," she would say and that was the end of that.

If she was the mother of the streets then these four were among her children. She told us the streets whispered to her what was happening to these children. Rebecca, despite her advancing years, made short work of the pimp and rescued the kids from a future of sexual slavery. We heard the pimp may walk again someday. He was brought to the emergency room of the same hospital he snared Peter at and had to wait thirteen hours, in agonizing pain. Sometimes the system does work.

She admits she would have preferred to kill the scum, but out of deference to Paddy, she spared his life. Paddy holds all life sacred, without exception. He will admit to the necessity of killing, but it has to be an extreme case. Even then only with great reluctance.

Rebecca brought the kids here to Bulfinche's. There are lots of reasons for that: We have the room and we have done this before. Paddy and Demeter, our chef, are recognized as foster parents by the City of New York. Paddy greases enough political palms to make our system run smoothly so he can keep the kids until adoptive parents can be found. We coach the kids on what to say to ensure there are no blockages thrown up. In short, they say that they have no living parents, give a phony last name and the like.

This may seem dishonest and it is; but it is better than sending a child home to parents who would molest or would dump him with less respect than most decent people would show a stray animal. This is what happens if they find out the truth. We know. It has happened to us before. A brother and sister they sent back "home" were found beaten to death by their parents. We swore we would never again let anything like that happen to a child. If we have to cheat, lie, or hide a child, so be it.

Today we were having a grand time playing hide and seek. Nellie and Shellie insisted on playing as a single team and had caught me last round. I guess my imitation of a barstool left something to be desired. Now I was the seeker.

You may be thinking this is an odd activity for a bar to be sponsoring, but it isn't. It was late in the morning, traditionally a slow time for a bar, but it was great for business. As lunch time approached business people in their suits and construction workers in their jeans would walk in and see this or another game being played. Sometimes we played even without the kids, but usually with. Before long, one of the children has grabbed the grownup's hands and soon they are hiding as well. Many folks come down and spend their lunch hours playing, getting their food to go. Something more grownups should do. We need to grab joy whenever and wherever we find it. Certainly it cuts down on stress for those who join us. On the weekends many of the folks bring their own kids in to join in the games. More than a few of the kids in the past have been adopted by couples who just stopped in for a drink once and kept coming back until they fell in love with a kid. Peter was one of these lucky children. A lovely couple had already started the paperwork for adoption; they come by every day after work and take him out.

Unfortunately for Peter, his imitation of a seat cushion was no better than mine was of a barstool. I caught him, giggling all the while, but only because Shellie, Nellie, Brian, Paddy, Demeter, and Dion had beaten me to base. Rebecca was feeling overcrowded but still had the girls on one knee and Brian on the other. Dion was asking where he got to sit and Rebecca was directing him to a table on the other side of the room. Dion put his thumbs on the sides of his head turning them into moose antlers and stuck his tongue out at Rebecca in response. Giggling, the three children planted on her lap returned the greeting in Rebecca's defense. Serious, Peter came over and broke it up.

"Go hide! It's my turn!" he cheerfully informed. The assembled obeyed with a smile.

Peter hid his eyes on the side of the table and counted. "Nineteen, twenty. Ready or not here I come."

As he began his search, two clowns walked in the door. No, I was not being mean. My description was accurate; however one was rolling himself in, seated on a wheelchair.

Both were dressed outlandishly; complete with whiteface. The taller of the two, by virtue of standing, had his right eye darkened up in parody of a black eye and his mouth and chin were painted red into a exaggeration of a look of grim determination. He wore giant boxing gloves, a good two feet long and a foot wide. They were fluorescent red. A tooth was blacked out. His thick, curly hair stood straight up. I would describe it as an out–of–control Afro except for the fact it was a brilliant blue. It resembled a toy troll after a trim. He wore huge orange trunks with a black waist band over his pants and a golden rayon robe with hood completed his ensemble

The gentleman seated by his side wore a purple trenchcoat. His long hair was an orange red; perhaps naturally so, held up on the top of his head in a topknot. Small, narrow triangles were painted in black, above and below his eyes. The pair above his eyes each had a stroke going up and toward the middle of his forehead, going over an inch before stopping. The pair below had the same stroke, only heading in the down and out direction, much like the expression on his face.

They both seemed confused at the initial lack of people. The confusion increased when each person they did see was crouched or hiding behind something and telling them to shush.

"Think this is one of those shy people bars?" asked the one in the wheelchair.

"Naw. Probably just trying to avoid paying their tab. The owner will hunt you down for that," said the clown with the boxing gloves. Pretty accurate description of the boss. Must have been here before, although his face was new to me. Well, maybe kind of familiar. I couldn't think where though.

"Why? The prices that bad?"

"No. First drink is on the house, at least the first time round."

"Is it self service?"

"Not usually," said the black–eyed clown, as Peter noticed them and started to-ward them. "Father Mike told me they had hired a new bartender. Maybe this is him. Excuse me son, your name Murphy?"

"No, silly. I'm Peter."

"I'm Rumbles."

"Those are big shoes you have."

"Actually those are not over–sized shoes. It's my feet that are big. Are you here to take our drink orders?"

"No. I'm not old enough yet, but you can have some of my soda. It's over there," he said pointing to a glass on the base table.

"Thanks. I will think about it."

"You're welcome." Touching the clown in the wheelchair's arm he said "Tag. You're it!"

"But I'm not playing."

"Hey, you are not supposed to talk. Can you pretend you are in a box or walk against the wind? I love that," said Peter. The other clown covered his face with the boxing glove, trying to unsuccessfully hide his laughter.

"I'm not a mime, Peter, although I would love to be able to walk against the wind."

"Told you to use flourescent face paint years ago but no, you thought basic black was cool. 'All the rock groups used it.'"

"I was thirteen. I went with the traditional red round nose to get you off my back."

"He made a great horse," Rumbles said to Peter and was rewarded with the laughter of a child.

"If you are not a mime, then why are you dressed like that?" asked Peter.

"I used to be a clown. The all–wise pugilist here thought it would be good for me to relive my past to make way for my future."

"You're still it," Peter informed him. Roy shook his head no.

"C'mon, Roy. You are a clown. Playing with children is what you do," said Rumbles, a mild tone of pleading carried in his words.

"Correction. What I did. Before this," he griped, indicating the chair.

"Fine. Be that way. Peter, my friend is feeling too sorry for himself to play, but I'll take his place. Give me a chance to hide first," said Rumbles, hiding behind his friend's wheelchair, in an exaggerated motion. Rumbles covered his eyes with his oversized boxing gloves, pretending that if he could not see Peter, Peter could not see him. Peter didn't buy it. He tapped the clown on the shoulder and watched as he timidly peeked out from behind the gloves. Peter squeezed his red nose and jumped as it made a honking noise.

"Tag! You're it!"

"So I am. Tell me, how did you find me so quickly?"

"Easy. I'm very good at this game."

"You must be. Tell me, can you get everyone else to come out of hiding long enough for my friend and I to get a drink?" he asked, smiling and waving at Rebecca. She returned the favor in a much less exaggerated manner.

"Sure. Ollie, ollie, oxen free," Peter shouted and out came the rest of us.

"Hey, Rumbles," said Hercules. "Long time no see."

"Too long. The circuit has keep me away from my hometown too long."

"Welcome home," said Paddy, shaking hands or rather hitting fist to giant boxing glove.

"I second that," added Dion.

"You a local boy?" I asked.

"Bronx born and bred. A lucky man I am. Lucky enough to have three homes. One with blood family, another with my circus family and a third with you guys."

"What you drinking?" I asked.

"Vanilla egg cream for me, with a shot of rum," said Rumbles.

"Same for me, only make it chocolate."

"Roy, the docs said no alcohol."

"No, they said watch it. I can handle it."

"Then ye will get it," said Paddy.

"The circus been feeding you okay?" asked Demeter, exchanging a kiss and a hug with Rumbles. "You look a little undernourished. How about I cook you up something?"

"Your cooking? That sounds great, but I can wait until after the game. I don't want to be a bother."

"Time out can be called from the game for a while. You could never be a bother, darling. Sending all of us a postcard from wherever you are, almost every week. Warms an old woman's heart, it does. I hear from you more than I do from my own daughter; I blame it all on my son–in–law." True enough. Her son–in–law, Pluto, was what you might call an underworld character. "Never forgave him for eloping and lying to my little girl. Telling her he invited me but I just didn't want to come."

"How is Persephone?"

"As well as can be expected. She seems happy, but for the life of me I can't figure out why. Their house is always so dark. Mood lighting, they say. Too cheap to put in lights is what I say. No children yet after all these years. I tell her I am not getting any younger. I want to be a grandmother, but alas that is denied me for now. Enough of my problems. Beef stew is your favorite; shall I get you some?"

"That would be heavenly. Thanks."

"You eat beef stew three times a week at the circus. Why would you order the same thing when you eat out?" asked Roy.

"You have to try it to understand. Demeter, could you get an order for my friend, Roy, here?"

"Sure thing. With cornbread?"

"Absolutely," said Rumbles as Demeter retired to her kitchen to work wonders. "Let me introduce my friend. This is Roy G. Biv. Roy. This is Paddy Moran, Dionysus, Hercules, and Hermes. Demeter is the lovely mature lady who is preparing our repast. The lady at the table is Rebecca," Roy shook hands and exchanged greetings with each. "This gentleman and the children, other than Peter, I don't know."

Shellie, Nellie, and Brian all introduced themselves and each bopped Rumbles' glove. My turn came.

"I'm Murphy," I said.

"Glad to know you, Murphy. Father Mike told me a lot of good things about you when we stopped up the block at Our Lady of the Lake to see him before we came in. So sorry to hear about Elsie. She was a lovely woman."

"That she was. Thanks," I said. Since Elsie left this world there is an emptiness in my life that probably will never be filled. Still, part of her lives on in each life she touched. Bulfinche's was a special place for her in the last months. I hated having to leave her alone while I was working to try to get enough money to pay for her medical treatments. The price was too dear, not in terms of money but in time spent apart. Elsie spent much of that time here at Bulfinche's, with friends special enough to be called family. A lot of her lives on here. Not enough to fill the hole in my soul, but more than enough to smooth out the rough edges.

"I'll be in town for two weeks. Perhaps I will come by and together we can reminisce, cry, and toast her memory together."

"I'd like that," I said, finally recognizing his face, I pointed out his likeness in 'Rainbow's End', which now hung proudly over the bar.

"Nice to meet you, Roy," I said.

"Same here, Murphy."

"Interesting name, Roy G. Biv. Tis ye given or taken name?" asked Paddy.

"Given. Why interesting other than as a way of remembering the spectrum?" Roy asked.

"Not only the spectrum but the rainbow. My place has an affinity for rainbows. You may be the first living one we have had walk in the door."

"What do you mean an affinity?"

Peter answered happy. He had just learned the meaning of that word the week before. "Rainbows lead people here so they can find help."

"And why would they do that? Some new advertising gimmick?"

"Oh no. Paddy is a leprechaun. His pot of gold bought Bulfinche's so now rainbows end here," Peter explained.

"Oh, really?" Roy said with a sly, unbelieving smile.

"Yes. And Dion, Hermes, Hercules, and Demeter are all gods."

"What kind of stories you people telling the kids around here? How about some truth?" Roy demanded.

"Okay, Peter exaggerated a bit," said Dion.

"Thank you for admitting it," said Roy.

"Hercules and I are only demi–gods. Our mothers were human," said Dion.

"Leprechauns, gods? And what are you supposed to be Murphy?" snarled Roy.

"The bartender," I answered mildly.

"Open your mind to different ideas and realities," suggested Rumbles.

"Rumbles, don't tell me you believe in these fairy tales?" asked Roy in exasperation. Rumbles merely gave a small smile and shrugged his shoulders.

"Believe in fairy tales," I said. "Especially the happy endings."

"Happy endings? What kind of happy ending is life as a cripple? Can any of you so called deities give me back my legs?"

"Probably not. Rumbles had already called me in to consult on your case. I saw you in the hospital, if you recall," said Hermes.

Roy looked for a minute. "I remember you now. You were different than the other doctors. You were the only one wearing a baseball cap and red high top sneakers with little wings," Hermes was still wearing them. "You spent time with me like my therapists and nurses did. Yours was the most thorough examination I had. You were the one who gave me the good news about the sacral sparing."

I whispered to Rumbles "What's that?"

"Means he can go to the bathroom by himself and still have kids one day."

Roy and Hermes were still talking.

"You also hooked me up with a truly great physical therapist. Pushes me to my limits and then some. Anything else within your power, Doc?"

"Please, just Hermes. Even I have my limits."

"I can accept that. But my legs were my life. It is almost impossible for me to accept the fact that I'll never walk."

"Probably never walk again," said Hermes. "Grant yourself the luxury of hope, but accept that it may never come. A tight rope to walk."

"Should be easy for you, Roy," Rumbles said.

"Don't talk to me about tight ropes."

"Why?" I asked.

"A tight rope did this to me."

"Didn't know clowns walked the high wire," said Dion.

"Normally we don't. Roy is a special case," said Rumbles, slurping his egg cream through a straw.

"I was born into a family of acrobats. I could flip between trapezes before I could walk. I was fourth generation. Not everyone stayed an acrobat, but everyone started out that way. Most who gave up flying through the air left the circus for life as lay people. Me, I was different. I was always a cut up. Had to try and make people laugh. It was in my blood, every bit as much as being an acrobat. Maybe more. Problem was,

I wanted more. I wanted greasepaint and big shoes. I wanted to be a clown. So at thirteen I begged and pleaded with Rumbles to teach me."

"Your parents almost killed me. Acrobats are incredibly strong."

"C'mon. You could have taken on my whole family with one glove behind your back."

"Maybe."

"No maybe, Rumbles. You knocked me down once in a fair fight," said Hercules.

"You knocked down Herc?" I said in amazement. Herc is easily the strongest man I have ever met. We were driving with Ismael Macob, a regular who makes his living as a taxi driver, when he got a flat. Herc changed the tire without benefit of tire iron or jack. Plus, Herc is the bouncer here and I have seen him handle some pretty rough customers. I had my doubts as to whether or not a Mack truck could knock him down. "You must be real good."

"Years ago, I was a golden gloves boxer, before I joined the circus. Gave my mentor the idea for my name and my act. My act is to be belligerent and pick fights with everybody. The strongman, the elephants, the other clowns, you name it. As time went by, I realized the best way to make fun of something is to know it inside out. I was already a good boxer, so I started studying other fighting forms. I have four black belts, two second degrees and one fourth. A few years back I placed fifth in a bid for the US Olympic fencing team. I think the fact I went dressed like this may have cost me third place but I have no regrets. I had only been fencing for six months at the time. Four years later, I took home the bronze medal."

"Despite all that, the man hates to fight," said Roy. "His favorite martial art is aikido. No offensive moves in true aikido. As he tells me, 'It is a sin to hurt someone, so by avoiding violence we do not sin ourselves and by stopping an opponent from hurting us, we prevent him from sinning.' Did more than preach it, though. My parents never attacked him with more than words. They couldn't understand why I wanted to be a clown, not an acrobat. Forbade me even. Did a lot of good, as you can clearly see."

"Roy had quite a tumultuous youth."

"Finally I combined my two loves, satisfying not only my family, but my soul. I was an acrobatic clown. Not unique in and of itself but I was better than most. Then came the day that ended it all. In my act on the high wire I pretended to trip over a banana, fall off the wire only to catch myself by one hand. While trying to get back on the wire I would almost make it before slipping again this time for real. Below a trapeze act, seemingly separate from my own was going on. I would coincidentally be caught, flipped back and forth before 'shakily" being deposited safely on a platform. One problem occurred on the last night I did this. Actually two. Someone moved the banana peel to cover a fray in the rope. I actually tripped over it as the rope broke. No one below was ready for the fall, so no one could catch me. I hit the ground hard. It was all in slow motion, like it was happening to someone else as in a dream. Snap. Pain. Shock. Numb."

"You performed without a net?" asked Dion.

"Not exactly. Dad wouldn't let any of us practice without a net, but the ringmaster and owner felt it was better showmanship to be without one. They compromised. Dad invented a spring loaded net, kept hidden beneath the sand. One of the crew had the job of standing with his hand on the release lever throughout the entire performance. One pull of the lever and the net sprung up, usually in time to catch anyone falling."

"Usually?"

"Every other time but mine."

"The important part is that you survived," said Paddy.

"That is what I have been trying to tell him," said Rumbles. "So have all his counselors. He just don't hear."

"I hear all right. They tell me the reason I am having so much trouble adjusting is that my entire self image and sense of worth are tied in to what I do. Now that I can no longer do what I did, I am cast adrift in the sea of self–awareness or some other clap trap."

"But you can still do what you did," Rumbles told him, perhaps louder than he needed to.

"Right. I can do some serious flips on the trapeze in this chair and ride across the high wire on one wheel."

"I am not talking about the acrobatics. I mean the clowning. I hoped wearing your old togs would bring back that realization."

"Right. People laughing at a cripple in a wheelchair. Real politically correct."

"Actually cripple is out. Physically challenged is the current term, as long as we are being PC," I said.

"Trying to be funny? Leave it to the professionals," Roy spat.

"I would, but you aren't doing a very good job of it," I retorted.

"You think it's easy to be funny?"

"Actually, I do."

"So how should I make you laugh? Start off with a monologue about how at least we get the best parking spaces?"

"That would be a start. Although I must say, it really ticked me off the other day when I saw one of you handicapped guys parking in one of our spaces."

Roy stared at me. Everyone else in the bar began to chuckle, Rumbles loudest of all. Finally Roy cracked a smile. Out of the corner of my eye I saw Peter sneak into the kitchen. Hungry, I guess.

"All right, I see your point."

"Life comes with its share of pain. How ye deal with it, laugh, cry, or go crazy, tis your choice. We do a lot of living, laughing, and crying here," said Paddy. "Feel free to join us."

"Thanks, but not yet."

"Don't give up the now. Tomorrow may never come," offered Dion.

As if on cue, Peter came up behind Roy and yelled "Ta–dah!" His appearance brought tears of laughter to our eyes. Nellie and Shellie had their hands over their faces in the disbelief of the young. Peter had gotten Demeter to help him dress up like a clown. Peter's face was white, covered in flour except for his eyes and lips which were circled in what appeared to be red lipstick. On his nose, a cherry tomato stood precariously perched while half a head of lettuce was tied on his head like a wig. He wore an oversized apron and two large paper bags tied around his feet. In his hands Peter carried a rolling pin and a spatula. He looked ridiculous. And adorable. Paddy took a picture.

"What have we here?" asked Roy.

"I want to be a clown. Just like you and Rumbles. Will you teach me?"

"I think Rumbles would be a better teacher. He taught me."

"Sure. I'll do it. Herc, will you do the honors?" Rumbles asked with a large wink.

"Certainly," Herc replied with a wink of his own. "It would be my pleasure."

The two in exaggerated form began to circle each other as if squaring off. Rumbles, boxing gloves flailing, made the first charge which Herc sidestepped. Rumbles went tumbling across the room. Rising to his feet, Rumbles made like he was a bull, scrapping his feet on the floor, then charged again. He held his gloves high on his head like horns. Instead of sidestepping, this time Herc picked up a metal serving tray off the bar and held it out in front of him. Rumbles hit it head first with a clang, then lurched and twisted around the room. I could almost see the stars and little birds circling his head. Finally he fell to the floor, back down with his feet and legs straight up in the air.

His last words were "Can't do it, Roy. It is up to you." Then he pretended to pass out. Peter ran over to him and shook the clown's shoulders.

"Rumbles, are you okay?" he asked.

Looking straight at Peter he joked, "Mommy, is that you? I don't wanna go to school today."

The kids laughed. Peter turned to Roy and said "Will you teach me to be a clown, Roy? Please?"

"I'm sorry, Peter. I don't do clown stuff anymore."

"Then why are you dressed like that?"

"Rumbles made me."

"That's silly, Roy. Even a kid like me knows nobody can make you do something you don't want to," said Peter. He hastily added "Unless they put a gun to your head or threaten to hurt you. I know. I have had that happen. Did Rumbles threaten to beat you up?"

"No, he didn't."

"Then you dressed up because a part of you still wants to be a clown."

"You thinking about taking up a career in psychoanalysis, Peter?"

"What's that?"

"What you just told me about me."

"You mean people can get paid for that?"

"Yes."

"Great," Peter said grinning from flour covered ear to flour covered ear. He stuck his palm out. "Pay me."

"Paddy, the kid has been hanging around you too long. He's gone mercenary," laughed Dion.

"It warms an old man's heart it does," said Paddy, wiping an imaginary tear from his eye.

Laughing, Roy handed Peter a dollar. "Here you go."

"You can have it back if you teach me."

"No, you keep it. I'm sorry, but I can't teach you."

"Then I think you better just leave. Then take that makeup off and never put it back on again," Rumbles, now standing, said solemnly.

"Rumbles...."

"No. You have had all the chances you are going to get. No true clown could turn down a kid like that. I was terribly wrong about you, Roy, and for that I am sorry. I thought your heart was your greatest asset. I guess it was your legs."

Roy wheeled himself in front of his mentor clown. "But, Rumbles I can't do it anymore," he whined.

"You don't know that. You never even tried. If you had never tried the triple somersault you never would have done it. You were afraid then. Not afraid of falling. It was the failure that terrified you."

"It was you who convinced me to try it. I couldn't do it."

"Not the first time. Or the third. But you kept plugging away and eventually you did do it. In front of an audience no less. But now fear paralyzes you more than your injury. Now you never will know if you could have succeeded. A pity. You were the best I ever trained."

"Rumbles, I'm sorry," Roy was crying.

"I don't want to hear it. Leave. You're embarrassing me," Rumbles voice was cracking. He turned away toward the bar and I saw the clown's tears streaking his face paint.

"Goodbye, Rumbles," he said, rolling toward the door.

"Yea, yea," Rumbles replied. The rest of us kept silent. It was his call. Well almost the rest of us. Peter merely walked over to Roy and took the cherry tomato off his nose and handed it to Roy. Roy looked at it, then at Peter and lastly back to Rumbles, anguish showing even through the long, thin red smile painted on his face. Roy turned as if to leave, then stopped and turned back.

Taking his own red nose off, he said "This is for you Peter," and he tossed the nose. In doing so, he threw off the balance of his wheelchair and fell backwards, screaming. Hercules rushed to help him but Rumbles' restraining hand held him fast. Rumbles was smiling. He never seemed the sadistic type.

Hands on the wheels, Roy propelled both himself and the wheelchair back up to a sitting posture. He didn't stop there. He threw his body forward, looking as if he was almost going to fly face first onto the floor. Again he caught himself, but the momentum never stopped. Soon the chair was spinning and lurching all over the bar, Roy acting every bit the captive of a mad machine imitating a bucking bronco. Finally, he brought the chair under his control. Then he rolled Peter's way. He reached behind Peter's ear in the age old gesture of the magician. I was expecting to see a coin or a bouquet of flowers appear. Neither did. Instead, Roy pulled a rubber chicken out. Peter was amazed. So was I.

Then the rubber chicken tried to 'fly' away; Roy stopped him. The chicken was none too happy over this and let Roy know in no uncertain terms by flailing and attacking him. It was all Roy could do to ward off the blows and it looked like the chicken was going to make soup out of him, but Roy got in a lucky shot which sent the chicken flying to the ground. Roy proceeded to run and back over it with his wheelchair several times. Then lining it up under the small front wheels of his chair, he popped a wheelie, only to crash right down on the rubber chicken's head, again and again like a hammer pounding nails. He paused for a minute and called Peter over. Ears were whispered into, heads nodded, and smiles exchanged.

When Roy next lifted his wheels to smash, Peter darted under them to save the chicken. He then hit Roy over the head with it. After shaking off the effects of the mighty blow, he gave chase to Peter and the chicken, brandishing the traditional weapon of the clown; a seltzer bottle. Peter ran to and fro, stopping directly in front of Rumbles. Roy drew a bead on his target, but at the last second Peter jumped away, leaving Rumbles to get a face full of seltzer. Never have I seen someone so happy to get hit in the smacker with water. Imitating fury, he rushed after Roy, catching him in a choke hold. Flailing his arms, Roy's head swung to and fro. The pair exchanged whispers and again Roy's chair fell over backwards. This time however, it took Rumbles with him, effectively flipping him over. Rumbles rolled about ten feet, head over heels before landing on his head with his feet up against the wall.

Roy was up again chasing Peter, who had chosen to stop in front of Paddy. Paddy is no man's fool. Bulfinche's has been around since the late nineteenth century. We have used lots of different equipment and Paddy hates to throw out anything that still works well. As Roy was taking aim, Paddy pulled out a seltzer bottle of his own, getting first Roy, then chasing Peter. Rumbles, getting a seltzer bottle from who knows where, together with Roy, intercepted Paddy and caught him in a crossfire. Dion and I, with bottles of our own, chased away the two clowns before turning our streams on the old man ourselves. Hercules was lobbing water balloons at the kids as well as the adults. Some of the business men and women were doing the same. Demeter ushered the children quickly into the kitchen. She had something planned. She isn't one to run from a fight. The two clowns had cornered Hermes and were about to soak him when he turned the tables on them and pulled out our fire hose and drenched them. Luckily, the floor has drains in it.

The children had returned from the kitchen bearing whipped cream cans and began spraying the lot of us, starting with Paddy. In actuality, they were herding him toward Demeter, where she stood waiting, banana cream pie in hand. Paddy saw it and stopped short. Not that he wouldn't have stopped tall if he could have.

"Ye weren't planning on using that, was ye, Demeter?"

"Wouldn't dream of it, Paddy."

"Good."

"I would however do it." With that, she slammed the pie into Paddy's face. He simply walked over to the bar and retrieved a spoon. Scooping some of the white off his face with the spoon, he tasted it.

"Not bad. A bit too sweet, though," he said. Criticism of her cooking annoys Demeter more than just about anything but her son–in–law.

"Why, you undersized runt," she said, pulling a can of whipped cream out of her waist apron. Paddy hates jokes about his shortcomings, I mean his height. Despite the words there was genuine love between the pair. Whenever I mention that to them, they agree, then remind me you always hurt the one you love. Within moments, Paddy was cream colored and Demeter was ready for a serious wet tee shirt contest. Meanwhile, Dion and I had joined Herc and the business people at the artillery range, lobbing water balloons.

The kids had teamed up and headed toward the one person who remained out of any confrontation. Rebecca had remained sitting at her table, a calm within the storm. The kids weren't about to let that go unchallenged.

The four surrounded her, creamers at the ready.

"Don't even try it," she said softly. The kids held back a second, hoping someone else would make the first, potentially dangerous, move. They got their wish. As Roy went speeding by, he sprayed the top of Rebecca's kerchiefed head. Her face went from solemn to shock and that was all the children needed to launch their attack. Within moments she looked like a cream–covered snow woman.

They ran expecting an attack, but to everyone's surprise she merely shook her head and said "Kids," before walking toward Hermes to get hosed off.

Eventually the kids ran out of whipped cream and the clowns ran out of seltzer. We still had water balloons and Hermes still had water pressure, but there comes a time when all things wet and wonderful must stop.

The crowning moment was a hug between Rumbles and Roy.

"I knew you could do it," said Rumbles laughing, lifting Roy up out of his chair in a hug that would crush a bear.

"You jerk! That was the same tactic you used to get me to try the somersault. Now please put me down," asked Roy. Rumbles lowered him down gently.

"It worked, didn't it?"

"Yes. With no small amount of help from this young man," Roy said, referring to Peter. "And as my way of saying thanks, how would you like to come to the circus tonight?"

"That would be great," said Peter, soggy and glowing.

"I have a better idea. Why don't you both come and be in the circus tonight. We can work this bit in," said Rumbles.

"You mean it?" asked Roy.

"Yep. Needs some polish, but we have time," said Rumbles.

"Will they let you put us in?" asked Roy.

"Sure. First up, I am head of the union. Second up, if you remember correctly, as part of your settlement you own a percentage of the circus, so if you say so they will have to put you in."

"How about the rest of us?" asked Shellie.

"Sure," said Rumbles.

The festivities had washed some of Rumbles face paint off, showing his dark skin beneath.

"Rumbles, are you black like me and Nellie under all that makeup?" asked Shellie.

"Yes, I am."

"Then why do you wear white paint? Are you embarrassed of being black?"

"Not at all, my dear. I wear it because of tradition. A clown is supposed to be for everybody and at the same time be nobody. Everybody can see a bit of themselves or somebody they know in a clown. The face paint hides what we may be on the outside so we can show what is on the inside. There are black , white and oriental clowns. Clowns are tall and short, fat and thin, ugly and beautiful, men and women. Now we even have one in a wheelchair to proudly count among our number. And if Al Jolson could get away with wearing blackface, I see no problem why I can't wear the traditional whiteface of my chosen people. Besides, even white people aren't this white. They are more of a tan or pink, wouldn't you say?"

"That's true, but can I wear black makeup instead of white?" asked Shellie.

"Sure, if that is what you want."

"Well, I think you will look goofy," informed Nellie. "I want to have white paint with big green circles around my eyes."

"I think that can be arranged"

"That invitation include the rest of us?" asked Paddy.

"Absolutely," said Rumbles.

"Who wants to be a clown?" asked Roy. The four kids raised their hands, as did Paddy, Demeter, Hercules, half the other patrons, and myself. Dion and Hermes agreed to cover for the rest of us. Rebecca surprised us, not by volunteering to be a clown, but for asking if she could go watch. Even insisted on paying for the ticket, until Roy convinced her that a certain amount of complimentary tickets were set aside for each show so they were meant to be free and no special exception was being made in her case.

It was a night of cotton candy and laughter, of magic and greasepaint spent under the big top. Actually under the high ceiling of Madison Square Garden. For a brief moment, we transcended the everyday and reached the surreal and fantastic. We were a hit, although nobody asked us to run away with the circus. The kids of all ages were in heaven. Our act was even better than the one in the bar. In addition, Roy had worked out a new act of his own and did a bit thrashing a clown car that supposedly parked in a handicapped space. He gave me no credit. Publicly at least. He was great anyway. He did ask me to consult on a new act he and Rumbles were working on.

Some tales have no definitive endings. Roy was not instantly cured of the loss of his legs, but he could handle it a little better. He had to. He was a fighter and his weapon was laughter. Pretty potent firepower. When everything is quiet, if I look closely in his eyes, I can still see the shadows of the pain of loss. I know that look. I have seen it in the mirror on occasion. The cause is different, but the eyes look like brothers. The loss never truly goes away. I will always miss Elsie. Roy will never have a day he doesn't wish he could walk. But we go on. There is something written over the door in the pub in Gaelic that sums up the hope concept. Happiness and hope never die. Especially in Bulfinche's.

SAFE SOX

Numerous folk stroll in and out of our door daily. Most of our patrons are memorable for one reason or another. A minority blend into the background like the gentleman who had just walked in. He was average. There was no other way to describe the man. Open up the dictionary and under average would be his picture or a reasonable likeness. I might have overlooked him completely if it weren't for his bald ankles. No socks on his feet. Nothing unusual in that, save it was a frigid January evening in Manhattan. The temperature was cold enough that if his exposed skin happened to brush up against a lamppost it would decide to leave him and stay with the metal.

Pulling his weary bones up to the bar he gave me his order and I got him his drink. It's my job after all.

This winter evening a light blanket of snow was snuggling up to the street outside. The man with no socks ordered the house special; hot buttered rum. Taking his wallet out of the back pocket of his jeans, he offered me some bills.

I turned him down. It's a strange thing to do, I know, but it's tradition. First drink's always on the house at Bulfinche's.

Drink in hand, he sauntered across the hardwood floors to a table and sat down. Thinking better of it he came back to the bar, stationing himself directly in front of the mirror. Sipping in silence, his gaze frequently wandered to the looking glass then wandered back. Whatever he was watching for was not there. Just to make sure, he threw frequent glances behind him in a downward direction. Nothing threw them back so he continued his work on the rum and ordered a martini. This time I let him pay.

Bags under his eyes, large enough to hold groceries, indicated he had not slept in days or even nights for that matter.

He ignored my attempts to converse, answering my questions with grunts and the occasional burp. Brilliant conversationalist he wasn't.

Dion, my fellow bartender and, as he so likes to point out, the god of wine and orgies, was up to the challenge. He looks like a fiftyish man with the beginning of a wine gut. Don't let it fool you. Dion has a way with people that is not to be believed. His love life is the stuff of legends. Not to mention several cults and two Off Broadway shows.

Dion moved to my end of the bar and attempted to bring "Sockless" back to normal time and space.

"Chilly weather, isn't it friend?" Dion offered.

"Yes" he answered, followed by a grunt.

"Your feet get cold?"

The man stared at Dion, a look of confusion spread across his face. Reaching over the bar top, Dion pointed at the man's feet.

"No socks," Dion said.

The man's eyes wandered down to his feet as if seeing them for the first time. He even wiggled his blue ankles to make sure they were his. Tremors that began in his torso worked their way upwards and out to his hands, causing the liquid to swish back and forth in his glass. Funny, I could have sworn he said he wanted his martini stirred, not shaken.

Draining the glass before any spilled, he plopped the glass down and ordered a third and a fourth. Half way through the fifth drink, the shivering subsided. Making an obvious effort, he inhaled deeply. We all paid close attention. We knew what usually came next, his life story, problems and so forth.

Words did come out of his mouth, not in the form of the expected story, but instead as a question.

"Have you ever wondered why socks disappear in the dryer?"

I nodded, offering, "The spinning of the dryer combined with the intense heat tears open small holes in the fabric of space and time. Occasionally a sock falls through and ends up in the dresser of some dinosaur." Not everyone agreed with my idea.

"The way I see it is the socks mutate into wire coat hangers which then somehow appear in my closet," Dion surmised.

Paddy Moran, ever the realist, added "No lads. The explanation is simple. Dryers have little spaces in which socks fall through. If the sides are taken off, you'll find your missing footwear."

Hercules and Hermes admitted to not knowing it was a problem. Demeter suggested they do their own laundry and learn for themselves. They responded with laughter. They enjoyed bringing their laundry to the dry cleaners, except for Hercules' trenchcoat. It's made from the hide of a lion he slew a few thousand years ago. He has to clean that himself with a horse grooming brush.

Still, they are an interesting sight coming from the cleaners. Only two folk I've ever met who get their socks and underwear pressed and hung neatly on little hangers.

"Socks are a lifeform with male and female genders," suggested Father Mike.

"How do you tell the boy socks from the girl socks?" asked Hermes, pulling his baseball cap farther up on his head. It had the Bulfinche's shot o' gold logo on it. The cap, not Hermes head.

"Easy," said Hercules. "The blue ones are male, the pink female."

"But what of green and yellow socks?" asked Paddy. Hercules had to think about that.

"Color has nothing to do with it. It's next to impossible for humans," –at this Father Mike got several stares– "or anybody," he quickly added, "to tell them apart. But they know. The mating ritual takes place in heat. Of the dryer that is. When the act is finished the female sock devours the male."

"Like a black widow spider," I said.

"Exactly. Sometimes the male escapes, explaining how holes mysteriously appear from time to time. It also tells why that sock you've never seen before suddenly turns up in your drawer one day."

At Father Mike's story, the man's ears perked up like a puppy's and in his eyes appeared the first glint of interest I'd seen all evening.

"You are very close to the truth, Father. Socks are alive. They perform ritual killing of their own kind for some unknown purpose," the bald–footed man said.

"I, myself, was unfortunate enough to witness this when one day I opened my dryer too early. A red tube sock was being forcibly restrained by blue ones over a shirt while a fifth argyle sock was poised for the kill. Too late they saw me and returned to their inert states, all save the executioner. He looked up at me and told me I knew too much. I was informed that my days were numbered.

"Was his name by any chance R. Guile?" Hermes asked. We all laughed.

"It's true, I tell you. They swore vengeance on me. I rid myself of all my socks and I refuse to wear any. I can't escape for long. They are everywhere" he said and ordered another double.

Something rare and unusual happened then. Dion turned him down. "You've had enough."

Dismayed, he looked with disbelief into Dion's eyes and turned to face each of us in turn. He sensed that we did not believe a word of his tale. Our giggling did not help his mood much either.

"Fools. Here I am warning you, but you don't listen. Fine, let whatever happens be on your heads," he said and rushed out into the snow covered streets. None of us followed. The falling snow soon filled the prints his feet had made.

To tell the truth, we all behaved badly. We should not have mocked his words, much less his pain. Usually we try to help folks and believe their stories, or at least humor them. Not so that night. Perhaps if his story was not quite so ridiculous we would have acted better. Perhaps things would have turned out differently. Perhaps not.

We forgot all about the strange man with the naked ankles until almost a month later. Paddy came in from his morning walk distraught, his expression grim. Taking a newspaper from beneath his arm, he threw it down on the bar top. It flew open to page three where the title said, "Foot Fetish Fiend". The article told of a bizarre killing. A man was found murdered in a locked apartment in Flushing, Queens. His feet were removed above the ankles and all the blood drained from his body.

Because the apartment was sealed, police were unable to determine how the killer got in or to find the man's feet. No blood was found, except for stains on a pair of argyle socks.

The man's name was Henry Walters and the picture, taken of him at an amusement park, clinched the matter. It was our visitor.

Paddy clipped the article. It now hung behind the bar to temper us the next time someone comes in with a crazy tale.

Other than that, Bulfinche's hasn't changed much with this failure. Except that none of us wore socks for three months.

2 VS. LOVE

Hermes walked in, looking far more weary than I had ever seen him. Even the tiny wings on his red high top sneakers drooped.

"Never again, Murphy," he said to me, stepping over to the bar and almost collapsing onto a stool.

"Never again what?" I asked.

"First give me an ambrosia." Being a good bartender, I did what he asked. Usually a sipper, Hermes gulped it down in a single chug. "Another." I gave: with a toss of his arm he emptied the glass. "That's better."

"What in the world could tire you out?" I asked. Hermes has been known to go out for a morning run and bring back croissants five minutes later. What's the big deal, you ask? The croissants were from Paris. Bulfinche's is in Manhattan. Not your usual morning dash, but then very little about Hermes is usual. He's the former messenger of the Greco–Roman pantheon, most of whose deities are no longer in the worship business. These days many of the old gods have moved on and Mount Olympus has been put on the market for sale or rent, from what I understand. A few of them found a home here at Bulfinche's.

The boss, Paddy Moran, is a member of the Gentry. More specifically a leprechaun. He's been possessed by wanderlust more than a few times in his long life. Back when Caesar conquered England, Paddy hitched a ride back to Rome, where he met Dionysus and a bunch of his clan. They bummed around the world for awhile, having a grand old time. Then back in the 1800's Paddy and Hermes hooked up again. Soon after, Paddy opened up the bar, hiring them on.

Hermes still does the messenger bit. He is quicker and more reliable than either Federal Express or the Postal Service, but now he works for Paddy. He moonlights as thief, doctor, con artist, protector, and anything else that tickles his fancy. Problem is, Hermes hasn't been laughing much lately. Hermes has not been around forever, but he comes pretty close. After that much time, life can get tedious. Hermes copes by doing things to the extreme. Takes risks that would make most men faint. Means nothing to him. Immortals are like that.

Hermes has been moping around the bar for the last few weeks. He has not wanted to do much. That's why Paddy sent him out on the job.

Hermes complained,"You want to know what could drain the life out of the sun? You want to have years of your life sucked away? Take a bus ride from the Port Authority to Niagara Falls."

"What the heck were you doing on a bus?" I asked. Hermes can become airborne easier than I can sneeze and he slides between time and space easier than I can squeeze out from behind the bar. For him, life moves so fast that the rest of the world seems like an audience of sculptures. That is one of the reasons he likes spending time in Bulfinche's. Here he is almost normal. As no powers or curses function inside the bar without the boss' permission, time passes normally for him. There are places in the universe where time drags at a fraction of its normal rate; a bus is one such place and it is not a mode of transport I can see him using. Not willingly at any rate.

"Paddy, the damn dictator," spat Hermes. Paddy is hard but fair. Anything he does he has a good reason for. . . at least in his mind. "You weren't here when that woman came in."

"Who would that be?"

"Madeline Raymond, professional busybody. Puts her nose where it does not belong. Came in here with some sob story about her daughter and her male friend."

"She didn't like the guy?"

"Just the opposite. Thought he was wonderful. The daughter agreed, but only to a point. The mother wanted dating, marriage, and grandkids. The daughter only wanted a friend. Madeline came looking for some sort of love potion and the midget offered to help," Hermes said, them screamed, jumping forward off his chair.

"Who ye be calling midget, baldy?" Paddy asked as Hermes jumped and squirmed, trying to reach inside the back of his jacket. "Stop being such a baby. I only dropped some ice down your shirt. You'd think I had stabbed ya."

Hermes started shaking his leg and three ice cubes fell out his pant leg. "Very funny, Moran. Who you calling bald, tiny?"

"You of the shiny forehead, unless you've gotten those hair plugs."

"You know they never took."

"Which is why you wear the baseball cap constantly and your hairbrush looks like a chia pet on steroids," Paddy shot back. It is also why he is always depicted with a helmet in classical rendition. Embarrassed by his male pattern baldness, even after thousands of years. "And who are ye calling a midget and tiny?"

"You see anybody else here that is four foot ten?"

"I am five foot easy."

"If you were being measured by a blind man with a faulty ruler."

"Good to have ye back, prevaricator," said Paddy with a smile, slapping Hermes on the back.

"Good to be back, leprechaun. Just telling Murphy what you put me through."

"You were helping a lass in distress."

"You pawned a troublemaker off on me," said Hermes. Paddy shrugged his shoulders innocently.

"I offered her a chance to learn and grow with ye as her teacher."

"What did she want?" I asked.

"She wished she could get a pair of Cupid's arrows and fix the problem she felt her daughter and her friend were having."

"She made an off–handed comment, and you tell her we have the winged rodent's address."

"Well, we do."

"He then volunteers me to be her guide," Hermes said to me. "Should have taken ten minutes tops. I offered to fly her there, but she refuses to fly before I even mention I was not talking about using a plane. Says she does not like trains either. Only travels by car or bus. So I asked Paddy if I could borrow Baby, but no."

"Baby is off limits. You know that," Paddy said. Baby was originally a V–16

1930 Cadillac. Paddy bought and modified her back in the days when the gang here used to run booze, during Prohibition. Baby has been remodified since then, mostly by Vulcan, but is still in vintage condition. Car collectors would kill to own Baby. Nobody drives Baby but the boss. Keeps her in the lower level of the parking garage under heavy security. "You could have bought, rented, or stolen a car."

Hermes continued his narrative. "What use do I have for a car? Besides, Madeline tells me it is too long a drive and she does not want to put me out. I tell her fine, I won't go then. She thinks I'm joking and off we go to Port Authority and the beginning of the longest journey ever undertaken by man or god. Our destination is Niagara Falls. Cupid, the little bugger, likes the area. With all the honeymooners and the images of him over hotels and motels, it is a place of power for him,"

"Of course there is not a non-stop bus there. There is no such thing as a non-stop bus, period. We made stops anywhere that could support human life and some places that couldn't. All the while, Madeline feels it is her duty to converse with me, telling me all the details of her first fifty years, that of her children, the gossip about her neighbors and the new spring fashions. It was the middle of February and she was worried about what she would be wearing in eight weeks,"

"Meanwhile, the roads were treacherous thanks to a snowstorm which the bus was fighting the whole way. It finally had to stop in a town called Andover. It was the type of place they used to call a one horse town. That was of course before the horse died. The storm became so bad they had to stop. There was no room in the local motel, so they put us up in the volunteer firehouse. We had been on the bus a good ten hours already and we had not even reached Buffalo yet. We waited out the storm,"

"Early in the morning the weather let up, and she insisted on taking me to a local attraction. It was a barn where a most unusual couple lived. Folks came from miles around just to watch them mate in the barnyard. I guess it beat watching the traffic light change colors. Inside the barn was a rooster and a cow. They were the couple, star crossed barnyard lovers. No one knew how it had started or what the attraction was, or why the cow seemed to enjoy the rooster's attention so,"

"I recognized the cause immediately–damned passion arrows. Told Madeline about it, too, that the person she was searching for was the one who did this. I detailed for her the lives Cupid has ruined by indiscriminately shooting his little arrows: Marriages destroyed; heterosexual people torn apart by urges for their own sex; homosexual folk confused after years of coming to terms with what was within them only to feel new urges. Cruelty toward eunuchs who could never act on the unquenchable fire he set within them. Tales of men and inflatable women. Ladies and department store mannequins. Priests and Nuns. Democrats and Republicans. An elderly man and his goldfish. An aged woman and her cane. My words only encouraged her. At least he is showing some taste in his old age. In the old days he would have used a bull and a hen. The aftermath would have been quite messy,"

"We got to the Falls by six in the morning. I actually had to go through customs. First time for everything. Asked me where I was born; I lied. The Canadian border guards did not believe my reason for going to the Falls. They wanted to strip-search me. Madeline explained that when I said we were searching for Cupid I meant it metaphysically. The guards did not buy it and detained me for questioning. I sent Madeline over the bridge. Then I beat her to the other side. The guard regretted his actions," Hermes said, pulling out a wallet and reading the drivers license. "His name was Harold Jones. His car looked quite regal as it sailed over the Falls. Once they fish it out and search the trunk, I'm sure they will find the cocaine he was trying to smuggle. Of course he probably first had to explain why, in the dead of winter, he was running naked wearing only a pair of rubber gloves on the American side of the border," Hermes is not one to suffer indignities well. He doesn't get mad, though. He gets even and then some.

"By then Madeline was exhausted and wanted to rest. The hotel she picked had more mirrors than a funhouse and a vibrating gel bed which my companion insisted on feeding quarters until she fell asleep. I went out every hour and paid the desk clerk while she rested. The woman even talks in her dreams. Madeline revisited the land of the waking by noon, ready for the completion of her quest. Again she refused to allow me to provide transportation. Instead we had to travel by more mundane means. Two tickets later we were on board the Maid of the Mist."

"Made you wear those blue rain ponchos?" I asked.

"They tried. I preferred my trenchcoat. The boat got as close to the Falls as it was going to get when I told Madeline to jump overboard,"

"She told me no. Then begged, 'Isn't there another way?'"

"Certainly, I tell her, but it involves a barrel. Taking my hand she jumped, shocked that we never hit the water. Instead we went into the Falls, ending up at Cupid's hole." I let that one slide.

"Was he home?" I asked.

"Of course. It was February 14, Valentine's Day, his day of power. On that day he never leaves the house. He greeted us with shouts of 'Go away and Begone,'"

"Madeline said, 'But I have traveled such a long way to seek your aid.'"

"'Keep going,' Cupid demanded, still hiding from us. The room had more mirrors than the motel we had stayed at."

"'I have brought you a guest. You shall receive her, cherub.'"

"'Who is that?'"

"'It is I, Hermes.'"

"'Leave me and take the woman with you.'"

"'We are not going anywhere. Get your butt out here now and say hi. Paddy Moran sent her.'"

"'Moran? Very well.'"

"Cupid stepped out from his hiding place so that we could see his muscular reflection in a mirror. He wore white shorts and we could not see his back."

"'Hello, I am Eros.'"

"'I was looking for Cupid,'" Madeline said, confused.

"Cupid laughed. 'I am known by many names.'"

"'More than two? You get a fake ID down on the strip?'"

"'Quiet Hermes. You are just jealous because I am more powerful than you, that my worship continues to this day. My graven image can be seen throughout the world.'"

"I yawned in retaliation," Hermes said.

"'You dare mock me?' he shouted, his face crimson. 'You whose claim to fame in these modern times is as a deliverer of flowers.'"

"He was right about that. I do hate that association. People forget I am on travelers checks, that my staff is the symbol of healing for physicians and even that my likeness is graven onto a wall in Penn Station among others. Still, it keeps me in the public eye and it gives me power so it is worth the embarrassment. Cupid has not quite come to terms with his own. Only time he interacts with people is when they are under the sway of his arrows. Doesn't socialize well and tries to compensate with threats.

"'I could strike you down where you stand,'" he threatened.

"'Not likely.'"

"'I am the most powerful of our family, more powerful than even Zeus!'"

"Your grandfather has left the mortal realms for points unknown. Or perhaps he has not. You need only speak his name twice more to summon him, if he has returned. Why not do it and give him a sound thrashing. After all, what hope could a thunderbolt have against one of your mighty arrows?'"

"'I choose not to flaunt my might,'" said Cupid as an excuse.

"'If you say so. I can respect that. But why then do you cower behind a reflection?'"

"'I do not cower.'"

"'Then come on out and meet the lady, unless you're frightened by a mere mortal?'"

"'Very well,'" Cupid said, walking out to greet us. Madeline kept her eyes up, expecting to meet the eyes of someone six four. Instead out walked a two foot cherub in diapers that made Paddy look like a giant, complete with the wings of a pigeon. "'Satisfied?'"

"'Where is Cupid?'" asked Madeline, looking behind him.

"'I am Cupid! I mean Eros,'" he shouted.

"'But you looked so much bigger in the looking glass.'"

"'Funhouse mirror,'" I told her.

"'Why do you look like that?'"

"'Actually any other day of the year I can look like my reflection. Tall, handsome, no wings. Wearing clothes even, but there is a price. I am weaker. There is no choice on Valentine's Day. On this day I am at my most powerful. Thought and belief are the source, but I must look like most people imagine me. Like an infant!'" Cupid said impassioned, flapping his arms and his wings until he was fluttering in front of Madeline's face. "'I can't even go out like this. What would people think?'"

"'That you were Cupid?'" Madeline asked.

"'Exactly! Sort of. Never mind, you would not understand,'" stuttered the cherub.

"'The heck I wouldn't. I won't leave the house without my accessories. First there is my push up bra, then my girdle. Next comes the makeup, which in and of itself takes an hour. Lastly I put on my wig. I have thinning hair, an embarrassing thing for a woman.'"

"'I can relate,'" I confessed.

"'That explains your hat. Hermes, have you ever considered a toupee?'" Madeline asked.

"'I haven't found an adhesive that could keep one on my head when I get really moving.'"

"'Too bad. Your long curls look good, if we could only get something on top. Ever consider combing it over?'"

"'Looks ridiculous.'"

"'Excuse me!'" yelled Cupid, dive bombing us from above. "'I believe we were talking about my problems.'"

"'Selfish little fellow, aren't you?'" Madeline said.

"'Insults are not the way to get my help.'"

"'Sorry.'"

"'Too late. My feelings are hurt. I don't want to help you anymore,'" Cupid said, floating with his arms crossed over his chest.

"'Cupid, take hold of yourself. I hate to see an Olympian pouting,'" I said.

"'I am not pouting.'"

"'You are too. Look, you are even sticking out your bottom lip. But before you make any hasty decisions listen to these two things I have to tell you. First, we saw your cow and rooster in Andover.'"

He smiled a proud, mischievous grim. "'What did you think?'"

"'I felt it was lame but Madeline here liked it.'"

"'Did you, really?'"

"'Why yes. I thought the man... cherub, who could do that would be just the one to help me.'"

"'With what?'"

"'That is the second thing.'"

"'I want to make my daughter and a male friend of hers fall madly in love but both of them vehemently refuse to take the path of common sense and romance.'"

"'They need some help?'"

"'Exactly. I thought your arrows might do the trick.'"

"'Why didn't you say so? I would be glad to help. Let me go get my quiver. Meanwhile Hermes, why don't you take a look at my lovebirds. Beautiful, aren't they?'"

"'Nice enough. Poor things were born to fly and you keep them locked up in a cage.'"

"'Perhaps you will feel differently in a moment,'" Cupid said, thinking me so unaware as not to hear him pull back his bowstring as he let loose an arrow, hoping to enamor me of the birds. I spun and caught the arrow between my thumb and forefinger. "'Oh Styx,'" he swore, unable to speak harsher words when stuck in his infant form.

"'Indeed. I think it is time I taught you the lesson I should have years ago,'" I said, as I backed him into a mirrored corner, closing in on him and an infinite number of reflections.

"'No, stop! Stay back, I command you.'"

"'Believe me, this will hurt you more than it does me,'" I said grabbing him before he could flutter away.

"'What are you going to do to him?'" Madeline asked.

"'Tan his hide.'"

"'You are going to spank him?'"

"'Why not? I am his father, after all, and he is acting like a spoiled brat,'" I am not one for physical violence, but sometimes it's necessary. Occasionally it's even fun. Cupid cried like a baby for a few minutes.

"'What do you say?'" I asked him.

"'I'm sorry I tried to shoot you,'" he said to me. Turning to Madeline he said "'During the rest of the year I have a specially designed Uzi I use. Unfortunately the effect is not as powerful as the arrows. And it won't work today,'" wiping tears on the back of his hand.

"'Will you still help me?'" Madeline asked.

"'I guess so. Here, take them. Enjoy. Now leave me.'"

"'Sure you don't want us to warm your bottle or change you?'"

"'Hush, Hermes. Leave him be,'" said Madeline, taking pity on the self–proclaimed lord of love.

"'Family,'" I justified.

"'I understand. Thank you,'" she said turning to Cupid.

"'You are welcome. Goodbye, Madeline. Farewell Hermes. Tell Paddy he owes me.'"

"'I'm sure he will take it off what you owe him.'"

"As we took our leave I asked, '"Do we have to take the bus back?'"

"'Please? I so rarely get a chance to travel. Besides...'"

"'Besides what?'"

"'It will give us a chance to spend some time together,'" Madeline said, pleading with her eyes and her smile. It was not an unpleasant sight. Madeline was exasperating, but far from boring.

"'Well, I suppose another sixteen hours in a box on wheels might have some bright points.'"

Hermes ended his tale as I gave him his fourth ambrosia. He was sipping now. "Where is Madeline now?" I asked.

"She went to use the arrows. I tried to talk her out of it with no success."

"You may have been right," said a woman who had just entered the place. I took her to be Madeline. No one gave her back. Introductions were made, as all good things should be, in New York. "It did not work."

"What do you mean it did not work?" asked Hermes.

"I used the arrows on my daughter. Nothing happened. She felt nothing. Yelled at me for sticking her. She didn't stop bleeding for ten minutes and when I left she still could not sit comfortably. The whole thing was a dismal failure. The two of them fought against love and won."

"Sorry to hear that. Don't fret about it. Some things are just not meant to be," said Paddy, with a consoling smile.

"Besides, you have better things to do with your time," said Hermes.

"Like what?" Madeline asked, with a smile both sly and hopeful.

"Like going ice skating," suggested Hermes.

"Where would I do that and with whom?" she asked.

"Me. Would you like to?"

"Perhaps if you asked me."

"Would you care to join me ice skating at Rockefeller Center?"

"Me? Really?" Madeline said, mocking surprise. Surprise barely seemed to notice and was not insulted in the least. "Why?"

"I find you to be a very interesting woman. You intrigue me. I find that both rare and attractive in a woman. I would like to get to know you better, so long as it is not in a bus. Deal?" Hermes asked.

"Deal," Madeline responded with a grin. "Why aren't you wearing my present?"

"And what present would that be?" asked Paddy.

"Nothing," said Hermes, trying to sweep the subject under the rug. Having no practical experience with a broom and the presence of the surrounding hardwood floor both conspired to defeat the action.

"Nothing? I bought that for you. You wouldn't want to hurt my feelings would you?" said Madeline. Hermes looked to Paddy and me for help, but we were with Madeline on this one.

"Fine," he said curtly, pulling a baseball cap from the pocket of his gray trenchcoat. He removed the one he was wearing, complete with the Bulfinche's shot o' gold, and replaced it with the one Madeline had given him. It was navy blue with "Niagara Falls" written in gold letters across the front. Hermes himself turned pink, as Paddy and I fought to keep in our laughter. The sides of the hat sported two fluorescent yellow wings. It was a baseball cap rendition of his classical helmet.

"What do you think?" he asked timidly.

"Do you like it?" asked an excited Madeline.

"Marvelous," said Paddy, almost choking on a chuckle. "Simply marvelous," I simply nodded in agreement, unable to speak lest I lose it.

Hermes ignored us, as, arm in arm, he and Madeline headed for the door.

"Have fun, kids," I said.

Madeline stopped and turned around, returning to the bar alone.

"I wanted to thank you for your help, Paddy," she said.

"It was my pleasure."

"I was saving these other arrows in case I needed them," she said, looking toward Hermes waiting at the door, with a smile and a wink, which he returned. "It doesn't look like I will be requiring them. Please take them as a gift."

"My thanks, Madeline. Now go on and enjoy," Paddy said. After the couple left, Paddy remarked "It is about time. Madeline should help get him out of his blue funk and start his fire again. Love is in the air."

"Is that what that smell is?"

"Yep," said Paddy.

"One question. Why didn't the arrows work?" I asked.

"Simple. They did. The two people involved already loved each other, in a non romantic way. The arrow, instead of causing new emotions, intensified the existing one."

"You knew that would happen and encouraged her?" I said.

"Of course. It got her off her daughter's back and will let her get on with her life now that she has done everything she possibly could."

"Nice and sneaky, all in the same gesture."

"It is what I do best."

"Well, not entirely. There was no saving of money."

"Not true. Hermes never hit me up for the bus fare."

"I stand corrected."

"You do it well."

FAERIE TALE

Imitation is the sincerest form of flattery and Paddy was thrilled. Our own brat pack had gone into the drink selling business. Of course since the oldest of the four kids was barely a teenager we had nothing to worry about in terms of competition. They were not selling booze. Nellie and Shellie, paired together as always, were selling iced tea on the sidewalk outside Bulfinche's. They were in direct competition with Peter and Brian, who were going the more traditional route with lemonade.

Each pair was "dissing" the other's product.

"They made their ice tea with bugs," challenged Peter.

"You made your lemonade with water from the toilet," countered Shellie.

"Well, you made your iced tea with prune juice," spat Brian.

"You peed in your lemonade."

"Did not!" shouted back Peter and Brian.

"Did too!" insisted Shellie and Nellie.

"Didn't!"

"Did so!"

"You smell!"

"Not as bad as your iced tea."

"Or your feet."

Kids will be kids and these kids, having gone through so much together, had become very sibling–like, right down to the bickering. In truth, it was all in fun. There were no customers around. Besides, they had set some ground rules: no real arguing in front of customers; a set price of fifty cents a glass to prevent a price war that would hurt both businesses. It wasn't as if they had no overhead. They had to pay Demeter for the raw materials to make the drinks and Paddy charged them a space rental fee of fifty cents a day for each stand. It worked out to a whooping quarter each. No sense in sheltering the kids from the workings of the real world. Not the normal stuff at any rate. Each kid had gone through their own personal hell, ending up as slaves to a pimp, until through the grace of God and Rebecca they ended up here at Bulfinche's.

After everything they had gone through, they had a pretty clear idea of the dark side of life. We made sure they learned about the lighter side and if they learned basic economics in the process, so much the better.

They were making out like bandits. The older kids, Brian and Shellie, realized most adults can't resist a sales pitch by a cute little kid and let Peter and Nellie attract the customers. They collected the money, poured and served the drinks. Even got me to buy more than once.

The squabbling halted the instant a potential customer walked briskly down the sidewalk. He wore a Shakespearean style floppy hat, complete with a feathered plume that bobbed back and forth as he stepped. A forest green trenchcoat covered up the rest of his outfit except for a pair of black boots. He carried a canvass sack over his shoulder.

"Hi, mister. Would you like to buy some lemonade?" asked Peter with a big grin on his face. The man paid him no more mind than the fire hydrant.

"That's right, sir. You don't want any of his lemonade. An inferior product for one of your discriminating tastes. Obviously a glass of our iced tea will fit the bill," said Nellie. Nellie had Dion help her write most of her sales pitches and took lessons from Hermes on presentation. She was a con–girl at heart. Still, he noticed her only long enough to step around her.

"Hey mister, what's in the sack?" Brian asked.

"Mind your own business, kid," the man replied curtly.

"There is no reason to be rude," said Shellie, jumping to Brian's defense. It was okay for her to be mean to him, but nobody else better try it when she was around.

The man started to trot. The kids followed him and saw him turn toward the garage attached to Bulfinche's.

"What's he going in there for?" asked Peter.

"I have no idea," answered Brian, scratching his head.

"Guys," said Nellie. "I think I saw something in the bag move."

"You sure?" asked her sister Shellie.

"Yep."

"I think I saw it too," said Peter. "What do you think it is?"

"He must have a dog or something in there. We gotta stop him before he hurts it," said Brian. Almost on cue, a small bark came from the bag.

The younger two, Nellie and Peter, ran off after him.

"Wait," said Shellie. "We're just kids. What are we going to do?"

"Don't be such a wimp, sis," Nellie shouted behind her.

Brian ran after them. "Don't worry. I'll keep an eye on them. Go inside and get some grownup help, Shellie."

She did. Meanwhile, Nellie and Peter had caught up to the man.

"Let the dog go, please," said Peter, grabbing the sack. "He didn't do anything to you."

The man turned to swing the bag away from the boy's grasp, but Peter wouldn't let go. The man was looking around desperately for a way out. Meanwhile Nellie had grabbed onto his leg and refused to disengage her grip.

"Would you children please let go of me!" the man shouted as Brian caught up.

"As soon you let the dog go," said Brian, adding his strength to that of Peter, pulling on the bag.

"It is not a dog," the man said.

"Yeah, right," said Nellie as she bit down and tried to take a chunk out of the leg she was holding onto. The result was the man letting go of the bag, screaming. Brian and Peter lowered the sack to the ground and loosened the drawstring around its opening. A beagle puppy crawled out and licked both the boys' faces.

"Looks like a dog to me," said Peter. "You're a liar."

"He looks like a dog but what he is is beyond your puny comprehension," the man shouted.

"Hey, don't you make fun of Peter. He can't help that he has Down's Syndrome," said Brian.

"Yeah. Peter is plenty smart and he dresses way better than a weirdo like you," said Nellie.

"That is not what I meant. Give him to me or there will be dire consequences." The dog was cowering behind the kids.

"What does 'dire consequences' mean?" asked Peter.

"I think it means he will beat us up. Bully!" said Nellie, kicking the man in the shin.

A door slammed open and six foot–four of silk–covered red head slammed into the man, knocking him to the ground.

"Not if I have anything to say about it," said the redhead, Jasmine. Actually, his real name was Jason Cervantes, but when he dressed as a woman he preferred Jasmine. He's a New York City detective and a regular. Jas made a bet with the boss awhile back. Paddy put a bunch of cash into an account. As long as Jas spends a certain amount of hours every week in women's clothes and goes by the name Jasmine, he gets the interest from the account on the last day of every year. It's a six figure sum. He even managed to work it into his job by volunteering to work the seedier, kinkier parts of town in drag.

Jasmine grappled with the stranger and had him in handcuffs inside of seconds. Shellie, who had gotten Jasmine, followed behind and was yelling at Nellie and Peter for running off so stupidly. She tended to take up the rule of surrogate mother for the group, doing her best to keep the others 'in line', even the older Brian.

Unfortunately, Peter, because of the Down's, has a decreased sense of safety awareness. He was trying to defend and justify himself.

"But he was going to hurt the puppy," Peter said.

"He could have hurt you worse," Shellie countered. "And you didn't even know for sure it was a dog. He could have had you arrested."

"But it was a dog," explained Nellie, exasperated at the suggestion that she could have been wrong.

"It was still a dumb thing to do," Shellie said.

"But..." said Nellie.

"No buts," said Jasmine. "Shellie's right. It was brave, but very foolish of you to do. You should have gone for help and not put yourselves in danger."

"It was okay. I was watching out for them," said Brian.

"I was talking to you too, Brian," said Jasmine, fixing his bra.

"Oh," said Brian, the wind knocked out of his sails. Shellie stood up taller, filled with righteousness.

Jasmine brought the kids and the stranger into the bar where yours truly was working. Hesitantly, the dog trailed in behind them. Jasmine handcuffed the stranger to the lower bar rail, the one used for resting feet on. The man kept muttering, "Damn cold iron."

Jasmine made a sarcastic offer. "Shall I warm them for you next time?"

"Murphy, we saved a puppy!" said Peter.

"Look, he followed us home!" Nellie said, looking at the beagle. "Can we keep him?"

"I think you better ask Paddy," I answered. Demeter took the dog into her kitchen for something to eat.

Almost as if he heard his name, the boss walked in the door. He was comforting a very distraught woman named Caylee. She was a semi–regular and had come to Paddy for help. Her son, Cornelius, had been playing outside her apartment when a strangely dressed man had kidnaped him. Neighbors rushed to tell her, but were too late. The kidnapper had escaped on foot with her boy. Paddy was assuring her we would do everything possible to get her son back. He was making phone calls, mobilizing the troops, faxing pictures of Cornelius to anyone who could help. Hermes was already searching. Jasmine used his radio to get the NYPD in on the act.

Caylee sat at a table, reeling and bewildered. She ordered and drank a double vodka straight. "Why would anyone do this?" she said.

"There is no explanation that could satisfy a mother," said Paddy. "Do you have any idea who it might be?"

"I do. I thought you might have better luck finding him and my son."

"We will find Cornelius."

"I hope so. The first thing I am going to do is hug him. Then I am going to kill the bastard that took him," Caylee said, fear driving her anger. "I'm going back out there to look for him."

"I'll go with you. We'll talk on the way. Remember, calmer heads will prevail," Paddy said.

"Before you go," said Jasmine, looking at the man on the floor who was desperately trying to avoid being seen by Caylee. "Can you give me a description of the kidnapper?"

"Gladys, my neighbor, said he was a tall man with brown hair, a green trenchcoat and a feathered hat," Caylee said.

Jasmine walked to the bar, uncuffed the stranger from the rail and recuffed his hands behind his back. He then yanked him unceremoniously to his feet and plopped the hat on his head.

"You mean kind of like this?" Jasmine asked. The stranger fit the description perfectly. At first he tried to avoid Caylee's eyes, but then he got a good look at them. Caylee on the other hand became much less agitated, almost dangerously focused. She walked up to the man and kneed him in the groin.

"Where is my son, you #!*@!" she demanded.

The man crumbled and slowly regained his composure. "What, no greeting?"

"You want a greeting, fine. Hello, Aliban. What happened? All the stores run out of milk? You think they would have gotten some in stock after seven years," Caylee asked, ice in her voice.

"Hello, Caylee," the stranger answered. Call it a hunch, but I figured these two knew each other.

"Hello? Is that all you can say? You ran out on me you..."

"It is not my fault."

"Right. Someone dragged you away."

"Actually, they did."

"You could have come back when they let go."

"No, I could not. My Queen would not allow it." Funny, he did not sound British.

Most of the rest of us were quietly trying to fade into the background. Domestic disputes can get dangerous and deserve some privacy, even in a public place.

Paddy chimed in. "Disobedience is always an option."

"Lord Moran," Aliban said curtly, with both respect and dislike.

"Hunter," Paddy spat flatly. I was having another hunch. Paddy knew him too.

"Disobedience is not an option for those loyal to the Sidhe."

"My loyalty to my people has never been in question. Any of the Gentry are allowed to disagree. Blind obedience is a most disloyal act, both to society and one's self. Least ye forget, Titania only rules one faction."

"But it is my tribe she rules and it encompasses much of Faerie," Aliban said indignantly. "As I cannot transport an unwilling passenger to Faerie on my own or through the one in Central Park, I came to use your nexus."

"Without permission?" Paddy asked. "You would never have survived long enough to make it to the lower garage."

"Did not see the point of asking for something you would never give. Survival is second nature to me," Aliban said. "Caylee, my love, I know this must seem very bizarre to you right now..."

"No, not at all. You tried to kidnap my son on some Queen's say so. I am only going to ask you this one more time before I start taking you apart. WHERE IS MY SON!" Caylee demanded, her hands grabbing the collar of Aliban's shirt and squeezing his neck.

"I did not know it was you that he had attached himself to. I just knew it was a mortal woman," Aliban tried to explain.

At this moment the kids, puppy in tow, came out of the kitchen. The puppy was acting almost self–conscious. It saw Caylee and its jaw dropped open.

"Mom?" asked the puppy.

"Corny?" asked Caylee, crouching down on her knees. The puppy ran into her arms and she squeezed it tight.

Peter and Nellie looked at each other, grabbed each others' hands and started jumping up and down, shouting, "We found a talking dog!"

"Hush, children," interjected Paddy. "All is not as it seems, is it Corny? Perhaps you had best come clean with your Mother."

"The Shapeling is not her child," said Aliban. Caylee stood, turned to Aliban and slugged him in the jaw. Aliban fell like a chopped tree.

"It's true, Mommy," Corny blurted out, between tears and sobs. "I'm sorry, but your real child died when he was a baby. I snuck in and took his place. I was supposed to just leave after a few weeks, but I couldn't; I loved you. Now the Hunter has come to take me back. I tried to fight him but he snuck up on me. I couldn't change fast enough to fight him. I never really practiced how to shape shift because I wanted to fit in with people. When I heard the kids talking about a dog, I had time to shift and since I came into the bar I've been trying to change back, but I can't. Now I'm stuck as a dog."

Caylee looked horror struck. Paddy softly chuckled and snapped his fingers. "Try to change now, Corny," Paddy suggested. The beagle morphed into a six year old boy.

"Does this mean we can't keep him?" Peter asked.

"Yeah. No fair," added Nellie. Shellie shushed the pair of them. Aliban pulled himself to his feet.

"No human can do that. As you can see, he cannot be your child, so with your leave I will be taking him back with me." Aliban said. Caylee knocked him down again.

"You idiot!" she screamed. "Not only is he my son, but he's yours, too."

"How is that possible?" Aliban asked.

"The usual way," Caylee replied, ice in her tone.

Turning to Paddy he asked. "Is that possible? With mortals?"

"I have children," Paddy answered with a smile.

"I could have hundreds of children!?" Aliban muttered to himself. Caylee hit him again.

"I have known that Corny was a Shapeling since he was three days old, the first time he morphed. I blamed it on his father being an elf."

"I am not an elf," said Aliban, offended.

"Well, fairy didn't sound PC, especially considering that you're straight."

"How did you know?" Aliban asked, bewildered.

"When we made love we flew around the room," Caylee said. The kids all put their hands over their ears and yelled "Ick!" Not big fans of mushy stuff. "That isn't the way it usually happens."

Aliban looked genuinely surprised at the revelation that not all lovers became airborne.

"Three weeks after you left, I found out I was pregnant. What I want to know is why you thought you weren't mine, Corny."

"I don't know," Corny said.

"I think I do. Something I've been on the lookout for a while now. About six years ago me cousin Shanna told me about one of her fellow Banshees who took a half breed to the Sidhe to grow up. Taught how to live as a Shapeling, something a mortal would be at great difficulty to do alone," Paddy said, eyeing Aliban disapprovingly. To my surprise, Aliban lowered his eyes in shame, finally believing Corny was his. "The child spent years being taught. Just before the child was to be returned, Titania found out and for sport demanded the child be told it was taking the place of a dead infant."

"Her Majesty lied?" exclaimed both Aliban and Corny, horrified and relieved respectively.

Paddy nodded. "What do you think of your Queen now that she's played you for a fool?" Aliban was at a loss for words.

"But Corny never disappeared until today," Caylee said, confused.

"Depending on the roads taken in and out, time passes different in Faerie. All that took place over the course of one evening," Paddy explained.

Corny grabbed his mother's neck and wouldn't let go. Tears of joy poured out of his eyes. "You're really my Mom!"

"I love you, Corny. Nothing could ever change that," Caylee said, matching her son's embrace. "But at least that explains why you were always asking questions about adoption."

Aliban was still in shock. "My son. I have a son. Come here, Corny."

"No way," Corny said pulling away. "You tried to kidnap me. You walked out on Mommy before I was born. I don't like you, even if you are my father."

"Could you give me a chance?" Aliban pleaded self–consciously, unaccustomed to begging.

"Maybe," said Corny, his face set in a pout.

"And you, my Caylee?"

She looked down at her son. "Maybe."

"Excellent. I shall move in today."

"Wait a second. Slow it down. There is no way you are moving in. You blew that chance when you walked out the door. You can have some *supervised* visits with your son and we will see how it goes."

Corny had made friends with our brat pack and the lot of them went outside, at Paddy's suggestion, to make sure no one had walked off with their drink stands. Jasmine decided it would be best to let Aliban go. The matter was technically out of his jurisdiction and he had enough problems explaining his wardrobe. He had no idea how to write this one up. He called it in as a misunderstanding, an unscheduled parental visit. Paddy offered to baby–sit while Caylee and Aliban sorted things out.

"Our son will need a bodyguard. Titania will not just give up. She will send another Hunter. And I will not be welcome in my homeland. I need a place to stay."

"You tell Titania that Corny and his mother are under my protection. She will leave them be," said Paddy. Aliban looked as if he had his doubts. "If you are too much of a coward to tell her, I will send Hermes," said Paddy.

"What about myself?" Aliban said, expecting an offer of the same.

"You, Hunter, are on your own," Paddy said flatly.

Caylee decided she needed to walk, so the pair headed out the door.

"I need a place to stay." Aliban said, trying to charm Caylee. Having been there and done that, she wasn't falling for it.

"Rent a place."

"How will I find it?" he begged.

"Classifieds," she answered.

"How will I pay for it?"

"Get a job."

"A job? How cruel can you be?"

"Not nearly as cruel as leaving me to go through fourteen hours of labor alone."

I didn't hear the rest of the conversation as they had left the bar, but I did see the kids hit both of them up for soft drinks. Caylee bought a cup from each stand. With some coaching, Corny got in on the act. Using guilt and childish wiles, he got Aliban to buy drinks, paying the equivalent of several hundred dollars of fairy gold.

The kids took the rest of the day off and got sick on all the candy they bought.

BLACK EYES

There was talk of violence, which is better by far than the real thing. Paddy and Hercules were going at it, in the debate kind of sense. It was still early in the discussion, so it was hard to tell who was winning. Both sides were making excellent points.

"Paddy, there are some times when violence isn't an option, but a necessity."

"True, Herc, but we differ greatly as to when those times are."

"If someone pushes you, you push back. Otherwise, you get trampled underfoot," said Herc.

"I'm not saying roll over and play dead. That doesn't make sense. It's a matter of the level of the response. You don't pull out a rocket launcher because some drunk throws a punch at you. That's overkill," said Paddy, referring to the incident that brought on this discourse.

"Normally, I wouldn't have done that, and you know it. I had just gotten it from Coco Joe. . ." Coco Joe's proper name was Cocijo and he was a Zapotec storm god. The Zapotec were a native tribe in Central America. Coco Joe still lives in the jungle, but needs to visit Bulfinche's periodically, or he'll fade from existence. Seems there isn't enough belief left to sustain him otherwise. The guy was visiting. He took a case of rocket launchers off some guerillas and gave one to Herc. ". . . and I hadn't had a chance to put it away yet. When the guy got out of line, I pulled it out."

"You could have hurt him," said Paddy.

"Paddy, it was in the bar. You know better than I do that conventional weapons won't fire in here unless you say so." It's part of the magic of Bulfinche's. "Besides, the safety was on. The guy left without causing any trouble. By using the weapon, I avoided violence. And taught him a lesson," said Herc.

"So now you're arguing that might makes right?" asked Paddy.

"That's the way of the world," said Coco Joe, who was downing margaritas like a sewer grate does rain after a storm.

"It doesn't have to be," said Paddy. "And that's my point."

"It's a poor point. Camelot didn't even last a century," said Coco Joe.

"The legend has," I said. "And the reality of Bulfinche's has passed the century mark."

"A legend? What good does that do?" Coco Joe was bitter that, aside from a few academics who think he was just a story, his legend has faded from the face of the world. He was jealous and resentful of those who were still either revered or famous. Considering his general attitude, his brown-nosing of Hercules made no sense. Herc is probably the most famous patron or staff member Bulfinche's has. Paddy believes in giving the benefit of the doubt, so I try to follow his example, but Coco Joe makes it a challenge. "Those who have the power tell those who don't how things are going to be. That's never going to change," said Coco Joe.

"I don't believe that. I can't believe that," said Paddy.

"I'm with Paddy on that part, Joe," said Herc.

"You kidding me? I figured a guy like you knew the score," said Coco Joe, licking the salt off his glass and motioning to me for another.

"I know the score, and even though it looks fixed, it isn't. It just takes honor and effort to flip the points around," said Herc.

"Maybe that works for a guy like you, who can take out any god or beast who comes up against him. The rest of us ain't that lucky. When it gets down and dirty, honor doesn't exist. Survival is all that matters," said Coco Joe. "Especially where mortals are concerned."

"Explain Gandhi," said Paddy.

"Lunatic," said Coco Joe.

"What about those that followed him?" asked Herc.

"Mindless sheep type lunatics," replied Coco Joe.

"Wrong. They cared more about a cause, about what was right, than about themselves. That's how you make a difference," said Herc.

"Like I said, lunatics. Look, what you guys are saying works great in a bar, but not in the real world," said Coco Joe.

"I can tell you don't hang out here much," I said.

"Why? Because I don't buy into that guano? Listen, the Zapotec Pantheon had dozens of gods and more demi-gods. Where are they all now? Dead. All of them gone into oblivion."

"All of them?" I asked.

"There are a couple I lost track of, but the rest I know for sure. First the Aztecs, then the conquistadors, wiped out or assimilated the people and their gods followed. That's the way of it. I'm all that's left and that's not because I shied away from a fight."

"You aren't around now because you fight. You're around because Paddy shares the manna of Bulfinche's with you," I said. Manna is mystic energy. Bulfinche's is one of the few sources on Earth that replenishes itself, which allows Paddy to dish it out to deities and others who need it to exist.

"Murphy. . ." said Paddy, trying to quiet me. He doesn't help others for the credit. I was embarrassing him. Coco Joe put on what looked like a forced smile.

"No, Paddy. He's right. But I can tell you that everyone else out there is nothing like our Mr. Moran here. Others would make me a slave for what he gives me freely. Let me ask you a question, Paddy. I already know Hercules' answer. What would you do if someone hurt you badly, in such a way that you couldn't stop them, and later on you found a way to hurt them back, just as bad. Are you telling me you wouldn't want to take your revenge?" asked Coco Joe.

"Of course I would want to. But would I actually do it? Probably. Would I torture them? No. Would I kill them? Not if there was any other option," said Paddy.

"Most of the time, there is no other option," said Coco Joe.

"You'd be surprised at the different options that can be found," said Herc.

"I thought you were on my side on this. I started out agreeing with you, Herc."

"I know, but I can't condone killing without looking at the other options first.

I've done too much of it to do that," said Herc, with genuine sorrow. "Paddy and I just disagree on to what extent we should go to when dealing with the scum of the Earth and Otherworlds."

"Who decides which options are worth trying? And to what degree?" asked Coco Joe.

"Each person has to judge what's right for him or her," said Paddy.

"Judge what's right? Paddy, those of us here are counted in the number of those who do the judging." Paddy sighed at Joe's comment. "And how do you do that in the heat of battle?"

"In a fight, you go from your gut, but mostly on reflex and instinct. I'm also not talking about self defense. What I'm talking about is when you have time to think about it or the power to do something else. Plus, there is always the chance for redemption."

"Redemption? Ha. That's a laugh and a half. Where I come from, piranha don't suddenly become vegetarians," said Coco Joe.

"Still. . ." started Paddy, when the front door flew open and in walked the kids; Shellie, Nellie, Brian, and Peter. Corny had tagged along, which wasn't unusual. They were late coming home from school, which happened all the time. They were making a beeline for the door behind the bar, which was weird. Normally, they have to be kicked out of the bar proper before they'll leave. Also, they had never not said hello to everyone. Peter had on dark sunglasses and Nellie was holding her arm oddly.

Paddy also noticed something was wrong and wasn't about to let the kids sneak by.

"Freeze," said Paddy. The youngsters each made like snowkids. "What's going on here?"

Brian and Shellie looked at each other, obviously hoping the other would have an answer. Both were disappointed.

"Peter, come here," said Paddy, going for the weak link, knowing who would break first. Peter obeyed. "Why are you wearing sunglasses inside?"

"To look cool?" said Peter. It sounded more like a question than an answer.

"Ye look fine without them. Take them off," said Paddy.

Peter did as he was told, revealing a huge black eye.

"Are you okay?" Peter nodded yes. "How did this happen?" asked Paddy, jumping out of his seat. The kids just looked at each other, their tongues tied. "Nellie, come here. What happened to your uniform?" The kids all went to the school at Our Lady of the Lake and wore the Catholic school uniforms. Being a private school, of a parish to which Paddy is a huge contributor, the odds of them checking out the background stories on the kids Rebecca brought to us was virtually nil. Safer all around, at least in that respect. "Move your hand please."

Nellie did so reluctantly, revealing a tear in the formerly white shirt sleeve. It was covered in blood.

"Are you all right, Nellie?"

"Yes, Paddy."

"What happened!?" demanded Paddy, his concern showing on his face.

"We got into a fight," said Nellie.

"A school yard fight might explain Peter's shiner, but not your arm, young lady."

"I got slashed by a razor blade," said Nellie.

"Who did this!" Paddy was yelling at this point, his cool was not only lost, but boiling over. "I'll kill them!"

Coco Joe snickered, a little too loud. "So much for sticking to your guns."

It wasn't a good time to gloat.

"Joe, either shut up or leave," Paddy shouted. Coco Joe cowered under the verbal onslaught.

"Sorry," muttered Coco Joe, as he stared into his drink rather intently.

"Paddy, calm down," I said.

"Calm down!?" said Paddy, throwing his arms out and knocking over a beer glass. It fell to the floor and shattered. Paddy took a deep breath and sat back down. I moved to clean it up. "I see your point Murphy. Why don't the lot of you tell me everything that happened?"

"We were at the corner playground, playing handball," started Brian.

"And these guys started picking on Peter," said Shellie.

"They were jerks. And mean," said Peter.

"They called him a retard and started pushing him around. Brian told them to stop. Instead they grabbed him and started hitting him," said Nellie.

"There must have been twenty of them," said Corny.

"At least," said Shellie.

"Maybe more," added Brian.

Paddy had heard enough bar tales to know when something was being exaggerated. He turned to the one he felt would have been the most level-headed in the situation.

"Nellie, how many were there?" asked Paddy.

"Six. Four boys, two girls. All of them were high schoolers."

"What were they doing picking on you guys?" I asked.

"They're in a gang. The Stormers," said Brian.

Coco Joe's head jerked up reflexively, before he caught himself and went back to staring into his margarita. He tried to look around to see if anyone noticed. I was the only one and I was apparently beneath his notice.

"Stormers are bad news, boss. They're coast to cost, and into some bad stuff. Big into dealing; ecstasy, coke, crack, and more than a couple of designer drugs," said Herc.

"These guys dealing to the kids on the playground?" asked Paddy.

"I'm not sure," said Brian.

"I think so," said Shellie.

"They are," said Nellie. Paddy nodded. Coco Joe looked nervous.

"What happened then?"

"The four boys started wailing on Brian. Corny ran off. Peter tried to stop the bullies and the biggest one punched him in the face. It knocked him down and gave him that shiner. Shellie jumped on his back and started hitting him on the head. He spun around like a bucking bronco and left Peter alone. Problem was, the girls went after him and he was still on the ground. One pulled out a razor blade and said she was going to give him a life mark," said Nellie.

"Life mark?" I asked.

"It's an initiation or rite of passion into some street gangs. The wannabe gangbanger picks a victim at random and slices them, usually on the face, where everyone can see it. It marks them for life," explained Herc.

"I threw the handball in her face and she dropped the razor. I managed to kick it away, but the big one had just thrown Shellie off his back, so he picked it up," said Nellie.

"He would have used it, too, if it wasn't for Corny," said Shellie.

"I thought Nellie said Corny had run off?" I said.

"I had to. I couldn't do any good as a kid and I couldn't change shape in front of the gangbangers," said Corny. Corny's mom, Caylee, was big into him keeping his Shapeling powers secret.

"What form did you take?" asked Paddy.

"A pit bull. I'm good at dogs," said Corny, smiling. He had been practicing using his powers since the truth had come out about him being a Shapeling, but he was rusty, not having done much since he was an infant. Also, changing shape is much easier in the magic-rich Faerie than on low-magic Earth, which didn't make things any easier.

"Corny bit his hand and he dropped the razor. He went for his gun, but it wasn't there any longer," said Shellie, handing a Saturday Night Special to Herc. Hermes had taken a shine to the girls, teaching them many things, including pocket picking. Shellie wasn't as good as her younger sister, but she was more skilled than most. "I got it from him while I was riding on his back."

"Did you have to use it?" asked Herc.

"Naw. Corny started acting like a crazy dog, barking and growling," said Shellie.

"Corny the pitbull was scary. He even started foaming at the mouth," said Peter.

"I did that on purpose," said Corny proudly.

"What happened next?" asked Paddy.

"Two cop cars arrived, their sirens blaring. Apparently someone called the police." And they say New Yorkers don't want to get involved. "The Stormers ran off. So did we. Then we found Corny's clothes. He changed and we came home," said Brian. Corny can use his powers to form clothes, but it requires a lot of effort on his part and after an entire day of that, he's exhausted. At least on Earth. Corny wears regular clothes and ditches them before he shape shifts, at least after the last time. Caylee had grounded him once after he shifted in his clothes, ripping them to shreds. He hasn't done it since.

"I'm glad all of you are okay. You handled yourselves well, but I think this is more than you should be expected to deal with. We'll take care of them for you," said

Paddy.

"Paddy. . ." started Coco Joe.

"What!?" snapped Paddy, expecting another wisecrack.

"I'd be happy to take care of this for you," offered Coco Joe.

Paddy's face softened. "Thanks Joe, but we take care of our own."

"Okay," said Coco Joe, but he seemed worried and disappointed. He downed the rest of his margarita and stood up. "I'm going to head out. Good luck."

Goodbyes were said all around and Joe left. If we had only known then what we learned later, we never would have let him go, but it was years before we discovered Coco Joe's connection to the Stormers.

"What are we going to do?" I asked.

"Murph, you are staying here and babysitting," said Paddy.

"Hey," said the kids and I in unison, but for very different reasons.

"Murphy, do you really want to go head to head with a street gang?" asked Paddy.

"No," I admitted.

"As for the rest of you, babysitting is just a word. You aren't babies, so don't be so sensitive. You all wait here until we get back," said Paddy.

"But—" started Corny.

"Don't worry, Corny. Murphy will call your mom," said Paddy. Corny nodded. "Now, Herc, you and I had best get a plan together."

"You want me to call in the rest of the staff?" asked Herc, referring to Hermes, Demeter, and Dionysus.

"It'll probably be best, even if it's doubtlessly overkill. After all, we don't want to hurt anybody," Paddy said with a smile and a wink. Herc smiled, but rolled his eyes back in his head.

In short order, they had a plan, and they had located the Stormers. It wasn't that hard. Paddy called Jason Cervantes and it turned out the NYPD had several addresses on them.

It took Hermes the better part of a minute to check out all the addresses in the city. He was being thorough, after all. Hermes found our culprits nearby. It was easy. Only one of the Stormers had a hand with a dog bite. They were comfortably resting in a store front redone as an upscale clubhouse. The Stormers did well enough that they had bought the building.

The front door was locked, which slowed Hermes down about as much as a gentle breeze, but he wasn't the one to go in first. Paddy was.

The boss walked in the front door silently. Leprechauns are good at stealth when they need to be. At first nobody noticed, so Paddy cleared his throat. That got their attention and a gaggle of guns pointed his way.

"Big mistake, old man," said one of the Stormers.

"I don't think so," said Paddy, snapping his fingers. The Stormers' guns all seemed to vanish, as if by magic. What nobody saw was that Hermes came in and took all the weapons in less than the blink of an eye. Not having seen it, the Stormers assumed Paddy had done it somehow.

Everyone stood and stared, until someone broke the silence with a question. "What'd you do with our guns?" asked a female Stormer.

"Give them back," demanded the Stormer Corny had bitten.

"Ye want yer toys back? Sure," said Paddy, snapping again.

The guns were returned the same way they were taken, although not quite in the same condition. Hercules had spent some time practicing gun barrel origami on the weapons so they were all useless, although Herc does make a lovely silver swan with a .45 magnum.

"How'd you do that?" asked one of them.

Paddy walked over to a reclining armchair, sat, and put his feet up, ignoring the man who appeared to be the leader of this Stormer chapter. The guy didn't like that, and reacted with violence, throwing a punch at Paddy's face. Paddy dodged the punch easily by rolling out of the chair and tripping the guy, who flipped over the chair and landed on his head.

He got up and rushed at Paddy.

Paddy lifted up his snapping fingers and the leader stopped short. "Don't make me do it."

The leader decided to risk it. Paddy snapped and the Hermes express went into action again. This time, instead of taking his gun, he of the red winged sneakers took the man's clothes and replaced them with a pink leotard, complete with pink fluffy tutu.

The subordinate Stormers started to laugh, despite themselves. The leader yelled at them to shut up, which only made them laugh harder.

"You," said Paddy, pointing to the Stormer with the bitten hand. "Come here." He hesitated, then Paddy raised his snapping fingers. He listened, moving timidly.

"Who was with you in the park today?" asked Paddy.

"I don't know what you're talking about," he lied.

"Those were my kids you were messing with. Right now, your lying is making me angrier than I already am. This is not a good thing, nor is it a healthy thing," said Paddy, frowning. "Tell me who was with you."

Before he could answer, one of the girls who had been there made a dash for the back door. A few moments later, her body was tossed back in, followed by Demeter.

"We got number two. Four to go," said Demeter.

"Thanks," said Paddy. Turning to dog-bite boy, he added, "I came with a few friends."

"Like we're scared of grandma there," said a Stormer, who was having trouble imagining Demeter as a threat. His mistake. Demeter walked right up to the guy and cold-cocked him. The wise mouth hit the floor like a sack of potatoes. The wise cracks died down after that.

"Let me invite in some of the others," said Paddy, snapping again.

Dion walked in, but he used the front door. Herc didn't bother, choosing instead to make his own in a side wall. The Stormers looked at Herc in his lion skin trenchcoat, then at the hole in the wall, and more than a few Stormers had downpours in their shorts.

"Of course, if you don't want to tell me, you can step outside with my friend here," said Paddy, indicating Herc. Dog-bite boy gave up his four remaining friends in less than four heartbeats.

"What are you going to do? Call the cops?" asked dog-bite boy. That got a few laughs.

"Come, now. We're men and women of the world. We know the cops won't be able to pin anything on you," said Dion, with his trademark smile. The eyes of all the women and about three of the men were glued in dreamy infatuation on him. Outside of the bar, his godly powers kicked in, and he was even more irresistible to women.

"We're going to take care of this ourselves," said Herc, with a smile of his own, but it had a more fearful aspect than that of the god of wine.

"How?" asked the leader in the pink tutu, his tone clearly worried.

"We are going to teach you something that seems to have been neglected in your formal educations. There are consequences to your actions," said Demeter.

"Like what? You gonna spank us," asked Mr. Pink Tutu, with a chuckle.

"Worse," said Paddy, snapping his fingers. I think he was beginning to enjoy having Hermes jump on his command.

The six Stormers from the park disappeared via the Hermes Express. Although they all seemed to vanish at once, Hermes actually took them individually and flew them to a height a few thousand feet above the New York skyline, then dropped them. They plummeted and screamed in terror, watching the ground coming toward them all too quickly. Just before impact, Hermes caught them, then returned them, physically unharmed, to the Stormer clubhouse. Mentally was another story.

The six lay on the floor, whimpering and shivering like terrified kittens.

"What did you do to them?" asked Mr. Pink Tutu.

Paddy stayed silent and just smiled.

"Now we have to take care of the rest of you," said Herc.

"The rest of us? Why? We weren't in the park. We didn't do anything to your kids," said Mr. Pink Tutu.

"But can you say you have never done something like that to somebody else's kids?" asked Herc. "To become a Stormer, you all had to give out a life mark. All of you have hurt people. Some of you have killed people." Herc was guessing, but the Stormers didn't know that and enough of them looked down at the floor for him to know he was right. "You laugh at the police. You thought nobody could touch you. You were wrong. We're here to avenge all the innocents you have ever hurt. First, we hurt you where it counts. In the wallet."

Herc nodded to Dion. Because of his nature, Dion has an affinity for mind-altering substances, so he was able to find their stash easily, not unlike a divine blood-hound. He walked over to a coffee table style trunk and opened it, revealing enough pills and powders to keep an addict happy for several lifetimes. These drugs weren't for personal use, they were for sale.

"Hey, those are ours. You better not touch those, if you know what's good for you," said Mr. Pink Tutu, trying to talk tough. With his outfit, he just couldn't pull it off.

"No touching, huh? Fine, I can take care of it from here," said Dion, and with a wave of his hand and a burst of light, the stash was incinerated. Most of the Stormers let out blood-curdling screams.

"What'd you do? We still owe almost half a million on that. We don't have that kind of cash. We're gonna get killed," said Mr. Pink Tutu.

"Stop your whining. The insurance will cover what you owe," said Paddy.

"What insurance?"

"On the building. I'd advise you all to vacate the premises quickly," said Paddy, nodding to Herc, who walked up to the support beams and walls, punching each of them.

"Over to the lady," said Herc, with a gallant bow.

"Time to shake things up a bit," said Demeter, snapping her own fingers, but what happened had nothing to do with Hermes. Demeter, a goddess of the Earth, had some powers of her own. A tremor, confined to the ground under the Stormers' building, began. The Stormers ran out, or rather those that could did, leaving behind the six who had experienced the wonders of free fall above New York City. So much for Stormer loyalty. Paddy and the rest carried them to safety.

Once Hermes had double checked that everyone was out, Demeter increased the tremor until the building fell in on itself, in a cloud of dust and rubble.

The Stormers stared numbly as their world crumbled to the ground.

"I think that this should convince the lot of you that payback is not only not an option, but an incredibly stupid idea. This time, we let you off easy. Next time. . ." Hercules let the implication hang in the air. The Stormers may not have liked it, but they knew he was right.

"You are starting now with a clean slate and a second chance. The insurance money will pay what you owe on the drugs," said Paddy. He and Hermes had already checked things out before they started. Paddy is very serious about protecting life, and wouldn't have risked the Stormers' lives just to prove a point. "Any or all of you can choose to leave this life and start a new one."

"Stormers swear a blood oath. The only way out is death," said Mr. Pink Tutu, fury overcoming fear.

"Then think of this as a one-time-only deal. Anyone who chooses to leave will be under my protection," said Paddy.

"Ain't no one leaving," said the Mr. Pink Tutu, who was tearing off the tutu, pulling a long leather jacket off a subordinate and putting it on.

"I want out," said a timid voice. It was one of the six from the park.

"You're dead if you do this," said the leader. Herc walked up to him, lifted him up with one hand and threw him into the wall of the building next door. It shut him up, but pure hate shown from his eyes.

"Whatever you do to him, I'm going to do to you," promised Herc.

"Don't do this, Dave," said the leader, pulling himself up to his feet.

"I have to, Turk," said Dave.

"Turk? An appropriate name for a turkey," said Herc, laughing. Tutu Turk didn't find it funny.

"Anybody else?" asked Paddy, sadly. He had hoped there would be more takers. There weren't. "Fine. The rest of you better be out of New York before midnight tomorrow. If you're not, we'll know, and we'll come after you." Several of the Stormers started to whine about that not being fair. "You have your lives and a second chance. That's more than most people get and more than most of ye deserve. Go now, before I change me mind," said Paddy.

Grumbling, but without a better alternative, the rest of the Stormers walked away. Hermes would make sure they did as Paddy told them.

Paddy did help Dave out. Turns out he was a sixteen-year-old runaway. The boss managed to help reconcile him with his family, and bought him a first class ticket home. Our kids were left alone after that. The newspaper blamed an underground gas explosion for the destruction of the building.

The only thing we should have paid more attention to was the fact that Hermes later mentioned that he had found Coco Joe hanging around near the Stormer's building. Hermes confronted the storm god, but Joe claimed he had followed in case the others needed help. Hermes didn't buy it, but didn't pursue the matter further. It would be years before we realized Joe had actually been there to warn the Stormers away, because he was their leader. Not only of that chapter, but of the entire international organization. By then, it was too late.

Coco Joe would eventually ally himself with certain vampyres and they would feed on his godly blood, giving them untold power. The first battle of blood would begin and it would be up to our friend Lucas Wilson, who we hadn't even met yet, to set things right. But that's a story for another day and another book.

BLOOD BROTHER

The mist followed him in, hot on his heels. Behind him, the first rays of sunrise started to bathe the Manhattan skyline in a warm, orange, luminescent lather. The haze on the city outside was slowly being eaten away by the lazy nibbles of the morning light.

A black trenchcoat draped his gaunt frame. From the company I kept, I knew that could be trouble. White skin and a look of desperation were drawn tight over high cheek bones. The face as a whole was as pale as the moon in twilight, yet his eyes almost glowed a deep crimson. The fact that they were bloodshot didn't hurt the effect. Straight black hair adorned the top of his head. It was grimy, unkempt, and made his skin appear even paler by contrast.

His two legs carried him into the bar easily enough, but then rebelled, forcing him to drop to one knee on the hardwood floor. The man began to tremble like a leaf caught in a hurricane. His eye lids were fluttering like the wings of a humming bird, and he appeared to be having trouble focusing his vision. The signs were easily recognizable. Bulfinche's newest visitor was a junkie.

"Help me," he begged, his raspy voice barely audible.

"What do you need?" I asked, not yet recognizing his particular addiction.

"A drink," he said simply. He had come to the right place; with no false modesty, we had the best stocked pub anywhere. Still, the pale man didn't look like someone going through the DT's.

"Name it. We have anything you could ask for," I said confidently, helping him off the floor and into a chair. The man moved oddly, almost lurching, as if he wasn't used to carrying his own body weight.

He decided to put me to the test.

"Blood," he blurted out, shame shining sorrowfully in his red eyes. He waited for an outward reaction from me. When it never came, he added, "In a dirty glass."

Odd request, but I've had odder. What could I do? I had said anything. Taking a sharp knife from behind the bar, I made a small incision over the vein in my left wrist. The draining blood filled two shot glasses before I shut off the tap. I put them and a third, this one of vodka, into a beer mug. Adding a twist of lime, I stirred it with a celery stick. I always said the morning shift would bleed me dry, but this was ridiculous. After sterilizing the cut with whiskey and bandaging my wrist, I poured a glass of O.J. for myself. I brought both glasses to the table and joined the man to make a toast.

"To your good health."

Ignoring my toast, he grabbed the glass and greedily gulped gobs of the scarlet liquid down. The concoction seemed to satisfy his hunger, as life flowed back into his weary bones. Straightening up from his slumped posture, he sipped the rest as if it was a fine wine.

"Good vintage," he said.

"Yes. O positive," I informed him.

"The universal donor. Not as tangy as some of the more exotic flavors, but very satisfying. Just my type," he joked. "May I be so bold as to ask the year?"

"'61," I answered.

"What do I owe you?" he asked.

"Nothing. First drink's on the house. Tradition here at Bulfinche's Pub."

"Thanks," he replied, swallowing the last few drops. If he had had a straw, it would be making slurping noises. Actually, he was making the noises without the straw.

"You're welcome. But the second one is going to cost you big time," I told him. He laughed and smiled. The fangs the grin revealed confirmed my suspicions about his addiction; it was one of the worst. My customer was a blood junkie: a vampyre.

"That's okay. This should do me for a day or two at least," he replied.

The sun had taken back the morning sky from the hold of the night, and its bright rays shone through the front window, landing on trenchcoat–covered legs.

"I don't mean to pry," I said.

"But you are going to anyway," the man added, good heartedly.

"Pretty much," I replied honestly. "Shouldn't you be dead? With the sunlight and all? No offense."

"None taken. Why do you ask?" he answered, amused.

"Well, I assume you did not drink that cocktail because you're anemic," I said overwhelming him with enormous insight.

"Right you are. I am a vampyre," he said, slightly surprised at hearing the words come out of his mouth.

"So why weren't you fried to a crisp outside, like in the movies?" Not that I wanted him dead. First off, he seemed like a decent guy. Second a body that sizzles and then decomposes makes a huge mess, and I would get stuck cleaning it up.

"A combination of the New York smog and this keep me somewhat safe from the sun," he said, pulling a plastic bottle out of the inside pocket of his trenchcoat. He handed it to me. It read "Sunscreen 199".

"Good stuff," he continued. "It has to be made special and costs a fortune, but it's worth it. For six months I hid from the day and embraced the night. It finally became too much for me so I put this stuff on and went out one morning."

"How did you know it would work?" I asked.

"I didn't. But I figured it was worth the risk. If I was turned into a crispy critter, at least I would feel the sun on my face one last time. Now I avoid mid-afternoon, but I can go out at dusk or dawn with no problem. I got my life back," he stated happily.

I nodded understandingly. Realizing then my lapse in manners, I introduced myself.

"By the by, my name's Murphy. Murph to my friends and blood brothers."

"A pleasure, Murph. I'm Lucas Wilson."

"What, no title like Count or Baron?" I asked.

"Nope. I guess Mister doesn't have the same kick to it," he said. Lucas went on to tell me he was a computer programmer. It was a good profession, allowing him to make a living despite his condition.

"You're taking all this rather calmly. A year ago if someone asked me for blood and then informed me they were a vampyre, I would be freaking out. You haven't even tried to make a bee line for the door or the phone. Aren't you worried that I might try for the rest of your blood?" he asked seriously.

"Not really. Any special powers or curses you have are neutralized here in Bulfinche's. Unless the boss gives you dispensation, you are mortal like anyone else. Then only ones with standing dispensations are his family and certain employees," I stated. Lucas looked confused.

"Go ahead. Try to turn into a mist or a bat," I suggested. He shrugged his shoulders, creased his brow in concentration. Nothing happened. Lucas was perplexed by this but decided to change the subject.

"Even so, meeting an actual vampyre must bother you a little," he said.

"Not in this job," I answered.

"What could be more bizarre than a vampyre?" he asked.

As if in answer to his question, the sound of women giggling permeated the room. It was coming closer. Footsteps were heard coming down stairs and the door behind the bar opened wide. Five women, smiles all, entered. To say they were beautiful was like saying the Empire State Building was a comfortable shack.

In the midst of this entourage was Dionysus. He led the women across the bar to the door and proceeded to give each a drawn out, passionate kiss. After the kiss was over the idea was for the woman to leave, but they kept getting back in line for another. Dion made no move to chase them.

"Popular guy," Lucas said, "I bet you enjoy his leftovers."

"Not really," I said. Lucas' ears perked up. "He never leaves any. Unfortunately. Dionysus takes all comers and leaves them smiling," I said.

"Dionysus, as in Bacchus?" Lucas asked. I nodded. "They sure picked the right name for him."

"Actually that is the real Dionysus."

"The god?" he asked, unbelieving. Again I nodded. He looked again at the women, but I could see he was skeptical. I poured a small glass of wine; made in–house, and passed him the glass. One sip of the heavenly vino later we had a believer.

"Incredible," was his rave review. "So you work for a Greek god?"

"Not exactly. My boss is a leprechaun by the name of Paddy Moran. Dion tends bar for him also."

"I don't get it. Why would the god of wine work in a bar for someone else?"

"Paddy has a much better head for business," I said. Talk about an understatement. "Besides, Dion likes to spend his time on other matters," I said pointing my thumb across the barroom.

By now, Dion had gotten all the ladies out the door save one. She refused to leave and fainted in an attempt to prolong her stay, just as Ismael Macob walked in. Together, they loaded her into the back of Ismael's cab and took her home. Ismael is one of our regulars. His is a strange story. Several years ago he picked up a fare down at the South Street Seaport. The man was poorly dressed and appeared down on his luck. It was a cold winter night, so Ismael took pity on the man.

He drove him around for awhile but the man kept changing where he wanted to go. It got too much for Ismael when the man said he refused to pay. So, not being totally without heart, Ismael dropped him off at a men's shelter. The man demanded to be taken somewhere else. Ismael refused and escorted the man out of the back seat. Furious at such treatment, the man cursed Ismael to wander the tri-state area, not knowing where he was and unable to return home or find any place a fare told him to go. Almost destitute, he found Bulfinche's. Once inside the bar, his curse was temporarily lifted. He was able to remember his home phone number and call his wife. They were reunited after four months. Paddy rented him a room upstairs for conjugal visits. Paddy was even able to find a loophole to the curse. If anybody was to tell him where to go, he couldn't. So Paddy suggested he not ask and just drive them wherever felt right. Turns out Ismael is infallible every time. He's made a fortune betting passengers that he knows where they are going without them telling him. Been in the papers as the psychic cabbie. With the extra money he has been able to bring the rest of his family over from Egypt and he now owns three houses, even if he has no idea where they are.

Hercules, Hermes and Dion are convinced the old man was Neptune. No way of proving it unless he stops in for a drink. Probably will happen someday.

His escapades completed for the morning, Dion walked over to join us. He doesn't look like the type of man women would contend over. His plump face is blanketed by a well trimmed beard, a smile that would put a Viking berserker at ease and he sported the beginning of a "wine belly." Whatever it was, I wish I had a fraction of it.

"Morning, Murph," he said.

"Morning, Dion. Slow night?" I asked.

"A little," he laughed. "But I did need to get at least fifteen minutes sleep." He turned toward Lucas as if they had known each other for years and introduced himself.

"Greetings," he said extending his hand. "I'm Dionysus and you are?"

"A vampyre," came the female voice from the door. Silhouetted in the light was a middle aged woman dressed in several layers of clothes whose styles spanned the last three decades.

A few years ago she would have been called a bag lady. Today she's called homeless. We call her Rebecca. She's another regular, although she only drinks hot tea and she brings her own tea bag. "Don't worry," she continued. "He's okay. He always asks before he drinks. He's on the narrow, if not the straight."

"How do you know that?" Lucas asked, incredulously.

"The streets tell their stories to those who listen," she answered. Lucas laughed, walked up to her and took her hand in his.

"My thanks for your approval, Milady," he said kissing her hand as he did so. Beneath the grime of the street that was her makeup, Rebecca blushed.

"If only you meant it," she said. "Murphy, we got us a hungry crowd out there. Snap to it."

I had almost forgotten the reason why I was up so early. It was my week to work the morning shift. Paddy has a multi-level parking garage attached to the bar. The ground level he uses to give the homeless a place to sleep. He supplies them with bedding and even with space heaters in the winter. The people in need find the place through Rebecca or Father Mike Ryann, another Bulfinche's patron. When his church, Our Lady of the Lake, stopped a similar program due to lack of funding from the diocese, Paddy picked up the slack. Now every morning he makes sure the hungry get food and every night they have shelter. Demeter, our chef and a goddess as well, prepares the meal and she, Father Mike, Rebecca, and the employee of the week dish it out. I left Lucas with Dion and hurried back to the kitchen to help bring the food out.

After the food was served, Father Mike offered to help find jobs for anyone looking. As long as someone was trying to find work they could stay and use Bulfinche's as a mailing address–a major necessity when job hunting. If someone wasn't looking, a three–night stay was all Paddy allowed. Paddy hates to part with money and abhors freeloaders, but he is willing to help those down on their luck. Hercules enforced the three day rule consistently, except during sub–zero winter days. Paddy seemed to develop "memory problems" with the cold. Children stayed as long as they needed and usually got a room upstairs.

Oddly enough, one of the few to not take advantage of what was being offered was Rebecca herself. She's helped hundreds of others but still stays on the streets. She had a soft spot in the old man's heart. She was the only adult exempt from the three day rule, even if she did not take advantage of it consistently.

Amidst all the people helping people, I was cleaning up, restacking the bedding, clearing the plates and such. Not too bad unless you count emptying and cleaning the port–a–potty that is kept there. Despite my begging and pleading, Paddy refuses to buy a modern, self cleaning model. He says as long as it works, it stays. Hercules has had to take a sledge hammer from my hands twice. And trying to overload it is counterproductive, since I'm the one who has to clean up the mess. Once was enough for me to learn my lesson. I just grit my teeth and do what I have to. Not my idea of fun, and I look ridiculous with the clothespin on my nose.

After an hour, I was finished and the garage was spotless. I rejoined the others in the bar smelling quite fragrant with my new cologne "eau de port–a–potty." Paddy had come in. Hercules was uncharacteristically awake. It turns out he was just getting in, not getting up. He was telling of past experiences with the undead element.

"...so of course I had no choice but to run him through the heart. Turns out he was the only one of the twelve not a vampyre."

I was not sure what the whole story was, but it actually had Lucas laughing. Hercules' gift for story telling is greater than the legends of his strength, most of which he started himself.

Father Mike had come in right behind me. Seeing the frocked priest Lucas averted his eyes. Mike took his usual seat at the end of the bar near the plate glass window and ordered an O.J. Ismael had returned also and was eating breakfast.

Lucas appeared deep in thought, as if debating something. Finally deciding, he went up to the good priest and looked him straight in the eyes.

"Father, would you please hear my confession?" he asked.

"Of course. We can go back to my church if you like. It's only right up the block."

"I don't think that would be a good idea. You see Father, I'm a vampyre. Holy ground and I don't mix well," Lucas said. I guess he was waiting for a reaction from Father Mike which never came. Hanging around in Bulfinche's builds up your shock tolerance.

"No problem. We can go to a more private place in the building."

"It's okay, Father. I'd like to do it here if it's okay with you. I feel comfortable here and I don't mind these folks hearing what I have to say," he said. Bulfinche's has that effect. It's almost as if the outside world no longer can hurt you once you walk through the door. It is the only place I have ever been in that can effectively block out the noise of an entire city. Bulfinche's radiates a feeling of well being, like being under heavy blankets in a warm bed on a cold morning.

Father Mike agreed to the request.

"Very well. Let's begin. In the name of the Father and of the Son..." he said. Lucas visibly cringed, more from habit than pain.

"Father, can we skip that part? It's usually very painful for me."

"Certainly, but I think you'll find it painless here," said the good Father, understandingly. Lucas crossed himself without incident.

"It has been five years since my last confession. In that time I have lied, been disrespectful to my parents, missed mass, stolen, and I killed a man," Lucas confessed. He had our undivided attention although to everyone's credit no facial expressions changed. All eyes did grow a tad wider though.

"Before I continue Father, I need to ask what the church feels about what I am."

"Vampyre? Off–hand, I'm not sure, but I'm certain it's not favorable," Mike said diplomatically.

"No, not vampyres. Homosexuals," Lucas said softly.

"Not favorable at all, I'm afraid," replied Father Mike.

"Why? We are people just like everyone else. But are we treated as such? No. I know vampyres who are treated better," he said. Then he realized his audience was not among that number and he calmed down. "Sorry Father, I don't mean to go off on a high horse like that. It's just I've been under a great deal of stress. It all began seven months ago. I was at a club where I met Jack. From the moment our eyes met, my will was not my own. Jack took me home and seduced me. I woke up the next morning alone with a small purple bruise on my right shoulder."

"The same scenario happened night after night for a week. Then Jack convinced me to let her into my house."

"Her?" asked Hercules, confused.

"Her. Jack as in Jacqueline. When we first met I thought Jack was a he. She was in drag. Once she was allowed in my house, I wasn't enough to satisfy her hunger. She went after Bill," he said, then delayed a minute before continuing.

"Bill and I had been involved and living together for four years. We had not been involved physically for almost two years since we found out he was HIV positive. I've tested negative every six months for the last two years. I didn't want to become infected and even safe sex wasn't safe enough for me. I was celibate for all that time. It was hard to do," he said looking respectfully at his priest confessor. Mike just nodded. "I wasn't going to leave Bill even when he developed AIDS. You don't abandon someone you love just because things get rough. But I still had needs. So I decided to go out for a one night stand. Not the most honorable thing and certainly not the best. That's how I met Jack," said Lucas, averting his eyes in guilt.

"She fed on both Bill and me for months, night after night. We were helplessly in her thrall. Meanwhile, Bill's condition had worsened. He was in and out of reality as his condition progressed. The doctors said that his brain looked like Swiss cheese on the CAT scans before this even happened. He had mini-strokes and other complications. Because of the vampyrism, he couldn't even get to a hospital. Nor could he die. He just lived on, a husk of his former self. Bill's only purpose was as a feeding ground for Jack."

"For a brief period he was coherent and he begged me to let him die. I couldn't bear to see him suffer any longer. I took a leg off our coffee table and sharpened it with a kitchen knife. I held him in my arms, kissed him on the forehead, and I...I..." he paused, choking on his words. He barely held back his tears. Finally he collapsed, sobbing in Father Mike's arms.

"I killed him. Put the stake through his chest. It was so hard. I had to try three different spots before I could hammer it in. His face never even changed expression. I wrapped his body in a blanket and put it on our fire escape before dawn. I pulled the black curtains that we had to live with and went to sleep. Awakening after sunset I took the blanket and his remains to the roof. Scattering his ashes to the winds, I sent a small prayer toward the heavens." Slowly he regained his composure. He took a moment to wipe the tears from his eyes before he continued.

"Before the next dawn, I moved all my worldly possessions to another apartment I had sublet from a friend. It had to be done before Jack came that night. I was successful and she has not been able to find me since," he said. He was done with his confession and bowed his head to wait for Father Mike to speak.

"The taking of a life is a horrible sin, but even that can be forgiven, in some cases there is no other choice. This is one of those cases. You acted out of mercy and from love. Lucas, you did the only thing you could do in the situation," said Father Mike. His words seemed to take a burden off Lucas' shoulders. What he did would be with him always. He would never forget. Lucas just needed to hear from someone else that he had done the right thing. It was obvious he had feared condemnation, but what he got was understanding.

"Have you ever harmed another person for blood?" asked Father Mike.

"No Father. I have a friend who's a medical technician that helps me out. I've also stolen from blood banks. I have no desire to put someone else into the same situation as me."

"Good, except for the stealing part. Now for your penance," said Father Mike thoughtfully. "I suppose normally you are unable to say the Our Father or Hail Mary?"

"Not out loud, Father."

"God hears even our thoughts, so pray to him that way. For the rest of your penance, I charge you never to harm another person to feed your hunger. And to not steal blood again unless absolutely necessary," said Father Mike. He did not have to state that appropriating blood would be less of a sin than drinking straight from the source. Lucas was able to say an act of contrition.

"Your sins are forgiven," said Father Mike.

"Father, I worry I may not be able to keep my penance. It is getting harder and harder to resist. I crave warm, fresh blood. This morning, before I found Murphy, I barely let an innocent go free. I wanted so much to have blood, but what I almost did horrified me. I ran away, but I couldn't run away from myself. I transformed into a mist in my haste to flee and the strangest thing happened. The first flickers of dawn flowed through me and formed a rainbow. It was radiant. On a whim I decided to follow it. Somehow I was able to. It led here. I tried to float in but as soon as I entered the doorway I couldn't remain a mist," he said.

Paddy explained to Lucas that one of the distinctive properties of Bulfinche's is that people in trouble tend to find it. Of course, this is true of many bars but the way in which they find us is unique. A rainbow leads them here. Sometimes the rainbow is a person, a regular. Occasionally it's the glint of the rainbow painted on the front window, above the drawn shot of gold which catches their eye. More often than not, an actual rainbow shows them the way. As near as I can figure the reason for this is that at the end of a rainbow lies a pot of gold. Paddy invested his pot to buy the bar. Therefore, the bar takes the place of the pot of gold and someone chasing a rainbow will not find wealth but a cold drink and some folks willing to help. Seems a pretty fair trade to me. Lucas seemed to have accepted this. Maybe the folks who tend to end up at Bulfinche's have a high shock tolerance to begin with.

Lucas was still worried about his increasing blood lust.

"It's ironic. Just about the only thing Jack was unable to convince me to do was join her in feeding on Bill. It annoyed her that she couldn't corrupt me completely. Now it may happen without her help. What can I do to stop this from overtaking me?" he asked pleadingly.

"I'm afraid I don't have an answer for you," said Father Mike apologetically.

"But I might," said Paddy. "Detox."

"What do you mean?" Lucas asked, a faint glint of hope gleaming in his red eyes.

"We wean you off human blood and onto a substitute like cow or sheep blood. We have plenty of that since Demeter kills her meat fresh," Paddy said. Demeter nodded and rattled off a dozens recipes on how to prepare an entree out of blood, every thing from blood pudding to blood pie. They had no appeal to me, but Lucas was licking his fangs. "I've heard of vampyres surviving on it before. It is not as nourishing as human blood and it will take constant effort on your part but if you are willing, we'll be glad to help you as much as we can."

"You would do that for me? Why?" asked Lucas.

"Why not?" was Paddy's only answer. It was the only answer Lucas needed.

"Thank you all," Lucas said softly, looking at each of us. Something was still troubling him though. He had the look of someone who wanted to ask something very important, but was afraid of pushing his luck. Taking a deep breath to steady himself, he went for broke.

"I realize that what I am about to ask will place a great burden on all of you, but I must beg a favor. If the detox fails or if I develop end stage AIDS like Bill, please see to it that I can't hurt anyone and that I am put out of my misery," Lucas asked. Many heads turned silently away, including my own. One voice answered him loud and clear.

"If the need arises, I will see to it," vowed Hercules solemnly. I had no doubt that he would. I doubt I could.

"Or I will," promised Rebecca. "There are some things no one should be forced to endure." It was obvious by his silence that Paddy disapproved. He believes there is always another way but Paddy, more than anyone, respects a person's right to choose their own path.

"Murph, show him a room upstairs," said Paddy, anxious to change the topic. Death is the one opponent who has been able to beat Paddy again and again.

I took him behind the bar to the door that leads up to our living quarters. Lucas stopped short as if he hit a brick wall.

"What's blocking you?" I asked.

"The bar is a public place; behind that door is your home. I cannot enter without being invited," he said.

I looked toward Paddy, who gave me a nod.

"You may enter as long as your promise to do no harm to any who dwell within," I said. "Do you agree?"

"I do," he said and came in. I showed him to one of our dozens of spare rooms. It had basic furnishings and heavy drapes. Lucas seemed to like it.

"Can I get you anything else? Extra pillow? Blanket? Few pounds of dirt? Garlic bread?" I asked.

"No thanks. This will be fine," he said as he plopped himself backwards onto the bed. Being a native New Yorker, the ground contained his native soil, but that apparently was not a big deal. Even if it was, Bulfinche's would allow him to stay without incident.

The events of the last few nights caught up to him. Lucas' eyes slapped shut and he was snoozing before I reached the door. Good thing he wasn't a vampyre in the days of old. His snoring would have lead the angry villagers straight to his coffin.

Most of the day was uneventful except for when Paddy chased down a businessman who tried to leave without paying his bill. After Paddy caught him he convinced the man that paying the bill, plus a fifty percent tip, would be in his best interest. Of course, once Paddy had him where he wanted him, the gentleman was in no position to bargain. It took the fire department twenty minutes to get the man down from the lamppost.

The eventful part came later. Dion had been serving a man in his mid-forties with messy brown hair and matching mustache. This gentleman was questioning everyone in the place. He was looking for a man who sounded very much like Lucas. First thing that crossed my mind was we had a vampyre hunter on our hands. Of the folks who were around this morning only Paddy, Dion, and myself were still about. We certainly did not volunteer information. How he approached Paddy did nothing to endear him to the old man.

"Hey, shorty," the man said. Paddy's eyes boiled over. Waiting for steam to come out his ears, I watched and was disappointed. One thing Paddy is very sensitive about is his height. The boss kept his cool. A few thousand years of short jokes had hardened him a bit.

"I'm not short," Paddy shot back. "I'm vertically challenged." The man was oblivious. The comeback sailed far over his head and was now entering orbit.

"Whatever. I have a few questions I want to ask you," the man said. "I'm looking for a man."

"Sorry it's not that kind of bar. Try down in Times Square or in the Village," Paddy responded. This one the man understood and he didn't care for the insinuation. Pity.

"Not what I meant. I'm trying to locate a man named Lucas. Don't know his last name."

"Why?"

"Personal reasons," the man said. Not good enough for us to give him anything. We knew he wasn't a cop; would have flashed a badge by now. Not that it would have made a difference.

"Got a picture of him?" I asked, knowing full well the answer.

"Strangely enough I haven't been able to find a single photo of him. Camera shy, I guess," the man said. He lay a fifty dollar bill on the bar in front of Paddy whose face turned into a smirk. Paddy may be a tad money conscious but it is from habit, not necessity. I don't know his net worth, but he made his first dozen million during prohibition and has been raking in the bucks ever since. He didn't even dirty his hands on the fifty.

"This is yours if you can tell me where to find him," the man said. Paddy shook his head no and shrugged his shoulders. Dion and I mirrored him.

"Damn it. I'll never find him," he said as his tough guy facade faded and tears reluctantly ran down his cheeks. More of a slow jog really, but their momentum and any hopes of winning the New York Marathon died out before even reaching his chin. He brushed them off on the sly, hoping no one noticed. We played along.

"Maybe if you told us why finding this gentleman is so important we might be more help," Dion chimed in, smile shining brightly. The man thought about it and decided he had nothing to lose.

"It's my daughter. She's been acting strangely for months. She quit her job, began staying out to all hours of the night and sleeping during the days. One night I followed her and she went to this guy's apartment. I started asking questions and I found out he was a fag. A couple of days later, I stormed up to his apartment, full of fire and fury, to find out what sick game this fairy was playing with my little girl. But I get there and the place is cleared out, like he left in a hurry. Nobody knows nothing. My little girl starts acting stranger, spends her nights searching for this weirdo. She can't find him and it makes her more frustrated. I thought I could help her but so far nothing."

By this point, we knew who his daughter was. She had to be stopped before she spread her contamination. Not only was Jack a vampyre but chances are she's HIV positive, which means her victims, if they were not killed outright, would eventually be condemned to a living death without end. Not a fun way to spend eternity. Not even a good way to spend a Monday.

"I think we might be able to help you. Bring her by at five AM. I'll send a cab," answered Paddy, a plan gleaming in his Irish eyes. They lacked their usual smile.

"Thank you. Here take the money," he said sliding the fifty across the bar top.

"No. Pay the cabbie with it. Tell Jackie not to be late," Paddy said. The man nodded, finished his drink in two gulps and headed out the door. Only halfway out did he realize he had never mentioned his daughter's name, and directed a great deal of suspicion and distrust Paddy's way with all the subtly of a traffic cop during rush hour. The boss responded by whistling and cleaning a glass with a dish towel.

Five AM came all too quickly, even without benefit of sleep and a set alarm clock. Lucas knew exactly what was going down and was jittery. He would not stop pacing and feared falling back under Jack's spell. All of our assurances could not dent his terror. Lucas expressed the desire to transform into a bat so he could fly and work off the nervous tension. The pacing was getting on everyone's nerves so Paddy granted him dispensation for one flight around the bar. It worked and Lucas sat still for about five minutes.

The grandfather clock next to the jukebox struck five. Outside, Ismael's tires were heard screeching to a halt. Everyone made sure they were ready. Father Mike and I had crucifixes beneath our shirts for protection. Since only we two believed, we were the only ones they would do any good for. Paddy, Dion, Hercules, and Hermes, who had just gotten back from an assignment from Paddy, were weaponless. The game plan was to try to convince her to join in the blood junkie detox program. If she chose not to, things would get ugly, even without her father's "good" looks.

Jack's father walked in, his hair combed this time, alone. Jack was nowhere to be seen. Ismael's cab could be heard speeding off into the half empty streets. The man was a coward but it wasn't held against him. I even admired him for it. If I was not so "brave" I would be in a safe cozy bed dreaming blissfully, albeit covered in a garlic sauce. Could not make me smell worse than after cleaning the port-a-johns.

"Where is she?" demanded Paddy.

"Jacqueline had some errands to take care of. She said she'd meet us here," he said. This turn of events made no one happy, but there was nothing we could do about it. Yet. Lucas decided to try the direct approach.

"Mr. Gill, I'm Lucas."

The man remained remarkably well controlled. His clenched fists paled to white, his teeth ground loudly, and veins popped out all over his purple face, but he made no move toward Lucas. Hercules was also providing no small incentive for this inaction as he was standing directly behind Mr. Gill.

"Damn fruit," he muttered under his breath. Lucas let it slide.

"Your daughter is a very sick young girl," Lucas began.

"Don't you talk to me about sick, you..." he stammered as he realized a hand the size of a portable TV was now resting on his shoulder.

"I think you should listen to what he has to say," Hercules said in a voice barely above a whisper. It got his point across louder than if he had shouted. Releasing his grip, Hercules sat on a nearby bar stool.

"Of course. How foolish of me," he said. I was impressed. He was able to keep his knocking knees totally silent.

"Jack has a disease. She infected me and someone I loved dearly against our will," Lucas continued.

"Infected you? Seems like she'd be more likely to get a disease from you," Gill started. Hercules rose slowly to his feet and Gill realized the rest of his thoughts were best left unsaid.

"Mr. Gill, your daughter is a vampyre," said Lucas.

"What kind of crap are you trying to pull here? Is this some kind of joke?" he asked, face bulging and turning a deeper shade of red. Looking around the room at the faces he saw, the unbelievable truth began the long process of sinking in.

"There are no such things as vampyres," he said as if begging the answer to a question. No answer came. "There are no such things as vampyres!" he shouted grabbing Lucas' collar and shaking vigorously, trying to force the answer he wanted to hear to come out.

"I'm afraid there are," Lucas stated, with no small amount of sadness shading his voice from the fire in Gill's eyes.

"How do you know, faggot?" Gill mockingly asked, as if talking to a slow child. This one Lucas wasn't going to let slide.

"Because I am one," Lucas said, baring his fangs in a smile, hissing for effect. Mr. Gill fell backwards over himself in his desire to get away.

"But these people can help her," Lucas said more congenially. Jack's father didn't respond at first. He was a man whose world had just exploded and his eyes showed he was not taking any visitors at the moment. He just kept muttering "Not my little girl." We were so involved in watching the father that the daughter arrived without us noticing.

"Isn't this sweet? Daddy dearest and Lukey," Jack said. She was of medium build with blond hair cut short and a neutral kind of face. Little cleavage to speak of. She could easily pass for a man or a woman depending on how she accessorized.

Now it was Lucas' turn to trip over himself running away from her.

"Lukey, you shouldn't have run away from me. You've been a bad boy. I'm going to have to punish you," she purred.

"Back off," Lucas said, regaining his footing. "I'm not afraid of you," he lied unconvincingly. Although his knees weren't knocking together, they were stirring up some fierce air currents.

"Honey," said Mr. Gill, his daughter's arrival bringing him out of his stupor. "These men said that..."

"Daddy, you can believe them. I'm sure it's no worse than the truth," she said.

"They said they can help you," he pleaded with his daughter. She was not interested in buying what he was selling.

"Help me? Why? I've never been so happy," she said, drawing a tongue the color of blood over the length of her right index finger as if licking something tasty off. A small, purposeful burp came forth from her mouth which she covered with her hand and a giggle. She tried to sound like a little girl, but the tint of evil in her voice prevented her from getting even close.

"Jack, where were you?" Lucas demanded, the horror of recognition in his eyes.

"My, so forceful. Not that it's any of your business, but I stopped for a bite," she said drawing her tongue over her glistening white fangs and dark crimson lips in small circles. Lucas cringed. Jack smiled a smile of darkest intent. Behind her Paddy nodded and Hermes turned the skeleton key and locked the door. Never before had I seen the front door bolted. We only lock the door behind the bar that leads to our living quarters. Even when no one is on duty that door remains unhooked along with the cash register, a rarity in this city. Pity Jack did not recognize this omen for what it was.

Jack looked around at the rest of us. A white collar attracted her attention. She moved toward Father Mike. Paddy tried to reason with her.

"Jack, we may be able to help you," Paddy explained.

"God helps those who help themselves. Isn't that right, Father?" she asked. Mike did not answer. He stood defiant. She put her hand on his chest and began stroking up and down in a sensuous manner. "And I help myself to what I want," she said, her hand traveling southward to areas strictly off limits. Mike grabbed her hand before she could have been arrested for trespassing in his nether region.

"C'mon, Priest. Think of all the commandments we could break," she said her other hand going toward Mike's upper chest as she was bending forward to lick his chin. With a start she pulled away, obviously in pain. Jack put her fingers in her mouth and sucked on them to soothe the cross shaped burn. "Smart man. Today you should always carry protection." Paddy had given dispensation for the crucifixes to work, but only on sight or contact so Lucas was not harmed. It worked through clothes.

The door rattled. It was the sound of a lock being picked. Hermes was inside so I had no idea who it was. The knob turned and the door creaked open. Funny what you think of at time like this. I just knew Paddy was going to make me oil the hinges later. Rebecca lumbered in, burdened down by a large object in her arms.

"You hurt one of my people," she spoke calmly, but with intense bitterness in her voice. "You are not leaving here alive." Jack was unfazed. Paddy was livid. We knew the victim. The lifeless body was that of the sweetest kid I ever met, our eight year old Peter. He had recently been adopted by a wonderful couple and he had moved out of the apartments upstairs to their home. His room had been next to Paddy's apartment. Paddy would spend hours with Peter, with all of the children. As they played, Paddy told them tall tales, and made music with his harmonica. I've never met anyone who loved children more. Jack had killed one of his. It took both Hercules and Dion to keep him from going after Jack. His rage was frightening to behold. The entire room shook with his rage. I knew Rebecca spoke the truth. Despite his distaste for killing,

Paddy would not let Jack leave alive. Hermes took Peter's limp form and laid it tenderly on the bar.

"Ah, yes, the child. Very tasty. Children are best, you know. Very little fat and cholesterol and no nicotine or drugs to taint the taste. Healthier for you than adults, really. Kind of like veal," she said.

"Jackie, how could you do such a thing?" her father asked, again returning to the real world.

"Don't be so sentimental. The boy was a freak. Just like Lucas here. They don't deserve life and I made sure this one won't be coming back. The freaks just aren't as good as we are. Isn't that what you always taught me? Besides, I go after freaks because I love you, Daddy," she said without the faintest trace of emotion. Mr. Gill didn't understand what she meant. Lucas did.

"She's been feeding on you, too. Check," Lucas said. Mr. Gill checked his neck. It was without blemish. Lucas explained that only an idiot or someone who wanted to be caught used the neck anymore. The shoulders were also clean.

"Check your inner thigh," Lucas suggested, shamefully. "It's a favorite spot of hers." Gill reached his hand down to palpate his leg and winced at the pain it caused. Jack was a very sick girl.

"I didn't want you to run dry," Jack said. "I would have to move all my stuff out. I guess I'll have to move out anyway. Maybe I'll go to the children's shelter. They always leave a window open, and its lights out at nine. I dine there in the special children section often. Best selection and prices in town."

Everyone lost it.

It was merely a race of who got to her first. Unfortunately, I won. Despite her lack of powers, she was incredibly strong and agile. She had me in a head lock before I could blink twice.

"Everybody back off or the undead get another convert," she said. Everyone stopped except Hermes and Hercules who were sneaking up behind her from opposite sides. I grabbed her hand and instead of trying to pull it away, I brought it closer. Contact with the crucifix on my neck happened a moment later. The pain loosened her hold momentarily and I was out of there. Hermes and Hercules were in and they grabbed her. Somehow she broke away and headed out the door. No move was made to stop her. It was a simple case of leaping before you look. The sun was rising. A swift U-turn was not swift enough. The door had been closed behind her. To my surprise, it was not Hermes who did the closing. It was Mr. Gill.

"Daddy, let me in. I'll be your good little girl again. Don't do this to me. I love you," she pleaded, in a deceptively sweet voice.

"I love you too, baby. That's why I have to do this," he said, tears moistening his cheeks. With a twist of the skeleton key, the lock was set. He collapsed against the frame. We all heard her screams for help but did nothing.

The doorway is a funny place. It is close enough to the bar that she couldn't transform into a mist to get away, but far enough away so it would not protect her from the sunlight. That, or Paddy granted her a silent partial dispensation. Lucas had informed us that she knew nothing about the sunscreen. She never even thought to run somewhere else.

As the sound of sizzling flesh got louder the screams became softer, until silence reigned. The room was absolutely void of eye contact.

The silence was broken by Hercules, who motioned for me to stay put as he went out to dispose of the remains. Hermes picked Peter gently up off the bar. He and Rebecca went to break the news to his new parents.

Mr. Gill was in a daze and the rest of us weren't doing much better. Hatred did not make the death easy. Nor the love her father had for her. We had only two comforts to get us through the day. First, no matter how horrible the deed was, we did the right thing, the only thing we could. The second was a drunken haze started when Paddy put his arm around Mr. Gill and bought him and everyone else a round of drinks. Lucas bought the second. We toasted poor Peter whose life had been taken too early and so unfairly. Then we toasted the woman Jack had been before and the woman she might have become. Only if.

EULOGY

I hate funerals. To this day, I don't know how I got through Elsie's. I managed not to cry until they lowered her into the ground. I think I was just too numb. I may not have been shedding tears on the outside, but that doesn't mean I was coherent. I don't even remember seeing Paddy and the rest of the gang, but they assure me that they were there.

Peter's funeral was very different. I cried like a baby. As horrible as Elsie's death was, she at least got to grow up. Peter was just a kid and he'll never get that chance. It was wrong, but even with all the divine powers of Paddy and the rest of the gang, there wasn't a damn thing we could do about it. Except cry.

Father Mike gave the eulogy, but didn't say the mass. Peter's adoptive parents were Baptists, so their minister officiated over the funeral. The minister had only known Peter a short time, but he did a good job.

After, we all followed the hearse to Calgary Cemetery in Queens, and Peter was laid to rest. I remember looking at his adoptive parents and thinking they were a mess. They had been through a lot themselves. They were recent immigrants from China, and, not unlike Peter's biological parents, originally illegal ones. That's where the similarities stopped. While his biological parents abandoned him, John and Nancy Chang took Peter in.

The Changs were fleeing from immigration officers when they ducked into Bulfinche's Pub. Seconds later, INS agents came in after them. Paddy told them the pair had run out the door that led into the parking garage, and everyone else backed up his story. The feds made a quick search of the bar, then chased after the fugitives, but never caught them. Paddy had stashed them in a trap door hidden behind the bar. He had originally built it during Prohibition as a place to conceal booze. The outline was virtually invisible, so even when the feds looked behind the bar, they noticed nothing.

Paddy managed to pave the way to get them green cards. It's amazing what money in the right hands can do. They wanted American names, so they choose John and Nancy. John was a tailor back in China, and Paddy helped find him a job down in the garment district.

Things were looking good for the Changs. They spent several nights a week at Bulfinche's, which is how they got to know Peter. John explained to us how that they had had kids when they were back in China. Their firstborn was a girl. The government there, concerned with overpopulation, allows every couple only one child. A male child is much more prestigious, so female children are often killed at birth by their parents. The end result is there are nine men for every woman in China. Eight of every nine men will never be able to marry. Not a dating pool I'd want to swim in.

John and Nancy weren't the type who were able to kill their own child, no matter what the neighbors did. They accepted and loved their daughter. Then the unthinkable happened: Nancy got pregnant again. They had a second child: a son. This was against the law in China, and the penalty was severe. Government thugs came and kidnaped John. He was taken to a government clinic and given a vasectomy against his will.

The surgeons where little more than quacks. It wasn't the type of vasectomy you'd get from an American doctor: the kind that could someday be undone. This was permanent and irreversible.

Life under the Chinese government was not what they wanted for their kids, so they arranged to send their two children with an aunt in the cargo hold of a rickety ship, bound for America. They were told the old ship never got here. It sunk somewhere in the Pacific, with no survivors.

Some time later, they decided to try the same route themselves. Things were bad enough to make the risk worth it. Hundreds of people were squeezed into a small cargo hold. They survived it, only to become virtual slaves. They had to work over eighty hours a week in sweat shops, making cheap clothing to pay off their passage. Eventually they were moved to New York. One day their sweat shop was raided. John and Nancy ran, and that's when they found us.

John and Nancy wanted to have more children, but the Chinese government butchers' work couldn't be undone, even by Hermes. Neither liked the idea of artificial insemination, which left adoption. They had fallen in love with Peter, and weren't put off by his Down's Syndrome. Plus, being Chinese, they wanted a Chinese child. A lot of people are that way, so I can't fault the Changs for that. Adoption agencies now actually give people grief if they want to adopt a child from a different ethnic group. I don't get it, but I realize not everyone thinks like I do.

Paddy again paved the way. He and Hermes forged documents that said Peter was Nancy's sister's child and that, before her recent death, she had appointed John and Nancy his legal guardians. It was just a few short steps and greased palms from there to finalizing the adoption.

Peter had been with them too short a time before Jack killed him. If only Jack's death could have brought him back. Instead, we had to lay him to rest in a newly dug grave. Nancy and John didn't have enough money to pay the funeral expenses and were too proud to take charity. Early on, Paddy had pulled the funeral director aside and covered most of the expenses, then had the director give them a much lower price, never hinting at the boss' involvement. The amount was still a lot for the Changs to handle, but a payment plan made it possible.

The Changs hadn't cried during the funeral, but they couldn't hold out as long as I did. They started as soon as they saw the open grave. Hercules, Hermes, Dionysus, and I were the pallbearers. We were all in black suits. It was the only time I'd seen the three of them wearing ties.

With the supervision of the minister, we carried the small wooden coffin to the side of the grave. Hercules could have done it one handed, but this wasn't the time or the place.

Paddy stood by the Changs, giving them what comfort he could. He was just as upset as they were, but he pushed his grief aside. He'd deal with it later. Demeter was keeping an eye on the kids. Despite how much she and the rest of us loved them, they were having trouble turning to anyone else for comfort. They had been through so much together, both before Rebecca rescued them and after, that they were a family. The rest of us were more of an extended family. Peter was their brother and his death was hitting them hard. Brian was playing the part of big brother. He had his arm around Shellie and she was crying on his shoulder. Nellie just stared ahead numbly, holding onto Brian's hand. Every so often a tear would trickle down from her eyes.

Hers weren't the only tears. Roy and Rumbles were crying, too. It took me a moment to recognize them, because it was the first time I had seen either without their clown makeup. Roy had wanted to be a pallbearer. Peter had been the catalyst to get his life back on track, but we couldn't figure out a way for him to carry one end of the coffin and push his wheelchair himself. He decided then he was going to build some sort of motorized wheelchair. I mentioned to him that they already had those.

"Not like the one I'm going to build, they don't," he said.

Rebecca was there, and for the only time I can remember, she was in an outfit that matched. It was a decade or so out of date, but it was all black. Lucas stood in the background, under the shade of a tree. His sunscreen worked well, but he felt it best not to push his luck by standing directly in mid-day sunlight. Lucas felt some guilt over Jack killing Peter, but Paddy convinced him there was nothing he could have done differently that would have changed the outcome.

We walked by, one by one, putting a flower on top of the casket. When it came Nellie's turn, instead of a flower she held a red clown's nose that Peter had gotten the night we performed with Roy at the circus. Peter used to wear it around all the time, trying to make people laugh. It had worked, but now it was more likely to make us cry.

"This was Peter's favorite thing. I was thinking last night that he should be buried with it. Could you please open the coffin, so I can put it in with him?" Nellie asked the minister.

He shook his head no. "I'm sorry, but it's sealed."

"Please, it's very important," pleaded Nellie.

"It's very unorthodox. You should have thought about it at the wake last night," said the minister.

"I know, but I couldn't sleep last night. All I could do was think about poor Peter. He used to wear this all the time, even in school. It would embarrass me and I'd yell at him for it. I wish now that I didn't. I know I should have done it before, but I didn't know they sealed the coffin. Please let me give it to him," begged Nellie.

The minister wavered. "Well, if it's okay with his parents..."

The Changs looked at each other and at Nellie. She and the other kids had been frequent guests at their home. They knew how close they all were and how hard Peter's death had hit the kids.

"It's fine with us," said John.

"You'll have to talk to that gentleman from the funeral home. He'll have to open the coffin and reseal it."

The man in question was the nephew of the man who owned the funeral home. He came across as a spoiled brat, upset that he had to work. I guessed the only reason he was still employed was his family ties. Nellie went up and explained the situation. The man was not sympathetic to her request, as it would involve him doing more work than he had to.

"No," he said simply.

"But you don't understand.." pleaded Nellie.

"I said no. Please move along," said the nephew, in a harsher tone of voice than was really necessary.

Hercules whispered something to the Changs. They nodded and Herc walked over and in a soft, deep voice he said, "Open it."

The sheer physical presence of Herc was enough to make him nervous.

"But. . . only the family can—"

"The parents already agreed. Besides, she's family," said Herc. The nephew raised an eyebrow.

"The deceased was Asian. This girl is black."

"Your point?" asked Herc.

"What relation is she?" asked the nephew.

"His sister," said Herc.

"I find that hard to believe," said the nephew snottily.

"Are you calling me a liar?" asked Herc, crossing his arms. The action caused the material of his suit to stretch over his flexing muscles. The nephew swallowed hard.

"No, sir."

"Then open it."

"But that requires a tool I left back at the funeral home. The seal can't be broken by hand."

"Do you have what you need to reseal it?" asked Herc.

"Yes. My uncle insists I always have it, in case there are any problems, but I can't take the casket back to open it," said the nephew.

"You don't need to," said Herc. He reached over and the lid opened with a pop. The nephew blanched.

Nellie stepped over and peered in. She looked up at Hercules. "Should I put it on his nose?"

"How about in his pocket?" suggested Herc. Nellie nodded and slipped it in.

"Thank you," she said to the nephew. He closed it and started sealing it back up, without saying a word or looking directly at Hercules. Nancy and John each gave her a long hug and they cried together awhile.

We headed back to the bar for a late lunch. Food, drink, and condolences were plentiful. Several hours and a few hundred tears later, everyone who didn't live upstairs had left the bar.

I was cleaning up. Paddy and the kids were helping out. The three of them kept whispering back and forth, looking at Paddy and nudging each other. I heard murmurs of "You ask him," and "No, you ask him."

Shellie pulled me aside. The other two casually moved closer. Paddy pretended not to notice.

"Murphy, we have a big favor to ask Paddy. What's the best way to ask him?" said Shellie.

"Probably just come right out and ask," I said.

"Murphy's right," said Shellie, turning to look at the other two.

"But who's going to do it?" asked Nellie. As if on cue, she and her sister turned their eyes on Brian.

"Why me?" he asked.

"You're the oldest," said Shellie.

"Please," begged Nellie. Brian rolled his eyes back in his head. He knew he didn't stand a chance.

"Fine, I'll do it," said Brian. Shellie and Nellie jumped once, before catching themselves. Very seriously, the trio walked over to the boss.

"Paddy, we have something to ask you," said Brian.

"Yes?" replied Paddy.

"Maybe you better sit down first," suggested Shellie. Nellie pushed a chair behind Paddy and he sat.

"This sounds serious," said Paddy, half smiling.

"It is," said Brian, taking a deep breath. It was obvious he was trying to get the nerve up to ask something. Brian finally decided to take the plunge. "Paddy, we wanted to say how much we appreciate you taking us in and taking care of us."

"It's been my pleasure, Brian," said Paddy. "You're all fine children. I couldn't be any prouder of ye if you were my own children."

"That's exactly what we wanted to talk to you about," said Brian. "We want you to adopt us."

"What?" exclaimed Paddy, caught off guard. "But I thought you wanted us to find you a home with human parents, like we did for Peter."

"It sounded good at first," said Shellie.

"But we already have a home. Here, with all of you," finished Nellie.

"Besides, when Peter left, we missed him so much it hurt. We don't want to be separated from each other," said Brian.

Paddy said, "I'm flattered, but. . ."

"But what? Don't you love us?" said Nellie, using a pouty lip and sad eyes any puppy would envy. Paddy pulled her up on his lap.

"Of course I love ye. I love all of ye, but I'm not human," said Paddy.

"What's your point?" asked Nellie, using the phrase Herc had said earlier.

"You deserve a mother and a father," said Paddy.

"You're like a father to us. Demeter is like a mother. Hercules, Hermes, Dion, and Murphy are all like uncles, not to mention everyone else who comes in here. We have more family here than most kids could ever dream of. Having only a mother and a father would be a step down for us," argued Brian.

"Look what happened to Peter, and he had a new mother and father," said Nellie.

"It wasn't John or Nancy's fault," said Paddy.

"I know. I wasn't blaming them. I was just saying that having two parents isn't everything," said Nellie. "Here, I have a brother and a sister. I don't want us spilt up either."

"We might find someone who'd take all of you," said Paddy.

"Who'd ever take all three of us? We're troublemakers," said Shellie.

"Whoever told you that?" asked Paddy.

"You did, last week when we were playing hide and seek and I got stuck in the back of the jukebox," said Nellie. Paddy laughed.

"I meant it in a good way," Paddy said.

"We talked it over before, and we'll understand if you don't want to adopt us. We won't get upset," said Brian, but even I could tell he was lying. They would hide it, but it would hurt.

"You can take all the time you need to think about it," said Shellie.

"Yeah, we're not going anywhere," said Nellie, still on Paddy's lap. She wrapped her arms around Paddy's neck and put her head on his shoulder. Shellie climbed on his other knee. Paddy shook his head and pulled Brian onto the unused portion of the leg Nellie was on. A group hug followed.

"Paddy looks like Santa Claus," I said to Dion.

"More like one of his elves," said Dion. Paddy gave Dion a dirty look, but otherwise ignored the short joke.

"Are you three sure about this?" asked Paddy.

"Yes," said Nellie.

"Yes," repeated Shellie.

"Yes," echoed Brian.

"All right then," said Paddy.

Paddy may not have been Santa, but their three young faces lit up like it was Christmas morning.

"That's it?" asked Nellie.

"We're adopted?" asked Brian.

"Not quite. We're going to have to go through a lot of red tape, and a lot of forged paperwork, but we'll make it happen somehow," said Paddy.

"Really?" asked Shelly.

"I must be crazy, but yes," said Paddy, smiling.

The screams from the kids were like mini explosions. All three tried to hug Paddy at the same time and they managed to tip the chair over backwards.

It was a touching scene.

"Dion, do you think Paddy would adopt me?" I asked.

"Not even if he was drunk," said Dion.

JINN & TONIC

The gusting wind felt colder than it actually was; no consolation at all to the wandering man. Edgar Tonic was more down on his luck than any man had a right to be. Of course, that was only his opinion, but until recently, it had carried a great deal of weight. Now it served only to add to his burden and drag him down further into his own sea of despair, without even hope as a floatation device.

Sunrise was hours away. Edgar swam through Manhattan's early morning human flood waters, avoiding the street sharks warily. Truth be told, they did not pay him much mind. Either he was an undercover cop, which they wanted no part of, or was so far down on his luck that he wasn't worth rolling. They knew he wasn't one of them. Attitude aside, a man in a five–hundred–dollar suit, no matter how wrinkled or soiled, does not take to street life nearly as easily as a fish takes to smog. First thing a street person had to do was swallow unnecessary pride in favor of survival. Edgar was choking and in need of a metaphysical Heimlich maneuver. All two and a half weeks on the streets had done was make him grumpy, angry, and in dire need of a shower. Friends were extinct in his world, killed by his requests for loans or hospitality. Most ignored his plight, unwilling to reach out a helping hand or even a kick in the butt.

Embarrassed and unwilling to seek out organized charity, Edgar had wandered the byways of New York City, certain he would find something. He did: sore feet. Three hundred dollar shoes looked fantastic, but were made for office, not city–wide, travel. Meals were supplied by the excess of others, deposited in waste cans and dumpsters. He never realized how good stale bagels could taste.

Edgar paused outside of a bar, Bulfinche's Pub by name. The window caught his eye, telling him he was it. Unwilling to play sight-tag, he simply stared. It sported a rainbow that ended in a shotglass o' gold, with coins that looked amazingly like bubbles. As he gazed his mouth watered at the thought of a cold glass of wine or even beer. It had been so long, but he might as well dream of lobster and steak. All were out of his financial grasp. The doorway was recessed into the building and offered some protection from the chilled breeze. Pulling the collar of his suit jacket up around his neck, Edgar huddled back against the doorway for warmth. Deciding it was not worth making the effort to bear his weight the door instead flew open, dropping him unceremoniously onto the floor. More shocked than hurt, Edgar stood, brushing himself off. The door gently closed itself, leaving Edgar bewildered but warm.

Edgar cautiously looked around the place and saw that he was quite alone, but somehow less so than he had been a moment earlier. He felt almost good. It made no sense and therefore had no place in his views of the world. What also made no sense was that a business in Manhattan would leave its front door unlocked in this day and age. They were just asking for trouble. Instead they had gotten him. He considered locking the door on the way out, but found he would need an old fashioned skeleton key, another of many things he did not have, so he let the matter drop.

His eyes were irresistibly drawn to the rows of bottles along the wall behind the bar. Bottles of all shapes, sizes and colors stood proud and tall, ready to be poured at a moment's notice. As far as Edgar was concerned, the moment certainly should be noticing by now. Problem was, Edgar had no money to purchase even the merest taste and no matter what he had been forced to become, there was one thing he was not, and that was a thief. As he thought about the possible benefits of larceny the cash register caught his eye. It was as old fashioned as the door, with big push buttons which displayed the amount of the purchase or "No Sale" on a flag in the glass window. Attached to it on the right side was a hi-tech credit card scanner. Drawn, he walked around behind the bar, careful not to step on a ramp running around its inside, all the while telling himself no one would be foolish enough to leave money in an easy open cash register in an unlocked bar. Once at his destination, his temptation and perspective of human nature were shattered by a simple, handwritten note done in excellent penmanship. The paper was attached by scotch tape and was yellowed around the edges.

It read:

"If you can wait until sunrise, wait. Help can be yours, friend. If not, there is fifty dollars inside. Take it, not as a gift but as a loan. Return it when you are back on your feet or pass it on to another in need and your debt is paid. First drink is on the house. Help yourself."

"This can't be for real," Edgar muttered to himself. But it was. Edgar poured a beer from the tap and drank it down quickly, almost afraid someone would jump out and take it from him. He instantly regretted it, as the amber liquid passed over his parched taste buds setting them atingle. Even depravation couldn't explain the fantastic taste. Rather than taking another he looked to the well stocked shelves where one bottle of Irish whiskey caught his eye. The label brand was the same as the name of the bar and had the same logo. The date was 1929.

Unsure of the price, he left five of his fifty on the shelf and sat down at one of the tables, debating on whether he would stay until sunrise. Problem was with so much time on his hands, Edgar found himself contemplating what his life had become. They were not exactly happy thoughts, and they shattered the little inner peace he had accumulated. Pride reared then fronted its quite unattractive head, flooding Edgar's emotional reserves with shame. Thoughts of how could he even think of letting another person see him in this sorry state, let alone explaining it, invaded and slowly conquered his perceptions. Finally, head held high but with his eyes lowered, Edgar found himself and his bottle born away on the wings of foolish pride out the doors and into the streets.

Pride not only precedes a fall, but often hangs around a while longer to see what other damage it can do.

Sick to his stomach, Edgar opened the bottle in an attempt to steady his queasy viscera. To his dismay, it was devoid of liquor.

"Damn it, Edgar," he said to himself, louder than was necessary. "Only you could buy an empty whiskey bottle." Raising it high above his head, he had every intention of smashing it on the ground but stopped. The bottle was his only possession. Possessions were important. What purpose would throwing it away serve? Surely he could find a use for it, even as a makeshift canteen. Sliding the bottle into his outside jacket pocket he sauntered away, unaware that he was being followed and had been ever since he opened the bottle. He was also unaware of the sigh of relief the figure standing in the shadows gave at his bottle saving action. Unaware at least until his shadow said "Thank you."

Edgar jumped at the words, unaccustomed as he had become of late to another human being addressing him directly, other than to tell him to get lost. Unfortunately, he had forgotten the polite way to respond, not that he had ever truly used it.

"What do you want?" he growled.

"Just to thank you for not destroying that bottle."

"Why should you care? You some kind of recycling nut?"

"No," he laughed. "Nothing like that. It is simply that that bottle has great significance to me."

"Really?" said Edgar, greed shining in his eyes. "What's it worth?"

"Its monetary value can be measured in cents, but its sentimental value is incalculable. Believe me when I say it wasn't for sale at any price. It was a gift from a very special lady. I would appreciate you returning it."

"A woman, huh? Nothing but trouble. It was a woman who got me into this mess. Still, if it means that much to you, I could see my way clear to give it back to you, if the price was right."

"I'm sure we can go back and get the five dollars you left on the shelf," the bottle connoisseur said. Edgar laughed at the suggestion.

"I don't think you understand basic economics," Edgar said. The other man gave a soft chuckle which Edgar impolitely ignored with a glare. "What we have here is the law of supply and demand. I have the supply and therefore I set the price."

"Of course the fact that I have no money may affect your asking price."

"What do you mean no money? Look at that suit you are wearing, and the coat. They didn't come cheap."

"Sure they did. At least at today's prices."

Confused, Edgar looked closer and noticed the style of the clothes was so far out of date that the man would not have looked out of place in a 1920's gangster movie. He even wore spats on his shoes. Only thing missing was the Fedora hat. On closer examination, Edgar saw that he held it in his hand. Probably bought the outfit at the Salvation Army thrift store.

"Damn it. I have lost it, trying to bicker over an old whiskey bottle," Edgar said, opting again to speak to himself.

"Great. Now if you will just hand me the bottle, I will be on my way."

"Not so fast, Spats."

"Call me Tommy."

"Tommy? What kind of name is that for a grown man in his forties? On top of that no last name?"

"None that I use anymore. What about yourself?"

"I still use my last name."

"No. What is it?"

"Tonic. Edgar Tonic."

"Pleased to make you acquaintance, Edgar Tonic," Tommy said, offering his hand. Hesitating but a moment, Edgar returned the grasp, trying to crush fingers in his grip. Tommy knew how to position his hand with the palm cupped so it did not hurt and merely smiled in response.

Having chosen not to try the macho response, Tommy simply let go and asked "The bottle, if you please."

"No. Possession is nine tenths of the law."

"So you plan to keep the bottle?"

"Not necessarily. If you have no cash, perhaps we can barter."

"All I have are my clothes."

"No. A bit outdated for my tastes. And I don't really care much for trenchcoats. Perhaps something else. What do you do for a living?"

"Nothing," Tommy chuckled.

"Nothing?"

"I don't qualify. Perhaps if you rephrased the question."

"What is your profession?"

"I grant wishes."

"You work for one of those foundations that grant sick kids last requests?"

"Not exactly."

"What did you do before that?"

"I owned and ran a major corporation."

"Didn't work out, huh?"

"No. Had no choice but to change careers after I died."

"Corporation went under? I can relate. Same thing happened to me. Damn wife's fault. How about you?"

"All my own doing, unfortunately. Now about my bottle."

"Oh yeah. You still doing the wish thing?" Edgar asked. Tommy nodded affirmatively. "How many wishes is the bottle worth?"

"Three is traditional."

"Okay. Three wishes for the bottle. Sounds good. Do we have to wait for the foundation to open up?" Edgar figured this was charity he had earned using his own wits, so he would have no difficulty letting Tommy help him get back on his feet. Only so much a charity can do, but at least he could maybe get an apartment, and a copy of the *Wall Street Journal* while the information was still accurate.

"This is no foundation. I work alone."

"But you said..."

"No, you did."

"But how can you grant wishes then if you have no money and no backers?"

"Easy. I am a Jinn."

"A gin? You are an alcoholic beverage? What color is the sky in your world?"

"No. J-I-N-N. As in genie. And the sky is a lovely shade of darkened smog this early morning."

"You some sort of psycho or something? Ringvue let you out for the night?"

"No. I am a Jinn, although I have had much counseling at Bulfinche's over the years. That is the bar you found the bottle in."

"I know what it is. I just happen to think you're whacked out of your mind."

"Perhaps. Or perhaps I tell the truth. Why not make a wish and find out?"

"Why not. At least then I will get you off my back. Let me think. All right. I got it. These last two weeks have been very lonely. What I wish for is an unforgettable sexual experience."

"Didn't you say you were married?"

"Was. Wife ran off and left me."

Tommy nodded and snapped his fingers. Out of a nearby doorway a man stepped out and walked toward the pair. Stopping in front of Edgar, he opened his long coat wide, exposing himself. Edgar's jaw dropped as he watched the flash without a camera to accompany it. Swiftly closing the coat, the man kissed Edgar's cheek. After ducking the punch Edgar responded with, the man ran off, disappearing down a cross street.

"Pervert!" Edgar shouted after the retreating figure.

"What? You didn't like your wish?"

"Wish? That wasn't what I wished for. I wanted insatiable blondes, brunettes, redheads, satisfying my every need."

"Perhaps that is what you wanted but it is not what you wished for. You have to admit that was a sexual experience you won't soon be forgetting."

"You tricked me, twisted my wish around!" screamed Edgar at a smiling Tommy. "Wait a minute. What am I saying? I'm talking like you really are a genie."

"Jinn."

"Whatever. If you really are a genie," Edgar said, adding as Tommy opened his mouth to protest, "Or Jinn and I have your bottle, don't you have to give me three wishes anyhow?"

"Perhaps."

"Why won't you give me a straight answer?"

"Is that what you wish?"

"Oh no. I'm not falling for that."

"So you believe me?"

"Let's just say I am leaving my options open. Let's talk as we walk," Edgar said, moving to continue the journey to nowhere he had begun before Tommy had stopped him. Tommy, by way of contrast, had remained immobile, huddled in a doorway. Actually, Tommy had his back pressed up against a wall for their entire conversation.

"Come on," Edgar called back. Reluctantly Tommy inched his way down the street, keeping his posterior glued to the store fronts. He walked like a man on a narrow ledge, twenty stories up, searching out each step with both a hand and a foot. When they reached the corner Tommy began to breathe heavily, almost nearing the point of hyperventilating.

"What's the matter with you?" Edgar asked.

"Nothing," Tommy snarled, his former easygoing manner replace by that of a terrified, cornered animal fighting for its life.

"Well then, let's cross the street."

"Let's wait for the walk signal."

"Wait for the walk signal? What kind of a New Yorker are you?"

Tommy ignored Edgar, instead concentrating on the crossing signal. His body tensed as the red "DON'T WALK" sign flashed on and off. He watched as it shined without blinking. When it changed to the white "WALK" signal, Tommy ran from the sheltering buildings across the crosswalk, covering his head with his hands and elbows, screaming like a banshee the entire while. He did not stop until he reached the safety of a doorway on the opposite side of the street, where the volume of his screaming was reduced to the level of a whimper. Embarrassed, Edgar followed at a distance, half covering his face with his hand.

"What is wrong with you?" Edgar demanded in whispered tones. People, awakened from their slumber by the wailing, were lifting up their shades to peek out.

"I am agoraphobic."

"What's that? Fear of angora sweaters?"

"No. I'm terrified of open spaces. Years of living in a bottle will do that to you."

"How the heck do you travel around then?"

"I don't get out much. I haven't left the bar in years. Didn't need to. Please just give me the bottle," Tommy begged.

"But how will you get back?"

"I will call someone. Paddy or Murphy will come get me. Maybe Hermes. Please, have mercy."

Edgar wavered, considering the request. His hand even reached to give the bottle to Tommy, but pride again intervened, grabbing at his wrist. It forced words out of his mouth.

"A deal is a deal."

Tommy started to curl up into a little ball. Tears, falling from glassy eyes, rolled down trembling cheeks. Pity overwhelmed pride, holding it in a headlock long enough for decency to take control. "But if you give me your word you will stick to it I will give you the bottle to hold onto until we complete our deal. Okay?"

The tears stopped and the eyes popped back into focus. "Okay," Tommy said softly, hugging the bottle close to his chest like a child with a teddy bear. He was still trembling.

"Why don't we try to get you into that alleyway. It has three sides. That should help you. So should this," Edgar said, pulling the tail end of the trenchcoat over Tommy's head effectively blocking out the wide world. Edgar guided Tommy into the alley and a voice rang out from the darkness.

"Keep walking. This alley is already spoken for."

"We only need it for a few minutes, until my friend gets his bearings. There's plenty of room," Edgar said, squinting at the figure silhouetted in the darkness. Definitely female. A kerchief covered her gray streaked hair. Her clothes appeared to have been assembled by a mad designer caught in a time warp high on drugs. Dozens of fashions were represented, many decades apart. Colors never meant to be together were resting comfortably. Despite this, the woman was not comical, having almost an air of anger and danger surrounding her.

"Don't matter. Get out. Have him sleep it off elsewhere. If it is funny business you want, rent a room," she demanded. Despite the fact she was much smaller and older than he, Edgar found himself very wary of the woman. Flames burned behind her eyes and there was steel in her voice. Again pride stepped in and spoke up.

"You can't talk to me like that. I used to own a multi-million dollar corporation."

"But what have you done lately?" she asked. Unable to give an answer he liked, Edgar changed the subject.

"No one owns alleys," he informed her.

"Sure they do, at least until sunrise. Sometimes later. Squatter's rights. Something you should know if you plan to spend any more time on the streets, mister poor rich man. Move on."

Pride wanted to press the point but fear was presenting some very convincing arguments for making an immediate exit. Edgar stood immobile and debating while the third player piped up.

"Rebecca?" Tommy whispered.

"Who's that?" she asked, lifting the coattails from over his face. "Bottle boy? That you Tommy?"

"Yes, it's me, Rebecca," Tommy replied.

"Never expected to see you on the outside. What's going down?" she asked, glaring at Edgar all the while.

"It is really none of your concern, ma'am," Edgar interjected. A mistake. Rebecca gently lowered Tommy to the ground and executed a swift takedown of Edgar, landing him flat on his back with her hand wrapped tightly around his throat.

"What happens to my friends and family is my concern. Nobody hurts them. Ever. Bottle boy here qualifies," Rebecca growled. Edgar tried to get up, to move away, but the feel of cool metal against his windpipe convinced him to remain perfectly still. He had never even seen her reach for the knife. "Now you behave, mister poor rich man. And don't call me ma'am," Rebecca ordered. Looking down, she saw Tommy hugging his bottle. "He take you out against your will, Tommy?" she said, tenderly cradling him with her one arm, the other still holding throat and knife.

"No. He just took the bottle. I followed him to try to get it back," Tommy replied.

"The bottle Bulfinche gave you?" she asked. He nodded. "Understandable. So he has not tried to hurt or enslave you?"

"No," Tommy replied. Rebecca loosened her grip around Edgar's throat, freeing him.

"My apologies mister poor rich man. Since you have the bottle back, hop in and I will take you home."

"I can't. Not yet. He still has two wishes left."

Rebecca's eyebrows rose. "Wishes?"

"A trade. Three wishes for the bottle," Tommy said. Rebecca nodded.

"You do what you have to, Tommy. You need anything call home, we will be there in a flash. Wingfoot will probably be there first, but the rest of us won't be far behind."

"I know. Thanks."

"And as for you, mister poor rich man: two weeks away from suburbia and you fall to pieces. Not good, Tonic."

"How do you know who I am?" Edgar asked, shocked.

"I know. The streets hold no secrets from their mother. But if anything happens to the Bottle boy, I'm coming after you."

"Don't worry. Nothing will," Edgar promised.

"Good. Just so we understand each other," Rebecca said, walking to the rear of the alley to retrieve a waiting shopping cart. Pushing it, she made for the front of the alley.

"You're leaving?" Edgar asked incredulously.

"Yes," she answered.

"But what about squatter's rights and all that?"

"He needs the alley more. That's what friends are for. Besides, I don't want to sleep the whole day away."

"But it must be only four in the morning," Edgar guessed as best he could without benefit of a watch. His Rolex had been torn from his hand his first night on the streets.

"Actually closer to five," she said reaching into her cart. She pulled out a large, folded cardboard box, a bottle and a salami stick and handed the lot to Edgar. "Let him rest up in the box for a while and he should be fine. And for mercy's sake, carry him inside the bottle while you are traveling."

"You mean you think he is a genie, too?" Edgar asked.

"Jinn!" yelled Tommy from the back of the alley.

"He prefers Jinn. Use it. Of course that is what he is. Based on your disbelief, I must gather you were in the bar after hours. Otherwise you would not ask such a stupid question. I keep telling Paddy to lock the door but he is too headstrong. Funny part is, he has never been burgled. The bottle is for the both of you. The meat stick is a meal. It looks like you have not had one in days. If you choose to stay on the streets, come see me. Bottle boy will tell you how. I'll teach you to survive. If you want to get off, Bottle boy knows some people who can help you with that also."

"If he really is a gen...Jinn, couldn't I just wish to be off the streets?"

"Sure. And you might wind up on a rooftop, in the East River, or worse, in a landfill in Jersey. Have to be specific or anything can happen. Like the old saying says, be careful what you wish for. You might get it."

"Couldn't I just wish for more wishes?"

"Nope. Deal was for three only. No more, no less. Besides Bottle boy has been through that before. Won't go through it again. As soon as Tommy's ready, be on your way and finish your deal so he can go home." While Rebecca spoke, she palmed the top to Tommy's bottle and took it with her, making sure Tommy would not be trapped in the bottle.

"Okay. And thanks," said Edgar.

"You're welcome. Goodbye," Rebecca said, fading away into the early morning darkness. Edgar unfolded the flattened cardboard until it was a refrigerator sized box and brought it back to where Tommy was sitting.

"Your castle awaits," Edgar said, as a light rain began to fall, trip, stumble and topple down from above. Each drop smashing itself on the hard ground, injuring themselves to the point where, had they been human, an ambulance-chasing lawyer would have been able to retire off the resulting lawsuits. Instead, they just joined together, forming small puddles and rivulets, running down drains and gutters to explore subterranean Manhattan. In the midst of this, Tommy crawled in the box on all fours and made himself comfortable.

"There is enough room in here for two. Much drier, too," Tommy offered. Edgar, not having a dry change of clothes, did not need to be asked twice. Settling in on the opposite side of the makeshift shelter, Edgar brought out the bourbon and the salami. After sampling each he offered them to a much calmer Tommy, who accepted.

"I don't need to do this you know," Tommy said.

"Do what?" asked Edgar.

"Eat. Drink. Once you die, nourishment is optional. Just a habit now."

"Are you saying you are not only a genie–"

"Jinn."

"But a dead jinn?"

"All but the very first jinn lived and died. You see, I'm in what my grandmother would have called Purgatory."

"You mean Earth is Purgatory?"

"No. Not for you. Not yet. Purgatory is a place where the departed go when then have not been quite good enough to get into a heaven, but haven't been bad enough to be condemned to a hell."

"A heaven? A hell?"

"There isn't just one afterlife. There are multitudes of options. For me, the punishment was made to fit my crimes."

"Which were?"

"Business related. I used to say everything I did was just business, as if that justified everything. It didn't. Profit was the top line, the bottom line and everything in between. To make money, I treated my employees horribly, and abused my power, making others into my wage slaves. God, I loved it. Then I died and found out the powers that be have the real power and you can't buy them off. So I was sent back as a Jinn. Very powerful, but subservient to whoever possessed my bottle. In short, a slave. That is why wishes have to be so specific. Jinn can be very bitter and it is the only way to strike back at masser."

"Sounds dreadful."

"It is. You better be careful yourself. I see bits of me in yourself. Clean up your act or get ready for an afterlife in a bottle."

"But I am not that bad."

"Denial is useless. Change your ways... I sound too much like Jacob Marley."

"Who?"

"Scrooge's partner in 'A Christmas Carol'. Enough about me. How did you end up in your present predicament?"

"I would rather not talk about it." Those were pride's words, not Edgar's. Pride was talking to the raindrops' lawyer, trying to get a gag order.

"You never know. It might help."

"It might help what? Me get my business back? Or my house? My money?"

"No. It might help you feel better."

"That is ridiculous," Edgar said, not believing a word, but desperately wanting to. Wavering, he started his tale. "Straight out of college, I started my own import/export business. Started with nothing and worked it up to the point where we had hopes of becoming a Fortune Five Hundred company. I employed thousands. Took home a million plus each year. During that time I married. It was the beginning of the end, though I wouldn't know it for nine more years."

"Were you in love?"

"I thought I was, but I guess I wasn't. It was more lust than emotion. God, she was beautiful. Probably still is."

"She left you?"

"Yes. For the postman, of all people. He didn't have to ring twice. Apparently he had his own key. This had been going on for almost two years, but I was oblivious to it. Not surprising, when you realize I was working twelve hour days, six sometimes seven days a week. Then, one Tuesday she left me, took off with the postman. Didn't even leave me so much as a note. I found out from one of my gossiping neighbors. Not surprisingly, she didn't leave a forwarding address. You know what the funny part is? I had always given him a huge Christmas tip. Anyway, I sort of lost it. Did not go into work for the rest of the week. Ran off three mailmen with a baseball bat. Got notified I would have to civilly pick up my mail at the post office proper. Of course by then I had gone back to work. Within two weeks I came home to find the bank had foreclosed on my home."

"Aren't they supposed to notify you?"

"They did. By mail and certified mail which I never picked up because they were closed by the time I got back from work. So there I am, locked out of my house, arguing with the bank's representative and a repo man who had repossessed my Lincoln Towncar. I chased him for the better part of a block, but I had abused my body for too many years with no exercise and ravaged it with tobacco, so I couldn't keep up with him. Man, I miss my smokes! Going back, I found they wouldn't even let me in my house to get a change of clothes. With only the suit on my back I walked back to the Long Island Railroad station, planning to head back to spend the night at my office. Wouldn't have been the first time. A cab ride later, I was facing another bank man who had taken possession of my business."

"Why were the banks taking back everything."

"I had sent them the checks, but my accounts didn't have the funds to cover them. It seems my wife took it all with her as a lovely parting gift. All my money plus a few million I didn't have. In short I was busted. I had spent most of my cash on the cab ride, used to using plastic which was now useless. I went to friends and employees for a place to stay the night, but each turned me away. Not that they didn't have some very creative excuses. My favorite was my secretary telling me her dog was allergic to men."

"It was after midnight on the last day of the month so my monthly train pass had expired. I was stuck in the city with no means of support or help."

"How have you survived?"

"Eating out of dumpsters. Sleeping in churches during the day but, believe me when I tell you, man was not meant to sleep in the kneeling position. At night the churches were locked up so I hit the streets until the doors opened again in the morning."

"A lonely existence."

"Not too much more than my previous one. Just without the illusions of companionship."

"Was there ever a time when you were happy?"

"Sure, when I started the business. Actually, I was real happy as a kid. I had great parents, God rest their souls. Spoiled me rotten. They weren't rich, but we never did without. Dad was a hot dog vender, working the corners. During summer vacations he used to take me to work with him and I would help him hand out the dogs, knishes, and pretzels to the customers. 'Always smile...' 'Always try to remember the customer's name,' he would tell me. He loved his work. Loved being outside and working with people. Learned a lot of wisdom at his feet. Still, as I got older, I realized he wasn't making as much profit as he could. He put twice as much chili, kraut, and relish on as he needed too. Would give away free food to someone down on their luck with no hope of ever getting paid back. I told him to change and he laughed at me. Told me there was more to being a man than making money."

"A wise man. He was right."

"Yeah, he was," Edgar said, sadly. "The rain is letting up. How about we move on?" Edgar said, draining the last of the bourbon. "Any sentimental attachments to this bottle?"

"None."

"No objections to me throwing it away?"

"Nope."

"Okay, why don't you hop in?" Edgar said, pointing to the other bottle.

"You finally believe?"

"No, but I figure once we get that little delusion out of the way, we can get on to helping each other out. For a crazy man, you're a pretty all right guy."

"Thanks."

"Let me fold up this box and hide it behind the dumpster," Edgar said, bending over and turning his back to Tommy. "You never know. We may need it later." That task finished, he spun around but Tommy was nowhere to be seen. Edgar had been nearer the mouth of the alley and he was certain Tommy had not passed him. "Tommy, where did you go?" he asked.

"In here," Tommy responded but Edgar still did not see him. He checked in garbage cans and under boxes. Finally he turned to stare at the whiskey bottle standing alone in the center of the alley.

"No. It isn't possible," Edgar muttered, picking up the bottle and looking down the neck. "Tommy?"

"Yep. You believe now?"

"Unless you are a ventriloquist, yes. How come I can't see you?"

"To fit in here I have to be fairly insubstantial. To stay visible requires great effort. However, should you wish it..."

"No, no. That's all right. Two wishes. Any limits?"

"Plenty, but don't worry. If you reach any, I will tell you."

Edgar put the bottle in his coat pocket and turned to leave as a woman walked in with three small children, the oldest of which was about eight and the youngest was no more than three years old. All three were skinny, dirty, and looked exhausted. The three boys were laughing and playing catch with an old sneaker they had found.

"Oh, I am sorry. I didn't know the alley was occupied," the mother offered by way of apology.

"Don't worry. We were just leaving," Edgar said.

"We?" the mother asked, looking around and seeing no one.

"Me, myself and I," Edgar covered. "You look hungry."

"Only a little. We ate at the shelter the day before yesterday."

Edgar reached in his pocket and pulled out the salami. More than half was left. "Here. Take this."

"No. I can't take your meal."

"Sure you can. I already had all I can eat," Edgar lied. "Besides, you have three mouths to feed. Please take it. It would mean a great deal to me."

"If you're sure."

"I am."

She took it, thanking him.

"If you don't mind my asking, how did you end up on the streets with three such lovely children?"

"My husband died in a car accident. He had no life insurance, I had no job. We were evicted three months ago. We have survived begging on the streets. Many are generous to my children. I hate to have them do it, but it's better than starving. I have been trying to get a job, but one look at me and I don't even get through the door," she said, suppressing a shiver. Edgar noticed each child was wearing a woman's coat, while the mother shivered in a thin sweat shirt.

"I'm sorry to hear that. Look at you. You're cold. Here, take my jacket," Edgar said taking the bottle out and helping the mother put it on.

"I can't take your coat. It looks so expensive."

"Nonsense. I found it in a dumpster up on Lexington by Bloomingdales. Got five more just like it in my shopping cart around the corner," he fibbed. Removing a necktie from his pants pocket, he tied the jacket around her waist like a belt.

"Thank you. You've been very generous to me."

"No need for thanks. I know where you are coming from. I wish I could help you more," he said, shaking her hand and leaving the alley. As soon as he did a voice boomed out of the bottle.

"Edgar, did you mean that?"

"You mean the wish?" Edgar hesitated only a moment. "Yes, I did. Can you do it?"

"Yes. But give me more to work with."

"I thought you had to take the wish as spoken?"

"Shut up and work with me. How would you like to help her."

"Well, she seems like a proud woman, so a handout wouldn't be the way to go. I wish she had a good paying job and a safe place to live for her and the kids, indefinitely."

"Done."

"Just like that?"

"Just like that. Go back to the alley and watch," Tommy suggested. Edgar did as he was told. The mother had divided the salami in three, not even saving a piece for herself. A door opened out onto the alley and light shot out bathing the mother in its radiance. Blinking, one could see she was ready to run. A voice from the doorway spoke.

"You the girl from the agency?"

She stood there numbly.

Tommy whispered from within the bottle "Tell her to say yes."

Edgar waved his arms over his head until he got the young mother's attention. Then he began furiously nodding his head. She got the hint.

"Yes, I am."

"They said you were a little down on your luck. You and the kids can move into the spare rooms above the kitchen. One for you, one for the kids. Only a shower, not a full bath and no place to cook, but you can eat in the restaurant kitchen. You can cook, can't you?"

"Oh, yes."

"And you are able to start this morning?"

"Definitely."

"Good. Put on the uniform and get cleaned up. After the breakfast rush dies down, I can give you an hour to register the older two kids in school. My missus watches out for our younger one and will be able to watch yours. Sorry the salary isn't very high, but we are only a small restaurant. That is why we'll throw the apartment in. We live next door," said the voice from the doorway as he ushered the mother and her three children inside. The voices faded as the door shut.

"Nice job, Edgar," said the voice from the bottle.

"Me? You did all the work."

"It was your wish. There may be hope for you yet."

"Yeah. I have only one regret."

"Which is?"

"If I had known that was going to happen, I wouldn't have stuck the twenty dollars in the coat pocket," Edgar chuckled. Tommy joined him in a guffaw as he and his bottle were carried down the street.

"Where are we going?" Tommy questioned from within his bottle.

"Don't rightly know. Need to find a place to stay."

"Head back to Bulfinche's."

"Maybe later. First, I want to decide what my third wish will be. I want to make it count and I have to be certain that the wording won't be misunderstood."

"You think about it then. I'll just hop in the Jacuzzi. Get back to me later."

Edgar held the bottle's opening up to his eye and stared in shock. What he saw was just the inside of a bottle. "You have a Jacuzzi in there?"

"It overlooks the golf course," answered the voice within the bottle.

Edgar looked harder with no greater luck. "No wonder you want it back. How come I can't see it? Are you scamming me?"

"Yep. There's no golf course. No room with the lake," Tommy answered with bottled laughter.

"Very funny. Now be quiet. I have to contemplate."

"How about a little thinking music to help you along," Tommy said as he began to hum a food jingle. He did it well. It was very catchy and Edgar began to hum along. He even began to sing, but caught himself in time.

"Hey! Stop it. I have no desire to wish myself into becoming an Oscar Mayer wiener."

"Sorry. Old joke. Couldn't resist."

"Try harder."

"Don't be mad. I would have changed you back. Probably. Now seriously, if you could wish for anything in the world, and you almost can, what would it be."

"To have my old life back."

"You don't mean that. You yourself said you were miserable."

"I said I wasn't happy."

"Same difference."

"Close enough for government work, I guess. Maybe money. Lots of money."

"You've been there, done that. It wasn't enough."

"If you know so much, why don't you tell me what I should wish for?"

At this point, the sun was rising and the morning light was dazzling the city with its brilliance. Early morning suits and overalls were on their way to work, covering people too bewildered by employment to realize what an atrocious hour it was to be up and about. Still, they had enough wits about them to take great pains to walk around the man arguing with his bottle and apparently losing. Edgar noticed and decided he did not care. He simply smiled and waved them on their way.

"I can't tell you what to wish for. I can only suggest. Search your heart and your soul. Look inside yourself for that missing piece and fill it. Grand or small, right or wrong, pick something that will make you content."

Still walking, Edgar said, "Something more to reflect on. I don't know if anything could fulfill me. Maybe a true friend, someone who won't abandon me when the going gets tough."

"Edgar, you don't have to wish for what you already have."

Edgar held the side of the bottle up at eye level. "Can you see me?"

"Of course."

"How many fingers am I holding up?"

"None. You are sticking your tongue out at me. Be careful. Those cops on the corner are looking at you funny."

Edgar turned and saw that they were, so he turned back to the bottle and straightened his hair and finger brushed his teeth, using his reflection in the glass as one would a mirror. The cops moved on.

"Thanks."

"For what?" asked Tommy. "Warning you that you looked like a madman?"

"No. For what you said before. The friend thing."

"Don't mention it."

"It meant something to me. What's more, I decided what I want my third wish to be. I want you to be free of having to grant wishes to whoever holds your bottle."

"Wish wouldn't work."

"Why not?"

"I will explain later. But thanks for the thought. Think some more. It will come."

"All right, I will. Just stop humming that song!"

"Sorry. Make a left at the corner."

Edgar did and traveled on in pondering silence, deviating only to follow the directions the bottle gave him. Finally, he spoke.

"I know what I want. I just have to make sure I word it the right way. Damn, its so hard to think under pressure when my body is screaming for nicotine. I wish I had a smoke."

Edgar stopped short and let his jaw drop open.

"I didn't just say that."

A lit cigarette popped into his fingers. "I'm afraid you did."

"Crap. I can't believe I did that," he said, taking only one puff before throwing the coffin nail away in anger and frustration. "Couldn't you have at least given me a carton?"

"They are no good for you. I don't want to help you kill yourself."

"What difference does it make now?"

"Don't talk that way. What was your wish going to be?"

"It sounds really silly but I was going to wish for a hot dog cart, like the one my Dad used to have. Completely stocked of course. Your influence, really."

"Me?"

"Yes, you. All that talk about when I was happy and humming that damn tune. Doesn't matter now. Won't happen."

"Maybe. Maybe not."

"You mean you'll give me another wish?"

"No, I can't do that. But I can introduce you to some friends. Just go inside."

"Huh?" Edgar said eloquently. "We're back at Bulfinche's."

"Yep. Head inside and I'll introduce you," Tommy said, exiting the bottle as soon as he was through the door. Inside I was setting up breakfast. It was my week again to be up at the crack of dawn to help run our early morning food assistance program for the hungry out in the parking garage. Not that I complain, not anymore than usual, that is. Get to meet some mighty interesting people at this unreasonable hour.

In attendance was the boss, Paddy Moran, Father Mike Ryann, and Rebecca, who had told us what had become of Tommy. It was good to have him home. He introduced Edgar and the two of them told us the tale of their meeting. Edgar thanked Paddy for the cash in the register and Paddy just told him to be sure to pay it back.

Still, Edgar seemed disturbed.

"Let me see if I have everything straight. A jinn has to grant three wishes to whoever holds his bottle and I could not have wished him free? And if his bottle is destroyed he doesn't have to obey?"

"Correct," said Paddy.

"Well then, that is easily enough fixed," he said raising up the bottle over his head. We all screamed "No!" but it was too late. It smashed down, bottom first on a tabletop. Tommy collapsed to his knees.

"Noble gesture, Edgar but unnecessary for two reasons," I said. "One, that isn't his original bottle."

"Then where...?"

"It was a gift to Tommy from my departed wife," said Paddy somberly.

"And second, she took care of his servitude just before giving him the bottle. That's why your wish wouldn't work," I said.

Edgar walked over to Tommy and put a consoling hand on his shoulder. "Tommy, I am so sorry. I thought I was helping you."

Edgar meant what he said and Tommy did forgive him. Edgar tried to make it up to him by gluing the pieces of broken glass together. Did a pretty good job of it too. Now the bottle has twice the sentiment attached to it for Tommy, but he doesn't live there anymore. Vacations there only occasionally. He has a new home not very far away.

Tommy went to bat for Edgar with Paddy. Got Paddy to give Edgar a loan, two percent below prime. Edgar argued for a better deal, but Paddy countered that once he declared bankruptcy on all his outstanding debts not even a loan shark would stake him the money, at any interest rate. Paddy even insisted on having Tommy co-sign the loan. The boss would have just loaned him the money interest free but he believes you have to work for something to really appreciate it. And by having Tommy co-sign that gave him a co- interest in the purchase. Edgar got his hot dog cart. Sells on the corner right outside the bar. Edgar says he is actually happy. Not everybody believes it, you see. He is often heard yelling at his bun warmer to stop singing. And if you listen close you can indeed hear Tommy crooning "I wish I was an Oscar Mayer wiener," from inside his new home.

HELLO, I MUST BE GOING

Voices swarmed into the open air, parading up and down the sound barrier, not to mention the borders of good taste. Boisterous singing rocked the rafters, trying to raise the roof. Only the weight of fourteen floors above and the laws of physics prevented us from succeeding. That was only one of our many abilities. Once we really got going, we gained the power to empty entire rooms with a single refrain. Acme Earplugs once even offered to sponsor us with the assumption that their stock would rise enormously if more people heard us sing. We turned them down.

We sang not for fame and fortune, but because the song needed to be set free from our souls. Once liberated, most folks understood why it had been locked up in the first place. Once begun, there was no turning back. Those unfortunate enough to be at ground zero had few options. Most would pray for or actively work toward deafness, but for a few moments something deeper, more primal yearned to join in. Probably an evolutionary throwback to the days before primitive man discovered weapons or fire, when he had only his voice and his wits to keep the beasts at bay. As the wits were as yet meager, he worked on his vocal defense. He learned certain notes and frequencies that even a rabid saber–toothed tiger would not dare approach. This method of defense was soon forgotten, after the invention of the spear and submachine gun, but those sounds and the ability to make them are buried deep within each of us. Many young children instinctively know how to make these noises in an attempt to bend their parents to their will. As for the rest of humanity, this normally only rises to the surface when drunk or alone in the shower.

Strangely enough, when given the choice between flight or merging their voice with the masses, most folks choose the later. Defying rationality, the active participants actually think the sound is a thing of beauty, and wonder why the police keep wandering in to break it up. The bar song is far from an uncommon phenomenon. Our masterwork varied from tradition in two respects: First, the singers were sober, or at least most were. It would not be a very good bar if someone wasn't drunk, though if the truth were to be told, most would admit to coming here for the atmosphere and camaraderie. The drinks are a very close second. Our imbibitions are the stuff legends are made of. Literally.

The second variation was we were on key. The difficulty was that we just couldn't find the right lock to put the key into. Each songster was convinced he or she was the crooning locksmith that would unlock the mystery of the music. Better serenading detectives than we have tried and failed. In the end, we simply enjoyed its splendor, exhilaration, and power, and ignored the complaints of the neighbors. The harmonic feeling was too good to last–but last it did, at least for awhile.

The chorus was comprised of a varied and unique group of employees and patrons acting happier than anybody had a right to be. And why not? It was a Wednesday night and we had nothing better to do. Very few bars these days still have singalongs. Karaoke is just not the real thing. A pity, really. There is nothing quite like the camaraderie of voices taking up arms against life, celebrating its joys or drowning its sorrows in a place called Bulfinche's Pub. Sitting with his front to the back of a chair was Paddy Moran. Paddy is a blues harpist supreme.

The blues harp is a harmonica, for those unacquainted with the term. His head just reached over the top of the chair. Reason for that is Paddy is untall. Paddy hates the term "short" with a passion most folks reserve for the tax man. His distaste for the tax man exceeds known measurement. He claims to have paid more taxes than three normal men, which is true. He opened the bar well over one hundred years ago, and has had to pay what he couldn't avoid ever since. For the amount of time the sum is staggeringly low. Paddy hates to part with money, especially if it's his. He has every tax code and possible deduction committed to memory. Every time they change the tax laws, Paddy goes nuts. He puts this knowledge to good use. One year the government ended up refunding every cent he had paid plus an additional ten thousand he proved they owed him. With interest. Since the IRS hates to give away money almost as much as Paddy, they ended up changing the tax code loophole he used. Worked, too. The following year they only owed him two thousand.

Dionysus, Hermes, Demeter, and Hercules were putting out some amazing four part harmony. Listening to them, I can almost understand why many of the gods left old Mount Olympus.

At the end of the bar, straddling a stool, sat Father Mike, cantoring sounds more at home up the block in Our Lady of the Lake Church. Ismael Macob, our resident cabbie, was singing like he was trying to imitate Elvis. Either that or his upper lip was going into spasm. Rebecca was doing a respectable showing, even if she made up her own words occasionally.

The door slowly swung open and wide, as a stranger wearily walked into our midst and into our song. He was an older man of indeterminate age, thanks mainly to hair and beard of gray. Draping his listless frame was a worn, traveled trenchcoat the color and consistency of dust. The trenchcoat, in and of itself, should have been a sign of what was to come. The odder patrons of Bulfinche's tend to wear an overcoat. A wide–brimmed hat rested lazily atop his head, comfortable as an old friend. Below the brim, eyes drooped from fatigue, looking as if they had seen all life had to offer before, and weren't thrilled with any of it the first time around. The neutral set of his lips was reminiscent of a statue. A bored statue.

All that changed as the euphony reached his ears, causing a chain reaction. It was rough going at first. His face was being forced to do something it apparently hadn't done in quite some time. The end result was a smile as he joined in. And when I say joined, I mean joined. If there had been a membership fee he would have paid in triplicate. To us at Bulfinche's, this was far from unusual behavior from a stranger. He lay his walking stick upon the wall and stepped into the circle. As his voice rose up, Hercules draped an arm over his shoulder and the pair swayed to and fro, keeping time for the rest of us. After what they were doing to it, none of us wanted it back.

As with all good things, the song came to an end... or an least an intermission until the next time. And the neighbors rested easy. As did the police. For all that Bulfinche's keeps out noise, it doesn't keep our noise in. Whenever they came in to register a complaint, they had to deal with our bouncer, Hercules. Hercules made even a top–notch bodybuilder look like the original ninety–eight–pound weakling, and despite his easy–going manner, took his job very seriously. He owed Paddy a lot. We all did. He was always polite when he refused to ask the bar to quiet down. He is even more polite when he extends the police an invitation to join us. Not one has refused. What mortal can refuse a force of nature? We have gotten more than a few regulars that way, including Jasmine.

Dion, Paddy, and I climbed back behind the bar to tend to business. Paddy is no dummy. Singing is thirsty work, and drinks were ordered all round. Irish whiskey for Father Mike, pineapple juice for Ismael. Rebecca ordered hot water and brought out her own tea bag. Life on the streets is hard, but even that will not make Rebecca take handouts. Lucas had some bloodwine, fermented from the blood of sheep. It is the drink of choice for the politically correct vampyre. Demeter made it herself, as well as over fifty other blood based drinks and recipes which kept Lucas happy and well nourished.

Hanging in the background until well after everyone else had been served was the tired stranger. He seemed unsure of what to do with himself, almost as if he had a pressing engagement elsewhere. In the end, he took a seat at my station and lay his hat down on the bartop.

"What will you have, friend?" I asked.

"Irish coffee," he replied, shifting uneasily on the stool.

"Is your seat uncomfortable?" I asked. "We can get you another." I handed him his coffee.

"Actually, quite the opposite."

"Is that unusual?"

"Yes. What do I owe you?"

"Not a thing. First drink is on the house. Tradition."

"Thanks." Things got quiet after that. I used the lull in conversation to make introductions.

"I'm Murphy, your friendly neighborhood bartender."

"Charmed," he said.

"How about yourself? You have a name?'

"Several. I guess you can call me Joseph. That was the first. Not that it matters. After today you will never see me again."

On that ominous note, Paddy came over. Introducing himself he asked "Why is that? Something wrong with the drink or service?"

"No. Both are quite good. It is quite a lovely place you have here."

"My thanks. We work hard at it," Paddy replied. What he meant was I worked hard at it. Other than sweeping the sidewalk in front every morning, Paddy left all the menial tasks to me. "Well then, are you planning to do something to yourself that would prevent you from returning?"

Joseph chuckled wistfully. "I should be so lucky."

"Then why?"

Joseph stood and placed his hat back on his head. The action seemed more one of instinct than of conscious effort. Now in the full, upright position Joseph seemed stunned. He remained perfectly still as if fearful any movement would break some sort of spell.

"Unbelievable," he exclaimed.

"What is?" asked Paddy.

"I feel wonderful."

"Were you ill when you came in?" I asked.

"No. But every other time I have been asked that question my body becomes racked with pain until I put some distance between myself and the one who asked. I have answered, before but only at great personal cost."

The gang became silent as a hush fell over the room. Luckily, it was not a long drop and it wasn't hurt. This had all the earmarkings of a tale. Joseph just needed a bit of encouragement. Dion provided it will a smile and a question.

"Will you share the answer with us now?"

Joseph nodded slowly. "I might as well, even if nobody will believe me. It has been lifetimes since I have been able to stay in one place long, due to a curse placed on my head long ago. I have tried unsuccessfully to fight it hundreds of times, but each time I lose. It is always the same. First comes the wanderlust, the overwhelming desire to be elsewhere. Sometimes the ache to be around other people instead of being constantly alone is stronger than the wanderlust. That is when the pain begins, small and barely noticeable at first, but the longer I remain in one place the more intense the ache becomes. Eventually, agony overwhelms me and carries me away. Then the cycle begins again. Why bother to learn names or faces when I know I will never see a single one of you again? Why care about people when they can be torn away from you in a matter of months or moments?"

The answer was in his weary eyes. Compassion. He cared regardless of his curse.

"Because you cannot help it," said Ismael, standing up and walking over to Joseph and laying a comforting hand on his shoulder.

"What do you know about it?" spat Joseph curtly.

"More than you might think. I live under a similar curse inflicted on me by an abusive passenger. I am forced to wander the Tri-state area, never recognizing anyplace I go or anyplace I have been. This would mean certain death for a cab driver such as myself. I was unable to find my home and family, unable to even remember their phone numbers. Eventually, after backing into a fire hydrant, I found Bulfinche's."

What Ismael was leaving out was that the spray from the damaged hydrant filled the air with a fine mist. The midday sun shone down and refracted into the colors of the spectrum which glistened toward Bulfinche's. In short, it formed a rainbow that pointed to our door, a beneficial side effect of Paddy buying the place with his pot of gold. Rainbows are better for our business than billboards. Cheaper too, which pleases Paddy to no end. The window is even painted with a rainbow ending in a shotglass filled with a golden liquid with coins for bubbles.

Ismael's cab was damaged and needed repairs. Following the rainbow, he came in expecting to use the phone to call a tow truck. Instead, he found his salvation. Inside Bulfinche's, curses are lifted and even gods and vampyres are the same as ordinary folk. Only way around it is with a special dispensation from the boss. The staff has limited dispensations. His family has a standing dispensation which makes for quite an interesting St. Patrick's Day when the Gentry come to town. Ismael was able to contact his family and found a way to make quite a good living off his curse. As I've mentioned, one of its unexpected side effects is the ability to know exactly where someone is going, as long as they don't say where it is. Betting passengers had quintupled his income. Plus, he can always find his way back to us.

Ismael's story touched Joseph in a small way. Someone could actually relate to his plight.

"How long have you been afflicted?" asked Joseph.

"Fifteen years."

"Seems like a long time?" Ismael nodded. "It is nothing! I have been wandering for two thousand years!"

"That is horrible," said Father Mike compassionately.

"You say it is horrible, yet your very life is spent in service to the monster that did this to me!"

"Excuse me? I serve no monster."

"You are a Roman Catholic priest, are you not?"

"Yes."

"By your very words you admit it. You serve the Christ beast."

There was more than some confusion over Joseph's accusations. But I had figured out who Joseph was.

"You're the Wandering Jew," I said insightfully.

"I have been known by that name."

"Wandering Jew? Why is there such hate in you toward Jesus? You don't believe in him?" asked Father Mike.

"Believe? I do not have to believe. I know he is real. Your Jesus is the one who condemned me to this everlasting journey though the nightmare of human existence. I happened to be unfortunate enough to be standing and watching along the side of the road to Calvary when the Nazarene was on his death march. The Romans were a vicious, lazy lot and made their prisoners carry the means of their own destruction. The crosses were heavier than a man could carry. It helped take the fight out of the prisoners. The populace, having nothing better to do, stood along the side of the road and watched the morbid entertainment. Stories of the Nazarene had spread and the crowd was especially large. Some were there to watch him take down the Romans, others to watch the end of a prophet, or the death throbs of a madman. The first time he fell, the crowd felt sympathy. The second time, they began the jeers, for no savior would allow himself to be treated as such. The third time he stumbled was at my feet. I mocked your Christ in his weakness, spitting in his very face. It is a moment I shall regret for all of eternity. The Nazarene had been pushed to his limits and beyond. Forbidden to strike back at this captors in order to fulfill his destiny he had no such orders regarding the bystanders. At my insults his head raised up and he assailed me with his eyes. Those orbs were afire with hatred, misery, and betrayal. In that gaze the entire world faded away like so much smoke. I felt his power. Had he been allowed he could have crushed the entire Roman Empire with a single word. With twenty five words he destroyed me. His gasps were thunderous. 'Mock me as you may. For your sins you shall be condemned to wander the earth until I return again in glory. This I swear.' "

"I tried to laugh at his words, but I could not. I was practically fixed to the spot, able to follow only at a distance, unable to leave until I witnessed his death. From that moment on, I have been a homeless wanderer. I, too, had a family. A wife and seven children. Unlike Ismael, I never saw them again. Without me to support them they must have starved and died, thinking I abandoned them. Now they are two thousand years gone. Is this the work of a merciful God?"

Father Mike remained silent. Joseph did not.

"I tried conversion to every Christian sect and have been baptized so many times that I have spent more time under water than a fish; anything to end my torment."

"Have you simply asked him?" questioned Father Mike.

"Asked him? I have asked, pleaded, cursed, threatened, bargained, appealed, petitioned, beseeched, implored, and begged. All to no avail. Suicide is useless. I cannot be killed no matter how hard or what method I try. Believe me, I have sampled them all, from the hangman's noose to the chopping block. Even with the highest of tips, I still walked away." [Back in the days when rulers actually said "off with their heads" it was customary to give the executioner a monetary gift so he would be sure to kill you with the first stroke of the blade. If he didn't, you were still alive but laying around, your head hanging partly chopped off. Not a fun way to spend the day, even the last day of the rest of your life.] "The ax would break, melt, or spontaneously combust. The natives typically would then try to burn me as a witch. The fire did little more than warm my feet. I fared no better with the guillotine, although I must say the Nazi's were by far the cruelest. They insisted their victims lie face up so as to have to watch the blade's long, cold travel down. I dived out of airplanes, sat naked on the frozen tundra, enjoyed explosions from the mundane to the nuclear. Every few centuries, I joined the masses in an organized suicide called war. I have more decorations for bravery than there are stars in the sky. I would always be the first foot soldier over the top, rushing headlong into the enemy. Most took me for a fool, albeit a lucky one. Not that they complained. The more I failed to die, the longer those with me survived. I often stayed on after hope had left me and the pain enveloped me, just to save those who still wanted to live. In doing so, I was able to take a little revenge against the Nazarene. During the Napoleonic Wars, I was with a group of soldiers who needed to hole up in Milan. By sheer luck, we choose the chapel of Santa Maria della Grazie, where Leonardo DeVinci had painted the beast's "Last Supper". We used the painting for target practice. I myself shot out the head of the Christ from the painting, almost obliterating it."

"Wouldn't that destroy the canvas?" asked Ismael.

"No. It was painted on the wall, not on canvas. The monks had already lost respect for the art and broken a doorway through their savior's legs. But no matter how much target practice we took, we couldn't destroy it."

"You weren't alone. In World War II, a bomb landed atop the monastery but the wall the painting was on miraculously survived," said Father Mike. Joseph merely shook his head sadly.

"He has more concern for a work of art than for a living being. Ever living despite poisons beyond counting. I ingested hemlock once a day for an entire year. Still, I have my health while others beg and pray to him for what I would gladly throw away. Why would a God treat his people so?"

"Sounds like he was angry and backed himself into a corner by making the promise that cursed you," offered Hercules insightfully. "He can't release you without losing face. Not to mention breaking the word of a god, which isn't an easy thing to do. A near impossibility. The stronger the God, the more impossible. Take my father, for instance. He never learned he shouldn't promise anything to a mortal. He would have been better off if he had never heard of the River Styx. No matter how horrible the consequences of the promise, no matter how much he wanted to undo the results, he could do nothing else but follow through on his word. I remember the time..."

"Later, Hercules," said Dion gently. Hercules, the master tale spinner of any generation became silent at Dion's request. He knew full well the folly of Zeus' promises. One had killed his mother. Herc would just wait until a better time to finish his story.

"I don't care. I just want to die."

"Life, no matter how long, is to be treasured, to be cherished at all costs," said Paddy, a despiser of death. He has had a running battle with the Grim Reaper for a very long time. Paddy has saved multitudes. Many still have perished with Paddy powerless to save them, his own wife, Bulfinche, and my dear Elsie among their number.

This meant nothing to Joseph, who asked "What do you, with your pittance of years, know of eternity?"

At his words there was subdued laughter and more than a few chuckles, the loudest of which came from Demeter. Joseph turned, focusing the anger of centuries on the humble matron.

"You laugh at my pain?"

"No, just your arrogance. Thinking you are so old," Demeter scolded, as if speaking to a child.

"And I suppose you are older," he asked mockingly. Demeter remained silent but smiled serenely. Joseph looked at her closely. "How old are you, Madame?" he questioned.

"Don't you know it is impolite to ask a lady her age? I will say this much. I am the fifth oldest of the women I play bingo with," Demeter said. Joseph stared dumbly. Then again, he didn't know who her gaming companions were. "You haven't yet reached the twenty–one hundred mark, correct?" Demeter asked. He nodded affirmatively. "Let me put it this way. I have a daughter older than you, young man. And you think she would know better than to marry that no–good excuse I have for a son-in-law."

"Hush, Demeter. There will be time for griping later," said Paddy. Joseph stared unbelieving.

"How old are you, Paddy?"

"Older than ye, wanderer. As are Dion, Hermes, and even young Hercules.

Joseph turned to me as if to inquire of my age.

"Don't worry. You have me beat," I said.

"I don't believe any of you," he said but he walked up to each of the long timers and looked them straight in the eyes, somehow searching for the truth. He found it mirrored in their souls.

"You aren't lying! I can't believe it. After all this time I have found other immortals. People who will not turn to dust in the passing of a heartbeat. I cannot tell you how wonderful that feels." Perhaps he could not, but the single tear free falling from his right eye could. "In the past, others have taken my journey with me. Perhaps I can persuade one or more of you to join me in my travels, for a century or two? Barely an eye blink for one of us."

"Let us speak of that later," Paddy said, with a glint in his eye—a glint that spoke volumes to those who knew him well. "If you could, what would you wish for, revenge or peace?"

"Peace. My hatred grows cold and my desire for serenity is almost greater than the pain. Besides, what can a mortal, even an undying one, do against the son of God?" He smiled at his own rhetorical question and proceeded to answer it. "I was present at a court case in Arizona in 1970, where a woman was suing God for damage to her house in the amount of one hundred thousand dollars. Her lawyer accused God of negligence in his power over the weather when he allowed a lightning bolt to strike her home."

"What happened?"

"She won. The defendant failed to appear in the court."

"How did she collect?"

"Exactly. He was found guilty and nothing could be done about it."

"If God created us in his image and people can do evil and be violent, it stands to reason that so can God," offered Lucas.

"Only one flaw with that theory. There are some people who can do only good. I spent some time with the Tasaday tribe in the Philippine Islands. Modern man has only recently discovered them. The Tasaday have no enemies, no weapons for war. They don't even have the words to describe war, hate, or even dislike. They neither hunt nor cultivate. The island provides them with all they need."

"What do they do with all that free time?"

Joseph smiled, gave a small cough, and blushed in his hairless areas of his cheeks. "They keep quite busy, I assure you. The tribe has quite a few singalongs as well." See, what did I tell you. Primal instinct. They must be much worse than the Bulfinche's crew. It is a simple deduction, once you remember that they have no enemies. Their singing scared them all away. I didn't share that bit of wisdom with Joseph. He probably would not agree with me anyhow. Besides, this information in the wrong hands could lead to an arms build–up of sorts. Voice stock–piling. Bad singing and little children standing on the borders of countries, microphones in hand, amplifiers at full blast. With the possibility of someone cutting in on radio and TV frequencies, no one would be safe. That, or the entire world would join in, but that would probably destroy what is left of the ozone layer. It's better this way.

"Wait a minute. If they are out in the middle of the Pacific Ocean, how did you find them? Not to mention get there and leave?" I asked.

"I have my ways," he answered with a grin. He inhaled deeply. "My wish would definitely be for peace."

"Very good. I am glad to hear you say that. I have wonderful news for you, Joseph the wanderer. Your journey has come to its end."

Unable to speak, Joseph's mouth swung open wider than a screen door on one hinge. "How is such a thing possible?"

Paddy explained to him how Bulfinche's negated and neutralized all curses, powers, and many causes of harm were void where prohibited. Joseph stood, then sat back down when he realized that it was true. It was why he was feeling no pain and zero wanderlust.

"You are welcome here and may stay as long as you want, Joseph."

Joseph was practically speechless. He managed to mutter a simple "Thank you" before he collapsed, weeping tears of joy at Paddy's feet. Paddy has never been comfortable with that kind of worship mixed with affection. He pulled Joseph to his feet and held him as he wept and laughed. Paddy shed a tear or two of his own. My eyes were misting over and I wasn't alone. It was one of those moments that makes me glad to be alive, glad of my job's intangible fringe benefits.

That is when the light hit.

The brilliance came down from the ceiling, making the fourteen stories above it seem nonexistent. Save for having to cover our eyes, none of us were affected. None of us save Joseph. He was knocked to the ground as if he had been hit by a giant luminescent sledgehammer. He was holding his head and abdomen, writhing in agony.

A cloud of anger covered Paddy's face.

"Stop," he whispered and Joseph visibly relaxed and rose slowly to his feet. Fear was slowly being washed away by the hatred of two thousand years. Paddy placed a calming hand on his shoulder.

"Who dares conspire to undo my work?" boomed the voice. Paddy calmly leaned against the bar as if half bored with the situation, but every muscle in his body was taunt. This was no drunk he was dealing with.

"That would be me," answered Paddy, with calm and nonchalance.

"And who are you?" the light demanded.

"Ye know quite well who I be," Paddy answered. "And ye have done quite enough to this man. He needs a rest. And ye need better manners, barging into my bar like this, uninvited. Use the door and materialize like everyone else."

"You have no right to judge me. By your nature, you are subject to my commands."

"No offense, but I think not. Ye must be thinking of my parents who ye father booted out of your kingdom. I wasn't born in your dominion, not even in Faerie like most of my people. I was born here in the mortal realm. Ye booted out my people from heaven, even though they committed no crime."

"They did not side with me in the great battle."

"But neither did they side with Lucifer and his Horde. They choose to stay out of politics and where did it get them? Exiled no different from the rebellious."

"The realm of the rebels was much different than that of Earth."

"True, but at least Hell was theirs. My people created Faerie with their own sweat and tears. Even so, it still crosses over to the mortal plane, so we couldn't avoid contact with mankind. With your coming, our power weakened and waned, yet we too had committed no crime."

"They did not make a stand."

"Yet I am making one now. You cannot condemn both my actions and theirs by your own admission."

The light grew silent.

"Nevertheless, I demand the taunter continue his journey, alone and unabated."

"I am afraid I cannot allow that."

The voice answered with a clap of thunder as the light magnified in intensity until its brilliance was blinding. I could tell even from under the table under which Ismael, Lucas, and I had taken cover. That is the macho way of saying the three of us were cowering in fear.

Paddy said "There will be none of that behavior in my bar." With a snap of his fingers, the nova flare subsided to a dull glow. Joseph was holding his temples. "Pain?" asked Paddy.

"Just a little. Very mild, actually."

"We can't be having none of that." Paddy closed his eyes and creased his brow in concentration. Joseph's hands returned to his side.

"Better?"

"Yes. Completely."

Paddy nodded. "Very well," said the light. "You leave me no choice. Father Michael Ryann, come forward," Mike did as he was told and knelt before the light. "Rise, my faithful servant. I have a great task for you, my son. Carry the scorner out of this bar and onto the street, where his punishment for his sins may begin anew."

This was trouble. Mike was one of the family. If he chose to listen, no one would lift a hand to stop him. Hercules would merely walk out and bring Joseph back in, but the damage would be done. Paddy would be able to forgive Mike, but Mike would never forgive himself. It would put a wall between them that the most skilled of mountain climbers would have trouble getting over. I could not blame him if he did. I'm Catholic, too. I don't think I would have the strength to refuse. Luckily, Mike did.

"No, my Lord. I cannot. I must follow my conscience and it says this is wrong."

"When my Father asked Abraham, he was willing to sacrifice his only son."

"It was wrong then, too," Father Mike said gently. The light seemed almost to nod in agreement. "I would gladly hear his confession and grant him absolution. As you yourself said 'If you forgive men's sins, they are forgiven. If you hold them bound, they are held bound.'"

"I have tried before to no avail," said Joseph.

The light agreed with him. "No. His sins are too great."

"You have got to be kidding me," shouted a voice from the back. It belonged to Rebecca. "All he did was insult you and spit on you when you were down. If his sins were so great, what about those whose sins were much greater? Where were you and your father when the innocents at Auschwitz needed you? Why did you not answer the crying children? Why did Adolph Hitler go virtually unpunished in his lifetime? Why were the blameless condemned?" Damn good questions. No answer came. Rebecca issued a further challenge. For the first time I can remember, including during the hottest of summer days, Rebecca rolled up her sleeves. The numbers on her forearm stood out stronger than the light. The light had no answer for her and was shamed by its silence.

The light turned its attention back to Paddy again. "You insist on giving him haven here?"

"Yes."

"You know what I can do?"

"Yes. But he and I are safe."

"But someday you will have to travel outside of your Bulfinche's."

"Perhaps."

"I could destroy it."

"Then you will have to destroy me as well," I said, placing my body in front of Paddy and Joseph. Paddy had saved my life and taken me in when I had nothing. I owed him my life and it was a debt I found myself willing to pay, even seized by terror. Lucas stepped in front of me, Ismael in front of him. Rebecca pulled the lot of us back as we locked arms forming a human wall. The light seemed unfazed.

"And ye will not be able to destroy Bulfinche's without destroying the entire island of Manhattan. Are you willing to destroy ten million lives to punish one guilty man?"

"'If even one good man is there, I shall spare the city.' The fact that so many are willing to do what is right proves there is more than that number in this bar alone," said Father Mike.

"True, I would not do that. At least not until the appointed day," spoke the light. That worried me.

"You always taught us to love our neighbor as ourself. To turn the other cheek when another strikes us. Joseph long ago struck you. Will you offer him your other cheek?"

The light contemplated. The bar grew still. "You are right, but I cannot lift the penance from him. I can only allow him to stay here as long as he wishes and to be able to return when he grows weary. Is this acceptable to you, Joseph?"

"Yes it is, Nazarene." Straining, Joseph managed to say, "My thanks."

"You are welcome. I promise you one day your travels will be completed. In the meantime, you have helped a great many people in your journeying who otherwise would have been at a loss. You may yet find redemption."

Joseph stared defiantly, squinting into the light.

"Scorner, you may set your mind at rest. Your family learned of your penance and bore you no ill will. In fact, they found a chest of coins when digging a well the next spring, which helped them live the rest of their lives in comfort. Farewell," the light said. I wanted to ask him why Elsie had to die, but I was unable to speak, perhaps because I was afraid he might answer me. Still, it didn't ignore me or any of us. Before it vanished it changed its aspect entirely. The light filled all present with a special grace and warmth. I swear it smiled. Then the light was gone and the ceiling returned, having the nerve to act as if it had never left.

"I cannot believe the Nazarene ended my torment," said Joseph.

"He is a merciful God," said Father Mike. Joseph nodded, not yet fully convinced. Two thousand years worth of aching feet is hard to forget. Or forgive.

"Don't kid yourself. He wanted this to happen," said Paddy.

"What?" said Joseph and Mike in unison.

"Joseph, you never did tell us how you found Bulfinche's."

"It was the oddest thing. I was walking when all of a sudden, the sprinklers at a church up the street turned on." That would be Our Lady of the Lake, Mike's parish. They water their twenty–square–foot lawn daily. It seems to me astro-turf would be easier. "The water streamed up into the air and a shaft of sunlight streamed through it, forming a rainbow which seemed to leap right to your door."

"What was the source of the sunlight?"

Joseph's eyes spread wide in wonder as he answered. "It reflected off the metal cross atop the church steeple."

"I rest my case," said Paddy. "He knew this was the only place where Joseph would be able to find rest. The thunder and brimstone was just an act."

"Did you know that at the time?" I asked.

Paddy stopped looking so smug. "No."

"But why could he not just lift the curse himself, or grant him a rest without leading him here?" I asked.

"Easy," said Hercules. "He couldn't break a promise. Even a regretted one made in anger. Like I said earlier, he needed an out in order to save face. Not unlike the time my father, shaped as a codfish, became involved with a fisherman's wife. She was very competitive with her husband and wanted to out do him in every aspect. One day after the husband had caught the biggest fish their village had ever seen, the wife became insanely jealous. So much so, in fact, that she tricked a promise out of Zeus for favors rendered. She demanded she catch the biggest fish in all the oceans, in front of the entire village. Sadly, father agreed. Back in those days, marine life was not classified in fish, mammals, and such, so anything that swam was a fish. So, alone in her boat but in full view of the villagers, the wife cast a line which almost instantly was caught in the mouth of a blue whale. She pulled on the line and up came the whale. Awed, she tried to bring it in but it was too much for her. Her request had never mentioned bringing the fish back to shore. The whale dove under, the line still caught in his jaw. The woman, too stubborn to let go, was dragged beneath the waves, never to be seen again. Zeus was saddened, until he learned of her sister's fascination with otters."

Joseph sat back and listened to Hercules' tale. Later he would share several of his own. But for now the walking stick lay in the corner, unused, and Joseph took off his coat. He was going to stay a while.

SOBERING VISIONS

The place was pretty full for a Tuesday. Some yuppies had wandered in off the street and seemed confused by the lack of sound. The silence is the first thing that hits you. Not that the bar was quiet–far from it. When someone walks through our door they leave the world outside behind for a while. Not even the street noise gets in. Most people find it comforting. The yuppies appeared almost frightened by it. It is quiet enough for you to hear yourself think, which was perhaps a tad uncomfortable for our new visitors. They might have been out of their element, having to leave the group mind behind and stand alone for a little while, even if only inside their own heads. Still, we try not to discriminate against any one here at Bulfinche's, so I put aside my personal views and tried to make them feel at home. Men call me Murphy, usually collect. Women tend to forget my number.

The yuppies settled at a table in the corner.

Despite its technical classification as a pub, most of us, staff and patron alike, consider Bulfinche's home. From the looks the newcomers were giving some of the regulars, they thought of it as more of a group home. Most of the folks could pass for normal, especially on the streets of New York. Take Father Mike Ryann, for instance. Looks like any Catholic priest, other than the fact he was racing around the tables at high speeds in a borrowed wheelchair, nicknamed Laughter's Chariot, to the cheers of the assembled crowd. He had borrowed the chair from fellow patron and racing fan, Roy G. Biv.

Looking at him now, one would find it hard to believe the man ever experienced any tragedy. Roy's back working full–time with the circus, the only professional clown in a wheelchair. Whenever the circus is in town, we see him more than his audiences do. Lucky us. His presence would bring a smile to a dead man. Roy was now chiding Father Mike on his poor performance. Roy had beat him by eight seconds. Blindfolded.

Also in attendance was the bossman, Paddy Moran. He had been anxiously awaiting the completion of Father Mike's final lap. His turn was next. Climbing into the freshly vacated wheelchair, he prepared for the starting gun, a bottle of champagne. It was held ready for popping by Dionysus, the chosen divinity of the inebriated. Paddy, while large for a leprechaun, was petite by human standards. He was having trouble settling into the wheelchair. His feet didn't reach the footplates and his arms had some trouble reaching over the armrests.

"Hey, Paddy!" yelled Dion, "Want me to get the telephone book for you to sit on?"

Paddy rasberried him before volleying his comeback. "Only if you want to sit on the bottle, letting me make the fine adjustments, O rotund one."

Dion simply smiled and raised his eyebrows twice in rapid succession, giving his best come–hither look. Paddy scowled and replied "Never mind. You'd enjoy it too much."

"Probably. Maybe I'll try it later," chuckled Dion, his ample belly jiggling in rhythm to his laughter. As Paddy continued to make his preparations for the race, Dion said, "Paddy, one more thing."

"What?"

The cork popped. "Go."

Though caught unaware, Paddy didn't lose much time pulling onto the make-shift track. As he was circling the first turn, one of the yuppies, dressed in a suit and tie, his armor of arrogance, stepped in front of the speeding Laugher's Chariot.

"Out of the way!" yelled Paddy, laughing and making up for lost time. The man barely moved and only Paddy's reflexes prevented the loss of any toes.

"Stupid imbecile!" the yuppie yelled in Paddy's wake, but wisely got out of the way for lap two. He made his way over to my station at the bar. 747s were swerving to avoid colliding with his nose. "That man is crazy. He almost killed me."

"Nah. Would have only given you a flesh wound at best. Roy won't let anyone else drive with the spiked wheels on. Claims they are great in the snow, though," I quipped. The man looked at me unbelieving, mouth agape, maybe even twogap, at the fact that a mere bartender would speak to him such. I was going to enjoy this. "Besides, it was your fault. You didn't even look before crossing the bar. You rudely walked right onto the track. He clearly had the right of way."

"You are defending that madman's actions?"

"Yep. But be careful about throwing stones. Madness is relative." Especially with some of the relatives that drop by here. "It must be one hundred and five outside in the shade, and you are wearing long sleeves and a jacket. And a blue suit with red tie. Very original fashion statement. It says 'Look at me! I am one of the faceless masses. Do me homage.'"

"One should grant me the respect due my station."

"Which one? Penn or Grand Central?"

"How dare you! I could buy and sell you."

"I doubt you could afford the payments. I'm high maintenance."

"What do you mean? You are a bartender. You can't be making more than me."

"Depends. How much you make?"

He told me.

"I got you beat. Not counting tips." Actually, I was exaggerating by counting in what my free room upsides saves me in rent as income. "Besides, even if you were a billionaire, you can't buy respect. Not here. As for what you want, it is back to that homage thing again. Let me tell you, homage doesn't go over big here. Even if it did, you would be last on the list."

"Such impudence must not go unpunished."

"Buddy, you ever listen to yourself talk? This isn't Masterpiece Theater."

"I have had just about enough of you."

"Oh good. Please do come back when you are ready for more."

"I demand to see the manager."

"What day is today?"

"Tuesday."

"Oh good. Then today's manager is me." We rotate the job, since nobody really wants it.

"Then I want to see the owner and demand he put a stop to this buffoonery."

"Buffoonery or otherwise, we here at Bulfinche's respect all creeds and beliefs." Even those of yuppies.

"I said I wanted to see and speak to the owner."

"Okay. If you turn around you can see him from here. He is on his fifth lap but you will have to wait until his race is done before you can speak with him."

"You mean the maniac in the chair?"

"Yes."

"Forget it. Give me five beers and two wine spritzers."

"Coming up." As I poured the brew and mixed the wine and seltzer, I decided I had come down too hard on the guy. He might just be having a bad day. "Try to relax, kick back, and enjoy."

"Enjoy what? Your making fun of handicapped people?"

"We aren't making fun of anyone. The clown sitting on the chair is a paraplegic, and the chariot races were his idea. Probably because he figures he can win them. He is still mad he lost the dance contest last night."

"Of course he lost."

"Right you are. Rebecca and Hermes are hard to beat."

"Are you saying he had a chance?"

"Of course. He and Rumbles took third. Right behind Demeter and Dion's number."

"But that's impossible. He cannot dance without legs."

"Who is making fun of handicapped people now?"

"Never mind. Just give me the drinks. What do I owe you?"

"Nothing. On the house."

"At last. Some respect. A peace offering to make up for your earlier rudeness."

"No. Tradition. First drink is on the house."

"Yeaa," stammered Mosie drunkenly, from his tenuous perch on the barstool next to the yuppie. "If Murphy had to give away a drink to every one he was rude to, the place would go belly up."

"You are too kind, Mosie."

"Yes, I am," he slurred, more plastered than most walls could ever dream of. Taking the tray of drinks off the bar, the yuppie looked down his nose in disgust at Mosie. He didn't leave me a tip. Imagine my surprise.

"Stinking drunk," he muttered.

Standing and smelling his armpits, slowly and one at a time, Mosie looked up and proclaimed, "Deodorant works the same whether I am sober or not. Right, Murphy?"

"Don't know, Mosie. Never saw you sober."

"Not a pretty sight, I can assure you."

Afraid to step back onto the track, where Lucas was doing his level best to beat the record still held by Roy, the yuppie had to get by Mosie. Instead of asking nicely or using a simple "excuse me," he grunted, "Get out of my way." To accentuate his point he lifted his free hand up to push Mosie out of his way, but Mosie knowingly side-stepped the attack. The yuppie, off balance, fell flat on his face, but not before Mosie caught the full tray. Spinning and lurching with the grace of a garbage truck, he placed the drinks down on the bar without spilling a drop. Hermes, waiting for his turn at the races, joined me in giving Mosie a standing ovation. He bowed modestly, then offered his hand to the fallen yuppie who angrily brushed it away.

"I can get up by myself."

"You certainly got down there by yourself, all right."

"I did not. You pushed me."

"I'm sorry. You must have the two of us confused. A dishonest mistake, I'm sure. Let me share with you an easy way to tell us apart. I'm the handsome one whose breath has the sweet smell of finely distilled whiskey, and you are the one wearing a tie. Simple, no?"

"Why you sonna...."

"Tut, tut my bad man. No need for profanity, although given the life you have made for yourself, it is understandable."

"Why I oughta...." said the yuppie.

"Why I oughta...." repeated Mosie simultaneously. Instead of being impressed by Mosie's talent he became even more annoyed.

"How did you do that?"

"How did you do that?" echoed Mosie, grinning. Most folks hate a mimic, vexed to be forced to endure hearing their very words repeated and twisted into sounds and meaning never meant for them to have. Mosie's synchronous parroting, although amusing at first, loses its charm, especially when he says what you were going to say even before you do. The yuppie learned of this when a very attractive woman from his party came over to the bar to see what the holdup was. Smiling Mosie beat the yuppie to the punch. Lifting up the tray, pulling it away just as the yuppie reached for it, he handed it to the woman.

"Sorry about the delay. It is this simpleton's fault," Mosie said before the yuppie could even finish the second word. The woman smiled, not unaware of her companion's faults.

"How much do we owe you?" she asked the yuppie.

Shyly he replied, "Nothing. I got this round." Surprised at the monotone sentence, he turned to stare at Mosie, who gave him a look of bemused innocence.

"Actually," I interjected, "The first round of a patron's virgin visit is on the house. Enjoy with our compliments." Under my breath, without even moving my lips, I whispered "And our insults for you," to the yuppie.

"Thank you," she said, first to me, then to Mosie. The yuppie waited, but none came his way, and he was left without a thank you to call his own.

The yuppie left us, to no one's dismay, save perhaps the drinking companions he returned to.

Meanwhile, back at the races, Hermes had finished in second, only half a second behind Roy. I was up next. Walking around the bar I made my way to the starting line and climbed in the wheelchair's cockpit. I had a pair of swimming goggles, a bandanna borrowed from Rebecca tied around my head and a long white dish rag that I tossed around my neck to wear much as a fighter pilot would wear a scarf.

"You ready, Ace?" Roy asked, kind enough to suggest I had a chance. I did but it wasn't worth mentioning. So I did.

"I'm going to beat your record, Roy and be the winner of the Bulfinche 500." Five hundred feet that is.

"Want to bet, Murph?" asked Mosie, putting down his club soda. Which was odd. The club soda, not the bet. Mosie never drinks anything without alcohol in it, but today he had been easing off. As far as the bet goes, it is a good policy never to make more than a friendly wager in Bulfinche's unless you enjoy losing. Paddy and Hermes are con artists: the old masters, one might say. Very rare for them to lose. Don't bet Ismael that he knows where to take you in his taxi without asking. Inside the bar, Heimdal held a note on a trumpet for five minutes without a break. Demeter got Jasmine the NYC detective to give up donuts in favor of granola. I once caught a leprechaun and got my job here for my trouble. Father Mike once gave a sermon that lasted less than ten minutes.

I guess you would have to know Mike to get the full impact of that occurrence. Mike is the greatest guy going, but he tends to get a little lengthy in his preaching at times. A plus in his chosen line of work and the sermons are good. Actually has me going to church more than twice a year. Mike has a gift of not talking down, but instead he lifts up the listener so that not only does he believe he can make his life better, but he wants to. In short, the impossible is done here daily.

Still, if you are adventurous, you can wager, but there are a few nevers even in Bulfinche's: Never forget to pay your tab; never intentionally hurt someone, and Mosie never loses a bet. Not that he isn't allowed. The old man and Hermes would love to hoodwink him just once. It just can't be done. Not without Paddy breaking a promise and cheating. Cheating he has no problem with, but the old man would sooner lose a finger than break his word.

So I resolved myself to my fate. I wasn't going to win. This wouldn't stop me from trying. Dion let loose the cork and I sped forward, racing around chairs and tables at speeds that belittled the adjective. Just for effect, I threw the scarf rag behind me where it stood straight back as if a mighty wind was holding it there. The coat hanger wire was practically invisible. It got a couple of chuckles.

My effort was respectable, even if Hermes was yelling that a tortoise was blinking for the passing lane. I would have to remind him of the race he lost to Paddy on camelback.

Respectability only carries one so far, but momentum can carry you all the way to the bar, which is what happened to me when something materialized right smack in front of me on the track. Roy would have been able to jump it or steer around it. Me, I did the only thing available to me. I hit it and became airborne, stopping just short of Mosie's feet. A folded dish rag cushioned the impact of my chin.

"Thanks, Mosie."

"Don't mention it, Murph. One bit of advice: despite the outfit, it is still a good idea to fly using a plane or other appropriate device."

"Yes. And Murphy, you didn't even assume the correct position for landing," yelled Hermes.

"Or return your stewardess to the upright position," chuckled Dion.

"Make sure you find the little black box so we can find out what really happened," suggested Roy.

"Actually it seems to be a small golden sphere that caused the problem," said Paddy, picking up the cause of my short flight. "And it appears to be addressed to you, Murphy."

"Me? Who would send me a small golden sphere? I've always wanted one but never found the time to shop. It isn't even my birthday."

"Open it anyway," suggested Dion. "It isn't like you will be getting any gifts then, so you may as well enjoy the experience."

"Okay, but how?" I asked. "The thing has no handles, buttons or latches."

"Try a hammer."

"Run it under hot water."

"Use a credit card."

"Drop it from the roof."

We tried some of the more reasonable methods. Nothing worked.

"You are going about this the wrong way," informed Roy, back in the saddle again in an undamaged Laughter's Chariot.

"And what do you suggest, he of the red nose?"

"Knock," he replied, tapping out shave and a haircut, two bits. The damn thing sprouted a hatch.

"How did you know that?"

"Didn't. I was just trying to be funny. Sometimes it is better to be lucky than funny," Looking down at his legs, he said "I was overdue." There was no complaint in his tone, just a twinge of sadness and acceptance.

Inside was what appeared to be a manuscript and a data disc. Paddy pulled it out. "A Wave Then Goodbye. By J. Murphy. Copyright two thousand and what?" exclaimed the old one, handing it to me. There was a yellow stickee on the first page.

It read:

"Murph,

  Enclosed is a story, all too true, written by yours truly. Or you, whichever you prefer. Same difference. You and the gang need to make preparations. Try to stop it if you can. We couldn't, and we got the same warnings. We can't change the past, but it is still the future for you. I do not need to mention the risks involved. This capsule is breaking all kinds of laws, not that that ever stopped us before. At worst, this becomes a self-fulfilling prophecy and the lot of you save seven million lives. Give Paddy my condolences.

  I know he hates the reaper with a passion, but this time it is unavoidable. The three million he was not able to save died quickly. I know you have no reason to believe this is anything but an elaborate practical joke, but there is a way to check it out. Paddy knows how. Do it.

  Good luck.

            True to yourself,

            Murph

P.S. - Give the Time globe to Vulcan. He developed it. The systems burned itself out, so in and of itself, it will tell him nothing. He didn't want to lose a challenge.

The mood of the bar quickly sobered.

"What do you think, boss? Is it legit?" I asked.

"Don't know. Could be. Vulcan has been working on time travel ever since he read Twain's *A Connecticut Yankee in King Arthur's Court* and Wells' *The Time Machine.* But by the time of that copyright, who knows."

"What does the story say?" Father Mike asked.

I scanned the pages quickly. Perhaps in another Bulfinche's collection I will share the whole story, years before I supposedly copyright it. The story, written in the remarkable Murphy style, tells of the destruction of Manhattan, and most of the Bronx, Queens, Brooklyn, and Staten Island. Worse, from our point of view, the destruction of Bulfinche's, which happens to be in Manhattan.

The city is destroyed by a mad god, who in his twisted mind has suffered one too many indignities at the hands of New Yorkers. The god is Neptune, the same gentleman who cursed Ismael to his aimless wanderings, a trick he has used before. Fed up, taking all he is going to take, he summons a tidal wave that wipes out the city. It is beyond the power of any and all of Bulfinche's staff and patrons to stop. The parts of the boroughs that survive, not to mention Long Island and New Jersey, are devastated by floods.

But all is not lost. Armed with the knowledge of the globe, we have made our preparations. Faking a nuclear bomb scare we manage, in just under three days, to evacuate the city. Almost. Some people, too stubborn, proud, or stupid to leave, don't. Even as the wave rises out of the sea, Paddy is using helicopters and submarines to remove the laggers, but even he has to run and cut his losses. Like the note said we saved seven million and our wine cellar, but ,we lost the building and much more importantly, three million lives.

One of the preparations Paddy makes is to build a space station called the *New York City* with five sections, one for each of the boroughs. In an out–of–the–way corridor, he sets up shop and opens Bulfinche's Pub the Second. He relocates as many folks as he can onto the station and life goes on.

I conveyed the info and Paddy read the pages, weeping at the end for the dead.

"This can't be for real," said Lucas.

"Yes it could. But how do we know?" I asked.

"The future Murphy said you would know what to do to prove it, Paddy. How can you do that?" Roy asked.

"Easy for me. Not so easy for others. Right, Mosie?" said Paddy.

"Right as pain, Moran. I will do as you ask. I owe you too much not to, but do you know what it is you ask of me? What it is for me to be sober?"

"Yes."

"Is there no other way?"

"No."

"Very well."

At this point I should interject some details about Mosie. To most people, even many of our regulars, Mosie is a drunk, pure and simple. A funny, friendly drunk to be sure, but a drunk just the same. There is a reason however, for his constant inebriation other than to avoid a hangover. Every drunk has his reasons for the drink, but Mosie is the first I have run across with a legitimate one. He has been a regular here for years, well before me. Other than the fact that he hasn't been sober over a decade, there are a few other areas Mosie has some distinction in. He has a running tab that is covered by the boss, regardless of the price. He is the greatest psychic to ever have lived. Makes Nostradamus look like a blind man. His visions are so powerful that he finds it impossible to live fully in the present. When he meets somebody, he knows all there is to know: their sorrows, joys, triumphs, and failings. Sober, he sees each person at their birth, death, and every moment in between, all overlaid, a series of infinite double exposures. He was in an institution, diagnosed with autism until he was seven, unable to interact with the real world.

His mother, a gypsy named Madame Rose, a psychic of some repute herself, had met and befriended Paddy years earlier. He had helped turn her fortune–telling scam into a billion–dollar business as a financial adviser. Together, she and Paddy became extremely wealthy. Her urging helped him invest all the money he made during Prohibition and avoid the stock market crash of 1929.

After years of having believed her son had autism, she began to suspect it was something else. Madame Rose turned to her friends in her time of need; she came to Bulfinche's. Paddy and his wife, now dearly departed, with the help of Dion and Hermes, figured out it was his uncontrolled psychic ability, running rampant, that was causing his condition. Hermes realized that the same drugs that would help the condition would make him an addict in short order and have horrible side effects. The least of them was alcohol. But we were still talking about a seven–year–old boy. Paddy suggested that they bring Mosie to the bar, where he could negate the ability. Of course, even Paddy has his limits. He cannot raise the dead or change a physical condition, such as to help Roy to walk again, but he thought he could help Mosie..

Madame Rose did as Paddy suggested. Once inside, Mosie's eyes became clear for the first time in his life and he smiled. Then he screamed. While the full blown power was too much for him to handle, the lack of it was unbearable. Used to living in all time simultaneously, the confinement to a single moment was intolerable and terrorizing. Made temporally blind, Mosie collapsed trembling into his mother's arms. They tried many things, but none worked, so they got a seven–year–old boy drunk, and have kept him that way into adulthood. Blasted, he can see only a few hours either way in time. Paddy promised Madame Rose to never again negate his powers unless he requested it.

Now Mosie was going to sober up completely to search down a time line for a specific event.

"How long do you need?"

"Not very. I have been cutting back since this morning. Any minute now."

"This is nonsense!" uttered the yuppie. "Tidal waves, mad gods, and the psychic bar network. I have never heard of anything so ridiculous in my life."

I started to open my mouth, but Mosie gestured me to be silent. "I will handle this, Murphy. You, sir, are Randolph Howell, supposed son of Nathan and Muffy, but actually of Muffy and the man who cleaned your pool. You were born May 2, 1962. You have many secrets in your closet, including having taken and abandoned a wife on a business trip to Mexico, all for the sake of sex. Your wife, Maria, curses your name and has had to become a prostitute in a border town to support your children. Twins, a boy and a girl." He gave more details of the situation and Paddy wrote them down. The woman would find herself the winner of some contest, giving her enough money to get her started on a new life. (Paddy will spend money well, but he would hound you if you owed him a quarter.) "Your business practices are despicable. You have been involved in insider trading for two years, and performed quite poorly, I might add. With the information you have gotten you should have made your third million by now."

"How do you know all this?"

"I know. It's what I do. It is what I am. But despite all the evil you have done to your fellow man, I still pity you." With that, Mosie hugged him and feigned wiping a tear from his eye.

"What!? What do you see?" begged the yuppie, now a believer.

"Soon, very soon, you will die a horrible, painful death. You will linger for months, unable to move or speak, until you finally pass, friendless and alone."

"Is this set? Can I change it?"

"Who do I look like? The ghost of Christmas yet to come?"

"Please!" he groveled on his knees, pulling on Mosie's pant leg. "I don't want to die."

"Very well. There is but one way I can see. You must give up your worldly possessions and become a Buddhist monk."

"Never!"

"A pity," Mosie said, then again hugged the yuppie. "Goodbye."

"No. Wait. I will do it. When?"

"Now wouldn't be too soon."

"Right. Thank you," said the yuppie, running out to the streets, on his way to a life of solitude and contemplation.

Paddy chuckled. "You didn't really see all that, did you?"

"No. Not exactly. I saw him going along and doing much of the same, ruining dozens more lives. Now he will actually do as I suggested. He will find happiness and in ten years he will save a woman's life. A good piece of work for a few white lies."

With that, Mosie's eyes rolled up, back into his head and he collapsed. Hercules caught him and very gently lowered him to the floor.

Dion and Demeter took over from there, each cradling him in their arms. Paddy held one of his hands, I the other. Every one else in the place—even the rest of the yuppie strangers—tried to hold Mosie, to ease his pain, each of us more than willing to take a piece of his pain for our own. Unfortunately, other than moral and physical support, it was beyond us. Did not stop anyone from trying though.

"How long does he have to be like this, Paddy?" I asked.

"I don't know. Five minutes should be enough."

It was the longest five minutes for most of us in the room. For Mosie it literally lasted years. By the end of it, Mosie had curled up into a fetal position and was sucking his thumb. He was incapable of taking a drink, so Dion and Herc held him still and kept his mouth open while Paddy poured five fingers of Irish whiskey down his throat. Demeter rocked him and sang softly to him his favorite drinking song. The rest of us joined in. Mosie's body relaxed as the liquor hit his stomach, then his bloodstream and slowly over the next several minutes his eyes began to focus again.

Finally he spoke. "Enough with the singing already. I have a horrible hangover you know. Been drinking for decades, you know."

"We can get rid of that easily enough," Paddy said, handing him the rest of the bottle.

"What? Do you think me a savage? A glass please. And a round for all these good people in thanks for their caring and compassion," Paddy raised his eyebrows. "Don't worry, Moran. I'm paying, not you. I have won the lottery, you know. At least eight times. A toast and my thanks. Slainte!" he said, using the Gaelic toast Paddy's wife had taught him when he took his first drinks, all those years ago.

We returned it. "Slainte!"

"Now, with that bit of business out of the way, I suppose you all want to know what I saw. Murphy's story is accurate for the most part. New York is doomed. Nothing can be done to change that."

"Can't you find Neptune?" Lucas asked.

"No," said Hercules. "We have tried several times, including once to try to have him lift Ismael's curse. He is protected."

"By what?" asked Roy.

"One of Demeter's amulets protects him from detection," Herc said.

"Zeus was hunting him," Demeter said. "I gave him the amulet as a favor. It seemed like a good idea at the time."

"What about the three million dead?" asked Roy.

Before answering, Mosie shot a look at me. "That has some leeway in change. More, perhaps all could be saved using the bomb scare earlier and having more rescue vehicles. But we have time. Years, many years."

"Regardless, we need to get started immediately. I will call Vulcan, ship him the time globe and have him send me blueprints for a space station." With that, Paddy disappeared through the door behind the bar and up the stairs to his living quarters. Everyone else spent a moment of silence in quiet mourning for the city we loved, hated, and spent our lives in. Unable to do anything at the moment, the races started up again, this time with the lady yuppie, name of Margarete, in the drivers seat.

Mosie pulled me aside. "Murphy, I saw Manhattan go under. I saw the horror and the heroism. Very few die. Nowhere near three million."

"I know."

"Sober, I knew why you told yourself that lie. Sober is now fading away from me."

"The answer is simple and written on a stickee stuck to the last page, which I palmed." A trick I picked up playing cards with Hermes. "Basically, we all know Paddy takes any death that he could have possibity prevented as a personal defeat. It may be an unreasonably harsh viewpoint, but it is his own. My future self felt that if Paddy thought saving the people of New York was a sure thing, he wouldn't work as hard on it as he could. He would thereby possibly doom more people to death, which he in turn would blame himself for. However, the specter of saving three million lives from certain death is a challenge that will fuel him to save them all and give him the greatest triumph of his life. All in all, an excellent justification for a few small fibs."

"Good plan. It works.

"But one possible flaw exists. You might let something slip."

"No worries there, my friend. Although foretold, the fifth kept silent. Pleading the fifth, if you will. Which is a good thing," he announced, raising a fifth savagely to his lips. "Because I hate the shout of liquor screaming as it rolls down my throat."

I laughed, but I could have just as easily made the switch to tears. Before today, the future had always been kind of a murky, mystery land which remained shrouded in mists of ignorance. True, the past and present gave us many clues to what may come next, but one never knew for sure. That was part of the future's charm. Irrevocably, that was changed forever.

"Murphy, knowing is the hardest part," Mosie confided in me. Poor guy knew everything, the good, bad, and mediocre in all of us. How he was conceived and how he would die and everything in between. Now the rest of us could understand just a fraction of his burden.

He was right. Knowing was the hardest part. We knew New York was going to die. We knew how and we knew when. But we knew other things. Things that counted. We had time and we had hope. In the end, they would be enough.

SILENT JUSTICE

It was an odd way to spend my day off. Not odd in the way that, say, dressing up in tin foil, claiming to be a potato, and asking people to bake me is. Besides, that was a one time deal, but only because I lost a bet. No, I was doing something more mundane. I was on the wrong side of a bar, if such a thing is possible. It was not just any bar. Today, instead of bartending, I was a patron. Amazing how a change of scenery can alter one's perspective.

I was here because of an invitation to share in a Passover Seder and I was a few hours early. Bulfinche's is a special place. People of all creeds and beliefs gather here in harmony. Some of the objects of beliefs have even stopped by or live here.

I was sitting with two men of legend. Although I could be counted in their company, I could hardly be counted in their number. I am legend only in my own mind. Makes one wonder about my stability.

To my left sat Joseph, the Wandering Jew, who like myself lived upstairs, albeit on a different floor. It was Joseph's first home in almost two thousand years. Thick grey hair and beard engulfed the better part of his head, leaving only his eyes, ears, forehead and nose to baldly fend for themselves.

On my right was seated Samson of Biblical fame. You may have heard of him— guy who hates barbers and Philistines. These days he wears his locks slicked back and tied in a pony tail. Dark wayfarer sunglasses cover hollow eye sockets. After his first and last trim, his enemies gouged his eyes out and left him blind for eternity. He still gets by, even uses a blind man's cane. Been coming to Bulfinche's for years.

The three of us were debating hockey, arguing who had the better chance for the Stanley Cup this year, Islanders or Rangers.

There were several others, regulars and strangers in the bar, but one gentleman stood out from the rest. Literally. He was sitting on a barstool but I had seen him walk in. He was seven feet tall if he was an inch. Built like a brick wall. Wore a navy bandanna tied pirate style around his head, covering everything above his eyes. His skin was an odd color, the shade of earth baked in the sun too long. He moved slowly and a bit awkwardly. He was definitely the tall silent type. Guy didn't speak a word. Used sign language to order his drink, then proceeded to simply stare at it longingly, without even an effort of raising it to his lips. Luckily, Paddy and Dion are both fluent in sign. Me, I know only the basics. He finger spelled his name. It was Judah. Judah had a look on his face that spoke volumes. It told of sorrow and pain, the kind that affects your whole life. Dion and Paddy had offered to listen, or rather look, if he wanted to get anything off his chest. Putting his index and middle finger together over his thumb he closed the fingers together like a snapping alligator. It was the sign for no, followed by thank you.

Although everyone at Bulfinche's loves to help people, we first and foremost respect a person's privacy. If he wanted to tell us, he would. Until then we simply did our best to put him at ease, to feel at home. Bulfinche's has the kind of people and atmosphere that make people feel like everything is going to be all right. Then the people do something about it, if and when they can. Sometimes it is something as simple as listening. Or not listening, as the case may be.

A sweet–looking elderly couple walked in the door, arm in arm, each helping the other. The dedication each had for the other was heartwarming to see. You could see the love in their eyes, but hidden behind that love, cowering above the fire they had for life, was something dark and disturbing: it was fear. A dragon invading a new lair.

The couple took a table in the corner near the dart board, but playing was not on their agenda. They each ordered a white wine, which Paddy brought to their table. They tried to pay him but Paddy politely refused, explaining one of Bulfinche's customs. First visit, first drink is on the house.

"Anything else I can do for you good people?" Paddy asked, his smile burning bright.

"Not unless you are a bodyguard," said the old woman.

Judah signed and Dion translated. "I was once a bodyguard."

"Hush, Sarah," whispered her husband.

"Why, Aaron? What difference would that make?"

"Why would you folks need a bodyguard?" asked Paddy.

The couple looked at each other, desperately wanting to speak but fearful the dragon would keep them silent. Staring into each others eyes, they found the strength to overcome their fear and, while not slaying the dragon, at least mortally wounded him.

"We have been threatened by those who demand we leave our apartment," said Aaron.

"It has been our home for almost forty years. We raised our children there," added Sarah, tears in her eyes.

"Why are they trying to drive you out?" asked Dion.

"Because we are Jewish."

"There is nothing wrong with that," said Joseph.

"It is a proud heritage as God's chosen people. Who is trying to drive you away?" asked Samson, sagely turning his shaded eyes their way.

"They call themselves the Aryan Knighthood," said Sarah. It seemed in this case the self-proclaimed knights were creating the dragon.

"What have they threatened?" asked Paddy.

"It is not what they have threatened. It is what they have done. First they beat Simon and raped his wife Julie. After they went to the police to report the crime, they were both found strangled in their apartment," said Aaron.

"Didn't the police do something?" I asked.

"They tried, but no leads. These people are not stupid. They may wear a golden swastika around their throats, but they do not paint them at the scenes of their villainy. That would get them publicity and prosecution for hate crimes. Now they are threatening us, and the police say they can do nothing unless the Aryan Knighthood does something overt. We are old, and it may be far too late by then. We cannot even prove they exist because they keep such a low profile. Regardless, they are deadly in their silence," said Aaron.

Anger rising almost as high as his height, Judah got up from the bar and signed. Dion translated.

"Others of us are deadly in our silence as well."

"That we are," said Rebecca as she entered the room, dressed as always in a mish–mash of fads and fashion that even by the furthest stretch of the imagination and poor eyesight would never be in vogue. Rebecca didn't care. Her clothes kept her warm in her life on the streets. Refuses to leave the streets for reasons of her own, but has saved numerous others from the same fate. Rebecca was our very own paradox. "I heard about the new hate mongers. I have come to help."

"How did you hear?" asked Aaron, confused.

"The streets confide what men may hide, if one is willing to listen," Rebecca replied. "You should not have to live though that again."

"You know?" asked Sarah. Rebecca nodded.

"Know what?" asked Samson.

"We are Holocaust survivors of the camp at Buchenwald, or should I say, man's own Hell on Earth. We are Russian Jews. The Nazi's herded thousands of us into their death camp. They also did the same with the gypsies, other Russians, and any other group that did not fit into their Aryan framework."

"They were butchers and monsters. Not only did we have to witness them marching off our loved ones, but we even saw what they did to them," Sarah said, starting to sob.

"It is all right, sweetest. You don't have to go on," Aaron said, laying a comforting hand on his wife's shoulder.

"It will never be all right. The soldiers meant to take me to the gas chamber. My mother volunteered to take my place. They refused until another man, claiming to be my father, added his life to the bargain, saying that he had lived a long and happy life. He was maybe twenty five. I was only twelve. My own father had been killed just two days before. The soldier agreed. I watched them march off together, hand in hand to the valley of death. I never even said thank you." Sarah was weeping openly now.

"Words fail in trying to comfort you," Samson said. "I am sorry."

Sarah nodded. "That is not the end of the story. A corporal had me working as his personal maid. As I was cleaning his quarters, I noticed a lamp. It looked familiar. When I realized why, I screamed. On its center were two strawberry color circles that overlapped. I had seen the birthmark before on my mother's back. They had skinned my mother and turned what remained of her into a lamp shade." She collapsed, sobbing, into her husband's arms. The lot of us bowed our heads in a moment of silence out of respect. After a moment, Sarah regained her composure.

"I apologize for my outburst," she said.

"No need for that. You are among friends here," informed Paddy, offering her his hand. She took it and smiled the saddest of smiles.

"I lost all of my family there but my brother, Simon, who these new monsters have taken from me. The only light in my darkness there was meeting my Sarah. Now we must leave in fear again. We are too old to fight them," Aaron said.

"I know your pain," said Rebecca.

"How could you know my pain?" said Aaron harshly.

By way of answer Rebecca rolled up her sleeve, revealing a row of numbers tattooed into her arm. "I was in Auschwitz. You were lucky your brother survived with you. All my family died."

"I am sorry. I did not know," said Aaron, bowing his head. Rebecca nodded her forgiveness.

"I came to America and New York. I found and fell in love with a wonderful man, Abraham. We were married soon after. We had three beautiful children. Moses, Judy, and Helen. It was not a perfect life, but it was a happy one. Abe helped me heal after the terrors. I only survived by pleasuring Nazis. I was eight. I was not the only girl forced to service our killers. One day a visiting SS general walked in on seven soldiers and one ten–year–old girl. He had all seven executed for soiling themselves on a Jew. The girl was actually a gypsy. Did not matter. It stopped for a while. Abe did not hold my past against me. But happiness was not meant for me."

"One cold night in July, I awoke to find a hand clasped over my mouth. A voice told me not to scream, that I was a filthy Jew and deserved what I got. His partner held my Abe at gunpoint while he started to lift up my nightgown above my knees. Abe lunged forward to stop him, but got a bullet in his head for his heroics. That only seemed to inspire my rapist. I groped in the dark and found a metal letter opener. It was not sharp, but it was all I had. I rammed it into his throat before he could ram anything into me. His partner, frightened, fled. I pushed his carcass off my bed and rushed to Abe's side, too late. I held him and whispered a last 'I love you' in his ears before rushing to the children's rooms. Again I was too late. They had been there first. They had killed my babies. Moses was eight, Judy was five and Helen would have been two in three weeks. The bastards had drawn swastikas with the blood of my babies. I buried my family," Rebecca said, as a single tear glided down hr cheek. For her, that was a tremendous display of emotion.

Paddy walked over to her and holding out his arms said "Come here."

"I don't need no comforting, Moran," she said.

"Ye can lie to yourself if you like, Rebecca, but don't ye ever lie to me. Get over here and take the damn hug."

"If you put it that way, I guess I cannot refuse," Rebecca said. Despite Paddy's smaller stature, he enveloped Rebecca in his embrace. As he held her she shed three more tears in addition to the first, one for each loved one. I think I finally was beginning to understand why Rebecca stayed on the streets.

Rebecca finally pulled back, but I could hear her whisper "Thank you," before going on with her story. "The police caught the man, but he was freed. Found not guilty because my testimony, that of a heartbroken woman who had only seen him in the dark, was deemed unreliable. As he left the court room a free man, he whispered to me 'I will come see you and finish the job.' I found him first and made sure he would never harm another baby or loving husband again. I could not bear going back to the empty apartment alone, so I started walking and I have never stopped."

"You must not blame yourself for the hatred of others," Aaron consoled. "There was nothing that any of us could have done to stop the Nazis, whatever guise they were wearing."

"My father thought differently. We had been relocated to the Jewish ghetto out-side Krakow, Poland. He had made a study of the Kabbalah, the Jewish book of magic. He and five others decided they could create a savior–to defeat the Nazis–out of dirt and clay, water and tears, pleas and prayers. A golem," said Rebecca. Judah became very interested in her story. "One of the men had been a sculptor. He fashioned the body of a giant. They performed the ceremonies as outlined in the book and the Golem rose off the floor. We named him Judah Maccabee, after the biblical hero– the ham-mer of God– who sacrificed his life to stop an invading army atop elephants by lying beneath them and stabbing at their unprotected undersides as they trampled over him. Judah stayed with us for many weeks as preparations were made for our revolt. He hid with many of us children, to protect us. The day before the revolt was scheduled, the cleansing of the ghetto began. Judah took us and hid us in a basement. The Nazis blew up the building. Judah held up the building as long as he could, using his body to shelter the rest of the children. He held it up long enough for all but two of us to climb out a basement window. The weight was too much for him and he fell as the rubble collapsed, burying him. The squad of Nazis who had blown the building soon caught the rest of us and moved us to Auschwitz."

Judah stood and walked toward Rebecca, signing something with his hands. It was not American sign but Rebecca understood it.

"Rebecca, is it really you?" Judah signed.

"Judah? It can't be."

"It is."

"Prove it," she demanded.

Judah pulled the bandanna off, revealing his bald head, and a word sculpted onto his forehead. The word was Emeth, the Hebrew word for truth. Rebecca moved forward and reached toward his forehead. Judah pulled back out of self preservation. If the 'E' is rubbed away from the forehead of a golem, it leaves the word 'Meth', which means "he is dead". As legend has it, the action would kill the golem. Rebecca removed her hand but still was not convinced.

"Take off your shirt," she demanded. Judah removed first his trenchcoat, then his shirt, revealing a torso that indeed looked sculpted, from the well–defined pectoral muscles to the developed arms. There was something that did stand out. Three small hand prints, one of which was on his left lower rib cage. Rebecca traced it with her own hand.

"It is you!" she said, wrapping her arms around Judah. He returned the gesture. When the embrace ended, Rebecca regained her composure and said "Two hugs in one day. I must be becoming a loose woman in my old age."

"What's with the handprints in his side?" I asked.

Judah deferred to Rebecca in the sign language they developed in the ghetto.

"Part of the ritual to create a golem involves leaving the golem alone to harden. We kids had been hiding and watching. When they left Judah's body alone, clay still wet, we did what any children would do with wet cement. We put our handprints in it. We did not do our initials because we did not want to get caught."

Judah switched back to American sign language and, falling to his knees, started rubbing a fist in clockwise circles on his chest "I am so sorry I failed you and the others."

"You did what you could."

"No! I was created to save you, to free you from the Nazis. In the first battle, I allowed them to herd us into a basement and bury us," signed Judah.

"Holding out as long as you did allowed seventeen children, including myself, to get clear."

"Clear for what? To go to death camps?"

"Yes. And to survive them. Eight of us survived, thanks only to you."

"I did not know. I thought they had killed all of you. When I fell, Jacob and Rachel were beneath me. As I fell, I crushed and killed them. I lay there for years, beneath the rubble, unable to move with two dead children my only companions. I opened my mouth to scream, but was denied that release. My makers had sculpted me well, but I had no voice box. No diaphragm to bring the air in, no lungs to hold a breath. Only a carved mouth with no throat. Eyes but no ducts for tears. Guilt drove me quite insane. Years after the war had ended I was dug up, comatose and catatonic. I was mistaken for a statue and spent some time in a small Polish museum."

"Later I was bought by a wealthy American collector who brought me to his personal gallery here in the United States. The gentleman had children who loved to play into the gallery, despite his yelling and threats not to. They would place their tiny hands in the handprints on my body. The one who came the most was a little boy named Doug. He would sit at my feet and tell me stories, some of them terrifying. His father beat him, often and badly. One day, while talking to me he heard his father coming in the gallery and tried to hide. In his haste, he knocked over a small statue, smashing it just as his father entered the room. The father picked up the largest of the fragments, raising it above his head to use as a club on the boy."

"Doug shouted out 'Emeth, help me!' Emeth was what he called me because of the mark on my forehead. The father shouted back 'Emeth cannot help you now.' But he was wrong. His cries, like those of other distant children, resonated in my soul, bringing me out of my stupor. I climbed down off my pedestal and ran toward the man. Hearing my thundering footsteps he turned, feeling the same terror he had inflicted on his own children. Cowering, he used the fragment now as a shield, which I took from his hands with the intent of again using it as a club. Before I could, he grabbed his chest and collapsed to the floor. A fatal heart attack stayed my hand. Doug told me to run and hide. Waving my good-byes I did, finding that, thanks to years of silently listening to English, I could understand it as well."

"I spent years traveling the country. I learned American Sign Language, did odd jobs until I ended up here today. As I crossed the street the sun was beating down. When I squinted, a rainbow appeared that seemed to end at your door. I followed it in."

"I collect rainbows," said Sarah. "Pictures, sculptures, anything. Rainbows give hope. I saw the window painting of the rainbow ending in the shotglass and suggested to Aaron that we stop in."

"Bulfinche's works that way," I said. "Rainbows tend to bring people here." It was bought and paid for with leprechaun gold, after all.

"We still need to do something about these Aryan Knights," said Paddy.

"Not we, Paddy. Us," said Rebecca. "They are after Jews. It should be Jews who stop them."

"I don't care who they are after. They need to be stopped."

"Yes, they do," said Samson. "And we need to be the ones who do it. I gave a life once for my people's freedom. I am not about to let anyone take it away."

"Try to understand, Paddy," said Joseph. "We aren't rejecting your help. If it is more than we can handle you will be the first we ask for help. I wasn't present at the Nazi concentration camps, but I did witness the Japanese camps during World War II. In one week in February, 1945, I saw 2500 Filipino civilians executed in the concentration camp at Manila. I was the only one to survive," Joseph spent a large portion of his eternal life trying to kill himself or have others do it for him. As an Eternal immortal, each try ended unsuccessfully. "I was unable to stop it then. I may be able to help stop the same kind of senseless killing now. These people need to be taught a lesson only we are qualified to teach. Do you understand?"

Paddy nodded. "I do, but I don't agree. I will respect your wishes."

"Thank you," said Joseph.

"I know where we can find them," said Rebecca. The four of them–Rebecca, Judah, Samson and Joseph, along with Aaron and Sarah, left Bulfinche's on their mission of justice. Aaron wore a hearing aide. As I watched him, blind Samson and mute Judah leave, all I could think of was the old phrase "Hear no evil, see no evil, speak no evil."

They returned solemnly several hours later, just before sunset.

"It is done," said Joseph solemnly. The rest shared his state. There was no joy in what they had done, only necessity. It was violent, but brief, and stopped short of death only out of respect for Paddy.

They had assured there would be no miscarriage of justice, no legal tricks or reduced sentences. Each member of the knighthood confessed fully and refused to plea bargain, which avoided the need for trial. Had they done otherwise, it would not have been the healthiest situation. Shows of brute power by Samson and Judah, the inability of bullets to harm either Joseph or Judah, and the fury of each of them, especially Rebecca, frightened them into pleading guilty and begging for the maximum sentence.

Shortly after their return, we started the Passover Seder. The kids–Brian, Shellie and Nellie–joined us. We listened to the readings, ate the unleavened bread and the bitter herbs in commemoration of the passing over of the Angel of Death during the last plague of the Jews' captivity in Egypt and the ending of their slavery. Samson lifted the cup left out for Elijah and spoke of the prophet Malachi. Following tradition, Nellie got up and opened the door. An older, bearded gentleman, in a dark two-piece suit came in as if on cue to take the reserved seat. He took the glass from Samson, but then put it down. He walked over to where Judah sat, frustrated at his inability to swallow any food or drink. The man put his hand atop Judah's head.

Judah did not pull away this time, merely bowing his head in respect. The man turned to Paddy, who nodded back at him, giving him permission to give a gift. As his fingers passed over Judah's forehead the word Emeth vanished from sight and with it, his vulnerability to instant death by the erasing of a letter. For the first time, tears flowed from clay eyes, down sculpted cheeks.

The man returned to his place and the Seder continued. At the end, he raised his glass saying "Next year in Israel."

"No,"Rebecca interrupted. "Next year in Bulfinche's."

The man smiled in agreement.

LOVE AND JUDGMENT

Today the sun shone brilliantly in its eternal battle. It was strong today; the clouds and smog did not stand a chance, fleeing temporarily from the New York skyline. They would return again to vanquish the sun. The conflict would continue until night came and ended it; battle lines would be redrawn at sunup.

I was stuck inside, looking out. This was not necessarily a bad thing. From behind the bar I could still view the outside world, and see the radiance illuminating the painted rainbow that ended in a shot glass filled with gold. Above the rainbow, I could see the lettering that spelled out Bulfinche's. No finer place to be in all the world, even outside. Here the air was clean, the drinks were cold, and all was right with the world.

The place was uncharacteristically empty. Just me and the boss. Paddy was quite an unusual man, a contradiction in terms. Cheaper than Midas and more giving than a dying man trying to buy his way into heaven. Paddy towered above his domain without trying, quite the accomplishment for a man who has never seen this side of five foot without artificial aids. A platform ran around the inside of the bar which gave the illusion of Paddy being almost six foot. I was told that back in the seventies he even wore platform boots, until he began taking more ribbing for his fashion sense than for his height.

Dion showed up for his shift. He came out of the wooden door behind the bar. Behind the door was the staircase which led to our living quarters.

As his relief had arrived, Paddy picked up a broom and stepped outside. He put his broom to sidewalk and summoned a cloud of dust and debris which soon found its way to the gutter. A daily tradition of his on sunny days. He sweeps the sidewalk, talks to the neighbors and passersby. As Paddy chatted, the front door opened and a kid came in dragging a kid. More explicitly, a young boy was pulling a reluctant young goat across the floor. On closer examination, I realized the puller was not a boy, but a diminutive gentleman, in baggy trousers, poorly fitting high–top sneakers and a red hooded sweat shirt pulled over his forehead. The goat decided it had gone as far as it was going and adhered itself to the floor. After several unsuccessful attempts at physically levitating the kid, the gentleman decided to tie it to one of the tables. Finishing that task, he approached the bar. I didn't understand a word he said; it's Greek to me, literally. I may not speak it, but I recognized the accent.

I merely shook my head in ignorance. I turned toward Dion's section of the bar, knowing he is fluent in about a hundred languages, but Dion was gone, vanished without a trace. The gentleman realized his mistake and in heavily accented, but well–spoken, English asked, "My pardon, innkeeper, but I seek the Lord Dionysus. He is also called Lord Bacchus. Is he here?"

Since Dion headed for the hills, further investigation was called for.

"That depends. Who are you and what do you want with Dion?" I asked. His eyes opened wide at my words.

"The Lord Dionysus allows a lowly personage as yourself to address him with such informality?" he asked. Now a bartender may not be the highest position on the food chain but it was far from the lowest. We serve drinks, solve problems and accept tips with a smile. I tried to hold down my annoyance at the implied insult.

"Sure, and I let him call me Murph. But you still haven't told me who you are and the nature of your business."

"My name is Fred, son of Pan. I am one of the proud people called Satyrs of the land of Nysa. I come to do Lord Dionysus homage. I have brought him a sacrifice," Fred announced, indicating the goat who was chewing merrily away on his leash.

I had more than a little trouble believing his story. "You're a satyr? I don't think so. Satyrs have horns coming out of their head."

With that he pulled the hood off, revealing two amber, twisted, and pointed horns as well as a head of coarse brown hair and thin, short, brown sideburns. Still, any good FX artist could do that.

"Satyrs also have cloven feet." Which means they aren't Kosher, I guess.

In response to my challenge, he pulled off his high tops, exposing feet very similar to those of the goat across the room, albeit larger and attached to legs covered in a brown pelt. The cloven hoofs were much too small to house human feet. If an FX artist did these, he chopped off some toes and metatarsals first. I believed him.

Now what was puzzling me was where had Dion vanished to? Not even Hermes could disappear that swiftly, at least not inside the bar. Dion had not mentioned acquiring a teleportation device, and the trapdoor was on my side of the bar. Casually, I walked around to his station. The plastic garbage pail was sticking three quarters out from its cubby hole. Moving the pail out further revealed Dion sitting on the floor, curled up in the negative space that by rights belonged to the pail. He looked up at me desperately, real terror in his eyes. His index finger was vertically covering his lips in a "Shush" sign. Now I was confused. Dion isn't afraid of anything. I once saw him take on a hold–up man armed only with a bottle of champagne. His opponent had a .38 special. Dion won, his magnum beating the hold-up man's. The cork shot out, jamming the gun barrel. The bottle followed suit into the man's jaw. Dion's only regret was the waste of the bubbly. He did count it as the robber's first drink though. Now why would he be scared of a simple satyr? Still, I would honor Dion's wishes. That's when Paddy walked back in.

"Sorry, but Dion is not available. If you would like to leave a message, I will make sure he gets it."

"What do ye mean Dion is not available? Tis his shift. Where is the overweight maker of swill?"

Fred turned and a smile lit across his face. "You must be the Lord Padriac Moran of the Gentry. I am Fred, son of Pan. It is my pleasure to meet you. Father speaks highly of you."

"Ye must send him my thanks for his kind words. Please, simply call me Paddy. We don't stand on formality here, and I never officially claimed the title of Lord. Ye are a long way from home, Fred. What brings ye here? And why is there a goat tied to me table?"

"A boat and a taxi brought me here. And the goat is a gift for Lord Dionysus."

"I see. So you have made a pilgrimage?"

"Yes, exactly," Fred said, head bobbing excitedly up and down in agreement.

"Murphy, get Fred here a glass of the house Red wine. Give the goat a bowl of milk."

"The goat? Do I look like a shepherd?" I asked.

"No, more like a sheep dog. Just do it. Fred, have a seat at the table while I see if I can find his lordship," Paddy said sarcastically, going around to the back of the bar. I heard the garbage pail slide. As I served Fred and his goat, the following conversation transpired in hushed tones behind the bar.

"Excuse me, your Lordship, but one of your subjects has come a calling ye. Do you think ye can be persuaded to leave the throne room and receive him?"

"Go away, Paddy. I don't need that kind of grief anymore."

"I remember a time when ye thrived on it. Ye still make a yearly pilgrimage to New Orleans for the Mardi Gras to revel."

"For the adoration, not bloody worship. I don't want it. If he wants to worship something, let him go to Father Mike and get baptized."

"C'mon, ye know those fools don't even believe his kind have souls. J.P. II and Mike know better, but that doesn't change the rest of the lot. Besides, he wants you. We cannot disappoint the lad. He has traveled around two worlds to see you. He is family. Your brother's son."

"Leave me be, you rotten, stinking, diminutive excuse for a friend."

"Nope."

"I will not do it."

"You will and you will like it."

"Dream on, runt."

"Do it now, Dion," Paddy said in that tone of voice which books no argument. Dion had no choice now, if he ever did.

"Fine, but I won't like it."

"That's up to you."

Rising up from the floor, the pair stood.

"Fred, I have located his Lordship," Paddy said with a sadistic chuckle. Dion shot him a look that would drop a mugger in his tracks. Paddy was unfazed. Fred was not as he leapt to his hoofs and then fell to his knees in homage.

"My Lord Dionysus, I have traveled far to be in your presence. I wish to dedicate my life to serving you," said Fred. Dion cringed.

"Fred, I appreciate the sentiment but I have no desire to be worshipped any longer."

"My Lord, is it something I have done to offend you? Whatever it is, I will fix it, I promise you. I have brought you a sacrifice," he said, indicating the goat. Sensing the meaning of Fred's words the goat finished its milk and again took to chewing the rope that held it. "How would you like the sacrifice prepared?"

"Medium rare," Dion ordered with a smile, his first since Fred entered. The joke flew over the Satyr's head.

"Is this your altar?" Fred asked, pointing to the bar top. "Shall I slaughter the animal here?"

Paddy blanched. The boss takes great pride in the cleanliness of his bar. The board of health tends to frown on animal sacrifice, as does the ASPCA. Dion's grin widened at the thought but before he could speak Paddy's voice boomed out.

"Don't even think about it."

"Fred, I am afraid I no longer seek or desire worshipers. I am sorry, but I cannot accept your pledge."

Fred's face dropped to the basement as his entire world crashed in on him. Eyes downcast he headed toward the door. Dion was touched with pity.

"Wait, Fred. You don't have to go just yet. Have another drink."

Fred looked sheepish. "I am afraid I cannot afford to pay for a second drink. The taxi ride here took the remainder of my money."

"How much did the cabbie charge you?"

"Six hundred and twelve dollars. Plus tip. I have only ten dollars to my name." Damn con artists can smell a tourist miles away. I'm surprised Hermes doesn't drive a cab; never known him to let a racket slip by.

"Don't worry. The first drink is always free at Bulfinche's. Tradition," I said by way of comforting.

"The second drink is on me," said Dion. "I will give you the money to get home."

"My Lord, I could not accept your gift. I will find a way to work and earn my keep. I still wish to explore the big apricot before I leave."

"The Big Apple," corrected Paddy. "I think I have a solution."

A look of terror again took up residence on Dion's face, for he knew what Paddy had in mind. Frantically he shook his head "no" but it availed him naught.

"Fred, how would you like to work here?"

"But I am not worthy, Lord Padriac," At Paddy's glare, Fred changed his nomenclature. "I mean Paddy. What do I need to do?"

"Stand up." Fred did. Paddy stood next to him and to his delight found he was two inches taller than the satyr. Paddy instantly liked anyone shorter than he, especially children. With the height issue settled, so was the hiring. "Welcome aboard."

Fred cheered. Dion moaned. I reserved judgment until I found out his job title. It was that of busboy. Speaking from a politically correct standpoint, he was a busperson or perhaps a transitsatyr. Didn't matter to me. I had someone to help out with all the hard jobs Paddy dumped on me.

"Thank you, Paddy. Please allow me to make the sacrifice to you," said Fred.

"It is really not necessary," answered Paddy.

"But I insist," said Fred.

"As do I," added Dion with a smirk, pleased at the turning of the tables. Those were not the only tables turned. The one the goat had been tied to twisted as the goat fled from Fred. The mostly chewed through rope broke the rest of the way, and the chase was on.

"I bet on Fred," I said. The satyr could really move when he tried.

"Wrong bet," said Dion.

"Why?" I asked.

"Simple," said Paddy. "It is an old story but a true one. Fred is running to make a sacrifice, or his dinner if you will. The goat is running for his life."

They were right. The goat, after a dozen laps around the bar ran into Demeter's kitchen, where it was rescued by Demeter herself, who chided Fred for his cruelty toward the animal. The three of us suddenly found important things to do, varying from counting the peanuts in the bowls to polishing clean glasses. Demeter did not buy any of it and chewed us out for letting the chase occur. She adopted the little fellow and gave him the name Rainbow.

Sometime after the chastising was completed and Rainbow taken care of, a man and a woman traveled through our door. Nothing unusual in that, save they were together and dressed unusually for two people together. She resembled something out of a time warp, a flashback to the days of flower children and Woodstock. The original, not the various sequels. She had long, straight, blond hair, a billowy shirt and bell bottom jeans with iron–on daisy's. She used a red bandanna for a belt. He, on the other hand, wore a somber but sharp gray suit, white shirt, and power tie and haircut. Judging by their differences and the fact they entered together, I guessed they were brother and sister. I later found out I was right.

They walked up to Paddy and she asked, "Are you the owner?"

"Yes. I am."

"Is the room prepared for The Teacher?"

"No. I don't think the teacher's association has made a reservation."

"Not an association. The Teacher. Grace Devine."

"Sorry, no reservation under that name."

"But surely you have heard of Grace."

"Amazing Grace?" asked Paddy. It was a name the media had bestowed. Grace Devine was called a teacher by some, although she was not certified by any agency. I would call her a roving philosopher. Some had labeled her a preacher, but she asked for no donations and refused the chance to receive fees for her talks. Others had labeled her a cult leader, but she asked nothing from her listeners, save that they open their hearts. A little corny but for now she was the media darling. Nobody could dig up any dirt on her. The tabloids were forced to say only good things about her. To their surprise, it sold even more papers than scandal. Turned their view of the world upside down. "I know who she is, but that doesn't change the fact she has no reservation," said Paddy. The flower child looked downcast at the news.

"But she told us to go to the docks and follow a man with a goat. He would lead us to the place where we would have our banquet. Grace said to ask the owner if he was prepared for The Teacher."

Paddy's interest was peaked. They had followed a "Rainbow". A sign that something interesting was about to happen. The man was in the process of pulling out his gold card when Paddy continued.

"I think we may be able to squeeze you in, even without a reservation," he said with a smile. That was certainly true. I had never seen the place this empty.

"Excellent," said the man.

"Bitching," said the flower child. Her well–dressed sibling gave her the evil eye for her choice of words. She smiled and ignored him while still making eye contact. A good trick.

"How many in your party?" asked Paddy.

"Twelve, and The Teacher," answered the flower child. "We should be back within the hour."

"Very good. See you then," Paddy answered. They left. Fred stayed and Paddy began his orientation. Fred was nothing if not enthusiastic. In his first hour he mopped the floor, washed the windows, and cleaned up a mess left by Rainbow. Rainbow had gotten loose twice and was causing no end of troubles from eating the garbage to knocking over furniture. I began to wonder if the goat was part demolition crew. I think Paddy was ready to sacrifice it himself if Demeter had not been there to protect it.

The hour deadline passed and the party arrived. A wider variety of people in one group is difficult to imagine. There were the siblings from before, and people dressed as a doctor, a lawyer and an Indian chief. A lady of the evening. A biker complete with leather and tattoos who was upset Paddy made him leave his Harley on the street. A women dressed all in black with black hair, eye shadow, and lipstick and five others of varying descriptions. The spilt between male and female was fifty-fifty and every race and creed seemed to be represented in the group. Last in the door was Grace herself, dressed simply in jeans and a sweat shirt. It had the phrase "BE GOOD" silk-screened on it. The news coverage on her failed to do her justice. Grace was enigmatic in appearance. Anyone would be hard pressed to guess her ethnic origin. Brown, shoulder length hair cascaded simply off her head. Her smile was a match for Dion's own in terms of radiating warmth, but it was her eyes that sold her. If eyes are mirrors to the soul, she was about as pure as they come. It was as if she had never done any evil. Grace introduced herself to the lot of us, and I showed The Teacher and her twelve groupies to one of our back rooms. I took their drink orders. Grace ordered one set of appetizers for the lot of them.

"Is that all you want?" I asked.

"It will be enough," Grace answered, smiling. Most of the orders were beers, so Paddy brought them in, carrying eight mugs using only his left hand. The handles of the mugs looped around his fingers. My hands are bigger and the best I can manage is six. I left the appetizers, a basket of garlic bread, and a pitcher of water on the table. Before Paddy left, Grace stopped him to ask a question.

"Paddy, may I have your permission to bless the food and drink and pass it among my friends?"

Paddy looked at her perplexed. "What ye are asking, Grace, is can you say grace?"

"In a sense, yes."

"Knock yourself out."

"Thank you."

"You're welcome."

With that, we left them to their celebration. In the bar a customer had walked in the door, first-timer by the look of him. He glanced around before coming all the way in. Satisfied with what he saw, he sauntered over to the bar. A look of darkness had claimed his face and his eyes were almost like two black orbs looking out into the night of his day.

"Give me the strongest you got," he muttered. His request lit up Paddy and Dion's faces brighter than the lights on Broadway.

"Really? You mean it?" asked Dion, beaming. "What is your name, courageous one?"

"Of course I mean it. Would I have asked if I didn't? My name is Nero Domitian."

"It is just that our strongest is much stronger than anything you have had anywhere else."

"I doubt it."

"Really," said Paddy sarcastically. "So you have had four hundred proof before?" With that, the dark stranger lifted an eyebrow.

"Four hundred proof? Two hundred proof is the highest alcohol can be. That would be one hundred percent pure alcohol."

"Our stuff is two hundred percent."

"How is that possible?"

Dion and Paddy exchanged glances with the pride with which most people exchanged expensive gifts. "Trade secret," they said in unison.

"All right. I will try a glass."

"No, you won't," said Paddy.

"Why not?"

"A glass would kill you," Dion said, taking a bottle wrapped in goatskin (no relation to Rainbow, of course) off the shelf behind him and tenderly unwrapping it. Paddy was pulling out a form and handing it to Nero to look over.

"First sign this."

"What is it?"

"Consent form, past medical history denying liver, lung, or heart trouble and listing next of kin," said Paddy. Nero raised his eyebrow again but filled it out and signed it. "Now," continued Paddy "Come over here to the scale so we can weigh ye."

"What for?"

"To determine the correct dosage," answered Paddy, putting a penny slug in the fortune telling scale. "One hundred and seventy-nine pounds, four point three ounces." Paddy ignored the fortune. I didn't. It read:

"Consider a change in careers because love will turn your world inside out."

Paddy brought the gentleman to the bar where Dion was measuring out the four hundred proof liquor using an eye dropper to pour it into a thimble sized shot glass. Dion handed it to the customer, who skeptically took it between his thumb and index finger. "How much for this?"

"First drink is on the house. Tradition. Of course you understand it is the only alcohol ye will be able to have for the next twenty-four hours," Paddy said.

"This drop? It isn't enough to freshen my breath, let alone get me buzzed. I have never been able to drink enough to get drunk. This certainly won't do it."

"I personally guarantee ye will be drunk after drinking that or double your money back."

"But Paddy, it was free," reminded Dion.

"Exactly," answered the old man. "I recommend ye sit down before ye drink. It packs quite a kick."

Scoffing, the man brought the miniature shot glass to his lips, looking more like he was drinking from a doll's tea cup. Then in surprise Nero's eyes lit up and his legs went wobbly. "Murph," shouted Paddy, but I was one step ahead of him as I pushed a chair beneath Nero before he hit the floor.

"Wow," was all the man could say, but he said it twenty-two times as the liquor raced through his system and he played with the air in front of him as if it was a ball of yarn and he was a kitten. He even hugged and kissed Rainbow before Demeter dragged him back into the kitchen. Rainbow, not Nero. The smiles lasted only a few minutes. The singing several more. The dancing lasted a quarter of an hour. Then the weeping started and it did not stop. All Nero could wail was "No," holding the vowel until his air ran out.

Dion placed a comforting hand on Nero's shoulder. Nero cringed away from the touch.

"No. Don't make me like you when I will only have to kill you later," Nero ordered. We all stood stunned and silent. Not the kind of confession you like to hear from anyone, especially a new drinking buddy. "It is not that I want to. I don't. The darkness that raised me demands it. I have no choice."

"Ye always have a choice, son," Paddy said.

"Choices are for normal people, not me."

"Why not?"

"I am the Apocalypse, the Beast from the Pit."

"Must be hell to put on a business card," I quipped.

"Why yes, it is," Nero giggled. "Except they won't let me put it on my card. Or tell anyone. All I have to worry about is the downfall of the savior and the destruction of the world, when Hell will reign supreme. A little bit more than your average person. Growing up, it was unimaginable. Back in my teens I envied my classmates who worried about acne, getting wasted, the opposite sex, and SAT scores. I never had those worries. My complexion was perfect, my SAT score was sixteen hundred, I had a dozen succubi to answer my every pleasure and before today, I had never been drunk. My thanks for that. I never had to worry about anything else. My every move is monitored. This is one of the few times in my adult life I have gotten away for more than a few hours. Not that they could stop me any longer. I have begun to come into my birthright." Nero began to look guilty. "I really should be moving on. The longer I stay in one place, the faster I will be found. I have no desire to endanger any of you."

"Don't worry about that Nero. Ye are safe here."

"You don't know who you are dealing with."

"Yes I do. Better than ye know. I do have one question for you. Why did you come in here of all the bars in Manhattan?"

"I saw the little man dragging the goat in. I figured any bar that allowed goats had to be an interesting place. But first I scoped out the neighborhood. Then I saw the Teacher come in."

"You mean Grace Devine?"

"Yes. Grace. The non–preacher. The cult leader who asks for no money, nor asks for any of the usual selling–flowers–in–the–airport or working–in–a–dark–factory type of blind obedience. Or at least that was the Grace one portion of the media portrays. The rest of the media gloried in ripping the poor girl to shreds, all of it fictional, most of it ignored. Her opposition was led quite vocally by the Reverend Jezebel Smith of Philadelphia, who condemned Grace for everything and anything she said, did, or implied. Finally The Rev. Smith challenged Grace to a public debate on her Christian cable station. I own it.

"The debate was remarkable in two senses: the two hours the debate lasted was the single longest period of time that the station had broadcast without asking for donations. Second, Smith did not cut off the debate when it began going badly for her. Apparently she tried but the equipment jammed in the on mode. Smith had started out blasting Grace for preaching without a license or some other such nonsense. Grace countered that she did not claim to be a Reverend, and in fact endorsed no church. Grace then brought up the fact that Smith had purchased her credentials for fifty dollars by mail in the sixties. The debate went downhill from there, quoting some scripture that says you shall charge no fee to preach the gospel; *Corinthians 9,* or some such nonsense. Grace rebuffed Jezebel successfully in every area and even produced a copy of her church's tax records for the last ten years. The crowd almost lynched her when they found out what their donations were spent on. I think they could have accepted the mansions, cars, jewelry, and vacations but the keeping of one dozen men and animals on church grounds for the satisfaction of her personal needs was too much. Only Grace's intervention saved her. The Reverend Jezebel Smith was one of my people. I owned her and her Christian Empire."

"Was?" I asked.

"Was. My organization isn't known for their tolerance of failure. I can get away with my actions only because I am the Beast. In three days time, I become all powerful, and what they say becomes meaningless. But absolute power shall corrupt me absolutely, of that I am certain. I was never allowed to be put in a situation where my every wish was not granted. I have never had to stand up for anything. I am weak and will fulfill my destiny. As Mark Twain once wrote 'The weakest of all weak things is a virtue that has not been tested in the fire.'"

"Why the regrets?" asked Dion.

"The last few times I got away, I decided to scope out the competition. My opposite number. The anointed savior of mankind."

"Grace Devine," I said.

"Got it in one. I listened to her speak. She made a lot of sense. Throw away prejudices, love unconditionally without condemnation, and harm no one. The truly religious heed what she says. Organized religions are worried. She has no strict rules to follow, no need for money, and condemns hypocrisy and hate. If everyone went her way, there would be no need for churches or collections. Every street corner and park would be a place of worship, everyone a minister for the heavens."

"You know her philosophy well."

"Know thy enemy. I knew it, but it took Grace to move me. After her speech, we conversed for hours. I left minutes before the hellhounds caught my scent," Nero said, with a starry look in his eyes. I would bet his heart was going pitter patter and butterflies were fluttering in his stomach. "I met with her since only briefly."

"You love her," I said.

"Yes," Nero answered with a combination of shame and delight. Makes sense. Grace would be his only forbidden fruit.

"So to sum up, despite being born of Hell and raised to destroy the world, ye find ye have no desire to actually hurt anyone," said Paddy.

"Sort of ruins both heredity and environment arguments," I said.

"To top it off, you are in love with your sworn enemy and the end of the world is scheduled to begin in three days."

"That's about it."

"Now let's see what we can do to change all that," Paddy said.

"It cannot be changed. Destiny is immutable."

"I do so love a challenge," said Paddy. At that moment Rainbow escaped Demeter again, leaping upon the bartop before he realized its lack of friction. Plopping on his bottom with his front legs outstretched the goat slid the entire length of the bar, scattering glasses in his wake before plunging to the floor with a crash.

"If you want a challenge, how about keeping that goat under control?" asked Dion.

"I do have my limits you know," he answered with a chuckle.

"You have just learned the world as you know it is about to cease and you are worried about a goat?" asked Nero incredulously.

"Which is the more immediate threat?"

"The goat, I guess."

"Exactly. It is all a matter of priorities. How does it begin?" Paddy asked Nero.

"Well, a nanny goat is standing in a field, then the billy goat comes along," Nero explained, grinning.

"No. Not the goat. The Apocalypse."

"Not much that will be seen by the general public. Grace opens the first seal of the Book of Seven and it begins."

"Where does she keep the book? We'll just take it from her," said Paddy.

"Won't work. She doesn't have it."

"Where does she get it?" asked Dion.

"I don't know where it is. I know only that my people will bring it to her. Don't look so surprised. Both sides will help each other out so we can get to the point where we can annihilate each other."

Paddy shook his head in disgust. "The first time wasn't enough. Bloodthirsty idiots. I won't let them destroy humanity like they did my parents and people. You are willing to stop it. Now all we need to do is convince Grace."

"Impossible. Her faith is too strong."

"What about her compassion? Is she willing to let billions die to satisfy the Lord of Heaven?" I asked.

"Don't bring Yahweh into it. Probably he wasn't even consulted. Humans aren't the only ones with free will. It is a grudge match between Michael and Lucifer, pure and simple. The only thing God will do is help those who get caught in the crossfire. How are they going to pull off the plagues?" asked Paddy.

"The side of the angels does most of the plagues." Nero slid a computer CD across the bar to Paddy. "It is all detailed in there. I downloaded it from my computers, in case I came up with a good use for it."

"Very good. I think the good use has materialized. I'm sure you'll understand if we do not share our plans with you," Paddy said. Nero nodded. "Now we find out if we can recruit Grace." Paddy went into the back room and came out a minute later with a puzzled look upon his face.

"Okay, who brought them the food and the wine?"

"What are you talking about?" asked Dion.

"The group back there is eating fish, garlic bread and drinking wine like there is no tomorrow."

"Oh there will be a tomorrow. It is next week that is in question," Nero quipped, then belched loudly.

"Paddy, I brought them one order of fish and garlic bread and a pitcher of water."

"But how?"

"She asked for your dispensation and you did give it."

"Ah," he said and headed back in.

"What are you doing, boss?"

"Getting the glass she is drinking out of and putting it in a safe place," Paddy answered. He collects artifacts. He will be the first one on the block to have the Holy Mug. Maybe it will heal like the grail, and questing beasts and knights will be trudging through here in search of it. Or perhaps our plan will work, the world will live and it will be worthless. Either way he wins.

Paddy had quietly taken Grace away from her admirers with a line about a phone call. Upon entering the bar proper, she recognized the Beast.

"Nero, what a pleasure to see you again," Grace said with the utmost sincerity, she even blushed. Must have been some incredible conversations they had.

"Hi Grace. A petey you won't be sayhing dat tree days from now." The alcohol was going further in his system and he was slurring his words.

"Nero, you're drunk. Why?"

"Woodn't yew be if yew had to destroy the world in three days," The seriousness of the situation was sobering him up. "No, I guess not. You are still sober."

"What are you talking about?"

"You, teacher, are the Lamb. The Light of Heaven. The Anointed One. The Savior."

"That is what some have called me."

"Come off the evasive routine. That is for the masses, not for the Beast, the dragon from the Abysses, great Abandon, Apollyon the destroyer."

"You?!" she said backing away, slowly. "But it's not the appointed time!"

"Why wait?"

"Exactly," said Paddy. "If we cannot come to an agreement, let us settle this here in the bar. Tonight."

"But Paddy, this is the battle for the end of the world," I said.

"We have a contract to cater Ragnarok." We did actually; it is a story for another day. "And we are not going to close just because it is the Apocalypse," Paddy said. Taking me aside, he whispered, "Besides if they fight here, the most dangerous thing they can do is throw darts at each other. In the bar, their powers and all the damage they can do is neutralized." Turning back to the pair he continued. "Well, what do you say?"

"Fine by me," said Nero.

"Okay," agreed Grace.

"No! You can't!" screamed the suit from earlier. The twelve had wandered out to see what was keeping their mentor. "No deals with the Beast. It is against everything you stand for."

"Bovine feces!" I screamed, surprised at my own voice. I too had listened to a home recorded video of Grace speak when it was played on public access cable. She made sense. "Grace, do you believe all that you have taught?"

"Yes, of course."

"Then all people are basically good. If you go through with this as it is outlined in Revelations, you are going to be condemning most of the Earth's population to torture for five months followed by the extermination of one third of the human race. And that is from your side."

Grace was actually shaken by what I had said. It had never been put to her in quite that way. The suit was steadfast in his pride. "The anointed ones of the Lord will be spared."

I ignored him, concentrating on Grace. "But who chooses the chosen? If there is good in everyone, how can you condemn one out of three people in this room to death."

The suit harrumphed. "We are among the anointed. Are you?"

"Beats me. Am I Grace?" I asked.

"I do not know."

"Am I not good?"

"Of course you are," she said.

"Then why are you not sure? Is there good in Nero?"

"Yes."

"Then couldn't he be among the saved?"

"I suppose."

"But he is the Beast! How could he be more worthy than one third of the Earth?"

"Steady, Grace. You are being tempted," the suit chimed in. He was beginning to get on my nerves. I never liked holier-than-thou types because all of them turned out to be hypocrites, hiding their own inadequacies under a cloud cover of righteousness and religious piousness. The truly holy don't have to tell you. You sense it in their ways, in their eyes. Like our regular, Father Mike. Like Grace.

"And for the sake of humanity, I hope you yield. Here at Bulfinche's, there will be a battle between good and evil with no innocents–or even the guilty–dying. How could that be bad? I am surprised you didn't suggest it yourself," I said. The suit started to lunge for me.

Grace smiled, putting a comforting hand on the suit's arm. "You are right, Murphy. Violence is not the answer." The suit hung his head in shame. Grace put her hand beneath his chin and lifted his head so their eyes met. In that instant his shame faded and he again stood tall. A little less righteous, a little more natural. "We will meet here. Now Paddy, what is this other offer you have?"

"Call the whole thing off. Do not battle at all. Do not open the Book of Seven. Do not break a single seal," Paddy pleaded.

I added, "Do not pass go. Do not collect two hundred dollars," but the crowd was not receptive. Only Nero and the flower child chuckled.

Grace stood flabbergasted. Again, the concept had never been suggested to her. Saving lives had made sense but shirking her duty was too much for her to take in. "I must complete my destiny."

Despite the sun shining just outside our window, then it was the darkest and praying for the dawn seemed inappropriate. I did it anyway. My prayer was answered from an unexpected quarter. Nero.

He bowed down before his adversary on bended knee, humbling himself. Half her disciples were looking smug and righteous that the embodiment of Hell, evil personified, was begging before their Teacher. The other half seemed genuinely interested in what he had to say. Grace looked torn.

"Grace, I beseech you. Reconsider. We are just pawns in the most horrible game in history. We soon will be more powerful than our puppet masters, but by then it will be too late to turn back. Now is our only chance to save our people. To save the children, the adults, the good and the bad. Less than two hours ago, I met a child in Central Park. Her name was Lilly. She asked me why I looked sad. I couldn't tell her. Still, she tried to cheer me up and succeeded in making me laugh. She showed me kindness simply because she was kind. How many more like her are there? The children are the first to fall in all battles, casualties of innocence. For their sakes turn back, please."

Grace stared down blankly for several minutes. Finally she shook her head numbly and said "No," in a tone barely more audible than a whisper. Nero turned his head in disappointment.

"I am sorry. I thought for sure you would want to stop the dying, but the four horsemen will ride. I ask one boon of you."

"What is it?"

"Place your mark upon Lilly and her family to spare them. And on Paddy, Dion, Murphy, Fred, and Demeter."

"On Lily, her family and Murphy I shall. The others I cannot because of their nature."

"Don't worry about Murphy," said Paddy. "We at Bulfinche's take care of our own."

"Very well. At the stroke of midnight then," said Nero, writing something on a napkin as he stood. Walking up to Grace, he handed her the napkin. "If you should change your mind you can summon me. Farewell."

"Goodbye, Nero," she said. He waved to the rest of us and we returned the favor. Nero headed back out into the streets.

"What did he give you to summon him with?" asked Paddy.

Grace's answer was a quote from scripture. "Wisdom is needed here; one who understands can calculate the number of the beast, for it is a number that stands for a person." With that Grace handed Paddy the napkin and Paddy completed the quote.

"His number is 666-HELL. Figures," he said.

"What?" I asked.

"It has a Jersey area code."

"Excuse me, I have to be alone now," Grace said, to the dismayed cries of her followers. "I need time to think. I'll return by midnight."

With that the lot of them left, but the flower child waited then slinked off on her own.

Once we were alone, Paddy called for a council of war in one hour. That would give the staff and regulars a chance to get here. Hermes was called and given the job of rounding everyone up. It would also give Paddy and Dion a chance to review the disc and determine if we were being conned by Nero or not.

"Paddy, I'll go up the block to Our Lady of the Lake Church and get Father Mike," I said. "I also want him to hear my confession. You know, just in case."

Paddy nodded solemnly, then pulled out his laptop and popped the disc in.

By the time Father Mike and I returned, the gang was mostly all there. The staff including Paddy, Dion, Hercules, Demeter, Hermes, Fred, and myself. The regulars included Father Mike; Ismael Macob, the cursed cabbie; Rebecca, bag lady with guts of steel and a heart of gold; Roy G. Biv and Rumbles; Judah Maccabee, the golem; Lucas Wilson, vampyre, computer hacker and programmer supreme was at the bar, keyboard in hand, typing away furiously; Mosie, the most powerful psychic of our day; his mother Madame Rose, a gypsy psychic of no small skill herself; Samson, blind hero of biblical fame; Edgar Tonic, our corner vender; Tommy, a jinn; Hermes' ladyfriend, Madeline Raymond; former staff member Heimdal, the guardian of the Rainbow Bridge to Asgard, (the only bridge to Manhattan that doesn't get tied up during rush hour); Heimdal's girlfriend, Mista, a Valkyri;. Jasmine, cop in a dress.

Everyone was seated comfortably with their drink of choice. Paddy began the war council.

"Hermes has brought ye all up to speed. My damned and undamned relations are fixing to have a final shootout. The problem is Earth, is going to be laid to waste in the process. As this will undoubtedly be bad for business, we have no choice but to stop it," Paddy said half seriously. "We can do nothing about the book, as we don't have the book. The breaking of the seals empowers the horsemen and the legions of Hell, as well as starts a massive earthquake. It needs to be stolen from the hellspawn and brought to a place of safety that will remain unknown to the lot of us. That task falls to Hermes."

Hermes nodded, grinning. For him that would be a walk in the park, nothing compared to his last stunt. Let's just say he has a sick mind, and the Statue of Liberty recently spent a brief period greeting visitors to the harbor without her dress. It was long enough for him and a tourist to take some pictures. Hermes has his perfect pics framed. The tourist sold his to a tabloid, where the grainy photos were printed but passed off by the public as a computer–enhanced double exposure.

"In the unlikely event that Hermes fails, the rest of us have to disable the remainders of their mechanisms of destruction. Using the disc Nero gave us, we learned how and where the disaster for each sounding of the trumpet will occur." With Father Mike's help we crossed-checked *Revelations* for the details. "The first blast is supposed to hurl down fire mixed with blood upon the Earth, destroying one third of the Earth's vegetation. Unfortunately, many of the surviving Rain Forests are in the target area. Starting yesterday, select factories began spilling out more contaminants into the atmosphere in an hour than they normally do in a year. Unchecked, the resulting pollution will indeed hurl down on the Earth as the worst occurrence of acid rain in history. We figure they are combining the second and third trumpets into the same project. At the second trumpet, a large burning mountain is hurled into the sea, destroying a third of the oceans and marine life. With the third, a large star burning like a torch falls from the sky. Recently a certain corporation, through a dozen fronts but owned by Nero, has taken on contracts to store and house nuclear waste. The same corporation that has recently been sending up satellites from private launchpads in Japan and Egypt. It is called Project: Wormwood, same as the star in *Revelations*. The satellites hook up together in orbit and are heat shielded against reentry. The mass is certainly more than a mountain and they are presently in synchronous orbit over the Pacific Ocean. One plunge through the atmosphere and all that waste is dumped into the water. Smaller satellites do the same over lakes and rivers. They have actually taken control of a US Star Wars satellite, and will use its laser to make sure the nuclear waste is cut free of the satellite casings, in case reentry doesn't do the trick. This will fulfill the passage 'Many people died from this water, because it was made bitter.'"

"The fourth sounding darkens a third of the sun, moon and stars. The Heavenly Host have taken control of four sites with no less than thirty missiles with nuclear payloads. They plan to detonate the missiles in the upper atmosphere, causing a nuclear winter to block out the heavens. This will diminish the amount of light coming into the atmosphere by at least a third. Since a side effect of the blast would be an electromagnetic pulse which could cause the loss of all electrical power on Earth for an indefinite period of time, their fifth and last earthborn attack would be non-mechanical in nature. *Revelations* almost perfectly describes the aftermath of the explosion, down to the smoke out of which 'Locusts came... onto the land' with the same powers of scorpions.' A fairly vivid description is given. A genetics lab in Mexico, unimpaired by any legal guidelines, has successfully developed a species of locust that is highly poisonous. Breeding has been underway for months now. The larva should be reaching maturity within the month."

"What happens next?" I asked.

"Nothing we can prevent. With the Earth's defenses down and electricity nullified, Heaven's armies ravage those unmarked by their seal. Then Hell gets the upper hand and does the same. Eventually, one side wins, but humanity pays the tab with its lifeblood."

"So what is the plan?" asked Father Mike.

"Yes, what is the plan?" came a voice from the darkened doorway behind the bar. Joseph had arrived from his apartment upstairs. Since the Wandering Jew found Bulfinche's, he has given up his wandering and taken a well–deserved rest. He is cursed to wander the Earth until the second coming, which was exactly what we are trying to prevent. Paddy had planned to talk with him privately later.

"Ye know what we are trying to do?" Paddy asked.

"Yes, damn it, I want to help. I'm hurt that you didn't trust me enough to ask me here."

"It isn't a matter of trust. I wanted to give ye time to make the decision alone."

"I was alone for two thousand years. I will decide among friends and my decision is to help stop this if possible."

"Ye know what that means if we win?"

"Yes."

"Glad to have ye aboard," said Paddy, smiling. "Now, the first order of business is stopping the output of those pollution factories and disarming the nucs. The trouble is, they are in control of the Star Wars satellite."

"Not any more," said Lucas, looking up from the laptop's screen for the first time since the meeting began.

"You got control?" asked Dion.

"Absolute," he said.

"How?," I asked.

"Simple. I helped design the system," Lucas said. "I always leave myself a backdoor. I am entering a virus now that will insure the satellite responds to no one but us. Paddy, this laptop is incredible. I have never seen a Decitume before and I've never heard of the brand. Vulcan. Who makes it?"

"Man of the same name."

"Same guy who built and does the upkeep on your car?" Lucas asked.

"The same. But he only redesigned 'Baby'. It was originally a suped up 1930 V–16 Cadillac we used during Prohibition to run booze. Now it does everything, including fly. Now that you have control of the lasers, can you knock out the factories?"

"With these coordinates, no problem." Lucas bragged.

"One problem," interrupted Rebecca. "If we blow up their factories, they will know we are on to them. They will never let the pair return here. Wait until one minute after midnight, then blow them up. Concentrate now on the Wormwood satellites and destroying them."

Paddy weighed the logic against the environmental damage and agreed. "Can you disable the satellites? So the damage won't be noticed until after midnight?"

"No prob. I have already written a program with the factories' coordinates that will destroy them at 12:01 New York time," said Lucas.

"Fine. I will arrange for phony bomb threats to evacuate the places ten minutes before," Paddy said.

"Now all I have to do is determine the best way to disable the satellites, add to their momentum and have them sail into space," said Lucas.

"Can you do that?" I asked.

"Don't know. Never tried before. Let me get back to you on that one," Lucas said, smiling, never once looking up or lifting his hands away from the keyboard. Mozart never played a keyboard with such precision. I don't know which was giving him more pleasure, saving the world, or playing with one of the world's most powerful computers.

Hercules cleared his throat, an act which when done by him got our full and undivided attention.

"Paddy, we still have to resolve some serious issues. First, what do we do if the parties involved try to take their conflict outside?"

"Ye have full dispensation for the duration. Ye will keep them inside."

"At all costs?" Hercules asked. What he meant was "Do I kill them if they try to leave?"

"No," was the boss' simple reply.

"Paddy, we cannot deal with them with kid gloves on," Hercules stated. Rainbow chose that moment to again get loose and plowed over the table in front of Paddy.

"I'm going to make me a pair of kid gloves if that goat does not get out of here," Paddy yelled. Demeter chastised him with a look, called Rainbow once by name. The goat then followed her back into his makeshift pen where Demeter proceeded to talk baby talk to him. The excitement ended and Paddy addressed Hercules' issue. "Herc, you know how I feel about killing for any reason. I admit sometimes it is necessary but not often. Especially in this case. I'm not sure the bodies wouldn't be reanimated," Hercules started to open his mouth with a suggestion. "Or recreated if we destroyed the bodies. They have to renounce their destinies from within, not from outside coercion. That may be the only way to stop it. We will minimize the damage they do by stopping what we have already discussed, which will at least give those who wish to resist a fighting chance against Heaven and Hell. So no unnecessary killing, but leave it to your best judgment."

Once Lucas finished his work with the computer, Paddy divided everyone into teams. One, made up of Joseph, Judah and Lucas, went to destroy the genetic lab in Mexico. Being a golem, Judah's stony clay skin and Lucas' vampyric ability to control vermin and turn into mist would grant them the most protection against the venomous locust. As an Eternal immortal, Joseph simply cannot be killed. The poison might make him sick, but he would survive. The rest were divided up into four teams headed by Demeter, Rumbles, Heimdal and Mosie. Each was given the mission of finding and disabling one of the missile sites. Mosie, Madame Rose, Tommy and Ismael were all put on separate teams, as each had abilities that would assist in finding the nucs if they were moved. Paddy, Dion, Fred, Hercules, and myself would hold down the fort.

Lucas reactivated the satellite's missile screen and made some improvements that would fire on any missile from anywhere. Unfortunately, the missile site were scattered, so the range of the laser, if kept equidistant between all four, was minimized. Paddy put a call in to Vulcan on his South Pacific island and ordered four laser-capable satellites of his own. Paddy is extremely wealthy. As the satellites were for a worthy cause he didn't blink an eye buying them, yet if a customer forgets to pay his bill Paddy goes ballistic. Go figure. Vulcan promised to have them up and launched by the end of the week. To show his confidence in our plan, Paddy even made an appointment for Vulcan to tune up 'Baby' next month.

At eleven thirty, crowds started showing up. First the disciples of Grace, even the flower child. Next came the contingency from Hell. The demons were in bad shape and looked like themselves warmed over. Strange thing is, once they walked in the door, they looked normal, human even, except the red eyes. Next in the door was their heavenly brethren. In appearance the Host were similar to the Horde, save for lighter colored clothes and albino blue eyes. The two groups took up positions opposite each other. Hatred shaded their eyes no matter what the color. Next through the door was a group of preachers and business people who must have been Nero's human followers. They also numbered twelve and took up positions in front of the hellfire Horde. They might as well not have existed for the response they received from their allies. Grace's twelve took up a mirrored position before the heavenly battlechoir with the same reaction their opposite numbers received, which is to say, none.

Outside, four men stood on the other side of the door. Fred went out to see what they needed. He came in more confused than he left.

"Paddy, there are four guys outside with horses. Weird colors too. Black and white are normal enough, but red and pale green? I thought humans didn't ride anymore."

"It is all right, Fred. They're expected. Tend to their mounts in the garage. Keep them on the first level and away from the sublevels, Cerberus, and Baby."

"Okay, boss," Fred said.

The first in was almost wasted away. Sunken cheekbones marked a pale face, hair thinly dispersed. A bloated stomach protruded forth and, despite the shirt that covered his gut, an outie belly button was easy to make out.

Next through was the sickest man I have ever seen. Pus oozed from dozens of open and bleeding sores. Bloodshot eyes rested uneasily above a mouth whose teeth were rotted clear down to exposed nerve.

The third was a big man in leather trenchcoat, chain belt and fatigues. He had red shaggy hair and beard. He was emptying his pockets of all weapons. It was taking a while, as he was reluctant, but Hercules was convincing in his polite requests. His last weapon was a huge sword which was causing more than a little bit of a problem.

"No. The sword is my badge of office. It stays or I go."

"Bye. Don't forget to write when you find work," Hercules said cheerfully, without a hint of malice. It took the belligerent man aback. "Next."

The last of the four was dressed in black. Full and total like the bottom of an abyss. He wore a trenchcoat. They all did but his was hooded. "I am sorry, sir, but you have to check the scythe."

"I AM RATHER ATTACHED TO IT."

"You will get it back when you leave, unharmed, I assure you. Rules are rules. I am sure you understand."

"YES. I DO. RULES ARE IMPORTANT. VERY WELL. TAKE GOOD CARE OF IT."

"The best," Hercules promised, putting the scythe in a special locked weapons cabinet. The large combative gentleman tried to get in the door. Hercules stopped him with an outstretched palm. "We have been through this, sir. Please kindly take it elsewhere. I will have Fred bring your horse around. It was the black one, right?"

"No, the red," he said. Hercules called Fred over. The man wouldn't give up. "Wait. I will fight you for the right to wear my sword."

"I don't have the time. The boss says no weapons. So no weapons. No excuses, no exceptions."

"You are a coward."

"Say what you will. You aren't coming in without checking the blade." With that Hercules slammed the door. Almost instantly, incessant pounding began on the door with the shouts of "Coward. Face me like a man with the sword as the prize."

"Boss?" Hercules asked a slight grin on his face.

Across the room, Paddy nodded affirmatively, adding, "Just don't break any furniture."

Bowing with a flair and a smile Hercules said "Enter and be beaten."

"In there? Ha. I knew it. Afraid to face me outside of the little man's protection." At the 'little man' comment Paddy turned crimson but made no move. The man got off lucky. Hercules himself was unfazed.

"Dion, spell me at the door?" he asked, putting on his trenchcoat, made from the hide of a lion who fell before Hercules many years ago.

"Sure," answered Dion, leaping over the bartop with a single bound, wine belly dancing like jello with the movement.

At that moment Grace and Nero arrived together. Hercules excused himself while he frisked the pair.

"They're clean," he said. Dion nodded. They entered. He exited. Grace smiled. Nero frowned. They both went to talk to Paddy, the full attention of the assembled on them. They spoke. Paddy nodded. I refilled the skinny guy's peanut bowl for the forth time and gave the sickly gentleman his third box of tissues and a plastic garbage bag to put the used ones in. He was sneezing up a storm and coughing up things that are better left unmentioned.

Paddy walked to the center of the floor before speaking.

"Ladies and gentlemen, heavenly Host and hellish Horde, welcome to Bulfinche's production of The Apocalypse. No cover charge and drinks are full price. Best place your orders now before the show starts, and remember to tip your bartenders and serving people well. Now, without further adieu, allow me to introduce the players. Grace Devine, known as the Teacher, represents Heaven and all things righteous. Her opponent, weighing in at one hundred seventy nine pounds four point three ounces, is Nero Domitian. Nero is the champion for Hell and all things dark and indulgent. They have agreed to meet here in this, our forum, in order to the spare lives of their fellow humans. Both contestants have agreed, by a binding handshake contract, that the results of this contest shall decide the question of supremacy between Heaven and Hell."

At that all sides, divine, devil, and human leapt to their feet screaming protests and arguments.

"Grace, think what you do," the suit yelled.

"Nero, you shall not betray your brethren," shouted a reverend.

"They are not to be trusted!" That came from both sides.

"We do not recognize your authority," spat a demon.

"We do not recognize your match," hissed an angel.

"Enough. It is our right to decide the field of battle," Nero commanded, fire in his eyes.

"And we have decided. Our decision is not to be questioned or undone," explained Grace, equal to Nero in her intensity.

"At least open the book," said one of the angels in white.

"Yes, the book. Open the book. I shall get it for you," said one of the demons in black, racing blindly for the door. He crashed into and bounced off of Hercules' chest. Hercules was smiling and wearing a huge sword around his waist. "Out of my way, oaf," the demon demanded.

"No," answered Hercules. "No ones leaves or enters once the show has begun."

"I have to get The Book."

"Wait until the library opens tomorrow."

"No," said the demon, attacking Hercules. Hercules sidestepped the clumsy attack, grabbed the back of the demon's neck and lifted him off the floor.

"Yes," Hercules countered convincingly before tossing the demon across the room to land on his chair. "Stay seated until I tell you otherwise. Please," he added as an afterthought.

"Yes, sir," said the demon meekly.

Meanwhile, back at the bar, Big Red was finally inside, putting down the drinks and whining to the skinny guy, who I had just given the twenty pound bag of peanuts, rather than keep refilling the bowl. "I can't believe I lost my blade of office. He is going to kill me." Big Red's right eye was blackened more than Cajun catfish and his left jaw was bruised. Two teeth were missing and he had limped to his seat.

"NO, HE WILL NOT," said the man in black who had come up behind him.

Big Red turned with hope in his eye. "Are you sure?"

The man in black tilted his hooded head in such a way as to ask "Are you serious". Instead, he simply said, "YES. I WOULD KNOW. TRUST ME." It was then I realized I could not see his face beneath the shadow of his hood. Furthermore, I decided I didn't want to.

"All right. Do you think he will give me a new badge of office, like a shiny machine gun?" Big Red asked. The dark one in the hood shook his head in dismay as one would with a slow child and walked away. Big Red turned to the skinny guy, who shrugged his shoulders and offered Big Red a peanut.

Meanwhile, back at ringside, the main event was about to begin.

"Thank you, Hercules. Now we can get down to the business, at hand," announced Paddy. "The method of combat has been chosen by the players."

"What is it? Guns, grenades, crossbows?" demanded a demon.

"Hooks, spears, astral combat, swords?" asked an angel. At the mention of swords, Big Red burst out weeping. The sickly gentleman handed him a tissue into which he blew his nose loud enough to do a trumpeter proud.

"None of the above," answered Paddy. "Darts."

"What? Are they at least poisoned?" questioned an enraged demon.

"Look at the tips. Plastic! How is that going to do any damage?" asked an angry angel.

"It isn't. I don't want holes in my walls. They will not be throwing the darts at each other. Instead they will be aiming at the dart board," revealed Paddy. The demons and angels moaned at the mockery their plans had come to, but had no choice but to go along with it. "Grace picked the longer of two straws and will go first."

Grace threw three darts and got three bullseyes. Nero went next and did the same. After a dozen rounds, including different variations, Paddy declared a tie. The two contingencies, outraged, demanded a second contest. Paddy obliged by racking up ten balls on the pool table. Nero broke and had a game Minnesota Fats would have been jealous of. He sunk every ball exactly as he called it. After he cleared the table, Grace got her turn and had every bit as enviable a game. After a dozen such games, Paddy again declared a draw. By this point several of the spectators had begun to get bored. A normal game keeps your interest because of the risk of error. These games seemed to be without risk and, other than having the fate of the world riding on them, were without interest. Again a new contest was demanded and given. A chess board was brought out to the moans of all save one. The hooded man in black, citing "PRO-FESSIONAL INTEREST", came over and watched intently as they played twelve consecutive games to a draw where only their kings remained. By this time, half the demons and angels and all but two of the twenty four humans had fallen asleep. Several were snoring. Two enemies, an angel and a demon, appeared unable to turn their eyes away from each other and had lost all interest in anything but each other.

A new challenge was half-heartedly made. Two pitchers of ginger ale, instead of the usual beer, were brought out. Nero's twenty–four–hour safety zone had not yet passed, even if the buzz was long gone. Paddy specified that only one round would decide the match. A few spectators actually woke up and cheered on their champion, the humans with chants of, "Chug! Chug!" To nobody's real surprise, they finished exactly together.

The next trial was arm wrestling. Grace and Nero sat opposite each other, elbows bent on the table, hands clasped together. The rules were simple. Best two of three with no one match lasting more than five minutes. An hourglass timer was turned over and the wrestling began. Straining, Grace's cheeks turned crimson, veins popped out on Nero's forehead. With less than thirty seconds' worth of sand left, Nero leaned across the table, bringing his lips to Grace's and stealing a quick kiss. Grace's eyes opened wide in shock as her arm went limp and down. Nero had actually won a match. The demons and humans on the dark side cheered their champion, slapping him on the back and lifting him up atop their shoulders to carry him once around the room. All the while the humans chanted, "Hell is number one, Heaven is number two." The morale of the side of the angels plummeted.

Round two began exactly as had the first. With less than a minute left on the sands Grace pulled the same trick, only more so. Locking lips with her opponent she used her free hand to pull his head closer. The kiss was so intense he forgot he was arm wrestling. Heck, he probably forgot his name. Grace did not and slammed his hand down onto the table top. Now it was Heaven's turn to celebrate as they lifted their champion up, the disciples returning the earlier chant with "Heaven is number one. Hell is number two." Calming down, the final match began, all the while both sides were screaming "Kiss him." "Get her in a liplock." With a full three minutes left on the timer they caved into pressure, more from their hearts than their cheering sections. Exactly in the middle their mouths met and exchanged greetings. This time they were both prepared so neither faltered, either from the arm wrestle or the kiss. The timer emptied, but the kiss lasted until Paddy actually separated them, ever so gently. Both sides were looking worried now, fearing that their defender might throw the fight. Nero and Grace stood facing each other, without having let go of the other's hand. In fact, both hands were embracing, even if the digital owners still stood apart.

The worry turned into action. The flower child moved toward Grace, an overweight reverend migrated to Nero's side. Neither looked happy. A crash sounded from the kitchen and Rainbow was loose again. The noise drew Hercules' attention and he saw the approaching aides. Something caused him to sprint toward the quartet ,but Big Red had chosen that moment to reissue his challenge.

"I demand you reface me in battle. I place my other weapons up against the sword, double or nothing. What do you say?"

"Out of my way!" shouted Hercules, tossing the large man aside. Big Red was sent crashing headfirst into the wall while Herc was still rushing forward, but thanks to the delay he would be too late. Each of the aides had slivers of broken wine glasses and were about to slit their respective masters' throat. So lost were they in each other's eyes they failed to see the threat behind them. Paddy was mediating an orchestrated, distracting dispute between an angel and demon and was also oblivious. I was too far away to do anything but shout. The slivers were raised but inches from tender and vulnerable jugulars. It seemed all but over, save for the bleeding. Before the unkindest cut could be made, Grace and Nero both were knocked off their feet by a small furry nuisance with horns. No, not Fred. Rainbow. The betrayers and would be assassins were left slicing empty air. It was enough time for Hercules to reach and disarm them. The Host and Horde disavowed any knowledge of the moles' existence or intentions. Paddy chose to let it slide.

Since Nero had been already knocked to his knees it seemed an appropriate time to ask a question that was burning inside of him.

"Grace, will you marry me?"

Her response was short and sweet. "Yes!" They embraced and kissed again.

"Fine. Then let's be bringing this to a close. One last round to decide it all. One flip of the coin. Grace is heads, Nero tails. Agreed?" asked Paddy. Nero and Grace nodded. Paddy flipped the coin into the sky. Time seemed to slow to a crawl as it turned over and over again, glittering from the reflected light. Paddy neglected to catch it, letting it instead land upon the hardwood floor. It hit and bounced, twice. It landed as all strained to see. The fate of the world had been decided by a coin toss. But what a toss!

"It landed on its side!" I shouted.

"It did indeed," answered a grinning Paddy. "There you have it. I officially declare the battle between Heaven and Hell an even tie and declare The Apocalypse ended. Hercules, you may now open the doors." As he did so, Hermes came in smirking from ear to ear. His mission had been successful. The Book of Seven was no longer in the possession of demon or angel. As to where exactly it was, I don't know to this day, which is fine by me. Lucas also entered along with Judah and Joseph and gave us the thumbs-up signal as he cut himself a piece of Demeter's blood pie. The genetics lab and the locusts had been eliminated. He checked the laptop and smiled wider, fangs glistening. The computer's targets were smitten from above and the nuclear waste was drifting off into deep space. The crowd left in disarray and anger, one by one. One pair, an angel and demon seemed more interested in each other than the loss. Big Red was weeping on the skinny guy's shoulder as he exited.

"Pleasure doing business with you. Please come again," Hercules said with a smile, taking inventory of his new arsenal. Big Red wailed louder. Demeter and her team had returned after successfully destroying their missile target. She was giving the sickly gentleman a bowl of chicken soup which actually stopped some of the sneezing. When he left, she told him to make sure he dressed warmly and always had a sweater. He promised he would. The hooded man in black had challenged Fred to a friendly game of chess and was shaking his head from side to side as he left, unable to believe his loss. The angels left slowly, but the demons took off like a bat out of... , well, let's just say they left quickly.

Grace's human disciples left her, all but one. The biker, name of Hard Rider, stayed behind to wish Grace all the best with a kiss on the cheek and a pat on the bottom. "I better be invited to the wedding," Hard Rider said.

"You will be. We'll have it right here," Grace promised, returning the kiss and the slap. "I just wish the rest of the gang could be happy for me."

"They will be. Eventually. It is just you took away their shot at sainthood and immortality. A hard thing to lose, especially when you never had it," philosophized Hard. "Shame about Judy and that reverend." Judy was the flower child.

"They'll have to live with what they tried to do for the rest of their lives," said Grace.

"Not to mention the damage Hercules gave them," I added. "I understand the reverend did it out of a misplaced guilt that he had betrayed God and was striking out against Satan, but why Judy?"

"They gave her an expensive set of jewelry. A thirty piece ensemble, very expensive. Made entirely from silver, by my understanding," said Grace.

"Well, let he who is without sin cast the first stone," offered Nero. Grace picked up a stone ashtray off the bar and tossed it to him.

"Okay," she said with a smile.

They thanked Paddy and the rest of us, even Rainbow, who they decided to adopt with Demeter's permission and Paddy's blessing, and left to start their new life together. They had made reservations to be married in a week's time here by Father Mike in a non-secular ceremony.

As they exited I said, "And we all lived happily ever after."

"Especially with that pest Rainbow gone."

"Actually I'm surprised Dion isn't more upset over Grace and Nero having taken his sacrifice with them."

"Why, Murphy?" questioned Dion.

"You usually get more annoyed when someone gets your goat," I said, barely dodging the lemon slices Dion threw at my head. It was then that we heard a meek voice rising up from a chair in the center of the room.

"Excuse me? May I get up now," asked the demon who had tried to get past Hercules.

"Yes," Hercules said, with a chuckle. The demon rushed out, past one of his own kind and a angel conversing on the street outside. It was the same pair who couldn't take their eyes off each other earlier.

"I must say Paddy, you were very calm and cool the whole time. You were that confident of our successes?" I asked.

"Of course. I can make a coin land on its side anytime I want to," Paddy said, tossing a quarter up by way of demonstration. It landed on tails. "Oops."

"Oops? We were one coin toss away from Hell triumphant and all you say is oops?" I said

"I was just kidding, Murph. I meant to do that. It was a joke."

"Prove it."

"Maybe later," Paddy said scooping the quarter up and putting it in his pocket. "Besides, I also had inside information, so I was able to rig the games with the kids' help. I knew that Grace had changed her mind and they both wanted out."

"How?" I asked

"Easy, they got together earlier and talked the whole thing out."

"You mean?" I asked, dreading the worst.

"Yep. Grace reckoned the number of the beast," Paddy punned. We moaned.

"Collect?" I asked.

"I'm sure she plans to," Paddy said, smiling.

"So we have just saved the world from ending. What do we do next?" I questioned.

"Go to Disneyland?" answered Lucas.

"Get drunk?" suggested the never sober Mosie.

"Limbo?" said Tommy.

"With apocalypso music?" asked Father Mike.

"Buy a vowel?" submitted Roy.

"A celebration is definitely in order. Drinks half price. Oh what the heck, two for one," said Paddy.

"Isn't that the same thing?" asked Rumbles.

"Only if you want to be technical about it. Murphy, drinks all round. On the house. Keep 'em coming," ordered Paddy.

"I never thought I would see this day," I said.

"What? You helping to save the world?" asked Lucas.

"No, Paddy sponsoring an open bar. Before tonight I would have said it was one of the seven signs of the Apocalypse. Are we sure we covered everything?" I asked.

"Except your mouth," said Paddy.

Dion and I took care of everyone. There was lots of loud celebration. I was feeling more in the mood for something a tad quieter. I took my beer and headed toward the front door.

"Where you going Murphy?" asked Roy.

"I thought I would watch the sunrise. Seems appropriate somehow. Sort of viewing the fruits of our labors, being thankful for another day. Good or bad, win or lose, today is everyone's to do with as they choose. Thanks to what we did here," I said.

"Sounds like a good idea," said Father Mike.

"That it does," said Paddy.

"Mind if we join you?" asked Rumbles.

"Not in the least," I answered.

Arm in arm, the lot of us went outside to greet the morning.

A demon–angel couple had beat us to it and were floating above a fire hydrant, locked in a passionate embrace.

LOVE AND JUDGMENT EPILOGUE:
BLASPHEMOUS HEARTS

Armageddon was never supposed to be like this. Bar games determining the fate of all that was, is, and will be. The beginning of something new as the world was fated to be ending. The new light shone in enemy eyes. Servant of Heaven and slave of Hell stared, seeing deeply, viewing things not meant for either of their kind. Yet there it was, burning and shining. Brighter than the heart of stardust, hotter than the lust of hellfire.

Love had just saved the mortal world. It was about to do even more damage. The endgame of existence ended in a draw. Heaven and Hell were invited to stay, to make peace in a place called Bulfinche's, just as their mortal leaders had. For the first time since the Fall, the forces of light and darkness agreed.

NEVER!

Unable, unwilling to put aside the battle that was their existence. The end would come still. This was only a delay. A new savior would be sought. A tainted beast pursued. The Horde and the Host returned home, save two. The pair ignored the paths of their fellows, losing their way in the eyes of the enemy. Choosing to defy Heaven and Hell, each approached the other, without animosity or hatred. In that instance their hearts met and were one.

Empty, dark and deserted, the Manhattan city streets took no notice of them. The pair returned the favor, as blind to their surroundings as their surroundings were to them. Each only conscious of the other, a fire hydrant between them.

"I'm Ryth," she said, beautiful and strong.

"I know," he said, handsome and delicate. "I am Mathew."

Ryth smiled a smile that had damned more than one man, yet now shone with something new. Innocence. "I know." The introductions were a show, for any of the Host or Horde who might still be lurking. This was not the couple's first meeting, but that secret was theirs to share.

"Our meeting is forbidden. Save on the battlefield of souls," he said.

"I know," she replied, tinged with sadness. "We could pretend we are fighting, if you prefer. Like the last few times." Her smile lit up the sky with a dark light, no longer wanting to pretend.

"We dare much, meeting in the open like this. We should not be here. Each of us belongs with our own race. Our return is foreordained. Our homes call to us. The Pit screams for you, Paradise sings for me," he said, torn, denying his words even as he spoke them.

"We are both breaking the rules, but neither of us is in a rush to leave. Why?" she asked playing devil's advocate, a role she was born for.

"I fear I know the answer," he said, hanging his head in shame.

"Me too," she said, a small glint in her eye.

"What are we to do?" he pleaded, begging for her wisdom.

"We've got a couple of choices. Ignore it, pretend it never happened. Let the feeling fester like an open wound and infect us. Or do something about it. I can't deny what I am feeling."

"To fulfill what I feel is to court madness and destruction."

"I welcome it."

"Ryth, you are more accustomed to defiance than I."

"Perhaps, Mathew. Even in Hell, order must be maintained, the damned kept in line. We have our share of rules to follow. The important thing is to not get caught."

"We cannot do this."

"We have to."

"I know. I am seraphim. My existence is dedicated to saving the wayward, yet I cannot even save myself from my willful heart."

"I am succubus, carnal mistress for demon and damned. I can't see myself happy in the seduction of souls after meeting you, sweetie. Anyone ever tell you that you are a good influence? And such a huge wingspan. Do you know what they say about an angel with a huge wing span?"

"No. What?"

Ryth smiled at Mathew's naivete. "That he is... a hugely gifted individual."

"Why, thank you," he said smiling, a slight blush coloring his cheeks as he finally understood her innuendo.

"If it's true, it's I who will be thanking you," Ryth said, licking her crimson lips.

"By the Host, we are behaving like love–crazed mortals."

"Isn't it wonderful?"

"Yes. It is also insane. Moments ago we were enemies."

"We still are. Technically."

"I would have eradicated you mere moments ago."

"Would you?" asked Ryth.

"No. But I would have tried," said Mathew.

"I would have tried to mess you up pretty bad, too. You know what? I would have failed miserably."

"These things no longer matter."

"Nope. They don't."

"We are damned."

"We are saved."

"They will destroy us if we do this, each betraying our kind. Even Heaven hates a traitor."

"I have no thirty pieces of silver to offer you."

"Nor any need. Ryth, you are all I need."

"So we are going to try?" Ryth stopped before adding "Finally."

"Yes, though it will lose me Paradise. After what has happened between us, I realize that even Paradise will be empty without you. Regardless, Heaven will not take you in my love. The Host would never trust you, forever believing you a serpent in their midst."

"If we turned to the Horde the Damned would know joy. A gift of an angel. A plaything to destroy. I would be exalted, Queen of the Pit. Yet I would sooner destroy myself than bear your torment."

"What are we to do?"

"We'll hide, here on Earth," said Ryth.

"Even here, they will find us."

"Then we will have to find a good hiding place. Better. We will find asylum, protection."

"Where would we find such a place, willing to oppose angel and demon?" asked Mathew.

"In the same place where we began."

"With the Gentry and the false gods?"

"Yep. In Bulfinche's. They will take us in. Our love may be wonderful to us, but love is nothing new. We aren't the first to feel love as we do. Perhaps just the first of our kind to find it with the other. Many have known what we know. The barman and the leprechaun have felt love. True, unending love," said Ryth.

"How do you know? Why would they trust us?"

"I saw it. In my line, you know the ones you can never have. Love's flame still glows within them, even though their mortal loves have been torn away. Love like theirs never dies. Nor does the memory. They could never deny us, whatever our nature."

"Even if we do find protection, leaving our homes for Earth is not without a price. We may yet live forever but we will have frailties. We will need food, shelter, money. We will need all these and more. Will they help us with these?"

"Maybe. Maybe not. It doesn't matter. I will die without you, Mathew."

"I could not live without you, Ryth. Then it is decided. We will throw ourselves on their mercy and beg for their aid."

"Mathew, honey, maybe you better let me do the talking. Pity is a good thing, but it must be built up gradually to work. But before we go in, how about you give me a hug and a kiss?" said Ryth, leaving herself vulnerable for the first time in her life.

"That very action could destroy us. Matter and anti-matter are not supposed to touch."

"That is a tale used to frighten us. Besides, chastity isn't one of my specialties," said Ryth.

"I have never known anything but," Mathew admitted, embarrassed.

"No fooling? Boy, do you have a lot to learn. I promise to be the most attentive teacher," Ryth said, eyes opened with all the purity she had never been allowed before.

"And I promise to be the most eager student. What do we do first?" Mathew asked, with an eagerness he had never before known.

"Do what comes naturally," Ryth said, as the pair moved awkwardly toward each other. "We will work on technique later. Kiss me, you fool."

With the decision made, worry faded away. Stepping around the hydrant, they approached. Fingers touched, sending sparks the third rail could never match. Unbearably slowly and with speed without measure, heads tilted forward to meet with destiny. Lips touched tenderly in an explosion that rocked two worlds. Arms reached out in dearest embrace.

Dark, leathery and batlike. White, feathers like a giant dove. Demon wings. Angel wings. Each caressing the other, beating together to the rhythm of two hearts made one. Each combining with passion, causing an ascension from the city street below. Love—more than wings—suspended them, silhouetted in the rising sunlight and smog. There they stayed, defying gravity, Host and Horde. Their actions forever denied them Heaven or Hell but together their hearts had found them paradise in each other's arms.

So enraptured were they that the presence of an audience went unnoticed, even after the applause began. We had seen their meeting earlier through the plate glass window of the bar. It was hard not to notice the attraction earlier inside the bar, even on opposing sides. We had guessed the rest when we came out to watch the sunrise and saw something just as beautiful in the early morning light.

Ryth was embarrassed, Mathew aglow. Locked together, they descended to meet us, Bulfinche's own.

"Thank you for you kind applause," said Ryth, focusing her comment on Paddy. "We find ourselves in a bit of a quandary."

Mathew cut in, bowing deeply. "Honored Gentry, we beseech thee for asylum. We have nowhere else to turn. Please do not view us as former adversaries, but souls in need."

Ryth and Mathew were worried about the fact that we had all been enemies in the very recent past. Rightly so. Still, we aren't the type to hold a grudge. Not usually, anyway.

"Honey, perhaps a more subtle approach is called for," suggested Ryth.

"I am sorry, dear," he replied.

"No need to be sorry," said Paddy.

"There isn't?" asked a surprised Ryth.

"None. We all have made mistakes. It seems like you two have risen above all that."

Turning to look into Ryth's eyes, Mathew said, "We have."

"Glad to hear it. Now why don't you come inside and let's see what we can do to help you kids." The lot of us went in to continue the celebration.

"That's it?" asked Ryth, heading in the door.

"Pretty much," said Paddy.

"How do you know this is not some plot of revenge against you?" asked Mathew.

"Nonsense. Any fool can tell by looking at the two of you that you are in love," said Paddy.

"So I have been told," replied Mathew. "We need a great many things. Food, shelter, money."

"Protection," added Ryth.

"I can help you with the protection," said Demeter. "For now, you will be safe in the bar, but you can't stay here forever. Give me a day and I will whip up some amulets that will hide you from those who would seek you."

"As far as the other things go, I can put you up until you get on your feet. Nothing is free you understand. You will have to pay me back," said Paddy.

"No problem," said Ryth.

"Now we need to find you jobs. What are you qualified to do?"

Ryth actually blushed. "My skills are in a very specialized area. I don't want to use them on anyone except pookie wings, here. Plus, I believe the oldest profession is illegal here in New York. A shame. You think with all that time under their belts, they would have been able to get some decent legislation through."

"I have no marketable skills."

"Sure you do," said Paddy. "Ever wash dishes before, Mathew?"

"No."

"Then you are about to embark on a journey of learning. Ryth, you could wait tables for us."

"I get to keep all my tips?"

"Absolutely."

"And fifty dollars an hour?"

"Dream on. You will get a fair wage and a room until you get on your feet. Deal?"

"Deal," they said together, Mathew shaking Paddy's hand, Ryth kissing his cheek.

"Welcome to the real world," said Paddy.

"Hope you enjoy your stay," I added. Looking at the caring way they cherished each other with their eyes and hearts, that would be pretty much a given. Love may not conquer all, but sometimes it comes close.

A WING AND A PRAYER

When I walked into the kitchen, the angel was up to his elbows in dirty dish-water.

"Hey, Murph," he said.

"Hey, Mathew," I answered.

"Got any more dishes for me?" Mathew asked, as he scrubbed happily away. Angel or not, it was sick and twisted for anyone to enjoy washing dishes that much.

"Naw. I think Fred brought in the last of them before he knocked off," I said. There wouldn't be any more tonight. Demeter had closed the kitchen two hours ago and went off to bed, which was where I was planning to head shortly. My bed, not hers. We're not that close.

"So then, to what do I owe the pleasure of your company?" asked Mathew.

"You're the only one around here who refers to my arrival as a pleasure." Most of my friends would be more likely to use that term to describe my exit. "I was hungry and that roast lamb Demeter fixed for the special tonight was calling me," I said, opening up the fridge.

"That's what that noise was," said Mathew, his voice mildly sarcastic.

"A joke. I'm impressed."

"I'm told it doesn't take much," said Mathew.

"I'm easy that way. I'm going to make a sandwich. Want one?"

"No, thanks, I'm good."

I put the remains of the lamb on the counter. Demeter makes sure everyone feels welcome in her kitchen, unless they're getting underfoot when she's trying to cook. If she's not around, the staff has standing orders to help ourselves to the food. When she is around, she insists on doing most of the serving herself. It goes without saying that we clean up after ourselves and don't touch anything that is being saved for a special occasion. No one wants to make someone who cooks like Demeter angry.

It wasn't unusual for the whole staff to hit the kitchen after a shift and round up some nourishment. It wasn't even odd to see some of the regulars wander in and help themselves. Paddy had no objections, but he did have a habit of charging people for the food.

"Paddy let you off early?" Mathew asked.

"Yeah. Just Hard Rider and Lucas out there now. Everyone else hit the road, so the boss figured he could handle it solo. I think your wife is knocking off soon," I said, as I cut two pieces of fresh-baked bread.

The kitchen door swung open and Ryth walked in. Actually, Ryth didn't just walk anywhere. It was more of a salacious dance that could lead a man to distraction or straight to Hell. Ryth had done both, but regretted the latter.

"Speak of the devil," I said with a smile. Ryth shook her head, rolled her eyes and smiled back.

"You must have been waiting a long time to use that line," she said, walking up behind her husband and hugging him from behind. If my arrival had brought him pleasure, Ryth's delivered pure ecstasy.

"Yep," I answered truthfully. Mathew dried his hands on a dish towel and turned around to hug Ryth back. Some serious making out followed, each of them oblivious to me standing just a few feet away. Finally they came up for air. Newlyweds. "Want a sandwich, Ryth?"

"Sure. Spending all night on my feet waiting tables is hungry work. Got some rare pieces?" Ryth asked. Demeter had a talent of being able to cook a good sized piece of meat so different parts were more done than others, so depending on where one sliced, the meat could be anything from blood rare, for folks like Ryth or Lucas, to practically burnt for those well-done fans.

I cut a couple of pieces that could practically go back out and graze with a couple of band aids and held them up for Ryth's inspection.

"Murph, you know how I like it," Ryth said. Without even being aware of what she was doing, she purred.

"I thought you promised not to tell Mathew," I quipped. It was only a joke. Ryth would sooner be submerged under holy water than cheat on her husband.

Mathew joined in on the fun. "So you're leaving me for Murphy?"

"For Murphy? Get real," Ryth said, making a face.

"Hey!" I said.

"No offense," said Ryth, with a wink.

"No problem." Mathew had the kind of blond, pretty-boy looks that teen idols only dream of. "Mayo, mustard, or gravy?" I asked.

"Mustard, and make it spicy," she said. Personally, I went for the gravy. I made sure that my bread slices were thick enough to not let it soak though. Couldn't understand Ryth picking the mustard, as good as it was. Then again, I picked cooked pieces of meat. Different strokes.

I handed Ryth her sandwich. She uncoupled from Mathew in order to eat. Mathew turned back to his pile of dirty dishes and got back to scrubbing.

"Thanks, Murph," Ryth said as she took a bite. Some of the meat's natural juices ran down her hand and Ryth lapped them up with her tongue.

"Go figure," I said.

"What?" she asked.

"I didn't think your side liked the blood of the lamb," I said. Ryth rolled her eyes again.

"You almost done here, PW? If not, I may end up hurting Murphy," she said. She called Mathew "Pookie Wings", but used such a sickeningly sweet, baby-talk type of voice that Hard Rider and a few others had made comments, so she usually shortens it to PW in public.

"A few more minutes, hon, and I'll be out of here," said Mathew, concentrating on a particularly stubborn stain.

"You want me to dry?" Ryth offered, looking at the pile of clean, wet plates.

"No, I got it," he said, "Why don't you go home and rest up?"

"Okay, but don't be long. I went by the lingerie shop and got a new outfit. It's not much, but I think you'll like it," Ryth purred.

"I'll hurry home," promised Mathew, looking longingly at his wife. You could feel the lust in the air, hoping to cop a feel. Angel and Succubus kissed goodbye and lust got it's hopes fulfilled when Ryth grabbed Mathew's buns and gave a playful squeeze.

"I'll be waiting. Night, Murph. Thanks for the sandwich," Ryth said, heading out. I told her she was welcome.

"Mathew, how's the new place working out?" I asked. When they left their previous employers, Heaven and Hell, they had lived upstairs with the rest of the staff. Free room and board is one of the many job perks at Bulfinche's. Problem was they were newlyweds. Not that there's anything wrong with that. I'd been there myself and it was the happiest time of my life, but with these two there were extenuating circumstances.

Mathew has been alive since almost the beginning of time and was a virgin up until he met Ryth. Ryth, while definitely not a virgin, had never actually been with someone who truly loved her, who put her needs before his own. I guess nobody ever asks a succubus if it was good for her, too. Kind of a demeaning life, even if the sex was good.

The end result was that they were constantly making love. Nothing wrong with that. The problem lay, no pun intended, in the noise levels involved. It was explosive. They were both screamers, and would go all through the night. It eventually got so loud, that the rest of us complained, even Dion. When the god who claims to have invented the orgy is objecting to the volume, you know it's bad.

At first Paddy put them on a empty floor, away from everyone else, but eventually they decided to get out on their own. We had just helped move them in a few days back.

"It's a nice place. A bit cramped, but not too expensive, and in a nice area. We're planning to have everyone over for dinner, as soon as one of us learns to cook something that's edible. We've still been eating most of our meals here," said Mathew, scrubbing the last stack of dishes.

"Understandable. I had one of Ryth's chocolate chip cookies yesterday," I said. Actually, it was a small bite.

"Brave man. I barely survived eating mine. I'm surprised they disappeared so quickly," said Mathew.

"Well, I don't need to tell you the effect your wife has on men. When Ryth offered them, everyone took one. Almost nobody took a second bite, they were so awful, but no one wanted to hurt her feelings. Paddy sent her into the kitchen to check on something, then pulled out the garbage pail behind the bar. For the next few seconds it rained cookies and napkins filled with spit-out cookies. Dion picked up the tray and dumped the rest in the trash. When Ryth came back, the cookies were gone."

"That also explained the tubes of pre-made cookie dough Ryth's been getting all day," said Mathew.

"Yep," I said.

I finished my sandwich, licked my lips, and washed it down with a glass of fresh cows' milk. It was the rich and creamy kind, not like the watered-down stuff you get at the supermarket.

"Can I give you a hand with the rest of the dishes? If you want, I'll finish up for you so you can get home to Ryth," I said. Being a widower, I had a soft spot for newlyweds, happy and jealous of what they are lucky enough to still have.

"It's my job. I'll finish it," he said.

"You may be the only person I know who enjoys washing dishes. It's sick, especially with what you have waiting for you at home," I said.

Mathew laughed. "Not really. It's not the dishes so much as the fact that I'm doing something physical. I'd never done corporeal work until Paddy gave me this job."

"Part of that may be because you didn't have a physical body before," I suggested.

"Well, not often at any rate. I find there is a certain satisfaction in doing hard work. It makes me feel good."

It had taken Mathew quite a while to do what modern technology could have done in a quarter of the time or less.

"You think with all the money Paddy has, he'd invest in a few modern appliances, like a self cleaning porta potty and a dishwasher," I said.

"As long as he didn't mix the two up," said Mathew, cracking another joke. There was hope for him yet.

"Won't argue with you there," I said.

"Actually, with Paddy's money, he could easily buy those things. He could hire Vulcan to build a device to do anything he wanted done, but then he wouldn't be able to help others out by offering them a job as a dishwasher. Or a waitress. Or a busboy. Or even a bartender," he said. A picture of a giant machine that mixed drinks flashed in my mind. Probably only take Vulcan an afternoon to build it. I shuddered.

"You've got a point there, about everything but the self cleaning porta potty," I said, bringing the milk glass and the dish I had eaten the sandwich off of to the sink, planning to wash them myself.

"Give it here," said Mathew, holding out his hand for the plate and glass.

"I can clean up after myself."

"I know, but right now washing is my job. I don't climb behind the bar and pour my own drink do I?"

"Okay," I said, handing the glass and plate over. Those were the last things to wash, so Mathew turned his attention to drying.

"Mathew, mind if I ask you some angel-related questions?"

"Go ahead."

"I know Ryth has to transform for her wings to grow. What's the deal with your wings? Do they get absorbed by your body or what?"

"No, my wings are always there, although I can cloak them or me. Problem is, if I used my own power to do that, the Heavenly Host would sense it and track me down in milliseconds. Thankfully, Demeter's amulet does that for me," said Mathew, holding up the gold medallion with the Bulfinche's shot o' gold on it. Ryth had a matching one. The boss gave them dispensation to work in the bar, although the aspect that hides him from Heaven and Hell was redundant inside Bulfinche's. "I don't like having to hide my wings. It feels wrong, but it's necessary."

"Proud of them?"

"Oh yes. I was very lucky to have bonded with my wings," said Mathew.

"You mean angels really do have to earn their wings?" I asked.

"Yes, but not always in the way mortals traditionally accept," he said.

"Then how?"

Mathew wiped and dried the last plate. "I'm done here, Murph. I'd like to get home to Ryth. Mind if I tell you another time?"

"No problem," I said.

"Let me say goodbye to the boss and I'm outta here," said Mathew. My expression changed and he picked up on it.

"What?"

"It's just when you say boss, I automatically think of. . . well you know," I said pointing up at the ceiling.

Mathew got real still.

"I'm sorry. I struck a nerve."

"It's okay. I still think that way myself. I ran away from the Host and the angels, not the Lord of creation," Mathew said.

"I don't understand."

"Let's just say humans would be contemptuous to think they're the only ones with free will and leave it at that. Night, Murphy. Have a good sleep."

"You too."

Mathew said his goodbyes to Paddy and the crew in the bar. He passed Hercules and Hermes, who were coming in as he was going out. They each handled him tubes of cookie dough.

"These are for Ryth," said Herc. Mathew laughed.

"Thanks."

Apparently, after she left the kitchen, Ryth picked up a box filled with cookie dough to take home.

Mathew headed out.

He walked home along the Manhattan streets. The air was a bit chilly, but all Mathew wore was a t-shirt and blue jeans. He didn't always wear a trenchcoat, like so many of our other patrons.

It was the wee hours of the morning and the streets were almost empty. As he went by an apartment building, his ears heard something that they hadn't been privy to in a long time; a prayer from above. In this case, it was literal, as the woman doing the praying out loud was standing on a third floor fire escape.

"God, help me, please. Prove to me you're up there."

Mathew was torn. He had been a seraphim, not a guardian angel. His interactions with humans were limited, at least outside of Bulfinche's Pub. Quite frankly, he didn't think he was qualified, but his doubt only lasted for a second. He counted how many apartments she was from the end and went in the front door. The security door wasn't shut properly, and opened with a simple pull.

Mathew climbed the three flights and figured out which door belonged to that apartment. The door said 3G. The angel knocked.

The woman answered, keeping the chain on the door. It took only a glance to realize that Mathew was a stranger and in most parts of New York, strangers are rarely welcomed, unless you count an act of rudeness or violence a welcome.

"What? It's two-thirty in the morning."

"I'm here about your prayer," he said, not sure of what else to say.

"What prayer?" she asked, fearing a lunatic was outside her door and wondering it the tiny chain would hold long enough for her to slam the door shut and call the police.

"The one where you asked for help and proof," Mathew answered, unsure.

"What, were you lurking around outside?"

Mathew still had problems with lying. Not that angels couldn't lie. Most just didn't like to. "Something like that. May I come in?" he asked.

"You must be crazy to think I'd let a complete stranger into my house at this hour of the morning," she said, starting to shut the door.

"I'm here to help," offered Mathew. I guess Mathew didn't look like a traditional angel. They wear white robes. I guess a white t-shirt wasn't enough to pull off the look.

"Get out of here or I'll call the cops."

"First, look me in the eyes, and then if you still want me to leave, I'll go."

Inside the bar, Mathew's eye's are almost a solid blue. Outside, his eyes are very different. To the casual observer, an angel's eyes look like a normal human's, but if you look closely enough, you can see something; something mystic, holy, and unexplainable. It's like a doorway to the wonders and majesty of the universe. It's an unnerving experience.

The woman looked and saw, then took the chain off and opened the door, barely able to believe what she was doing, even as she did it.

"Thank you. My name is Mathew."

"I'm Jen."

"A pleasure to met you Jen. What's troubling you?" said Mathew. He still often spoke like he was in an old Bible movie.

"Troubling me? I'll show you what's troubling me," she said, opening a bedroom door. Inside, an eight-year-old boy was asleep, hooked up to far too many medical gizmos and gadgets. Each had a function, and several were working to keep track of his life signs.

"Your son?" asked Mathew. Jen nodded. "What's wrong with him?"

"Danny has a tumor on his brainstem. The doctors say the surgery to remove it would kill him. We tried chemo and radiation, but it didn't help."

"That explains the baseball cap."

Danny was eight, and no eight-year-old wants to be bald. He wore the hat almost constantly.

"Yes. The tumor is still growing. They say he has another month or two, tops. He wanted to come home, so today he did. All those monitors are set up to let me know if his heart stops or he stops breathing, which is what will happen once the tumor gets big enough to push on the brainstem. It's only a matter of time. I can't even nap. I'm afraid he'll die alone while I'm asleep."

"Where's his father?"

"Took off for points unknown five years ago. Haven't heard from him since."

"I'm sorry," Mathew said, genuinely sad. Jen could sense that, and it disconcerted her.

"I'm not. He was a bad husband and a lousy father. We're better off without him."

"So what is it exactly that you want?"

"I guess I wanted to know what kind of a God would do this to a child, but I already know the answer. There is no God."

"But Jen, there is a God," said Mathew.

"Right and the next thing you are going to tell me is he loves me."

"He does."

"So God's a man?"

"He can be."

"Let me guess. Now you quote from the bible and try to convert me to your religion."

"The Creator of all doesn't get as hung up on religion as some people do," said Mathew.

"So why doesn't he just heal my son?"

"God doesn't work like that."

"Right, like you can prove it," said Jen.

"Maybe I can," said Mathew, contemplating his actions. He was a renegade from the Heavenly Host, so some of their rules, especially those about visitation, no longer applied to him. The big question was the risk factor.

"How can you prove it?" demanded Jen.

"Risk be damned," he thought to himself with a chuckle, and then out loud added, "Like this."

Mathew took off the amulet, but didn't let go of it. It still cloaked him, but he was able to concentrate enough to make his wings appear, not as a hazy outline, but as solid and real. The wings gave off a beautiful glow that brought Jen to tears. Mathew kept his power expenditure minimal enough to not attract unwanted attention.

"Oh my God," said Jen, the tears streaming down her face at the sheer beauty of the sight of an angel's wings unfurling.

"No, but hopefully enough," said Mathew, opening his arms. Jen fell into them, weeping and letting out all the frustrations that had been building for months. His wings wrapped around and cradled them both. Mathew slipped the amulet back on. The wings vanished mere moments after Danny had woken up. It was enough to astonish the boy.

"Mom, he's an angel. Are you here to take me to Heaven?" asked Danny in awe. His mother sat beside him, putting her hand on his shoulder.

She turned to Mathew and asked, "Are you?"

"Maybe not yet. Can I borrow your phone?" Mathew asked.

"Sure. Who are you calling?"

"A friend of mine."

"Another angel?"

"Not quite."

"A doctor?"

"A step or too above that. He's a Greek god and a superb physician. If anyone can help Danny, it's him," said Mathew as he dialed. Into the phone he said, "Paddy? It's Mathew. Is Hermes still there? Could you put him on? Hermes, it's Mathew. I have a favor to ask of you."

Mathew explained everything, listened for a bit and hung up.

"Your friend is coming now? In the middle of the night?" Mathew nodded. "I can't even get my doctor to make a house call during the day. How much time until he gets here?"

Just then there was a rap at the window in the other room.

"That would be him now," said Mathew.

"But there's no fire escape by that window, and we're on the third floor."

"Then you better open the window and let him in, before an insomniac neighbor notices him," suggested Mathew.

Jen did. Hermes stepped in, carrying a little black bag. He shook Jen's hand and introduced himself.

"Where's the patient?" Hermes asked.

"Follow me," said Jen. "Do you want his MRI?"

"Don't need it," said Hermes. Jen looked confused, but was still too overwhelmed to question anything.

"I like your baseball hat," said Danny. Hermes was wearing a Bulfinche's Pub softball team hat, with our trademark shot o' gold on it.

"I like yours. Want to swap?" said Hermes.

"Sure," said Danny. He took his cap off, then was embarrassed. "I wear the hat because I'm bald."

Hermes took off his hat, reveling his secret shame. "Me too."

Even though Hermes had more of a bald spot than a bald head, Danny laughed. Hermes examined Danny, playing the clown, a role he rarely plays around adults. He prefers the role of trickster. Danny kept laughing the entire time.

"Well, I have good news. The tumor didn't spread and I think I can shrink it down enough that I can operate to get it out," said Hermes, not adding that in some cases he would have been just as helpless as anyone else.

"Really?" asked Jen.

"Absolutely."

"When?"

"Now."

"What hospital should we go to?"

"Right here will be fine," said Hermes, opening up his bag and mixing up a potion. Jen reached out to stop him, but at a nod from Mathew held her hand. "Drink this."

Danny did and giggled. "It tickled my nose. What's it do?"

"One, it'll shrink the tumor. Two, it will numb the area where I need to operate. Three, it will put you to sleep."

Danny was out cold before Hermes even finished his last sentence.

"How long until it shrinks the tumor?" asked Jen.

"Less than twenty minutes, then about ten minutes for the surgery," said Hermes. "I work fast."

"You mean in less than one hour, Danny will be cured?" said Jen.

"The tumor will be gone, but it'll still take several weeks before he recovers completely, provided all goes well," said Hermes.

"Thank you. Thank you both," Jen said, hugging Hermes and then Mathew.

"Our pleasure, right, wing boy?" said Hermes.

"Absolutely," said Mathew.

Jen collapsed into a chair. "I don't know what to do with myself."

"When's the last time you ate?" asked Hermes.

"It's been a few hours," Jen admitted.

"I have cookie dough," said Mathew, pulling out two tubes.

"Is that some sort of angel food?" asked Jen.

"No, it's just my wife is a really bad cook," said Mathew. Jen looked confused. "It's a long story."

"You're married? I didn't know there was marriage in Heaven," said Jen.

"I don't live in Heaven any more," said Mathew.

"Where do you live?"

"Just a few blocks from here." Jen still looked confused.

"Mathew emigrated here. It happens," said Hermes, saving Mathew an explanation.

"I'm glad it does," said Jen, reaching out to squeeze Mathew's hand. "Now, how about that cookie dough. Let me go out to the kitchen and get us some. . ." Hermes vanished for less than a flicker of an eye and reappeared holding three utensils. ". . .spoons. How'd you do that?"

"It's a gift," Hermes said, handing one spoon each to Jen and Mathew. He saved the last for himself. They cut open the top and scooped out some chocolate chocolate chip.

Jen excused herself and went into the kitchen with some of the cookie dough. She made some cookies for Danny to have when he woke up, after the surgery. When she came back, Hermes had a question.

"Danny's about ready. Do you want to watch?"

"Can I?" asked Jen.

"Sure," said Hermes.

"What about a sterile environment?"

Hermes snapped his fingers and a glow burst rippled across the room. "Got it covered."

"Thanks. Will you stay until he's finished?" Jen asked Mathew.

"Sure, but I'll need to borrow your phone again."

"Why?"

"So I can call my wife to let her know I'll be late."

EVENING'S LADY

There was a suspicious guy in the corner. I couldn't say exactly what made me wary of him. Instinct, I suppose. He didn't seem the type to go into a bar for enjoyment or sorrow. Also, he was trying desperately to go unnoticed, which made him stand out brighter than if someone had lit his hair on fire. Folks who come into a bar to be alone don't try, they just do it. Here in Bulfinche's Pub, those types find they don't have to, nor do they want to remain alone for long.

He just sipped his beer and stared inconspicuously, more often than not at Father Mike Ryann. Mike was one of our regulars, a parish priest up the block at Our Lady of the Lake Church. I didn't know why Mike was so interesting. Maybe the guy wasn't used to seeing a priest have a good time.

Father Mike was playing a friendly game of poker with a few buddies. Friendly meant no cash, losers bought the winners next round. House rules were in effect, which meant only one rule–anything goes as long as you don't get caught. The players were sitting at a table near the bar. One was Ryth, succubus on the run from Hell for the crime of loving an angel. Punishable by damnation where she was from. So was most everything else. She was winning. It was her last night of employment with us. She'd been waitressing, but had saved enough to start her own business. She wouldn't tell anyone, but Paddy Moran what it was.

Paddy was also in on the game. He was sad to see Ryth go, but that wasn't stopping him from trying to clean her out. He was trying but not succeeding. Hermes was not faring much better. Mike was second in winning, followed closely by Lucas Wilson.

The game was interrupted as the door swung wide and Rebecca came in, carrying a young woman over her shoulders.

"Some help here. Wingfoot, do your thing," Rebecca ordered. Wingfoot was Hermes and he was trained in all medical arts. Rebecca and Hermes lowered her into a chair.

"What's wrong with her?" Hermes asked, taking the girl's vital signs.

"You are the doctor, Wingfoot. You tell me," she said.

"Rebecca, work with me here," Hermes pleaded.

"She has been on the streets. Not the first visit. Her money ran out a few days ago. Offered her help and advice. She took the advice, turned down the help. I've been keeping an eye on her and she collapsed half an hour ago. Piled her into the shopping cart and lugged her here. In short, I would say she is messed up bad," Rebecca observed, rubbing out a kink in her back and plopping down into a chair next to the patient.

"Could you be more specific?" asked Hermes, looking into her eyes.

"Sure. My guess is lack of food. Dehydration. Withdrawal. Plus a bun in the oven," Rebecca informed. She had some practical first aid skills, learned in her years on the street.

"She's pregnant!?" Paddy asked, jumping up from the game.

"Great. There goes this hand. I had a full house," said Lucas, trying to lighten the mood. He was just as concerned for the girl as the rest of us. Except the guy in the corner. He just watched.

"Don't worry about it, Lucas," said Ryth. "I had four kings."

"I had five aces," said Father Mike. House poker rules allow one deck, but unlimited cards.

"Oh, then I don't feel so bad now," Lucas said. "How is she, Hermes?"

"Better than she looks. She just passed out from dehydration. Murphy, bring me my bag," Hermes said. Since Murphy was my name, I did as he asked. He pulled out a needle and an IV bag and set up a drip. I got him the coat rack to hang the bag from.

"I'm more worried about the baby. She is months from term. The shock to her system may have affected it," Hermes said.

"Can't you find out?" Ryth asked.

"Yes. But I need something," said Hermes.

"Ultrasound?" asked Lucas

"No, the midget's permission," Hermes said. Paddy was so concerned for the girl that he gave his dispensation with a nod, letting the short joke slide. Hermes is a great healer, but no powers work in Bulfinche's without the boss' say so.

Hermes put his hands on her belly, still small, and did his thing.

"The baby is fine."

"Thank God," said Father Mike. The stranger in the corner raised his eyebrows.

Fred walked in though the upstairs door behind the bar. He took one look at the sick girl and said "Who's the babe?"

"Who you calling 'babe'?" asked the girl, coming around.

"She speaks," said Rebecca.

"Bag lady? Where am I? You bring me here?" she asked.

"Who else?" Rebecca said.

"What the hell is this needle doing in me? I'm pregnant for God's sake. I have been trying to avoid them for weeks and you go and stick one in me?" she said.

"Easy," said Hermes. "When Rebecca brought you in, you were unconscious and dehydrated. We had to get fluids into you quickly. Don't worry. Both you and the baby are fine. I'll make you a deal. Drink half a gallon of orange juice and I will take the IV out."

"Give me the O.J.," she said.

"Here you go," I said, handing her the bottle.

"Wait. I can't pay," she said.

"First drink is always on the house. The next one will count as the baby's first drink. Enjoy," said Paddy.

"Thanks."

"You got a name?" Paddy said.

"Toni Ann Andrews," she said, as introductions were manufactured.

"You got a story?" Ryth asked.

"Doesn't everyone?" Toni said.

"Care to tell us?" asked Fred.

"Why should I?"

"Because it might help. And you look like you could use a friend," said Lucas.

"Friends are for suckers. They are only nice to you because they want something."

"Then we must be suckers," said Paddy. "Let's see. Instead of leaving you on the street to rot, you were brought here, where we, in our selfishness, gave ye the care ye need to get well. Of course, all this was done for personal gain."

"I'm sure I'll get the bill."

"How? You have no address to send it to. I doubt you have insurance. Besides I don't charge for my services," said Hermes.

"Remind me of that next payday," said Paddy.

"I meant to patients," Hermes shot back.

"Lucas and I unloaded ourselves of emotional baggage when we found this place," I said. "Then the folks here helped us find solutions to our problems."

"Why should any of you even care?" Toni asked.

"Because we do," said Fred, trying not to stare into Toni's eyes, and failing wonderfully.

"Fine. I am a lady of the evening. A hooker," she said hoping to shock us. "None of this high class, glamour 'Pretty Woman' stuff. I don't use dental floss. I prefer heroin. I have to keep my toe and finger nails painted so the track marks don't show.

"How did it start?" asked Fred.

"The usual story. I didn't always have the addiction. I was a normal teenage girl in search of big city dreams. Stepped off a train at Grand Central Station and instead of dreams, found a nightmare. Not that I hadn't been used to nightmares, even in the light of day. I lost my virginity at nine to my father while my mother watched and cheered him on, stoned out of her mind. Dad was sober," Toni said. We kept silent, but Toni took notice that there was not one unclenched fist in the house. Not even the stranger's.

"I put up with that for five years. Finally I ran away. First night out I got picked up by a street shark. His name was Jojo Smith and he offered me a place to stay with him and three other girls. He said he would be my friend. I accepted both offers. That night I was woken from my sleep. The three girls held my arms and legs while Jojo shot me up in my belly button. A few days later I started coming down, hard. The only way to get back up was to do what Jojo wanted. Just a little work on the street corner. Hop into cars with strange men and drive around the block with my head in their lap. Or go with them to a strange motel room. It didn't matter. I would do whatever to get my high back. Then the dreams were real. I barely noticed life as it whirled around me."

"I rarely ever used protection. It is amazing I am still alive. In one of my lucid moments, I knew something was wrong. Drugstore bound, I got a home test and found out I was pregnant. Me, a Mommy. What right do I have to bring a life into this world when I couldn't even take care of my own? I went to get an abortion but I couldn't. No one was ever there for me. I could not bear to kill my unborn child with the same disregard that I had been treated my whole life. That night I resolved to quit cold turkey for the sake of my baby. Of course I had already earned that night's hit. Jojo handed out the syringes. I looked long and hard at the tip of that needle. It would be so easy to slip back into oblivion. I rolled off my sock. I pushed the plunger down to get rid of the air bubbles. And I shot up the whole charge... into a potted plant."

"That resolve saved my life. Or maybe I saved my baby's life, so it saved me back. Whatever the reason, I was alive the next morning, alone with four corpses. It was a bad batch. All the syringes were empty and Jojo and the other girls were dead. I freaked. Instead of grabbing Jojo's cash stash, I ran out the door with only the clothes on my back and I never looked back. That night I met Rebecca. She offered me help. I wasn't in my right state of mind. I was shaking like a leaf. My gut was on fire. It felt as if bugs were crawling around inside my skin, trying to chew their way out. Rebecca taught me how to breathe to focus past. It didn't stop the pain, but I could bear it, for my baby's sake. After three days together, Rebecca offered to take me to where people could help me. I told her I would make it on my own. She gave me a video rental card someone had lost. I asked her how that would help me. Turns out it had a magnetic strip that would open the door of a bank ATM atrium. She told me they made good shelters. She was right. I got by, barely. One guy offered to help me for a price, even gave me some sort of contract, but he disappeared. Problem was I started having morning sickness and withdrawal pains the same day. Things get kind of fuzzy after that. It was like a hallucination. I remember seeing a rainbow and stumbling toward it. It superimposed itself over Rebecca's face. Next thing I remember I was being called a babe by short and hairy here."

"You are," said Fred with a smile.

"Withdrawal is getting so bad. I don't think I can hold out much longer," Toni said.

"You have to," Lucas said. "For both your and your baby's sake. Addiction is hell. I know. The cravings never go away, but the pain does. Trust me, I know."

"Mamma told me never to trust a man who said 'trust me'. Then again, she was wrong about everything else. What was your addiction?" Toni asked.

"Blood," he said.

"Blood?"

"Yes. I am what Murphy likes to call a blood junkie. A vampyre," Lucas said.

"Maybe all the junk isn't out of my system yet."

Lucas smiled and showed his fangs by way of proof.

"I know all about Hell, too. Quite intimately," said Ryth.

"You a blood junkie too?"

"No. I'm a succubus."

"You do what to a bus?"

"Only occasionally. Actually, it's a classification of demon, which is what I am. Retired and presently hunted," Ryth said.

"What about the short people?" Toni asked Paddy and Fred.

Paddy answered first. "I am a member of the Gentry. In layman's terms, a leprechaun. I own the place. Bought it with my pot of gold so now rainbows tend to precede the arrival of troubled folks, which explains your hallucination."

"Okay. I am exhausted enough to be buying this. What about you, hairy?"

"I am a satyr," he said, pulling off his baseball cap. It, like Hermes' cap, had our trademark on the front. A rainbow ending in a shotglass of gold. What was underneath it were a pair of smal,l curved horns. The stranger barely kept his seat.

"I guess that explains why you are acting so horny. What about you, Murphy?"

"I get horny sometimes too," I said.

"No, I mean what are you," Toni asked.

"Mixologist by trade, human by birth, sarcastic by nature," I answered.

"Hermes?"

"A god by birth and nature. Healer by profession. Thief by disposition."

"What about you, Padre?" Toni asked Father Mike. Before he could answer the stranger in the corner jumped up and began shouting.

"I'll tell you what he is. A heretic and infidel."

"Excuse me," said Father Mike indignantly, but with a smile, "Who are you?"

"Father Kevin Kerner, Universal Watch."

"What's that? New time piece?" I asked.

"No," answered Father Mike with a frown. "Universal is the meaning of Catholic. Watch is meant as patrol or guard. It is a secret organization under the Council of Cardinals, that answers to the Pope."

"You mean he is the church police?"

"Basically. I was approached fresh out of the seminary," said Father Mike.

"And ultimately rejected us, betrayed the order. Another crime to add to your list," ranted Father Kerner.

"To do what the Watch demanded of me would have been betraying my conscience."

"You would have been forgiven by the Cardinal in confession."

"I don't play that way. Besides, that wasn't my only reason. I choose not to join a group of assassins, spies, and converters by use of force: the same people who brought the world the Spanish Inquisition and more than a few witch hunts. From the shadows, of course."

"The Pope gives us his blessing."

"The Pope recognizes the Universal Watch as a necessary evil. Even he doesn't know a fraction of what the Watch does."

"We tell the Cardinal, whose job it is to pass on the information to His Holiness."

"You don't believe the Cardinal is going to tell the Pope everything. The pontiff would have him excommunicated before the sun set."

"I wouldn't know about that," said Father Kerner.

"Because you choose not to."

"Perhaps, but I will tell you what I do know. You, a Roman Catholic Priest, consorting with agents of darkness and minions of Lucifer."

"What are you talking about?" asked Father Mike.

"Don't try to deny it. I heard everything. Spirits and fairies. Vampyres. Demon succubus and of cloven hoof," ranted Father Kerner.

"Excuse me," said Fred. "But satyrs are not demons."

"I don't think he cares, Fred," I said.

"And the worst of it. Sacrilege! Worshiping a pagan god!"

"We were playing poker," said Father Mike. "Hermes and the rest are my friends, not my lords. I worship them no more than I do Murphy."

"I think I'm insulted," I said.

"Actually, I think the rest of us should be insulted," said Hermes.

"Lucas and Ryth have fought the darkness within their souls and won. Can you say the same?" Father Mike challenged.

"But you admit she is a demon?" Father Kerner said.

"Sure she is a demon, just as her husband is an angel. Do I get brownie points for hanging out with him?"

"A member of the Heavenly Host, sanctified with this demon? Unthinkable!"

"Actually, I'm a demoness," Ryth interjected. "And let me tell you, Kerner, your kind make my old associates' job much easier. Your intolerance, prejudice, and hatred are breeding grounds for the sin you claim to be working against."

"Do not mock me, Demon," shouted Kerner, holding up a crucifix in front of him.

"Do not mock me, Demon!" Ryth mocked in a little girl's voice, holding up a card from the deck.

"I cast you out..." Kerner began.

"Don't waste your time," I said. "That stuff don't work here unless the boss says so."

"Nothing can stop the power of Christ," Kerner countered.

"Actually, Jesus had to play by the rules when he came here, too," I said.

"Jesus here? You jest."

"No. He wanted us to give up a customer. We wouldn't do it, even though he ordered Father Mike," I said.

"Blasphemy!"

"No. Father Mike helped him see the light and reach a compromise. In the end, he admitted Mike and the rest of us were right," I said. He probably agreed all along, but had to put on a show because of the promise snafu.

To Mike, he said, "You had a visitation? Why did you not report it?"

"Didn't seem like the right thing to do," answered Father Mike.

"We will have to examine the site, see if it was true. Maybe build a shrine..." said Kerner.

"You even try and I will kick yer butt out of my bar," said Paddy. "We have no need to be proving anything to the likes of ye."

"Regardless, Father Ryann has sinned against The Church and must be brought for justice," said Kerner.

"How do you plan to do that?' asked Father Mike.

"I order you."

"Want fries with that?" I asked.

"Easy, Murphy. The Watch is no joke. Their power is real. That doesn't mean I will jump on their say–so. Not now, not ever," said Father Mike, staring down Kerner.

"Then I will take you by force if necessary," answered Kerner, moving toward Mike.

"I don't think so," said Paddy, as he and the rest of us flanked Mike. He then veered off to take a frame off the photo wall. "Besides, if ye are going to arrest Father Mike, ye are going to have to arrest your boss," Paddy said, handing Kerner a picture of Paddy and the Pontiff taken in the bar.

"This can't be. The picture has to have been doctored. Or maybe it is that actor who plays His Holiness on the television talk shows," said Kerner, reeling. His view of reality was being challenged.

"It's real, I assure you."

"Besides, your church took pagan holidays for its own and set up Saints to take the place of gods in the people it converted. You yourself may even have worshiped me without knowing it," said Hermes.

"Impossible!"

"You ever have a St. Christopher medal?" asked Hermes.

"Of course," answered Kerner.

"Ever wonder why he isn't considered a Saint any longer? I'll tell you. Last time the Pope was here I told him that the deeds and miracles attributed to St. Christopher were all done by me. After all, I am the god–small G–of travelers. He couldn't in good conscience let my saintly status stand, all friendship aside, so I was decanonized."

"You lie!"

"Check it out."

"There are still forces of darkness at work here," said Kerner.

"The same forces of darkness that just helped save a young woman's life? The same forces that fund my and Rebecca's breakfast for the homeless program every morning while the diocese cut off the funding? And Paddy pays for the food seven days a week. The diocese didn't let us give out the food on Sunday, as it might disturb worshipers. There are plenty of ills in the world you could be fighting. Don't waste your time with me."

"With all the bad press The Church has gotten lately with priests being accused of molestation of wives and children, one of our own worshiping demons and pagan gods in public is unacceptable," said Kerner.

"I understand your position, but that isn't what I am doing," said Father Mike. "Those problems disturb me every bit as much as you. As priests, we are expected to be perfect role models. Any mistake is magnified. These horrendous crimes are made that much the worse having been committed by men devoted to God and covered up by the Church. People lose faith in the Church and even in God. But for every bad apple, there are hundreds of golden ones. We do our best. Yes, we screw up, but despite the collar we are only human. We just do the best we can with what we have and pray to God it is enough to do the job."

"I have unimpeachable sources on what goes on here," said Father Kerner. "I heard you all admit what you are and evil must be destroyed."

"Different is not evil," said Paddy.

"Who is this source?" asked Father Mike.

"His name is Ramos, a pious man concerned with the fate of the church," said Father Kerner.

"The man who offered to help me was named Ramos," said Toni.

"I knew a demon Overlord by that name. He might be the one heading up the hunt for me," said Ryth.

"Maybe you were being misled by the self same forces of darkness you are trying to fight," suggested Lucas.

"Impossible! The Cardinal himself introduced us. Father Ryann, I have to take you in. The Cardinal's orders. Nothing will stop me," said Kerner.

"You don't have a chance against me," promised Father Mike. "Remember, there was a reason the Watch tried to recruit me. Leave here in peace, my brother."

"No. I am no brother of yours."

"We'll just have to go over your head, Kerner," said Paddy, reaching behind the bar, picking up his cellular phone and his personal address book. He flipped through a few pages and dialed a number.

"Who are you calling?" asked Father Kerner.

"Shh," ordered Paddy, before speaking into the receiver. "J.P.! Top of the day to you, your Holiness, This is Paddy. That's right. Paddy Moran. I'm fine, thanks. How are ye doing? Sorry to hear that. Yes, I had read about it in the papers. Hope you are feeling better soon. Why yes, I could send you some of Demeter's chicken ravioli soup. I will have Hermes bring it to you later this evening our time. So when are you coming back to America? It has been too long between visits. Well if and when you do, make sure you stop by for a sherry. Sorry to bother you at home, but we are having a bit of a problem with one of your boys from the Universal Watch. Seems he wants to arrest Father Mike Ryann for hanging out here with us pagans. Yes, I told him he would have to arrest you too, but it did not seem to sink in. Seems to be taking his orders from some Cardinal. You know him? Good. Sounds like you might want to look into it and clean house a bit. He may actually have been influenced by the Pit. Associating with a possible demon overlord. No, have not had any problems since we stopped The Apocalypse,"

Kerner's eyebrows rose high on that one. I could hear him now. It was sacrilegious of us to save the world. If Heaven demanded the extermination of billions, they must have their reasons. Wonder what he would say if he found out that the almost savior had been a woman this time around? "Yes, he is here with us now. Name is Father Kevin Kerner. Sure, I will put him on," Turning to Kerner he handed him the phone. "J.P. wants to speak with you."

"Your Holiness?" Kerner asked in disbelief before bowing his head as he realized who he was speaking to. "Yes, what he said was true. I was just following orders. Yes, I realize that was no excuse. Sorry. Of course. I will report to the Vatican immediately to debrief you. Yes, your Holiness. Goodbye," Kerner hung up the phone, his mouth wide.

"I am sorry, Father," Kerner apologized, visibly straining to get out the words. "I was misinformed. I regret any inconvenience this may have caused you. I have to leave for Rome on the next flight."

"Next time you are in New York stop by for a drink. You can crash with me in the rectory," said Father Mike.

"You would break bread with me after this?" asked Father Kerner, amazed.

"Of course. We have been lecturing you all night on tolerance. What better way to teach you than by example," said Father Mike.

"Thank you, Father. I will consider it. Goodbye," said Father Kerner. Shame and bigotry did not allow him to speak or look at us directly as he made his exodus outside to hail a cab.

"And that brings us back to your dilemma, little lady," said Paddy, turning toward Toni.

"First off, who are you calling little? Second, I ain't no lady," said Toni.

"Of course ye are," said Paddy. "Ye said it yourself. You were Evening's Lady. It seems you are between both jobs and homes. I may have a solution to both. I have just lost my best waitress."

"Paddy, I was your only waitress," said Ryth.

"True," said Paddy, with a smile. "I find myself in need of a new one and you find yourself in need of gainful employment. Perhaps we can help each other out. The job includes medical coverage, from the house physician, Hermes, and free room and board upstairs. Hermes and the rest of us can help you with the rest of your withdrawal."

"It will be a daily battle. If you need to talk to someone who has been through detox, give me a holler," said Lucas.

"Thanks. I might just do that," Toni said. Turning to Paddy she asked "What's the catch?"

"He works your butt off," said Fred. "Which would be a real tragedy in your case."

"Enough already. Stop with the comments before I hot wax your fur covered legs," Toni threatened.

"That might be fun," replied Fred, grinning.

Turning back to Paddy, Toni asked "Does goat boy come with the package?"

"Unfortunately," chuckled Paddy.

"I'll take it anyway," she said.

"Glad to have ye aboard," Paddy said. As she had finished the orange juice, Hermes took the IV out of her arm and replaced the empty juice bottle with a full one. "Fred will show you your room and then bring you a meal. Three squares are included, but drinks come out of your pay. Because of your condition, I doubt that will be a problem for a while yet."

"Definitely not," Toni promised. "So fuzzy legs, you going to show me my room or what?" Toni asked.

"Absolutely," said Fred, leading her behind the bar, through the door and up the stairs. "It is right down the hall from mine. Isn't that great?"

"I'm all atingle," she said as their footsteps retreated up and away.

"Rebecca, there is always a room for ye here, you know," Paddy offered.

"No. My place is on the streets, saving folks like night girl from themselves and the street sharks," Rebecca answered, gathering herself up to go.

"Toni is the Evening's Lady."

"I like night girl better." Rebecca names people herself. Some names she keeps, some she creates. "Bye Moran. So long Wingfoot, Bloodsucker, Hellfire slut. You too, Murphy. Tell Goatlegs I said goodbye." And then she was gone.

The rest of us settled in at the poker game. I had managed to palm Mike's five aces. With the three of my own, I should at least win the first hand.

"So Father Mike, were you worried he was going to arrest you?" I asked.

"No. Even if he had, I would have gotten off on a technicality," said Father Mike.

"What's that?" asked Paddy.

"He never read me my rites," said Mike. He was buried under a rain of pretzels, peanuts, and seventy-five playing cards.

NEW HEIGHTS

Russ came in, almost bouncing. A huge change from his norm of late; he had been letting his work get to him too much. It happens when you work with crazy people. I know. Of course, the people he works with are his patients, and would probably object to the term crazy. They might prefer the term troubled, while others might like "reality challenged." Russ is a shrink, formally called Dr. Idolatrous. He hates it when I call his patients crazy, but it is a word I would use to describe some of my closest friends, so no insult is intended. He thinks the lot of us here at Bulfinche's are nuts, delusional even. Not an unreasonable attitude, considering who hangs out here, but it is unusual for a regular to be such an adamant non-believer.

Part of Russ' problem is he takes his work to heart. Russ knows that only people can make themselves better, but he still blames himself when they don't. In short, he breaks the counselor's cardinal rule–he has trouble keeping his emotional distance, a very real liability in his line. It is a two-edged sword; his empathy gives him an edge that can cut him because of the short emotional distance.

Lately, Russ has been a bit depressed himself. He corrects me and tells me he is not clinically depressed, merely has a lowered affect, then he laughs. His idea of a joke. I have no clue where he gets these ideas from, but I wish he would leave them alone. They will only lead him down the road to social ruin.

His specialty is phobias. He has even been helping Tommy get over his agoraphobia with some success.

Russ sat down at my station.

"Hey, Russ. Glad to see you so chipper," I said.

"Yep, Murph. Today is a beautiful day and the world is a beautiful place. Give me a beer," Russ said, grinning. "I'm up for the Director of Psychiatry at Ringvue. Very prestigious. If I get it, I would be the youngest man to ever hold the position."

"Congrats. Make sure you stretch first. You will be able to hold the position longer."

"Thanks. On top of that, a patient and I made a major breakthrough. After months of therapy, he has conquered his fear of heights."

"All right. How'd you do it?"

"He," Russ corrected me. "Beat it mostly by using aversion therapy."

"You mean starting out standing on a chair and ending up on the top of a sky-scraper?"

"Basically, but with some visualization techniques tossed in. Yesterday we stood on the roof of my office building, thirty five stories up, and not a twinge of apprehension."

"You are a miracle worker, Doc."

"No, I just showed him the way. He did the work."

"Then you're an amazing trail–blazer. This one is on me," I said, topping off his beer.

"How can I refuse? Cheers," Russ said. "That patient is on his way up to the eighty-sixth floor observatory of the Empire State Building today to celebrate."

At that moment, an electronic buzzing began.

"Russ, you got a bee swarm in your coat? There are easier ways to get honey," I said.

"Not at all. It's my cell phone. It's all the buzz. I have nothing to hive," Russ said with a chuckle. See what I mean about his jokes? Makes even my worst seem good by comparison. "Probably a client. I give them this number for emergencies." Into the phone he said, "Dr. Idolatrous. Oh hi, Tony," covering the mouthpiece he whispered to me, "The patient I was telling you about."

Russ returned to the phone conversation. "Tony, no need to thank me again. Seeing you up there on the roof yesterday made it all worthwhile... You're on the observatory deck and no fear? Excellent. I am very proud of you Tony... No, Tony, I don't think you should climb up there. The fence is there for a reason. Tony, no!" Russ shouted into the cell phone. "I can be there in ten minutes. Five minutes then. Tony, don't do it. It's not worth it. I'm begging you, Tony, please don't. Oh, dear God!"

Russ held the phone numbly to his ear for a few more seconds, then visibly cringed. He shut the flip top and let the phone drop to the bar top.

It was one of those awkward moments when all I could do was state the obvious. "He jumped?"

"Yes," Russ said, a small tremor in his voice.

"Why?"

Russ inhaled deeply, trying to steady himself. "He never told me why conquering his fear was so important and you know I never even asked more than the basic 'whys'. Just now, for the first time, Tony told me he had wanted to commit suicide for years but didn't have the courage for poison or violent means. Felt he would chicken out at the last minute. Needed something he couldn't back out from. A suicide jump was his answer but the fear of heights kept him from doing it. Today he had no fear. Today he died."

"Are you sure? Maybe he didn't do it. Maybe it was a cry for more attention. Maybe..."

"Murphy, he didn't hang up. I heard the impact."

"I'm so sorry. Are you going to be okay?"

"Honestly, Murphy, I don't know. Eventually I'm sure I will be, but it is tomorrow I am concerned with."

"What are you going to do tomorrow?"

"Haven't got a clue. I guess I will worry about tomorrow when it gets here. First, I have to worry about right now."

"Anything I can do to help?"

"Yep, Murphy, there is. Give me a triple bourbon, and keep them coming."

MOONSHINE

A strange aroma hung heavy in the air, barely detectable and yet overwhelming. It was a combination of love spurned, fear, and pity, with a touch of testosterone. Combined with the full moon, it seemed to be affecting anyone of the male persuasion. Men of action, men of reaction, of derring–do were daring don't. Bulfinche's Pub–usually a haven–had become a hideout. Hiding from the enemy. Who could turn a large, passionate crowd of menfolk into such a sorry state? Not as sorry a state as Jersey, of course, but pretty darn close.

So as not to offend any Jersey residents who are not near New York City, let me assure sure you my words are nothing personal. Just a feud dating back to the beginning of time. Folks in Jersey use New Yorkers as the foil of their jokes. That's okay because people need someone to blame their trouble on. Everyone has someplace they make fun of. Here in New York we make fun of New Jersey. Even folks in Cleveland have a place to make fun of. It's called New Jersey. Now back to our regularly scheduled story already in progress.

What could possibly be the cause of these men's sad emotional decline? Women, of course. Some of them even from Jersey.

It was the first spontaneous, semi-annual, guy's night in. No one actually asked the women–folk to leave. They just felt the mood in the air and joined Demeter on our second floor balcony. I contemplated going with them, but that would be an unforgivable sin against my gender. Sometimes one has to be a man whether or not one wants to–it's a guy thing. Yes, I am aware it makes no sense to women, but remember it is a guy thing. We understand it. Or make believe we do, at any rate, and humor women when they do the same thing.

The reason retreat crossed my mind is that I didn't think any of the woes were all that bad, comparatively. My woman troubles had them all beat. How do I have them beat, you ask? Even if you didn't, you should have. You could at least pretend you care. But don't worry about my feelings. I'll get over it. These days most people call me Murphy, but once, far too long ago, a special lady called me John. Unfortunately, the only time I hear my wife's voice these days is in my memory. My Elsie is dead. What I would not trade to have one more minute with her, to laugh, even to fight. My male compatriots did not realize how lucky they really were. They cared enough to fight and would soon make-up. One on one, I would have said something, but in a crowd this size I kept it to myself. No reason to ruin a perfectly good moaning and griping session with something really depressing.

The complaints were going round-robin style in the tradition of fish tales. Each one trying to top the others.

"Mista," Heimdal complained, "spends too much time carousing with the Valkyries."

"Madeline doesn't spend enough time with her friends. No, she saves that blessing for me," said Hermes, rolling his eyes back in his head.

"Women just want a commitment. They don't understand why I don't want one.

Unless it is the right one," said Hercules.

Ismael Macob, an Egyptian immigrant and New York cabbie, was complaining about his Missus, Mona.

"My wife complains I am never home."

"Ismael," I said. "You haven't been home in over fifteen years."

"I didn't say she wasn't right. Only that she complained."

"I can relate," chimed in Joseph, the Wandering Jew. "Hard to have a steady relationship when you can't stay in one place for any length of time."

"That's nothing," said Hard Rider. Hard was your typical looking biker, from his leather vest up past his full face bushy beard to the red bandanna tied around his head. He even wore his heart on his sleeve. Jokes his doctor missed class the day they went over transplants. Actually it was a heart shaped tattoo. The word inside the cardiac rendition was 'MOM'. Apparently she did the work herself, a gift for Hard's sixteenth birthday. It's not bad. "My lady doesn't appreciate my sensitive side. She pays more attention to her career than to me."

"Corporate vice-presidents are like that," scoffed Nero Domitian. "Speak up when you have some real problems."

"Like you have woman troubles," said Hard, sarcastically. Nero was supposed to destroy the world a while back. He was the Beast mentioned in *Revelations*. Problem was, he actually found people he cared about, including his opposite number, the Savior. He and Grace fell in love and, to make a long story short, decided to call the whole thing off. Hard had been one of Grace's twelve disciples. "Grace is perfect."

"Exactly my point. Grace is perfect in every way. Never makes a mistake, never forgets anything, never gets angry no matter how bad I screw up. Do you know how frustrating that can be?"

"Sounds rough, having someone so nice," said Edgar Tonic. He had closed his hot dog stand down for the night. "My ex-wife ran off with the mailman and millions of my dollars, leaving me heart-broken and penniless."

"Come on," said a doubting Tommy the jinn, visiting from his new home in Edgar's bun warmer. "Your pride was wounded, not your heart."

"I never claimed her leaving made me sad. It was losing the money that hurt. Just can't trust women," Edgar shot back.

"I agree with Edgar. Women can be treacherous," said Samson of biblical fame, hiding his sightless eye sockets behind darkened glass. His pony tail snaked over his right shoulder like an affectionate boa.

"That was a long time ago, Sam," Hercules said.

"Maybe, but it's hard to forget Delilah's betrayal when every time I open my eyes all I see is darkness," Samson said. He may still have tremendous strength, but it doesn't make his world a brighter place. "I didn't say I don't trust all women. I'm just very careful who I place my trust in, and I've moved beyond using physical beauty and sex as a basis for it. I guess you might say I see more clearly now," he said with a bitter chuckle.

"What I hate is when I date a woman I know exactly how everything is going to turn out," complained Mosie. Truth is he does. His sight took in four dimensions, the fourth being time. He sees so well he needs booze goggles to blur his psychic vision.

"I don't understand them at all," said Fred, our satyr busboy. "My father made it sound so easy." Fred's father was Pan. Fred had been desperately trying to follow in his father's lecherous footsteps, to be crude, lewd, and rude, but it was an effort. He was just too nice. Women wanted to pick him up, hug him; horns, hairy legs, and all. Problem was, that was all they wanted. That and to be friends. Real friends. Fred had been sent out into the world a bit younger than most satyrs and less able for lechery. His body was years away from being able to produce the pheromones that would drive his lady friends wild. It was simply making Fred crazy. Thoughts contemplating the possibility that sex is something you only do with someone you love have crossed his mind and lingered. A possible first for a satyr, and a considerable source of personal embarrassment and fear. What would his father say if he found out?

To worsen the situation, Fred thought he was in the big "L". Love. He could not bring himself to use the word yet. "Toni won't even give me a tumble, no matter what I try." Toni was our waitress and the object of Fred's affections. Her location was in the nosebleed section, hiding out with Demeter and the female contingency. Toni was hiding for two. She was with child. Pregnant, it was quite impossible for her to be without child, at least for a few more months. Let's say no father is in the picture and Fred found himself more than willing to smile in the family portrait. As his emotions for Toni got stronger, his attractions for other woman were lessening, though far from gone. Toni cared about him too, but had gone through some major traumas recently and was not ready to be in a romantic relationship right now.

"Try what you heart tells you to do. It is all you can do," suggested Dionysus. Dion has a way with the women that makes Casanova look like an amateur.

"C'mon," said Rumbles. Rumbles was a long–time regular who in his working hours holds the honorable position of clown. He claims to have held several other positions, but being a gentleman, refuses to elaborate. The only time I've seen him out of makeup and costume was Peter's funeral. Otherwise, I'd think he had the grease-paint tattooed on his face and didn't want to tell anyone. White face decorated deep brown skin broken only by a blackened right eye. Two giant boxing gloves followed his hands very closely, so much so that his left hand had begun to suspect his right hand did not know what it was doing and had hired some professional help to find out. A gentle soul, he used an act of belligerence to entertain the masses. "Dion, with all your women, you have to have some system."

"The only system I have is what I said. That, honesty and love," answered Dion, sitting back and patting his ample middle. "That and being built for comfort instead of speed. Gives the ladies that much more to love."

"Have you been in love, Dion?" asked Roy G. Biv, Rumbles' clown compatriot. Roy had upgraded his self–customized wheelchair, 'Laughter's Chariot', so he could either push it or drive using an installed motor.

"Many times. Sometimes even many times a night," answered Dion with a glowing smile that could melt a heart of ice easier that a thermonuclear blast could liquefy a snowball.

"That's not the kind of in love I mean. I mean the kind in all capital letters, the kind of love that sets your soul on fire," asked Roy, his enthusiasm betraying his soul's inner need to find just that.

"Not in a very long time," said Dion sadly. "How about you, Roy?"

"Not yet. I'm waiting."

"You are young yet kid. You got plenty of time," said Rumbles.

"You ever been in love, Rumbles?" asked Ismael.

"Yes. Twice, or so I thought at the time. Looking back on it I'm not so sure."

"What about this true love stuff?" asked Fred.

"No such animal," said Dion.

"I certainly don't believe in it," said Samson.

"I do," said Hard Rider. "Never had it, maybe never will, but I believe in it."

"I don't believe," I said.

"Murphy? You a nonbeliever?" asked a shocked Dion.

"The opposite. I don't need to believe it. I know. I was lucky enough to experience it," I said. I knew if the boss was here, Paddy would agree with me. Mathew chimed in before I could get too melancholy.

"I, too, know it," said Mathew.

"But just a few minutes ago you were complaining about the fight the two of you had tonight," said Samson.

"I didn't say we were without our problems. Ryth is a demoness from the pits of Hell. I am an angel from Paradise. We are going to overcome our share of obstacles. True love is hard work. Only the lust comes easy. The point is, you do it together. The person you love completes you, makes you a whole person."

A lot of heads nodded agreement. The mood was softening.

"What is wrong with lust?" asked Fred.

"Nothing," answered Dion, the rest of us mere students at the master's feet. "Just how you approach it makes it right or wrong."

"What if you can't do anything about it?" asked Fred.

Our bouncer, Hercules, hero of legends (many of them his own) spoke up. "You can always do something about it, Fred."

"Really?"

"Absolutely," said Hercules. "I remember the first time I had sex. I was very scared."

"You were?" asked Fred, having a difficult time picturing the pillar of strength that sat before him frightened of anything.

"Absolutely. There I was, all by myself..."

"Ah, c'mon," shouted an annoyed Fred over the laughs of the rest of us.

"That reminds me of the first time I had a ménage à trois."

"What's that?" asked Fred.

"Sex with two other people," answered Dion.

"Really? You, Murphy?" said Fred, eyes wide with wonder and awe.

"Don't act so shocked. It happens more often than you think. I was a teenager then. I remember it well. My parents had gone out for the night. I had the entire house at my disposal. The lights were low, the music was soft and romantic. It was just me and two hand puppets," I said. Fred's face turned beet red at the good–natured jibes and laughter at his falling for that one.

"What about sex with someone else. A female someone. I have no experience yet," Fred admitted, a major act of courage and trust.

"Don't feel bad. Plenty of guys are inexperienced," said Hard Rider.

"Any of you guys?"

We all exchanged looks. It was not the type of crowd where you had to act macho and brag.

"Can't say I am," said Dion. He was not boasting, just stating fact.

"That goes without saying. As an infant, you made a pass at your nanny," said Hermes. "Damn youngster beat me to it."

"I was untouched by a female until I met Ryth. I was ages older than you and still virgin," said Mathew.

"I haven't been with a woman in a long time," said Tommy. "I don't get out much and living in a bottle for so many years wasn't a good way to meet women. The bun warmer is working out better in that respect."

"What about you Judah?" asked Heimdal.

Judah Maccabee was the strong, silent type. Golems are like that. He was not built with a working voice, but he's fluent in many forms of sign language. Most of us know enough to get by. Dion translated for those less versed.

"I have known woman," he signed.

"Rebecca?" asked Nero. Judah often stayed with Rebecca on the streets..

"No!" he signed, quickly snapping his index and middle fingers down on his thumb, embarrassed. "I have known Rebecca since she was a child. I do not think of her that way."

"Wait," I asked, signing as I spoke. Judah heard fine but I needed the practice. "How is that possible?"

"I was shaped in the form of a man. In every respect."

"You mean they did not bother to give you a voice box but made you anatomically correct?" I asked.

"It is all a matter of priorities, Murphy. I too remember my first time. It was with a Venus De Milo look–alike," Judah signed.

"The Venus De Milo is a statue," said Joseph, confused.

"So was Edith," signed Judah, the hint of a smile creeping up on his mouth. With a face of clay, the journey took a long time.

"But that is so wrong," said Dion.

"Why?" signed Judah.

"Haven't you ever heard of statutory rape?" asked Dion

"Cute, but not appropriate. She consented fully."

"How was it?" asked Hermes.

"A beautiful experience but the aftermath was messy."

"What do you mean?" said Heimdal.

"I never heard from her again. She never called. She never wrote. She had a heart of stone. I felt so cheap and used," Judah signed, his grin reaching from ear to ear, his head bobbing in silent laughter. Those of us more skilled in the art of noise joined him in his mirth.

Meanwhile, the front door opened. It was something it was very good at. After all, it had been doing it for years. Did it with skill and grace, obviously taking great pride in its work, not even making a squeak. Probably did not want to break the mood. In walked Lucas Wilson. Walking was something Lucas was quite skilled at as well. Next to him crawled in a nude man on all fours. The man acted as if it was a natural state, but his awkward limbs seemed to betray him. Lucas, ever the gentleman, took off his black trenchcoat and covered his companion, who gratefully took the garment and stood slowly. While not a fluid movement, he exhibited only a mild strain and did not stumble. He did what he set out to do, so while he scored poorly on technique, on substance he fared better. Overall a score of 6.0.

"Is it sunrise already?" he asked, dazed.

"No. Not yet," answered Lucas.

"Then how can I be standing upright?" he asked, shocked.

"Went on a bit of a bender, huh?" I asked. It happens. Life gets a bit much. People try to drown their sorrows in drink. Heck, I have done it myself a few times, just not much since I found Bulfinche's. Most of the regulars are the same way. We don't have many drunks, other than Mosie.

"No. I haven't had a drink all night."

"Then what's going on? You getting into some kinky stuff in your young age, Lucas?" I asked.

"Nothing like that, Murphy. My love life is still rather tame," Lucas replied with a sad grin. "This gentleman was heading this way when I happened upon him. He was about to get into more trouble than he could handle, so I helped him out a bit."

"I remember following the rainbow. It was shooting down from the moon. I took special notice of it because when I am like that I can't usually see in color," the man said. "But how did you do it? When I get like that I'm not exactly easy to control."

"Easy. I have powers and abilities far beyond those of most mortals. I am a vampyre."

The man took the revelation in stride, not doubting a word. He obviously had experienced some weirdness of his own. Even in Manhattan a naked man crawling down the streets on all fours would stand out, except maybe in parts of the Village.

Turning to me, he asked "Why did you ask him about the kinky stuff?"

"I will defer that. Lucas?"

"You could tell him Murph. It is not something I am ashamed of. Got over that by the end of college. I'm gay."

"Oh," said the man now giving him a subtle double take. Obviously a bit uncomfortable, he pulled the coat closed around himself.

"Don't worry. You're not my type. Too hairy," Lucas said. The man laughed, but the rest of us didn't get the joke, as the man wasn't exceptionally furry.

"Can we get you something?" asked Dion.

"Afraid I am all tapped out. No pockets, no cash."

"No problem. First drink is on the house," I said.

"Great. Then I'll have a large coffee, black, two sugars."

"Coming up," I said.

"What's your name?" asked Dion.

"Ted. Ted Brand."

Dion introduced himself and wrapped up acquainting Ted with the rest of those present. We would worry about the unaccounted for later.

"So how did you end up unclad and quadruped on our doorstep?" asked Hercules.

"It's a long story," Ted said with a weary sigh. The exhalation implied he need not even bother telling it because we would not believe a word.

"The good ones always are," Hercules replied. He should know. He is the best story teller I have ever met. Once he kept a dozen people enthralled for six hours telling a tale about the first time he went roller blading. Personally, I found it difficult to believe he actually bladed down the support beams of the 59th Street Bridge blindfolded, but the video Hermes took doesn't lie.

Ted hesitated, looked around at the bunch of us. He had our undivided attention, but it was not an intense focus. Our manner told him he was welcome to tell his tale or simply belly up to the bar. We might prod, but never pester. He steeled himself with a sip of warm java and decided to give us a try. He could always lie later and say he was drunk. "I've, quite simply, lost control of my life. What's worse, I think I have fallen in love," Ted said.

The crowd all moaned agreement. Here was something they could all relate to.

"You aren't alone. Love troubles seem to be in the air tonight. Probably the full moon. Makes people crazy," said Ismael.

"That is exactly what is causing my trouble. The moon," said Ted.

"I never bought any of that crap, about heavenly bodies affecting our destiny. Of course, the more feminine heavenly body can easily affect one's judgment," said Hard.

"It's true, I assure you. Especially in my case," said Ted.

"Tell us about your lady," said Rumbles.

Ted hesitated before describing her. "Her name is Shan. She is unique, different than anyone else I have known. I never would have imagined a romance with her in my wildest dreams. To be honest, I am embarrassed by the whole thing. I can only see her at certain times and I can be with her even less."

"Why? Does she live far away?" asked Tommy.

"No. Just up in the Bronx."

"Then what's the problem?" asked Joseph.

"I got her into trouble with her family. I got her pregnant."

"That does add a twist to the picture," said Dion. "Does her family know?"

"Yes. She had the twins three weeks ago."

"Have you seen them?" asked Roy.

"Only from a distance."

"Why?" I asked.

"The zookeepers mainly."

"Her family are zookeepers?" asked Fred.

"No. She lives in the Bronx Zoo."

"They have apartments there?" I asked, confused.

"No."

"But she lives there?"

"Yes."

"What is she then?" asked Fred, his curiosity piqued.

"I guess you would call her a bitch."

"I certainly would not. That is no way to talk about the mother of your children! You should marry her, not insult her," Fred shouted.

"Impossible to marry her. No institution would recognize our union."

"You should try anyway," said Fred.

"Sometimes love just is not enough. Worse, I fear her family may try to kill the twins because they are different."

"Then why aren't you doing anything about it?"

"I was heading toward the Bronx, but the number six line wasn't running because of a fire on the tracks."

"You should have ran on foot then," said Fred.

"I was doing that when I ran into the trouble Lucas had to get me out of. Damned animal control people."

"But..." argued Fred.

"Easy, Fred," said Dion. Turning to Ted he said "I take it your lady love isn't human, then."

"Not exactly. Actually not at all. She's a wolf."

"You had sex with a wolf?" asked a shocked, but strangely interested, Fred.

"Yes. But I wasn't myself at the time."

"Who were you?"

"More like what. Changes come over me. A poet might say Diana rises high in the night sky, riding her chariot, calling out her siren song to me, or a vast silver sphere ascending into a black tapestry takes control of my mind. I wouldn't be able to describe a full moonrise myself except from memory. Haven't seen one for months. At least not though human eyes. On the nights when the moon is ful,l I see with the eyes of a wolf. A werewolf," Ted said, walking to the window and looking up into the sky at the moon. "But perhaps now I am cured."

"Not exactly," I said. "Being in Bulfinche's cancels out curses and powers."

Ted took in the implications instantly. "So I could spend the three nights a month when the moon is full here and stay human?"

"If you wish," answered Dion. "But why are you worried about your offspring?"

"What if they have my affliction but in reverse? What if they turn into human infants when the moon is full? Sure, there are legends of wolves raising human children, but would it happen for real? The wolves in Shan's pack did not take well to me. They could sense that I was different from them. I was tolerated simply because I was larger than their alpha male and defeated him in combat."

"You killed him?" asked Fred.

"No, nothing so barbaric. When wolves fight, the loser merely needs to surrender. No kill is made then. I chose not to assume leadership of the pack. I simply claimed a willing Shan as my mate."

"That is beautiful," said Fred

"That also explains how Lucas was able to guide you here," I said.

"Not necessarily. I have hypnotic control over people, too. My control over vermin is greater," said Lucas.

"Vermin?" Ted asked indignantly.

"I didn't make the rules or coin the term. Rats, bats, and wolves, and their close relations, are all subject to my control. No offense meant."

"None taken, I guess," Ted said.

"How did you become a werewolf?" asked Edgar.

"I don't know. I started getting horrible migraine headaches three nights a month. I tried drinking, medicine. Nothing worked. Worse, I kept losing nights. I would wake up naked in my bed, not remembering taking my clothes off. Then one morning I woke up naked in a cage at the animal shelter. They thought I was some sort of animal rights kook and gave me clothes before throwing me out on the street. After that, I started remembering my nights. Lucas saved me tonight from being caught by the dogcatcher a second time. I was heading toward the zoo when the rainbow caught my eye. I was overwhelmed by an urge to follow it. And with Lucas' help, here I am. But Shan is still there with our children. If I step out the door I will lose my humanity and much of my intellect. I may not be able to get there."

Playing devil's advocate despite having given up the job, Nero asked, "Can you forget about her and leave her and the pups to their fate?"

"No. I am now part wolf, and by nature, wolves mate for life. Even human, my feelings for her are true."

"Do you love her?" asked Samson.

"Yes," answered Ted.

"Then the matter is settled. I'll go to the Bronx Zoo with you and we will save your children. Anybody else with us?" asked Samson, rising to his feet.

Everyone chorused in the affirmatory.

"I'll keep an eye on the place," said Dion.

"Problem is, how do we all get there?" I asked.

"I can take someone on my bike," said Hard.

"I can squeeze six in my cab," said Ismael.

"That still leaves nine of us," I said.

"If we had the clown car from work al,l of us would fit in it," said Roy.

"Of course, we couldn't move over 15 MPH, and would leave a cloud of smoke in our wake," added Rumbles.

Others had ideas of their own. Hermes smiled, a glint in his eyes. Trouble was brewing when he got that look. "I have the perfect solution. We take Baby."

"Oh no!" shouted Dion, throwing his hands over his ears. "I don't want to hear this." Baby was originally a 1930 V-16 Cadillac Paddy used to run booze during prohibition. At the time, it was bulletproof and could do 120 MPH. Since then, Vulcan has modified it so it is the fastest thing on the road and has more accessories than a

Swiss army knife. It still has most of the original body and paint. Paddy is overly possessive of it. It's his pride and joy. As Baby has gotten older, Paddy declared nobody else is allowed to drive it but him. Hermes has been trying to get back behind the wheel for years with no luck.

"Baby will fit the rest of us easy," Hermes said.

"Fit is the right word for what Paddy will have when he finds out," Dion said.

"Who says he needs to find out?" asked Hermes.

"You may be good but nobody is that good," said Dion.

"Fifty bucks says I am."

"You're on."

"You can't tell him."

"No problem."

"Hercules, Murphy, you are with me." said Hermes, pulling on his gray trenchcoat and straightening his baseball cap.

"Hey, how did I get dragged into this?" I asked.

"We are doing this for love. How can you not help?"

"Details. How are you going to get past Cerberus?" I asked. Like I mentioned, Paddy is very protective of Baby. He has an incredible security system on it. That is not enough for his peace of mind; he borders on the paranoid sometimes. Attached to the bar is a parking garage. First level doubles as a homeless shelter during the night. The upper levels are used for parking for the regulars and storage. The lower levels are another matter. The bar was bought and paid for with leprechaun gold, and has taken on many supernatural properties for that and other reasons. It acts as a foci or nexus. People in trouble are drawn to us by a rainbow much like Ted. Bulfinche's also allows folks from other realms and bygone realities to exist and sometimes even to cross over to our world. The lower levels literally lead to other realms. The Sidhe, where Paddy's people live, can be reached from here. So can many realms of the dead, including Hades, which is ruled by Pluto.

Pluto, as I've mentioned, also happens to be Demeter's son-in-law, a situation neither of them is happy with. By long standing agreement, Persephone, the wife and daughter, spends almost half the year with her Mom. Pluto gets lonely and comes up to the bar to spend time with his missus. During one such visit he had put up Cerberus, the three–headed hound of Hades, as collateral in a poker game. He lost big time to Paddy, so Cerberus now belongs to the boss. Paddy has security systems that prevent people from going either way into the garage, but sometimes even the best security systems prove inadequate. That's where Cerberus comes in. He sort of protects Faerie and the other realms from mankind and vice versa. Pluto has to call ahead so he can actually get through.

Paddy actually visits him almost every day. Brings him food and plays the harmonica for Cerberus. The pooch loves it. No one ever showed him any kindness before, or for that matter, fed him on a regular basis. He would die or kill for Paddy. He guards Baby very intensely. I had no clue how we were going to get past him.

We headed down the ramp, Hermes deactivating each alarm as we went. Minutes later, we were in sight of the hellhound and the Caddy.

"What now?" I asked. "Going to have Hercules wrestle him while we grab Baby?"

"I've done it before," Hercules said.

"Yes, but the first time he got away from you. You chased him down and didn't catch up with him until he was in Eurystheus' throne room. You barely stopped him from killing the guy."

"But he thought I did it on purpose. The look on his face was priceless," Hercules chuckled.

"Don't worry. We shouldn't have to resort to violence," Hermes assured us. "I hope," he whispered under his breath.

I have met Cerberus before, but always with Paddy. Around the old man, the tri-headed mutt was a sweetheart. We were approaching without him and a friendly continence turned into a deep–throated growl that filled the air thicker than the smog on a bad morning.

Hermes he would let pass into the underworld and anyone with him. Part of his duties. Problem was, we were not headed to Hades. I stopped short.

"What is the matter, Murphy? Frightened?" asked Hermes.

"What, me frightened by a three–headed hellhound that is bigger than a mini-van, with jaws that could take off an arm with a single nip? Why would I be scared? Terrified is more akin to what I should be."

"Don't let fear overtake you, Murph," advised Hercules. "Animals can smell fear."

Cerberus chose that moment to lunge forward, almost ripping his chain out of the wall.

"That isn't fear he smells, Herc. I think I may have soiled myself."

"C'mon, Murphy. You are made of sterner stuff than that. What is the plan, Hermes?"

"One that has worked time and time again on the guardian of the underworld," Hermes said, pulling a flute from beneath his gray trenchcoat. "Music hath charms to soothe the savage beast." Hermes moved closer and made ready to play.

"Hermes, I have a suggestion that may help you," I said.

"Murphy, please. I have done this a dozen times. I don't need any advice," Hermes boasted. Hermes had the biggest ego of anyone I've ever met. Problem was, most of it was justified. That is probably why I enjoy his screw-ups so much. Cerberus tip-toed forward, making as if he was getting ready to listen. When he was close enough, his center head grabbed hold of the end of the flute, yanking it out of Hermes' hands.

"True, you may have done this before, but have you done it since Paddy length-ened his chain? If you had taken the time to listen to me, I would have suggested that you step back. But in your wisdom you of course knew that, didn't you? Just wanted the dog to have a musical instrument of his own," I asked. Hermes was beginning to turn red from embarrassment. Hercules was speeding the blush to his cheeks with his uproarious laughter. Cerberus meanwhile seemed to be trying desperately to play the flute, with as much success as a duck taking to lava.

"We could go back and get another instrument," Hermes suggested. He played over two hundred of them expertly.

"Or I could take a hand in matters," offered Herc, tightening the belt on his lion skin trenchcoat.

"Or you two could leave it to me. We are short on time," I suggested.

"You?" asked Hermes, with his eyebrows raised high enough to rival a penthouse elevator.

More encouraging, Herc said, "Go for it Murphy."

I walked up to the imaginary line where Cerberus had to stop. Standing tall I held out my hand, palm up, like Paddy had shown me. Cerberus' growl grew silent as he sniffed, perhaps aided by the scent of my own personal fertilizer.

"Hi ya, fella. Remember me?" I asked. Cerberus' center head licked my hand in response. I scratched it behind the ears. Each of the remaining pair of heads demanded and received equal treatment.

"Great. Maybe he will pet him to sleep?" scoffed Hermes.

"Hush. You are just jealous Murph is showing you up," said Herc.

I had some words of my own to say.

"Cerberus, I know Paddy told you to guard Baby, but we need the car, and Paddy isn't here." Cerberus took a step back and growled. "I know. You don't want to make him angry. I don't either, but we need to get to the Bronx to try to save a pair of children. Wolf cubs. Their father has reason to believe they may be in danger. You wouldn't want babies to die, would you?"

"By Bulfinche's taps! I think Murphy is getting through," whispered Herc.

"Paddy, if he were here, would be at the front of us in an effort to save them. You know that," Cerberus' three heads seemed to nod in agreement. "Hermes felt the best way to get the lot of us there would be to take Baby. He will safeguard it."

"What!?" exclaimed Hermes.

"I am sure he will swear to keep it safe. On the Styx."

"Wait a second. We are almost right over that river."

"Go on," said Herc. "You better keep it safe, oath or no oath."

"Very well. I swear on the River Styx to keep Baby safe from all harm until I bring her back."

"And on Bulfinche's grave," Herc demanded. The Styx oath, centuries old, still carries a lot of weight, but the second oath was closer to home. Bulfinche was Paddy's wife and Hermes or Hercules would die before defaming her memory.

"Very well. I also swear on the grave of Beatrice Gerald Bulfinche Moran that I will keep Baby safe and return it when our task is done."

Cerberus laid down on his stomach and allowed Hermes to pass, staring him down with all three sets of eyes the whole while. Baby started up on the first try. Hermes drove clear and Hercules climbed in. Before doing the same, I turned to Cerberus and said, "Thank you." Again, he nodded thrice.

"Excellent job, Murphy," congratulated Hercules.

"Yes. You did good. Even impressed me," said Hermes.

"Thanks. Hermes, I just thought of something. Couldn't you just race ahead and bring the cubs back in a matter of minutes?"

"Sure, but this way is more fun. Remember, Murphy, do it with style or not at all," Hermes answered.

Reaching the entrance of the parking garage, we found the others waiting. It looked like a trenchcoat convention. Ismael had already loaded up his cab with Judah, Samson, Nero, Mathew, Joseph, and Tommy, who was in a wine bottle held by Edgar. Tommy still had a fear of open spaces. Years of living in a bottle will do that to you. Hard Rider had Fred on the back of his bike. He and Roy had jury rigged a tow cord so he could pull Roy's wheelchair behind him. I asked Roy if that was a good idea.

"Not to worry, Murphy. I modified Laughter's Chariot myself. In addition to its clown gimmicks, the wheelchair is part dirtbike. Can do up to forty on its own. Problem is, the gas tank only holds five gallons and I forgot to fill up today. This way will be better. Trust me. I will even wear my helmet." His helmet was metallic orange with a pinwheel in the front, a propeller on top between two antenna.

The rest of the gang piled into Baby, including Ted who had transformed back into wolf form outside of the protection of the bar. Lucas used his vampyric abilities to keep him calm and focused. Hermes insisted Mosie sit in front as clairvoyant co-navigator to make sure nothing happened to Baby.

The lot of us convoyed onto the FDR Drive and cut across onto Ward's Island and over the Triborough Bridge. They tried to stop Roy from going through, even under his own steam. Probably thought he was trying to escape from the Manhattan Psychiatric Center located on the island. But Roy is not one to be out done. I mean he dresses as a clown wherever he goes.

"I'm sorry, sir. I can't allow you on the bridge. That is not a registered motor vehicle."

"Why don't you admit the real reason," asked Roy.

"What do you mean?"

"I offered you the toll. You won't let me on the bridge because of prejudice. Because I am handicapped and a minority. A paraplegic clown. I will have you know that I am the president of the N.A.O.P.C."

"The what?"

"The National Association Of Paraplegic Clowns, and let me assure you that your actions may be opening up the city to a slew of lawsuits. Not only are you violating the Civil Rights Act, but also the Americans With Disabilities Act."

The toll collector was left speechless and meekly accepted the token, letting Roy pass. The rest of the trip was uneventful. Problem was, when we got to the zoo gates, they were closed.

"It'll be easier to go over and proceed on foot," said Hermes.

"Easy for you to say. You can fly over," I grumbled, looking at the twenty–foot–high fence.

"I told you that you should work out more often," joked Hercules.

"Will you watch Baby?" asked Hermes, scanning the neighborhood, slightly worried.

"And my cab?" asked Ismael.

"And my hog?" requested Hard.

"Of course," answered Herc. "Just get moving. Hermes, you go on ahead and protect those pups."

"Two human babies nursing at a she-wolf. What could possibly come of that?" Hermes asked sarcastically.

"Ask Romulus and Remus," Herc answered, as Hermes vanished into the sky toward the wolf habitat.

"I think I'll join him," said Mathew, taking to the air. Squinting, one could make out the luminance of angel wings carrying him aloft. It was a strain and a risk for him to fly. He betrayed Heaven to love Ryth, his wife. His abilities were limited now as a result of this decision to leave Heaven for Ryth. They were still looking for him. He wore the amulet that Demeter fashioned to hide him, but nothing is foolproof.

"Last one over buys a round when we get back," challenged Lucas moments before transforming into a bat and flying over the top. The lupine Ted squeezed through the bars. Fred tried the same and got stuck halfway through. Heimdal got a running start and leaped up and over the fence. Hard, not wanting to be left behind, started climbing. Edgar handed Tommy's bottle through the bars to Lucas. Nero had also gotten to the other side, but I didn't see how.

Roy headed up the wheelchair ramp. "Nobody ever locks handicapped entrances," he said. Unfortunately, the Bronx Zoo apparently does. Luckily, Judah was behind him and gave the gate a good shove. It creaked open allowing Roy, Rumbles, Edgar, Judah, and myself to pass.

Samson had taking pity on Fred's plight and pulled the iron bars apart so Fred could squirm free until the opening was wide enough for both him and Joseph, as well as Ismael to pass.

The only one still on the outside was Mosie.

"Guess drinks are on you," said Lucas.

"It will be worth it," Mosie replied.

"C'mon. There are two ways for you to get in," I said.

"More than that, Murphy," Mosie said, pulling on the main front gate. It opened at his touch and he walked in.

Hard was panting and breathing heavy after his climb. "Don't you think you could have mentioned that earlier?" Mosie shrugged his shoulders and smiled.

Not knowing where we were headed exactly, we followed behind Ted, who was trotting. Each of us jogging to keep up. Trenchcoats were flapping in the wind.

We reached the wolf exhibit. The Bronx Zoo tries to keep its charges in exhibits as close to nature as possible whenever possible, so we had another fence to circumvent, which was done in short order. Roy stayed behind to keep lookout.

"Anyone see Hermes or Mathew?" I asked.

"I don't," said Samson. "Of course, I may not be the right person to be asking," he said weaving his cane to and fro in order the navigate the fields.

"No sign of either," said Rumbles.

"I'm going to shift into wolf form," said Lucas. Between Ted and I we should find them quickly." Ted yipped in agreement. They ran out to search, leaving the rest of us to our devices, which might have worked if someone had thought to bring batteries for the flashlight. We split into two groups to cover more ground. I was with

Edgar, the bottled Tommy, Mosie, Fred, and Judah. The rest went with Joseph.

After a minute we heard the howls.

"They've caught our scent. They know we're here," said Mosie.

"You know, this seemed like a good idea a while ago, but now I'm questioning the wisdom of invading wolf territory," I said. Edgar nodded agreement. The rest of the group didn't seemed worried.

Mosie walked over to a tree and said, "I suggest the lot of you start climbing."

Knowing better than to question a psychic's recommendations, I moved toward a tree. Joseph, Fred, and Mosie were already halfway up when Edgar started. Still five feet away I heard Mosie say, "Murph, freeze. Don't move for a moment. Now turn around. Slowly."

I did and, with only a slight downward tilt of my head, was face to face with a pair of fur-lined, lupine faces not twenty-five feet away. I knew that running would only encourage them to give chase, and that was one gift best left ungiven.

"Oboy. Anybody up for a game of fetch?" I asked.

A low flying bat answered me. "Sure. What do you want me to throw? Please don't get any slobber on it," Lucas suggested.

"Go away, Lucas. I am a bit busy here."

"Yes. The ladies seem to be very interested in why you are here."

"Ladies, you say? Hum a song for me, will you? Now I have to decide which to ask first," I said. Turning to the larger of the two, I asked, "Madame, would you like to tango?"

"What are you doing?" asked Edgar.

"Why dancing with wolves, of course."

The larger she wolf did not find my joke amusing and growled to prove it.

"You can lead, if you want. Doesn't even have to be a close dance. On opposite sides of the zoo would be fine," I said. The smaller furball started growling as well.

"Murphy, stop smiling at them," said Joseph.

"Why?" I asked.

"Baring teeth is considered a sign of aggression."

"Oops. Lucas, do you think you could do that control over vermin thing here?"

"I'm trying."

"Very."

Judah was slowly advancing toward me in a manner so as not to scare the wolf into attacking. The smaller wolf, bored with me, went to sniff around the base of Edgar's tree. While trying to climb even higher he dropped the bottle Tommy was traveling in. It hit the ground with a thud.

"Hey!" Tommy shouted.

Meanwhile, the larger continued to advance toward me.

"Murphy, take a dive," ordered Mosie.

"I wasn't planning on fighting, let alone winning," but I understood the suggestion. Slowly I lay down on my back, in a position of submission and surrender. If a wolf does this another wolf will not press the attack. Question was, how would she react to a bartender doing it?

The she wolf approached slowly. Judah closed the distance as well. She came right up to me, sniffing all the while. She must have liked my aftershave because she licked my face.

"It's okay, Murphy," Lucas said. "You can get up. I have her under control."

"About time," I said. I noticed the smaller wolf was sniffing and licking Tommy's transport bottle.

"Get away!" shouted Tommy. The wolf pulled back, looked inquisitive, and resumed sniffing.

"How about Tommy?" I asked Lucas.

"Don't worry about me, Murph," Tommy said. "Just watch this." Tommy materialized outside of his bottle just long enough to say "Boo!" The wolf backed off with her tail between her legs.

"Got them both," Lucas said, transforming from bat to wolf in mid–landing. "We found the kids. Ted was right. They inherited his curse. Both are human infants for the duration of the full moon. Ted stayed with his family. The mother seemed very perplexed by the whole situation. Hermes and Mathew are waiting with them. I already found the others. They're on their way."

So were we. We found the den, mostly by following the sounds of infants crying. It was quite crowded outside where the werehumans were playing. One was a boy, the other a girl. They seemed to be at about the size of a six– month–old. Ted was nuzzling each of them, as any loving father would, given the circumstances.

Suddenly, with our fronts to a man-made wall, we found ourselves surrounded by the rest of the pack.

"It turns out that although Ted was right about the young ones shape–shifting, he was wrong about the immediate danger. The wolves view the man cubs as members of their pack and us as invaders," said Mathew. "They have no intentions of letting us take them."

"But even if they mean them no harm, that doesn't mean they couldn't get hurt. Neither can stand, let alone walk. Accidents happen," said Joseph.

"We need to protect them, for the time being," said Rumbles. "Maybe we will find a way around the curse. Until then they will be safer with us." Ted barked agreement.

"How do we convince them?" I asked pointing to the wolves who had encircled us.

"Let me try to reason with them," suggested Lucas. Still a vampyre in wolf's clothing he closed his eyes in concentration, sending mental images of the possible danger the cubs were in and our honorable intentions. The wolves fell silent, each turning to the largest gray male, the leader of the pack. Solemnly, the leader backed up and turned aside, head bowed. "They agree. But first they want to say goodbye."

Each of the wolves nuzzled the baby boy and girl, then turned to the mother, Shan, and did the same.

"Why are they saying goodbye to Shan?" asked Fred.

"You can't expect the children to go without their mother, can you?" asked Mathew.

"I guess not," answered Fred. "Why not take all of them?"

"The others may tolerate Ted, but they do not accept him. It is better this way." Mathew answered.

The wolves escorted us out of their territory and we left their enclosure. Mathew carried the infants while Lucas led Shan and Ted. The sorrow of the pack was deep as they said then what might be a final goodbye, in the manner of their race, in the tradition of time. Howling into the night, they sang to us of their anguish and pain at having to lose members of their pack and family. The beauty of the wolfsong lasted several minutes, bringing tears to our eyes.

After hooking back up with Roy, we walked toward the exit when the sounds of humans approaching caught our attention.

"Security guards," announced Rumbles.

"Let's move it, people," ordered Heimdal. "No reason to have to explain this. We may need a diversion. I'll handle it."

"No, let me," said Samson, smiling.

"You sure?" asked Heimdal.

"Yep," said Samson, beating his cane loudly against the pavement, headed in the opposite direction.

The rest of us got back to the vehicles with no problems, choosing to use the gate this time. Herc was leaning against Ismael's cab, whistling and cleaning his nails.

"Everything go well?" Herc asked.

"Well enough," I answered. As I climbed into Baby, I paused to look up and saw six large, teenage men hanging high up in branches. "Interesting trees they have in these parts. What kind of fruit are they?" I said to Herc.

"Bad apples. Tried to steal a few parts off Baby. I showed them the error of their ways by getting to the core of their problem. Never been punished before."

"Easy as pie, you might say."

"You might, if you were being saucy."

Meanwhile, the two security guards had picked up Samson's obvious trail, soon catching up with him.

"Excuse me sir," one said. "The zoo is closed. What are you doing here?"

"What do you mean zoo? This is Southern Boulevard. I know. I counted the steps," Samson insisted.

"Maybe it's too dark for you to see, but you are a long ways off Southern Boulevard."

"I wouldn't know how dark it is. I'm blind, you see. Or I assume you do at least." As Samson spoke he flicked his cane, knocking the pairs' flashlights out of their hands.

"Those were our flashlights, Mister," growled one guard.

"Easy, the guy is blind," said the other guard, whispering as if Samson could not hear him. "I am sorry," he said, speaking louder to Samson.

"So am I."

"What are you doing here?"

"Selling pencils," he said, holding up a cup he had fished out of the trash. "Would you gentlemen like to buy one?"

"There are no pencils in your cup."

"What!? I've been robbed! Help, police!"

"We are the police."

"Sort of."

"Help, I've been robbed by the police!"

"Easy sir. We didn't rob you."

But Samson kept screaming, "Help! Help!" and maneuvering so the guards could not get a hand on him.

"Sir, did you have a dog?"

"A dog? You found my dog? Lucas, is that you?"

"Of course it's me. Easy on the over–acting. Even this pair doesn't look that stupid. We are loaded up and ready to go."

"Excuse me, sir. Did your dog just talk?"

"What? Oh sure. Speak for the man, Lucas."

"Woof," went Lucas.

"Woof?" asked the guard.

"What else would a dog say?" asked Samson.

"More of a bark," suggested the other guard.

"Bow wow?" tried Lucas.

"You sure he can talk?"

"Absolutely. Let me prove it. Okay Lucas, what's on the top of a house?"

"I hate that joke. I won't do it," said Lucas.

At that, a honking noise was heard in the distance. It rapidly got louder and louder until Laughter's Chariot, with Roy at the helm, blew by the two bewildered guards, bumping into Samson so that he landed sitting on Roy's lap. Lucas went to bat mode and took wing as Roy sped himself and Samson to the rest of us.

As far as we know, the guards denied ever seeing a thing, even when the mother wolf and cubs were noticed to be missing.

We took the long way home. Hermes got Baby back unscathed and returned it to Cerberus' care. Paddy actually did find out we borrowed Baby, but since it was for a good cause and no damage was done, he continued to let Hermes think he had pulled one over on him. That, and the satisfaction the boss got by watching Dion lose the bet to Hermes, ensured Paddy's silence. Paddy also made the lot of us hit our heads by asking why didn't we just have Tommy wish the kids to safety. With everything happening so fast we honestly didn't think of it.

Once inside the bar, Mosie did buy the first round, including a bowl of water for Shan and two saucers of milk for the pups who had reverted to wolf form. We found out the girl was named Waff and the boy Nal. They were very friendly and intelligent. Ted, despite being human again, had a bond with his family that transcended species. He was a proud papa.

Paddy owns some land in upstate New York. Actually, he owns almost the whole county. He fenced off about one hundred and forty acres for Shan and her family to be relocated. He also rented a house on the grounds to Ted to live in. It's a two hour commute for him to work, but he does not complain. He is with his wife and kids. Yes, Shan and Ted were married the next cycle when the moon was full. Paddy officiated the unusual wedding. He figured if a ship's captain can marry folk, then why not the owner of a bar? I think Ted said it best: "You spend your whole life searching for that special someone. Some people never find their soulmate. I was lucky. I have. Shan makes me feel complete, happy. I want to spend the rest of my life with her and my kids."

Hopefully he will. They had a beautiful ceremony. Ted was given dispensation to be in wolf form. The kids weren't so they too could be in their fuzzy state. The entire wedding party was nude and fur covered, except for the bow tie Ted insisted on wearing as a collar. The wedding pictures are truly unique. The vows were more spiritual than verbal, but Lucas translated the images as best he could. At the close, we all joined the happy couple in howls of joy to celebrate their new lives together.

Now, for at least three nights every month, Ted loads the family into the mini van and brings them to the bar. Turns out the hound of hell has a soft spot for the pups. Cerberus sometimes even baby-sits for part of the night while the two parents have some quality time alone.

Some people might think Ted's actions sick and twisted. It fills me with pity, not for Ted and Shan, but for the close minded. They will never see beyond the narrow confines of their little worlds, while others are creating universes filled with beauty and tolerance. Happiness must be seized with both hands and felt with the whole heart.

No, the world is not perfect, but at least there are those who are trying. You can find some of them bellying up to the bar in a place called Bulfinche's Pub. Follow the brightest rainbow in the sky. Let it lead you past the ills of the world to a safe haven where the drinks are cold, the food hot, and the company exceptional. The bartenders are pretty darn good, too. Next time the pot of gold calls to you, come in and see us. First drink is on the house.

OF RED TAPE AND ROSES

The woman walked in like she had a bug wedged into a bodily orifice normally reserved for stuff on its way out. The way she was dressed only enhanced her demeanor. She wore a business suit and skirt with a white collarless blouse, which was buttoned all the way to the neck and fastened with a cameo brooch. Her hair was pulled back in a bun so tight she was getting a non-surgical face lift out of the deal. She even wore little granny-style glasses and carried a briefcase.

Ms. Prim-and-Proper stood in the doorway for a moment, dictating into a microcassette recorder, then putting it away. She replaced it with a clipboard, which she immediately started writing notes on. That task finished, she wasted no more time in approaching the bar.

"What can I get for you?" I asked.

"I can't drink. I'm working," she said smartly.

"We have plenty of non-alcoholic beverages," I said.

"I suppose it has been a trying day. I could go for a spot of tea," she said.

"You might as well have the full cup. It doesn't cost any more," I said. Ms. Prim-and-Proper frowned.

"Pointless humor is the sign of a slovenly mind," she said.

"Why thank you," I said.

"It wasn't a compliment," she said haughtily.

"Really? I'm so glad you pointed that out. Us slovenly minded folks are a little slow sometimes," I answered sarcastically. The frown deepened and little crinkles formed around the corners of her eyes.

"Just the tea, please," she said.

Rebecca stood up from where she was sitting at one of the tables and walked over to the woman. Rebecca's wardrobe was as eclectic as always, but it did set her aside from polite society. Luckily, the portion of society she chose to be around was us, and we have been known to be pretty impolite around her. From our regulars, impoliteness was tolerated, and in some cases even expected. However, Ms. Prim-and-Proper wasn't a regular, so the way she was staring disapprovingly at Rebecca down the barrel of her nose wasn't acceptable.

Rebecca pulled an envelope out of the folds of her clothing and took a fresh tea bag out, offering it to the lady.

"I have extra," said Rebecca, holding it out. The woman seemed flabbergasted that Rebecca would even dare approach her.

"No thank you," said Ms. Prim-and-Proper, turning her back on Rebecca in much the same way an ostrich puts her head in the sand, in hopes that something would simply go away.

Rebecca shrugged. "Suit yourself."

"Not too particular about your customers, are you?" asked Ms. Prim-and-Proper.

"Naw, so you're welcome to stay if you like," I said. Ms. Prim-and-Proper smiled a smile devoid of any humor.

"Very comical. Now it's my turn to amuse. This is a surprise inspection," she said, pulling a credential wallet out of her briefcase.

"Board of Health?" I asked. If she was, she hadn't been around before.

"No, social services. Are you Padriac Moran?"

"No," I said, as the side door to the garage opened. Paddy walked in with Brian and Shellie. The kids saw Rebecca, shouted her name, ran toward her, and gave her a hug. Normally, Rebecca is not the most physical of people. Under the onslaught of a hug, Rebecca typically cringes or makes the hugger regret their familiarity in a very physical way. Most people don't try. The kids are different. Them, she hugged back. "That's Paddy, over there."

The lady turned and made a bee-line for the boss.

"Mr. Moran, I'm Emma Jenkins. I'm with the Department of Social Services. This is a surprise inspection, pending final approval of your adoption of Shellie and Nellie Taylor and Brian Meyer."

"A pleasure, Ms. Jenkins," said Paddy, extending his hand. Ms. Jenkins shook it with a wrist like a dead fish. "I must confess that I'm surprised to see you. I thought we had everything settled with your colleague, Mr. Wiggens."

"Mr. Wiggens is the reason I'm here. It seems he took some bribes and he is no longer with Social Services. It has fallen on me to double-check all of his cases, in order to assure that the welfare of the children involved was not compromised."

Paddy's face remained smiling, which was impressive, because he had paid out to Mr. Wiggens. Normally, Paddy would do anything possible to avoid paying a bribe on principle alone, but the adoption issue was different. All the paperwork was forged, down to the last names on the kids. The child guardianship papers, granting Paddy custody, were signed by parents that never existed, even before their fictitious deaths. The girls' mother was really dead, but they had a father or fathers they had never met, whose names might be listed on their birth certificates. Brian's mother was alive, but had stood by and let his step-father do unspeakable things to him, then didn't believe him when he told her about them. If who he really was were found out, Brian would be returned to them, and Paddy might even be falsely charged with kidnaping. Needless to say, the boss didn't want anyone looking too closely, so a pay-off was the best way to go. It seems he wasted his money.

"A very wise decision. How can I help you?" said Paddy.

"I'm going to spend a few hours inspecting the home site. I've read Mr. Wiggens' report. Am I to understand that you live over this bar?"

"That's correct," said Paddy.

"That's not a very wholesome environment for children, is it?" asked Jenkins.

"What would make you say that?" asked Paddy.

"Drinking leads to many forms of deviant behavior. What assurances do I have that the children won't be exposed to negative influences?"

"We run a very family-oriented place here. It's not just about the drink. Bulfinche's is a community."

"It's a bar, Mr. Moran. The East Side is a community," said Jenkins.

"Please call me Paddy."

"I prefer to keep things formal, if you don't mind Mr. Moran. And I'm not sure that I approve of the people you have here," said Ms. Jenkins, looking at Rebecca, who was talking with the children. "Should you really be allowing the children to be so close to a homeless person?"

Several things happened at that point. One, Paddy controlled his temper. He doesn't like it when his friends are insulted. Two, Paddy moved in such a way that Ms. Jenkins couldn't see Rebecca jump up and storm toward her. Hercules, who had been losing a game of chess against Fred, managed to intercept and calm Rebecca down, before any damage could be done to either Ms. Jenkins or Paddy's case.

"Ms. Jenkins, I'd expect a social worker to be more sensitive to people and their feelings. Rebecca is a remarkable person and I find your comments toward her personally insulting." It wasn't as if Paddy could tell Jenkins the truth, that Rebecca had rescued the kids from a street shark that had planned to make them slaves and prostitutes. Besides the legal issues, it would drill a hole so big in the boss' story that it would sink to the bottom of the Hudson, never to be seen again. "She deserves an apology."

"You do realize I have the power to end the adoption process with my report, Mr. Moran?"

"You do realize you've insulted a dear friend of mine, and that if you are going to be so petty as to threaten me over this, I promise you I will not only report to every appropriate agency for discrimination against the homeless, but I'll call your superior," said Paddy.

"I'm in charge of my department, Mr. Moran," said Ms. Jenkins, smugly.

"I meant the mayor," said Paddy.

"The mayor is far too busy to take calls from every New Yorker with a gripe. Besides, I'm only following city regulations, something I'm sure the mayor would have no objections to. I do not act differently in a case because of threats. Besides, it's very hard to even reach his secretary. Yours is an empty threat Mr. Moran," said Ms. Jenkins, laughing. She shut up when Paddy went over to the wall, pulled down a signed picture of him with the mayor, and handed it to her.

"We'll see," said Paddy, smiling, pointing to Rebecca in the background of the picture.

Ms. Jenkins, knowing she had been beat, turned toward Rebecca.

"I apologize," said Ms. Jenkins, with more than adequate insincerity.

"I'll tell you where you can stick your apology," said Rebecca.

"Rebecca, please," said Paddy. If anybody else had asked, she would have ignored them, but this was Paddy.

"Fine," she said, turning and walking away.

"Would you like to meet Shellie and Brian?" asked Paddy, since the kids were five feet away, taking in everything and staring at her. They were worried enough that they were staying uncharacteristically quiet.

"In due time. Wait, there are supposed to be three children," she said, looking at her clipboard. "Where is Nellie?"

"Out with Hermes."

"Who is this Hermes?" asked Ms. Jenkins.

"I guess you could call him an adopted uncle," said Paddy.

"And you trust him with the children?"

"Implicitly."

Jenkins flipped some clipboard pages and skimmed some notes. "I see here that you and the children are not the only ones who live above the bar. Is that correct?"

"Yes."

"Does this Hermes live here too?"

"Yes."

"Is he related to you?"

"Not by blood, although his brothers. . ." Technically half-brothers, but that was an explanation Paddy didn't want to get into. "Hercules and Dionysus also live and work here. As does his aunt, Demeter, Dionysus' nephew, Fred, Murphy, our waitress, Toni, and her daughter Beatrice Gerald. Plus various guests at any given time."

"You trust all these people around the children?"

"Completely. They're family," said Paddy.

"But not by blood."

"Love is more important than blood. I would think someone in your position would already know that."

"True, but this environment seems pretty crowded."

"Nonsense. I own the entire building, all fifteen floors. Everyone has their own apartments," said Paddy.

"Even the children?"

"Their rooms are next to mine."

"I see. I'd like to inspect the living area," said Ms. Jenkins.

"Easy enough to do. Now, if you like," said Paddy.

"Fine. First let me pay this gentleman for the tea," said Jenkins.

"Don't worry about it. First drink's on the house," I said.

"Are you trying to bribe me?" she asked.

"With a cup of tea? You've got to be kidding," I said.

"I am not. I'm not allowed to accept gifts."

"Murphy wasn't trying to bribe you. We have a tradition here. Everyone's first drink is free," explained Paddy.

"How do you stay in business giving away drinks?"

"It's only the original visit that rates the freebie."

"Perhaps it was an innocent mistake. I insist on paying," she said, pulling out her wallet.

"I'm afraid I can't take it. When my wife and I opened this bar, she insisted on starting that policy. She wanted to make people feel at home here. That policy has never been broken and I won't start now. If it will make you feel better you can order a second and tip Murphy the extra," said Paddy. Worked for me.

Jenkins gave me the once over and put her wallet away. "I don't think that will be necessary." She looked down at her notes again. "You are widowed?"

"Yes."

"Are you prepared to raise three children alone?"

"I'm not alone. You've pointed that out yourself."

"True again. I don't have your age down here. How old are you, Mr. Moran?"

"Old enough," said Paddy. Jenkins would never believe the truth. Paddy's been around since before the Roman Empire.

"Your age is a concern. You seem to be at the age when most men are enjoying grandchildren. Will you even be around when they start college?"

"I can assure you I will be."

"I'm just voicing my concerns," said Ms. Jenkins.

"Which you should do. How about I take you on that tour of the children's rooms and you can ask me the rest of your questions," suggested Paddy.

They disappeared through the door behind the bar and up the stairs. Paddy later told me there was a sticky discussion of his religion, followed by a discussion of things like Santa, the Easter Bunny, and the Tooth Fairy. Paddy said he was for the first two and against the third. The boss said he felt it was a bad precedent to set for children to have them start selling body parts for money. He said it didn't go over well.

While that and more was going on upstairs, Brian and Shellie had climbed onto two stools in front of me.

"Murphy, should we be worried?" asked Shellie. It was obvious they were both already fretting.

"I don't know, but I do know Paddy can handle almost anything," I said.

"I hope you're right. I would hate to leave," said Brain.

"Hey, I don't want to hear any of that kind of talk," I said. Paddy was right about us being a family. It would rip my heart out if the kids weren't here. I could only imagine what it would do to Paddy.

The actual living-area inspection went off without a hitch. The main requirement was that each child have his or her own room, and Paddy had that covered. Ms. Jenkins finally decided it was okay to speak directly to Shellie and Brian, and she interviewed them. They breezed through it. They had their cover stories down, forward, backward, and in ancient Sumerian. Well, maybe in pig Latin. Then she interviewed the rest of us who lived above Bulfinche's, except for Hermes, who was still out with Nellie.

By the time Ms. Jenkins got to interview Dion, it was getting dark out. That, and it was the first night of the full moon, which meant the Brand's were down visiting. Ted was still in human form; Waff and Nall were still wolves, as was their mother, Shan. The moon was about to rise, so Ted was stripping down to his boxers, to make sure he didn't destroy his clothes when he wolfed out. Paddy gave dispensation for Waff and Nall to go human, as well as Ted to go wolf. Ted had decided it would be a good idea for his kids to learn more of what it was to be human, and had asked the kids to babysit and play with the pups. Waff and Nall had already stopped by to visit with Cerebus.

Problem was, Ms. Jenkins was walking out of her interview with Dion as Ted was doing his striptease. The lady was so enthralled by Dion, that she didn't notice at first. Enthralled may be an understatement. Ms. Jenkins looked like she was in heat. She had let down her hair and loosened the top two bottons on her blouse. The cameo and granny glasses were nowhere to be seen. She was holding onto Dion's arm and looking up into his eyes. I wondered if Paddy had given the wine god dispensation to use his divine charm at full throttle in order to enchant our visitor.

If only he had cranked the charm up to turbo, maybe she wouldn't have looked Ted's way. As it was, she did a double-take before she realized Ted was almost starkers.

"What is going on here! Why is that man in his underwear?" she demanded.

Brain and Shellie moved to intercept, each of them held one of the pups.

"We're babysitting his kids for him, while he and his wife have a night together," said Nellie, holding up Waff.

"Dear, that's a puppy, not a baby," explained Ms. Jenkins condescendingly. "And that still doesn't explain the half-naked man."

"I'm not half naked," said Lucas Wilson, who was sitting and eating at the bar. He usually came by on nights of the full moon, in case Ted and his family needed his help. His vampyric ability to "speak" wolf didn't hurt, either. Lucas knew the moon was rising. Ted and his pups were already starting to transform. It was a bizarre progression between human and wolf, one that would be hard to explain.

"Not you," she said.

"Something wrong with seeing me naked? Are you sexually harassing me, miss?" asked Lucas.

"How ridiculous," she said.

"Well, if not me, who are you talking about?" asked Lucas. The werewolf's and the werehumans' changes were complete.

"This gentleman over there," she said, turning and pointing to where Ted had been standing. He was still there, only much shorter now. "Where'd he go?"

"Where'd who go?" asked Lucas.

"The man in the boxers," she said, looking down at Brian and Shellie, who were now holding two naked toddlers. "You were just holding puppies. Where did the babies come from?" She looked over at Ted. Even in his wolf form, he was still wearing the boxers. "Is that dog wearing boxers? Where did he come from?"

It was obvious that Ms. Jenkins was very confused.

"You don't look well. Why don't you sit here," said Lucas, standing and giving up his stool.

"Thank you. I could have sworn I saw. . ."

"What?" asked Lucas, smiling, but not enough to show his fangs.

"Never mind."

"Are you going to be okay?" asked Lucas. Ms. Jenkins' was holding her face over his plate.

"Of course," she said, then opened her eyes. She pulled her head back real quick. "What kind of food is that?"

"Blood sausage," said Lucas. "Want some?"

"No. That's disgusting," she said.

Ted had managed to pull off the boxers with his teeth and was climbing on top of Shan. In wolf form, his inhibitions were minimal.

"Oh no ye don't. You have a room upstairs for that," said Paddy. Ted stopped, but didn't put his paws on the floor. Paddy picked up a seltzer bottle. "Don't make me use this."

Lucas nodded toward the door. Ted got the message, and he and his furry missus trotted to the door. Ted opened it with his nose and the pair headed upstairs. Ms. Jenkins watched, but her jaw had dropped significantly.

Waff and Nall were hungry. Paddy, Shellie, and Brian brought them into the kitchen to see Demeter and get fed.

"That was unusual," Ms. Jenkins said, as the door swung open and closed. It's like that, swings both ways.

Hermes and Nellie came in. Nellie was bouncing off the walls, she was so excited. She was wearing a pair of red sneakers with wings that were several sizes too big for her. They looked just like the pair Hermes perpetually wore, except they were more worn.

"You guys won't believe what happened. Hermes took me flying," blurted Nellie.

"Kid's a natural. Handles moving in three dimensions like she was born to it," said Hermes.

"This must be the missing Nellie. You went up in a plane?" asked Ms. Jenkins.

"Plane?" asked Hermes, sarcastically.

"We don't need no stinking plane," said Nellie. They didn't either, not with flying sneakers.

"Then what did you fly in?" she asked.

Nellie started to open her mouth, but before she could speak, Rebecca spoke up. "I think you are forgetting something." She had her arms open.

Rebecca never asks for hugs from the kids, although she accepts them. Nellie didn't pick up on this, but happily obliged. As Rebecca whispered what was happening in Nellie's ear, Hermes asked me, "Who's the suit?"

"Ms. Jenkins, from Social Services, about the kids' adoption," I said.

"I thought that was all taken care of."

"It seems Mr. Wiggens was caught taking bribes," I said. Hermes raised an eyebrow.

"How terrible," said Hermes, looking at Paddy, who had just walked in with Shellie and Brian. They had left the toddlers with Demeter. Paddy didn't make eye contact back. Hermes was against the bribe. He wanted to try blackmail first, but Paddy nixed it.

Nellie walked back over to Ms. Jenkins. "We went up in a helicopter."

Ms. Jenkins nodded. "Ah. Where?"

"Down by the piers. They give aerial tours of the city," said Hermes.

"You must be Hermes." He nodded. "Why did you only take one of the children? Do you play favorites?" "No. Me and Shellie are scared of heights," said Brian. Hermes had taken both of them up with just him wearing the shoes, but the heights freaked the other two out, so Nellie was the only one to get to try out the shoes.

"Shellie and I are scared of heights," she said, correcting his grammar.

"You're scared of heights, too?" joked Brian. Shellie elbowed him. "Just kidding."

"Very funny," she said. For some reason she gave me a dirty look out of the corner of her eye. "Nellie, I need to ask you some questions. Mr. Hermes, don't go far. Your interview is next."

"I await with baited breath," said Hemres.

"That's what you get for eating worms," I said softly, and was generally ignored. Ms. Jenkins noticed Nellie's footwear.

"Why in the world are you wearing those big red shoes? Doesn't Mr. Moran buy you shoes of your own?"

Nellie was fast on her feet. "I want to be a clown. . ." That was a lie. Nellie had announced recently that she wanted to be a ninja. ". . . so I asked Hermes for a pair of his old red shoes."

"I see."

They went off and did their interview, then it was Hermes' turn. When she came back, more regulars had arrived. Samson, Joseph, Heimdall, Fr. Mike, Jasmine, and Ismail were playing poker in the corner. Jenkins saw Samson's dark sunglasses and his blind man's cane and went to investigate. She stood to his side and waved a hand in front of his face.

"That's very impolite," said Samson. Ms. Jenkins seemed unnerved that he knew she was there.

"This man's blind," she said, looking at Fr. Mike.

"Excuse me, I'm right here," said Samson, annoyed.

"How can you be playing cards against him?" she said.

"Not very well. He won the last three hands," said Fr. Mike, palming a king from under the table.

"And you just cheated! And you're a priest!"

"Fork it over, Mike," said Heimdall, holding out his hand. Mike handed him the king.

"House rules allow for that, unless you get caught," said Joseph.

"What does that teach children about the real world?"

"How things really work?" said Jas. He was wearing a lovely peasant skirt and a yellow blouse. Jenkins looked at him for the first time.

"You're wearing a dress."

"So are you," said Jas.

"But you're a man." That was obvious. Jas didn't exactly doll himself up. He didn't do makeup and he hadn't shaved. His face or his legs.

Jas didn't want to bother explaining. "I'm Scottish. Be around later and you can check me out when I play the bagpipes."

Ms. Jenkins walked away shaking her head. That was about when Mathew and Ryth arrived.

"Attention everybody. I have great news. Tomorrow my business is officially open. To celebrate, I'd like to buy everyone a round," said Ryth.

"And I'd like to let you," chimed out Hard Rider, who was playing pool in the corner.

There were congratulations all around.

"What kind of business is it?" asked Ms. Jenkins. It was something that I wanted to know, too. Ryth had been very secretive about it ever since she left her waitress job here to start working on it. Other than her hubby, only Paddy knew the details.

"Well, we can all watch the commercial," said Ryth, dangling a video tape.

"Commercial?" I said.

"Yep," she said, handing me he tape. "It starts running on TV tomorrow. Pop it in the VCR, Murphy."

I did and hit play. There was a sizeable crowd around the TV. Ryth had been very popular as a waitress here, and the group was mostly regulars tonight.

The scene opened with fire across the screen, and faded to focus on a attractive woman dressed in a skimpy devil's outfit, complete with horns, tail, and a pitchfork. She then picked up a phone, her face tightened up, and she moaned like she was in physical ecstasy. Words appeared on the screen: FOR A HELL OF A GOOD TIME CALL 900-555-SINN.

"You started a phone sex line?" said Jas.

"You can have sex over the phone?" said Fred. "Why am I always the last to know these things?"

"Does this mean you are going to charge me when I call you guys at home?" I said.

"Murphy, you're still welcome to call anytime for free," purred Ryth.

Hard Rider had grabbed a napkin and was writing the number down. Paddy looked at him with raised eyebrows.

"It's for a friend," said Hard, blushing.

"Ryth, how come you're not in the commercial? You're much prettier than that girl," said Fred.

"Let's just say I didn't think it would be a good idea to have my face shown around the clock on TV," said Ryth.

"Oh, right," said Fred, realizing that being in the commercial would make it much harder for her to keep hidden from Hell's Hordes or the Heavenly Host.

"You used to work here and you left to start a phone sex service?" asked Ms. Jenkins. Apparently, she was a bit slow on the uptake.

"Yes."

Ms. Jenkins turned to Mathew. "You're her husband?" Mathew nodded. Ms. Jenkins then noticed the "whites" of his eyes were as blue as his wife's were red. "You two have very unusual eyes. Do you wear special contacts to get those colors?" The couple shrugged. She turned back to Mathew. "How do you feel about this business?"

"I'm not thrilled, but it gives her a chance to use her skills," said Mathew.

"Talking dirty isn't a job skill," she said. Mathew wrapped his arms around his wife.

"To each her own," he said, hugging his wife.

"I've seen enough. Mr. Moran, I need to speak with you."

"Yes. Ms. Jenkins?" said Paddy.

"This is not a proper place for children. Unfortunately, even with my recommendations, I'm not sure if the court will remove Brian. Shellie and Nellie are another matter."

"What do you mean?" asked Paddy.

"Children belong with families of the same race and ethnic background, whenever possible. True, it's not always possible or even desirable, but it's been policy for several years now."

"That's ridicules. Children belong with people who love them," said Paddy.

"Very sentimental, but not in keeping with current theories. Studies have been done showing the detrimental affects on these children, even in caring homes. Everyone will know they aren't your natural children. It will open them to prejudice and social abuse, not to mention a long term identity crisis."

"Nonsense. My girls can handle it. And another thing—"

"Paddy, may I?" asked Dion, interrupting. Ms. Jenkins' eyes went wide and she started breathing heavy, like she had after Dion's interview. Paddy nodded. "Emma." She didn't chastise him for using her first name. "You seem to have some issues here and I don't think all of them are because of this visit."

"I don't know what you mean."

"You are very protective of the children, which we can appreciate, but your judgement seems impaired by emotion. Do you have any children?"

"No," she said, looking down at the floor. Dion looked at the wedding ring on her finger.

"You are married?" She nodded. "Do you want children of your own?"

Dion had a way of breaking through people's emotional barriers with his manner and his words. Ms. Jenkins was no exception. A breakthrough that might have taken a trained counselor months to achieve, Dion did with a look of his eyes and one question.

Tears were falling from her eyes. "More than anything. I'm. . . barren."

Dion opened up his massive arms and pulled Ms. Jenkins close. There was nothing sexual about it. The poor woman was sobbing hysterically. Dion patted her head and whispered words of comfort.

Ms. Jenkins pulled away, embarrassed. "I'm sorry. I don't know what came over me."

"There's nothing to be sorry about. Have you been to doctors?" asked Dion.

"Yes, and every fertility specialist we could afford. That's how I know it's me and not my husband."

"Doctors don't have all the answers," said Dion. He turned to the boss. "Paddy?" Paddy nodded his dispensation.

"I have some skill at fixing problems like yours," said Dion. Which was true. He was a fertility god, after all.

"You think you might be able to help me?"

"I might."

"How?"

Dion placed the palm of his hand tenderly on the side of her face. "Do you trust me?"

"I have no reason to, but yes, I do," she said, tears flowing again. Dion took her by the hand to the privacy of the back room and sat her down on a table. Later, he filled me in on what happened.

Dion unbuttoned her jacket, taking it off. Ms. Jenkins sighed at his touch. With Dion in power mode, it was an involuntary reaction on her part. She couldn't stop it any more than she could stop her heart beating. Dion pulled her white blouse out of her skirt, then undid the buttons. When he moved to pull it off, her eyes went wide with fear and apprehension, but no objection. She sat there in only her skirt and bra. Dion bent down and put his face on her belly and closed his eyes. She did the same and put her hands on his head and pulled him close, breathing heavier. Dion gently pulled away and stood up.

"I can help you. Do you want me too?"

Tears started flowing from her face again. "Oh yes."

"Okay," said Dion, softly.

Gently, he placed both his hands on her belly. Ms. Jenkins stared down. His hands started to glow as he gently massaged her midriff. With a sudden thrust, his hand passed through her skin, into the inside of her body, yet there was no blood.

She stared in wonderment for an instant, then throw her head back, moaning loudly, her hands behind her on the table, in an attempt to hold her in a sitting position. As Dion's energy flowed through her body, her head thrashed back and forth, her hands gave way and she slid onto her back. Her moans turned into screams of ecstasy.

Even though the contact was not sexual, Dion's power had the side effect of probably being the best sex she never had. Jenkins climaxed as Dion pulled his hands out. There was no mark or scar.

Slowly, Ms. Jenkins sat up, and she was doing something she hadn't done all night: she was smiling.

"That was. . . amazing. I'm ovulating, aren't I?" Dion nodded. "I don't know how, but I can feel it. I need to get home to Doug."

"No. We have a small window of opportunity. We'll bring your husband here," said Dion, handing her back her blouse. She looked down and realized for the first time that she was half undressed. She fixed that condition quickly, but something in her had changed. The top three buttons stayed undone, and she didn't bother to tuck it in as she followed Dion out to the bar proper.

"We need to get Emma's husband here quickly," announced Dion.

"I can get him," offered Ismael. His cab was in the parking garage.

"No, we need him faster than that," said Dion.

"Is your husband home?" asked Paddy.

"No, he's at the office."

"Give Hermes the address and he'll bring him here," said Paddy. She did and Hermes headed out the door.

"This is all happening so fast. How long will it take him to bring Doug here?"

Just then, Hermes came back in the door, with a bewildered and disheveled Doug Jenkins in tow.

"Not long," said Paddy, smiling.

"Doug!" she squealed, running up to her husband. She jumped up, wrapping her legs around his waist and her arms around his neck. This greeting was followed up by a passionate kiss. From the look on his face, this was not the kind of behavior he expected from his wife, but he wasn't unhappy about it.

"Emma, what's going on? You wouldn't believe how I got here. That man asked me my name, then picked me up and flew me here," Doug said. At least she didn't make him call her Ms. Jenkins.

"Honey, forget about that. Something wonderful happened. I'm ovulating."

Doug's jaw dropped. "What? How? Are you sure?"

"Yes, but we have to. . . make love right away," she said, hopping down.

"Ick," said Shellie, as she Nellie and Brian covered their ears.

Looking around at the crowd of strangers who seemed to be paying far too much attention to him and his wife, Doug was embarrassed.

"But. . ."

Dion stepped in. "No buts. You two need to get busy right away. There's a baby to be made."

"Who are you?"

"Call me Dion," he said, shaking his hand. A glow passed between them. "There will be time for introductions later. Move it."

"But. . ."

"Honey, for once shut up and go with the flow," she said, giving him a kiss that would mean they were engaged in some cultures. Then she grabbed his butt and squeezed it hard.

Paddy picked up the seltzer bottle. "Don't make me use this."

Ms. Jenkins actually laughed.

"Go up to the third floor. Fourth door on the left. It's an empty room with a bed. Enjoy," said Paddy, opening up the door behind the bar.

Like a couple of hormone-overloaded teenagers, they ran through the door and up the stairs.

"Dion, what was that glow when you shook his hand?" I asked.

"A gift. As to what, let's just say his sperm count just tripled and he has no need for Viagra."

It was a few hours before we saw the Jenkins again. They came down the stairs much more slowly than they had gone up, but they were still hand in hand. It seems that in the throes of passion, neither could count very well. They went in the third door and apparently interrupted Ted and Shan. It was about ten minutes before either couple noticed.

They were smiling. Doug sat at the bar. He was drenched in sweat and looked exhausted. He ordered an O.J.

The guy was in a talkative mood.

"I just went five times. I never did that many in so short a time, even when I was a teenager," shared Doug.

"Your doing?" Ms. Jenkins asked Dion. He nodded. "How long will it last?"

"About three days," said Dion. Her face lit up with a two-hundred-watt smile. Dion put his hand over her belly and smiled. "Congratulations. You're going to be a mommy and you're going to a daddy."

A cheer went up from the bar. The menfolk picked up Doug onto their shoulders and carried him around. We love good news.

"What!?" said Doug, from his precarious perch. "How can you tell?"

"He just can," his wife said, smiling.

"Wow. Is it a boy or a girl?" asked Doug jokingly, as the guys put him down.

"Do you really want to know?" asked Dion.

Wife and husband exchanged a look. "No. It should be a surprise," she said.

Doug's eyes went wide and he stared down at his trousers. It looked like someone had pitched a tent. "Honey. . ."

"What, dear?" she asked, then noticed. "Again?"

The guys in the bar gave another cheer and Hard Rider gave a suggestion. Doug blushed.

"I can't explain it, but I'm real happy about it."

"Me too," she said, looking at Dion. "We better get home."

"Ismael, can you give these folks a lift?" asked Paddy.

"Sure," said Ismael.

"We live at—" started Doug, but Ismael threw his hands over his ears.

"Don't tell me!"

"But how will you know where to take us?" asked Doug.

"I just will," said Ismael, heading out the door to the garage.

"Honey, would you mind going to wait out in the cab. I have some things to take care of here before I leave," she said.

"Sure," he said, holding his suit jacket in front of his zipper as camouflage. He kissed her and headed out.

The boss walked over to her. "Ms. Jenkins—"

"Please, call me Emma. I apologize for being an idiot before."

"Apology accepted," said the boss.

"Is the offer to call you Paddy still open?"

"Yes."

"Well, Paddy, you run a strange place here, but that's not necessarily a bad thing. I can see that now. There is love here, and magic. I can't think of a better place for kids to grow up and I'll put that in my report," said Emma.

A cheer went up from the regulars in the bar, but the loudest were from the kids themselves as they began dancing around. Hermes got out an electric guitar from behind the jukebox and began to play a rocking tune. Heimdall pulled a trumpet out from the same place and joined in. Before long there was a conga line moving through the bar, with the kids in front. Both Paddy and Emma looked over and smiled.

"I trust you'll leave out some of the more unusual details?"

"Yes," said Emma, then she turned to Dion. "Not being able to have kids put a strain on my life and my marriage. I think that strain is over now. I never thought I'd ever be a mother. I never came to grips with it, and every day I was reminded of it at work. I can't thank you enough for that, Dion. Not to mention what you did to Doug."

"It was my pleasure," said Dion.

"Mine too," she whispered, blushing. Emma stood for a moment, staring up at Dion. Then she stood up on her tippy toes and kissed Dion on the lips. It wasn't the same kind of kiss she gave her husband, but it wasn't a peck either. Emma blushed again and ran out to Ismael's cab.

When Ismael got back, he complained that they hadn't even waited until they got home before they started round six.

The celebration went on into the night. The kids were allowed to miss their bedtime and Paddy even kept them out of school the next day, so they could spend some time together. The rest of the adoption process was just a formality at that point.

After dinner, the girls coerced Brian into asking Paddy a question.

"Paddy, can we change our last names to Moran like you?"

"Yes," said the boss, getting all misty eyed.

Shellie decided to ask a second question.

"Can we call you Dad now?" she asked.

The old man started crying like a baby. He gathered the three of them up into his arms and squeezed them tight.

"Yes."

HELL'S COVENANT

Silent night... at least, Christmas Eve had started out that way. Now joyous voices were in the process of larceny, stealing the silence from the night. Father Mike Ryann heard the commotion even deep in his room in the back of Our Lady of the Lake rectory. They need not even have bothered with the doorbell. It was just a formality. He opened the door upon the gathered crowd.

"Merry Christmas, Father Mike!" the assembled shouted.

"Merry Christmas, to you, Pagan gods."

"And proud of our heritage we are," said Dionysus smiling. "Now don't forget you Christians stole this holiday from us Pagans."

"Saturnalia, true enough. Isn't there a Christian among you?" Mike joked, never one to discriminate for any reason.

Leading the assembled was Paddy Moran. The pagan gods included Dionysus, Hermes, Hercules, Heimdal, Demeter, and her daughter Persephone. Lucas Wilson was there. As was Rebecca and Judah Maccabee.

"I'm Catholic, Mike. You know that," said Lucas.

"But you're a spawn of Hell, so you don't count," kidded Mike.

"I can too. Watch. One, two, seventeen, twelve," joked Lucas.

"Perhaps you better stick to your computers. You okay being here?" Father Mike asked seriously.

"No problem. The rectory isn't holy ground, even with your holy self living here. Sorry to disappoint you," said Lucas, smiling, fangs glistening, black trenchcoat blowing in the winter wind.

"It's devastating to hear, but I'll get over it somehow," said Father Mike, his hand atop his forehead and head tilted back.

"You holy rollers. Think you can keep your holidays all to yourself. Don't need to have water poured on your head by some stiff in a collar to hope for peace on Earth and goodwill toward folks," said Rebecca.

"True enough," answered Mike. "Actually, I'm glad you came. It was quiet all through the house."

"Were any creatures stirring?" asked Paddy.

"Actually, up until a little while ago, no," said Mike. "But the silence was getting to me, so I passed out hot cocoa and spoons to all the mice. Now the little creatures are stirring to their hearts' content."

"You are so good, even to the small creatures of the earth," said Paddy.

"You're too kind," answered Mike. "Persephone, I didn't expect to see you. Where's your husband?" Demeter harrumphed. Persephone shot her a look which stopped any further comments.

"Pluto is off shopping. I asked him to bend the winter–only thing so I could come see Mom."

"It's good to have you here," said Mike.

"Yes, it is," Demeter said, giving her daughter a small hug.

"Where are Shellie, Nellie and Brian?" asked Father Mike.

"Caylee invited them over for dinner with her and Corny. They'll meet us at Bulfinche's later."

"Shall we tune up?" asked Heimdal. He was answered by a chorus of "Sure," , "Why not?", and "Why? Do I look like a car?"

"Okay. Ready. Mee, Mee, Mee, Mee," Heimdal sang.

The assembled crowd sang back "You, you, you, you."

"Very good. Now lets try 'you, you, you, you.'" Heimdal said.

A chorus of "Me, me, me, me," filled the air.

"Excellent," Heimdal said. "I believe we are ready."

"And I believe Judah, compared to these, your voice is golden," said Mike, covering his ears in mock pain.

Judah smiled. Golems are not noted for their voices. In fact, as a rule they are mute. Judah put his open hand palm down on his chin and lips and moved it forward exposing the palm. It was the sign for "Thank you."

"You're welcome. I see the Bulfinche's Community Singers are not out in force this year. I thought you wouldn't be starting until midnight."

"We will still be going then, as well, with the rest of the gang. Just wanted to get a jump on the crowds," said Hercules. "Will you be joining us, adding your Christian voice to our number?"

"Sorry, but I can't right now. I'm putting the polish on my homily for tomorrow. Then after morning mass, it's off to my sister's in the burbs of Long Island for the traditional Ryann family feast. I should be free within the hour. I'll join you on the midnight run."

"Wonderful," said Demeter. "Remember to dress warm and wear a sweater."

" I will. Now aren't you going to sing a carol for me?" asked Mike.

"Absolutely," said Hermes.

"Which one?"

"Grandma Got Run Over by a Reindeer. In C," said Hermes.

"Oh good. My favorite," smiled Father Mike.

Soon the song was finished, as was poor grandma.

"Paddy, with all of you out here, who is watching the fort?"

"Murphy's tending bar. Toni and Fred are there for backup. Probably overkill. I doubt we will be getting too many folks before the midnight celebration starts," said Paddy.

"Probably. See you then," Mike told the gang, as they said their good-byes. Closing and locking the door behind him, Mike returned to his room, picked up pen and paper, and began his homily-polishing out loud.

"In conclusion, the most important gifts we give to each other are not the ones wrapped in pretty paper and put under the tree on Christmas morning. No, the most important gifts are the ones we give every day of the year to each other, wrapped in the love of our hearts."

"Bravo. Excellent."

"Thank you," said Father Mike. Turning around he saw nobody. Walking out into the hall he called, "Steve? Jimmy? That you, guys?" No answer. Re-entering his, room he noticed the television was on. "Probably voices from the T.V. Must have been turned on by a power surge." Mike picked up the remote and clicked the off button.

The set came back on immediately. "Don't touch that dial." A coal–haired and thin–bearded man, in a black suit with a lava red shirt and tie, commanded on screen. With a snap of his fingers he enforced the point by sending the remote flying out of Mike's hand.

"What are you?" Mike demanded.

"I must commend you on such a fine sermon. Will save many souls tomorrow, I'm sure. But we will get them back. How many will be able to live up to your high standards?"

"All of them."

"You optimist, you. No, that would take hard work and denial, things most souls are not willing to do. Not for long periods, at any rate. If people died at Christmas, so many would be saved. All that goodwill and all. Pity we lower the death rate around the holidays, isn't it? Although suicides go way up. By the end of January the road becomes hard and less traveled. They switch to the one paved with good intentions. Most don't even mind the traffic. Many seem almost to prefer it. Safety in numbers and all that."

"I asked you a question. What are you?" Mike demanded.

"You don't want to know."

"But I do. What is your name?"

"No. Too much power in a name. Would not want to give you something to hold over me, Father Michael Patrick Ryann."

"Tell me you name, now."

"Demanding sort, aren't you?"

"Tell me you name now, I command you in the name of Jesus Christ."

"Ow. Not that cursed name. Third time is the charm. You may call me Ramos."

"And what is your nature?"

"You get very stuffy, when you do this stuff. You have the blessing and the power. You don't have to be so formal."

"I command you in the name of..."

"No, not with the name again. I will not be telling you anything you don't already suspect. I am a demon. Pardon me. I am being modest. I am the Archduke of Hell, second only to our Lord and Father, Lucifer."

"This is holy ground."

"You know that's not so. We are just near holy ground."

"And why are you in my T.V.?"

"Trying to catch up on my favorite soaps. No, actually, this device has helped hand us so many souls that I thought it would be amusing to possess one."

"So you have come to tempt me?"

"No, nothing like that. Not that it wouldn't be fun, but trust me, my employees have tried. You should have been easy prey. A Roman Catholic priest who hangs out with not only Pagans, but their gods. You are one of the few blessed with a visitation by the one whose name you invoke. You have seen and spoken with him, the cursed Nazarene. You crossed him. Oh, yes. I know that and more. He ordered you to perform a task for him. What did you do? Behave like a good little servant? No. You followed what was in your cursed heart and defied he who you serve for an almost stranger. And what does the Nazarene do to punish you for your disobedience? Nothing! Then you criticized him for it, throwing past actions and scripture in his face. Did he strike you down with lightning? Perhaps damn you to my realm? Nope. Agreed with you in silence. Conceded your righteousness. Blessed you before he left. It's enough to give a demon fits."

Mike merely smiled, remembering the meeting with his Lord. Inner peace overwhelmed him and his tormentor.

"Stop it! I know you have known lust. You were no saint before you took up your collar. You still feel it. Yet you do nothing, despite the pull of your loins. You believe the rule of chastity for priests to be wrong, yet follow it because you gave your word. Sickening. But I know your dreams are not always so chaste."

"I cannot sin in a dream."

"Unfortunately so. You associate with a demon from the Pit."

"Ryth, a lovely girl. And her husband, Mathew. An angel from Heaven. Been over this before."

"A finer succubus damnation has never known. Left all that Hell had to offer for that preening peacock. On top of that, you people conspire to keep them hidden from us. No matter. We will reclaim our own. That leads us to why I am here."

"Upset over losing Ryth?"

"Yes, but it is more than the loss of a mere succubus that draws my presence."

"Should I be impressed?"

"You should cower in mortal fear. I could devour your soul whole."

"I don't think so, hell minion."

"I am no mere minion."

"That is right. Lucifer's lap boy. Licking the hoofs clean or some such important job. No wait, you were an archway of Hell, correct? Right under the abandon all hope sign?"

"Do not mock me, priest."

"Why should I stop now? According to you, my whole life makes a mockery of you and everything you stand for. Why would I stop something I am so proud of, now that I'm really beginning to enjoy it?"

"Do not push me."

"Yea, yea. Yadda, yadda. You have a point to all this?"

"You and that leprechaun and all your loathsome friends ruined the Apocalypse. My Apocalypse. I had planned and orchestrated everything. Then a bunch of barflies and a damn goat ruin everything. Damn, Nero, that traitor! Unfortunately, by his and Devine's very nature, they are immune from my wrath. You, Moran and the rest are not so lucky."

"Guess we should cancel our 'Las Vegas' night then."

"I have had enough of you, priest. I will destroy you!"

"No. I will destroy you, demon. I cast thee out in the name of the lord Jesus Christ. I expel you in the name of my savior Jesus Christ." The T.V. began to spark and smoke but Father Mike did not let up. "I banish you to hell in the name of my God, Jesus Christ." Before he could mutter the last words the television exploded, showering glass and flaming debris around the room. Mike did not flinch. Nor was he harmed.

Exhausted, he collapsed on his chair and wiped the sweat from his brow. The phone next to him rang. He answered it.

"Guess who?"

"Ramos!"

"Good job. Now tell me, Father, what are you wearing? I am feeling so hot."

"Hellfire will do that to you."

"Actually, I'm at a sewage treatment plant across the river in Jersey."

"How is that possible?"

"I know. Hellfire would have been more pleasant. I got out before you finished your little exorcism so, yes, I am still free to roam the Earth. A word of advice. In the future, bind the demon from escaping first, otherwise he will just jump ship at the last moment."

"I bind you to this spot and cast you out..."

"Oh stop it already. I am not in the phone to cast out. I'm merely calling. If you didn't want to talk to me, you should have gotten caller ID. Besides, you had your shot. You blew it. Impressive screw up though. The Pope couldn't have done any better. Mother Theresa, maybe. On top of all that, the warranty on your T.V. expired yesterday. I have some connections in retail who could hook you up with a replacement, even a satellite dish."

"What do you want?"

"World War and the damnation of billions. Is that too much to ask? I didn't call to discuss most of my plans for the future. I'm just going to tell you the ones that affect you personally. I am going after your friends. Because of your nature, I cannot corrupt you, but I can kill you. Go hide in your church. It is holy ground. I can't touch you there. Father Steve's homily for midnight mass sounded very good. Not in your class, but enjoyable. Listen to it. Hide. Pray. Warn your friends if you like, but stay out of it. Or die. The choice is yours."

"Not a hard choice."

"Perhaps. But just to make matters more interesting, I have positioned a sniper across the street from Our Lady of the Lake's main entrance with a constant feed AK 47 assault rifle."

"That's not a sniper's weapon, it's a machine gun."

"Impressive, Father. You're correct, but what it lacks in accuracy, it makes up in volume. If you make any attempt to leave, he will shoot you. If you are not standing on the front steps after mass, he will start blowing away parishioners as they leave. A blood bath. Just what I wanted for X-mas. And don't think of calling Bulfinche's. The phone lines are being cut as we speak."

"They have cellular phones."

"But you don't." With that, the phone went dead.

"Damn," said Father Mike.

Meanwhile, I was back at the bar, blissfully unaware of any troubles. What could go wrong on Christmas Eve? I was waiting for the big guy to show. I had all the preparations made. Fred tried to help himself to the goodies. I slapped his hand away. I shouldn't complain. Fred is well behaved, for a satyr. He is young for his people–in his sixties–but that still put him decades older than me. He was just hitting puberty and was beginning to develop more stereotypical behaviors associated with satyrs. Namely chasing women. He had encountered a few problems. First, he still didn't know what to do when he caught them. Since he is Dion's nephew, Paddy suggested he buy him a book. Hermes suggested renting a movie. Hercules offered to take him out for a night on the town. Fred went and had a great time but did not experience anything beyond a slow dance. He has found that women, while liking his hairy chest, are put off by his fur covered legs, not to mention the hooves. Fred has not given up hope yet. Adult satyrs are famous with their ways with the women. Almost as famous as Dion himself. But the adult satyr has one advantage Fred does not: pheromones– little chemicals their bodies put out that drive women wild. Usually develops in their seventies. Fred is counting the days. To add to his frustrated agony, he has a major crush on Toni, our waitress. The day was not complete unless he hit on her and was rejected at least twice.

Toni really cares about Fred. A lot. Although she would never admit it, I think they may one day get together. Right now she is busy getting over some pretty intense stuff that has left her pregnant. She is due next week. Still insists on waitressing despite her oversized belly and waddling gait. We know better than to try to argue. We have offered to find her a more prestigious and better paying job, but she refuses. Toni has something here that she has always wanted- family. Bulfinche's is her home now, and no amount of money is going to make her leave. Kind of like how I feel about my job as bartender. Her kid is going to have more aunts and uncles than an orphaned child millionaire.

The three of us were sitting around, being sappy. Comes with the holiday. Fred was still upset from when I slapped his hand.

"Tell me again. Who are the carrots for?"

"Santa's reindeer."

"So he is too cheap to buy food for his own animals?"

"No. It is a gift."

"Now if I eat the carrots, will I be able to fly too?"

"Probably not," Toni said. Fred stuck out his tongue at her.

"Who are the cookies for?" Fred asked.

"Santa Claus."

"An old, fat guy who dresses up in a red suit, breaks into peoples houses using the chimney and leaves them presents."

"Right."

"And is too cheap to buy food for his own animals and too stupid to use a helicopter."

"Wrong."

"And you think this Santa guy is going to show up here tonight?"

"Absolutely. Everybody else does."

"Murphy, you are a grown man. There is no Santa Claus," Toni lectured.

"Wrong," I said.

"Have you ever seen or talked to the man?"

"No, but Paddy says he has."

"Yes, but Paddy also says his car can fly," Toni answered.

"It can."

"Even so, that doesn't mean Santa Claus is going to come down our chimney. Fred could barely fit," Toni said. Fred is about four foot eight. "How could a large fat man manage it?"

"Magic."

"Magic doesn't work in the bar. Or had you forgotten?"

"Paddy gave him standing dispensation years ago. He'll be here. If we believe," I said.

"Okay, assuming that this Santa guy exists, what is his angle?" asked Fred.

"Just a nice guy," I answered.

"Nobody is that nice," Fred said.

"Santa is."

"How does he know what everyone wants?" questioned Fred.

"Kids write him letters or sit on his lap to tell him what they want."

"Toni, did you ever sit on Santa's lap?" Fred asked.

"Sure. Lots of times," she answered.

"I think I just figured out his angle. If I dress up in a red suit and dye my beard white..." Fred said.

Toni interrupted. "What beard? You mean that peach fuzz?"

"You mean my flowing mane. Anyway, if I do that will you sit on my lap and tell me what you want."

"In your dreams."

"It would be a disappointing dream if all you did was sit," boasted Fred.

"Besides, I'm huge. I'd crush you," intoned Toni.

"I'll risk it. It does not matter how big you are. You are still beautiful," he flattered.

"Thank you, sweetie. You can be pretty cute yourself," Toni said, holding a bit of mistletoe over his head and kissing his cheek.

It went straight to Fred's head. He started leaping around the bar yelling, "Cute. She thinks I'm cute."

"That is enough, young man. No more Rudolph Christmas specials for you," I chided.

"What's the deal with this mistletoe stuff?" Fred asked, caressing his cheek.

"Tradition. If you stand beneath it, you kiss the next person of the opposite sex you see," I answered.

"Or if you get caught beneath it with someone you care about," added Toni.

"You have got to be kidding."

"Nope. Only works at Christmas time. Watch," I said taking the mistletoe from Toni and holding it over her head. "May I?"

"Yes," she answered. We exchanged a quick, friendly kiss on the lips.

"Hey!" shouted Fred. "What about me?"

Holding it above my own head, I said "Sure. Why not? Give me one right on the cheek."

"That's not what I meant, Murph," Fred pouted, sulking away to the far end of the room, staring at the Christmas tree. With good reason. It was beautiful, decorated in a style unique to Bulfinche's. Instead of the traditional star or angel on top, there was our trademark: a shotglass shaped pot of gold with a rainbow pouring into it. The ornaments, made by our patrons and staff, reflect each of them and their beliefs, transcending just one faith.

"This mistletoe is dangerous stuff. In the wrongs hands it could be dangerous," I said.

"I couldn't agree more," said Toni, taking the mistletoe away from me.

"Hey!" I said.

"Don't worry, Murphy. I'll hang it over the door, where it belongs."

In the interim, Fred's face brightened and I could almost see the light bulb turn on over his head. Taking me aside, he whispered, "Do you think this Santa guy would get me a mistletoe belt buckle?" Fred was practically drooling.

"He might. But are you going to be the one to explain it to Toni?"

"Oh," Fred said, some of the air let out of his sails.

It was then we got our first customer of the night. A new bearded face attached to a body dressed in a black suit with a red shirt and tie. We were only expecting our regulars for the Christmas party, but we were still open for business.

Fred grabbed my plate of cookies and met the man at the door.

"Excuse me, but are you Santa Claus?" Fred asked.

"No. I am Ramos, Archduke of Hell," he replied haughtily.

"Oh. I guess you don't get any cookies. Sorry, I am new in this country. I have not been here a long distance, as they say. The suit is supposed to be red and white, not red and black. At least I do not have to clean up after eight tiny reindeer and Rudolph. You can get a drink at the bar."

"Seems like a good place for it."

"That's what I think," Fred said returning the plate to the bar. Ramos reached up and pulled down the mistletoe from where it was hanging and put it in his pocket, before coming over to the bar himself.

"Fred, who is he?" I asked.

"Ramos. Said he was royalty of some sort."

"Actually, I am the Archduke of Hell," he said, extending his hand to be shook. I did not return the gesture. He had the red eyes demons took on when they entered the bar. I had seen it before. It was not pretty, although demons themselves could be. I never had much use for most of the demons who have stopped by for drinks. Other than Ryth.

"That's nice. Still doesn't give you the right to steal mistletoe."

"Oh this. If it bothers you so, take it back from me."

"No need. I will simply count its cost as the cost of your first drink, traditionally free. Should you choose to return the flora before you leave I will give you a drink. Otherwise, bottoms up. Choke on a berry."

"No, I have a much more important use for it," Ramos said, putting the leaves above his own head. "Toni, how about a kiss for your old friend?"

Toni look at him and blanched. "You!"

"What? Aren't you happy to see old Ramos?"

"Get out of here, you son of a..."

"Tut, tut. No cursing. My delicate ears might be damaged by your harsh words."

"You know this hell guppy?" I asked.

"Why, of course she does. I'm the one who sent her here to Bulfinche's. Indirectly at any rate. Now I have come here to collect my due. We have a contract," Ramos smiled, pulling out a piece of paper. "Signed in blood."

"Can't afford a pen?" I asked.

"More binding and valid when signed with a body fluid. Proof, if you will," said Ramos.

"Toni, don't tell me you sold him your soul?" I asked in dismay. Toni hung her head, unable to meet my gaze. I had my answer.

"Nothing so crass, my boy," said Ramos.

"I ain't your boy, brimstone breath," I said.

"Oh, such tough talk. But I bet I could offer you something that would make you be."

"I doubt it."

"Really? Not even the return of your dead wife to your side?"

"What, so you would dig up her corpse and reanimate it? No, thank you."

"Don't knock necrophilia until you have tried it."

"Shut your sick mouth!" I shouted, almost jumping over the bar.

"Or you will what? No, I mean her, as she was. You could be together again. Love again. It is in my power. All I ask is your soul. Or you betraying Paddy to me. Help me in a little scam I have cooking."

"Would be the same thing either way. No."

"Then how about a succubus looking like her? Or more beautiful than even Ryth? Or a dozen, gorgeous, horny women with only one goal for all of eternity. To get in your pants and stay there."

"I missed the beginning of this conversation. What is this I hear about a dozen horny women?" Fred asked coming over.

"For a price they could be yours, young satyr."

"How much?" Fred asked, pulling out his wallet.

"He wants your soul, Fred," I said.

"Oh. Never mind. I'll just wait for my pheromones to kick in."

"It doesn't matter. I will accomplish what I need to without your help. It would have been sweeter to destroy Paddy using his friends. Pity. I am nothing if not adaptable."

"I'm afraid I'll have to ask you to leave," I said.

"You should be afraid. Very afraid," Ramos said.

"That stuff don't wash here. Hit the road. Now," I said.

"Make me. If you can. You have gotten too comfortable, under the protection of this bar. Too dependent on others' strength, until you have lost your own. You were never much of a fighter, John Murphy. You can't take me."

"I said out," walking around the bar, grabbing Ramos by the neck of his suit jacket and forcibly escorting him to the door. Fred opened the door. As I tossed him he brought his arms up so his hands grabbed the inside of the frame, stopping his exit.

"You'll be sorry you laid hands on me."

"Definitely. Probably take me hours to get them clean again," I answered.

"I have unfinished business with Toni," Ramos gloated. Toni had gone inside herself, shutting out Ramos. She had a rough time of things before she found us. Rougher than I thought by the looks of things.

"You're finished," I countered.

"Far from it," Ramos said, as demon wings started sprouting from his back. He then pushed back on the door frame, knocking me down and walking back into the bar.

"That is impossible!" I shouted.

"Nothing is impossible with Hell," Ramos said, opening his mouth and belching a river of flame at me. I saw the fire ready to engulf me. He was going to reunite me with Elsie after all. Then I heard someone shout my name.

"Murphy!"

The someone was Fred. First he shouted, then he hit me running all out, knocking me from harm's way.

Ramos covered his mouth demurely and said "Excuse me. Jalepenos always do that to me."

"Try brushing between meals," I gasped.

"You okay, Murph?" Fred asked.

"Thanks to you. I owe you," I said.

"Can I have one of Santa's cookies, now?" he asked smiling.

"Knock yourself out. Just save him a couple."

"What happened? How did he do that? I thought all powers were nullified inside the bar," Fred asked.

"They are," I answered.

"Is the bar not working right?"

"Impossible. The only people who have full use of their abilities are those Paddy gives dispensation to. The only group with a standing dispensation are the boss' family. Ramos must be a relation."

"Very good deduction," Ramos said.

"Pity I can't take it off my taxes. What relation?"

"Second cousins. Once removed."

"How is that possible? Paddy's no demon," asked Fred.

"Angels, demons, and leprechauns all come from the same stock, way back," I said.

"But we demons are the best looking of the bunch."

"The demons and the Gentry got kicked out of Heaven at the same time. The demons to Hell for rebelling, the Gentry to Earth for remaining neutral, where, as the boss puts it, the gravity stunted their growth," I said.

"Pity you couldn't kick me out of the bar the same way. Now there is no need for you to get hurt. Just step aside and let Toni and I conclude our business and we'll be on our way."

"Never!" shouted Fred, placing himself between Ramos and Toni.

"Ditto," I said, folding my arms and standing by Fred's side.

"Oh wait. I think you misunderstood what I meant by we. I didn't mean Toni and I. I meant myself and Toni's baby. You can keep the slut. We'll probably get her in the long run anyway."

Toni rejoined our struggle, already in progress.

"My baby?" Toni growled angrily, coming back to life.

"Why yes."

"Why?" she demanded.

"Simple. We need a new beast to replace the one Moran lost me. It seems only fitting that I replace it with one of his own."

"My baby is a person with rights."

"Not where I come from. Parents give up their kids all the time. Well within the rules. And you will give me the baby."

"I won't give up my baby," Toni proclaimed.

"You have no choice. We have a contract you signed in good faith."

"Take me instead," she suggested.

"Ha. You are useless to me. I need a newborn."

"What are you going to do? Rip it from her womb?" I asked.

"Certainly not. She is going to have the baby soon. Tonight."

"Toni?" Fred asked.

"I've been having contractions for the last hour, but I wasn't sure if it was it. I didn't want to worry anyone."

"How noble. A pity you will live. It is ordained after all. The mother of the beast and the savior's mother must live until the opening of the Book of Seven. While the savior would anoint his mother, the beast will kill hers."

One problem with that scenario. Hell no longer had the Book of Seven. Neither did Heaven. Hermes had stolen it from Hell and hidden it in a place only he knows. No reason to reveal our trump card. Regardless, we were out of our league. More like twenty thousand leagues under. We were not going to let him take the baby without a fight, but truthfully, I didn't think it would matter much. Like sending mosquitoes against a tank. We needed the big guns. Fred was the faster of we two so I made the decision.

"Fred, run! Get the boss!" I shouted, rushing Ramos to distract him. He didn't even notice.

To Fred's credit he sprinted to the exit that leads to our parking garage, since Ramos was between him and the street door. Problem was, Ramos was faster, materializing between Fred and an exit. Hard to outrun teleportation. But I tried, sprinting for the now unblocked front door. Ramos was there well before me. He had caught Fred by the neck and was holding him off the ground. A clawed hand was waiting for my throat. I felt his grip tighten as he yanked me off the floor.

Toni meanwhile was dialing furiously on the cellular phone we keep behind the bar. Ramos took notice and we had high hopes of her succeeding. After all, Ramos did have his hands full. Unfortunately, not only was Ramos good with his hands, he was good with his eyes. If his looks could kill, we would have all been dead. Fortunately, Ramos' looks only melted phones.

"I will be with you in a moment, Toni. Let me just take care of these two," Ramos promised.

I struggled in vain; the veins in my neck struggled in vain. Fred was not faring any better. The world started to get dark. Not that it didn't have its dark aspects already, but I had been blessed with knowing people who keep the light burning in the window and in their hearts.

Looking into my dimming eyes, Ramos said, "I told you, you would be sorry."

He was right. Sorry I did not call in sick to work today. Actually, that's not true, but I was sorry. Sorry I couldn't speak so I could die with a wisecrack on my lips. Sorry I was silent so I could not leave this world the way I came in: kicking and screaming. Sorry I let down people I loved.

Sorry, Fred, I couldn't save you like you had saved me. Sorry, Toni, I could not save your baby. Sorry I let you down, Paddy.

"You're the one who is going to be sorry," said a voice from the blurred distance. I could barely hear it over the pounding in my head. It was Toni, with a last ditch pitch. Several of them actually. Bottles smashed. Liquid and broken glass hit my almost numb face. Toni was throwing everything within her reach at Ramos. The pressure stopped increasing, but didn't let up. The end was still coming, just taking its own sweet time.

"Toni, please, I am trying to work here. Of course, should you hand the baby over willingly, I will let them live," said Ramos. Loosing his death grip on Fred and myself he said, "Tell her, boys."

"Don't do it," Fred gasped.

"Ignore Rumpelstiltskin, Toni," I whispered, sucking down as much sweet air as my lungs could hold.

"Wrong answer, boys," Ramos said,

"Oh, I don't know. Sounded pretty good to me," said a voice behind us. Suddenly we were dropped, forgotten.

Ramos had something new on his face. Fear. I was looking shocked myself. Father Mike was standing in our doorway, a belt of ammo wrapped diagonally around his chest and holding an AK-47 assault rifle in his hands, two others strapped on his back and a .38 special tucked in his waistband.

"Hope you don't mind me crashing the party, Ramos, but I brought the party favors."

"Oh, Father Rambo. Welcome," crooned Ramos, regaining his cool. "I must say I'm surprised you value the lives of your friends more highly than those of your flock, if for nothing more than the superior numbers."

"All life is sacred. I saved those in the greatest danger first."

"Impossible. I had three gunmen."

"Impossible? No. I grew up on the streets. Had my share of trouble later on. I can handle myself. You say you had only three? I guess the fourth one must have been a mugger. Good thing, too. He was the one with the cellular phone. I made a few calls to arms, you might say," said Father Mike.

"But they're not here. I guess you'll have to shoot me then," said Ramos, flapping his huge batlike wings for effect. I was impressed. Mike was not.

"Why? Bullets wouldn't stop you. Might hurt you a bit though. Doesn't matter. Guns don't work in Bulfinche's without dispensation," said Mike.

"Why would you bring useless weapons to face me?"

"A Christmas gift for Hercules' weapon collection. Besides, in here they will not be causing any trouble. Of course I did bring some protection," he said tossing me a crucifix identical to the one he was wearing. Since neither Toni nor Fred believed, it wouldn't do them any good.

"Ha. In here those are junk jewelry," Ramos said. To prove his point, he went to grab me. He touched the crucifix instead and pulled back his smoking hand in pain. "Cursed pain! The trinkets of the Nazarene should be powerless in here!"

"Normally true," I said. "But these have special dispensation." Mike and I had used them once before, against the vampyre who cursed Lucas. I slipped it around my neck quickly so it wouldn't be torn away from my hand. Meanwhile Mike had positioned himself between Toni and Fred, and Ramos. I joined him.

"I believe we have what is referred to as a standoff," said Mike.

"Not for long."

"Before you try anything rash, I should warn you about this holy water. With full dispensation," Mike said demonstrating a good habit he picked up hanging around Paddy and Hermes–he was lying.

"Why would Moran do that?"

"We had a baptism here. This is left over," Mike informed, picking two glasses off the bar and pouring a third of the water into each glass, saving the last third for himself. "This is the holy oil we used, Murphy. He comes near you, blast him. You two don't need to believe for it to work." Of course Ramos needed to believe or he would find out Mike was bluffing. "This stuff will scar your pretty face, here and in Hell."

"That stuff will do me no more damage than a gentle rain." The bluff was called.

"Try me, demon," Father Mike said, a hard smile on his face. The bluff luckily had call waiting.

Then the rest of the cavalry arrived. Ramos was knocked over in a flying tackle by Hercules and Heimdal, who he threw off like rag dolls. Judah, Rebecca, Demeter, and Persephone piled on top of him. Thinking Judah the greater threat, he dealt with him first. Mistake. Rebecca cut him in the gut and cut him deep. It would not kill him, but it hurt. Persephone dislocated his shoulder and Demeter smashed him in the groin. Lucas joined the fray and was tossed aside like yesterday's trash.

"Vampyre! You should be siding with your own kind!" Ramos demanded.

"I am," he replied proudly.

"Then you shall be the first to die."

I could have thrown him the crucifix. Lucas believed. It would have worked. It also might have destroyed him. So my legs threw the rest of me in the way. I claim no bravery, only concern and reflex.

At the sight of the crucifix and the threat of the holy oil treatment, Ramos pulled back, still holding his wounded stomach, liquids of red and blue pouring out. He ran into the raging fists of a clown called Rumbles, who showed up early. Each punch caused the demon pain. Hercules grabbed him from behind in a choke hold. In an open space, Rebecca replanted her knife in his upper right shoulder blade, while Heimdal had gotten his sword and ran Ramos through as Hercules let go. Ramos screamed in agony, in despair. Rumbles got in a quick one–two to the jaw while Judah broke Ramos' left arm in two places. In a fit of agony–induced rage, he threw the lot of them off. Then he began to shift, to change, to grow into something not even vaguely humanoid.

A creature from nightmare towered over us and shouted in a deep, gravelly voice "I will destroy you all!" Darkness seemed to envelop everything.

A light shone through. "No, you will not," said the calm voice of reason. The immense beast began to cower from a little man with white hair and mustache who had just walked in the front door, followed by Dion, who had gone to find the boss. "Family dispensation revoked, except for immediate relations to be named later. Tis over, demon." And it was. Paddy had returned. The creature had reverted to its human form with the red eyes. "I am not very happy with what I see here, hellborn."

"You could simply close your eyes," suggested Ramos. Paddy frowned and took a step toward him. He cowered. "It was just a joke."

"Um-hmm," Paddy muttered, taking a step closer.

Worried, trying to stop the tide of blood and ichor flowing out of his many wounds using only his hands, Ramos asked, "What are you going to do with me?"

"That depends on what you were trying to do," Paddy said. Father Mike and I brought him up to speed.

"Toni, did you sign the contract?" asked Paddy. Toni could not bring her head up to make eye contact.

"Don't ask her! She is street trash, a slut, a drug addict. She will lie through her teeth. I can supply handwriting experts to verify the signature and genetic engineers to verify the blood," Ramos shouted.

"Shut up," Paddy said. "And stop bleeding on my floor." Both happened. "Toni?"

Finally she looked up, tears in her eyes. In a voice barely more than a whisper, she confessed, "Yes, Paddy, I did." Ramos appeared shocked by her honesty. "I didn't know he was a demon. I thought he was a pimp. He promised me haven in exchange for one of my possessions to be named later. I didn't know he knew I was pregnant or I wouldn't have signed."

"Well as long as that is settled, I will just hang around until the birth then take the infant to its new home," Ramos said.

"Not so fast," I said. "For it to be valid you have to prove you led her to Bulfinche's."

"Exactly," said Paddy.

"Go ahead. Prove it," demanded Dion.

"I don't have to. What was promised happened and that is all that matters, in a court of Hell at least."

"You are not in Hell now," said Father Mike.

"Depends on your definition," quipped Ramos.

"You will not harm one of my children," Rebecca said, lifting her knife to Ramos' throat. At present, he could be killed.

"Get away from me, old woman," Ramos demanded. Rebecca ignored him. "Hey, isn't anyone going to stop her?"

"Why should we?" asked Hercules, cleaning his fingernails.

"Because even if you kill me, the contract is with Hell, not me. Only Our Father can make the contracts personally. Someone else will come to collect."

"She will be safe here," Paddy said.

"But she or her child will have to leave the bar someday, and we will have them then."

"Possibly. But hopefully we will find a loophole," said Paddy.

"C'mon. What do you take us for? Some of the best lawyers who ever died are working in our legal department. It is getting harder and harder to get out of one of our contracts. This one is airtight in its simplicity. But there is another option."

"Which is?"

"You take her place, Moran."

"I am not going to sign any contract with you."

"Ah, I do not speak of contract but of wager. Bar games like you made the beast and savior play. You win, she gets out of her contract."

"I lose, you get my soul?"

"No. Better. Your bar."

The rest of us shouted "No way!" and "Never!" Paddy simply waved us to be silent and looked at Toni, who was having contractions closer together. Demeter had sat her down and was acting as midwife.

"Let me think about it," was all he said. He walked off in a corner alone, pacing for several minutes. Then he called me over.

"Murph, do you have a dollar on you?" Paddy asked me.

"Sure. Why?" I asked. Whispering, he told me his plan and slid a napkin toward me to sign. I did. Before he did the same he gave full dispensation to any regulars who might walk in the door later and everyone in the bar except Ramos. We shook hands, I gave him the dollar and he gave me the napkin.

"Okay, Ramos. I will consider your deal," Paddy informed the wounded demon.

"Excellent," said Ramos

"But with some modifications," spoke Paddy businesslike. "The game is air hockey. First, if I agree to the wager, Hell loses all hold over Toni, her child, descendants, and loved ones forever," Paddy said. Pretty smart, because that would protect everyone in the bar from reprisals. "Second, if I win, you are banished from Earth for all time. Third, if you win you get your choice of any bar I presently own."

"That won't be a hard choice," Ramos said, his evil smile tainting the room.

"I have written it all up in this wager agreement, as fully binding as a contract," Paddy said handing him the agreement, written on the back of a placemat.

Ramos looked it over frowning. "I don't like some of the wording."

"Tough. Take it or leave it," Paddy said smiling.

Ramos nodded his head. "Fine. I will take it. Where do I sign?"

"On the dotted line."

Ramos smiled exposing fangs that were almost as impressive as Lucas'. He lifted his left index finger to one and punctured his finger tip and signed his name in his blood.

"Not like he needed to open a new wound to do that," I whispered to Heimdal, who chuckled.

Paddy took out a bottle and a fountain pen and signed his name in whiskey.

"It is supposed to be signed in blood!" demanded Ramos.

"'Tis a Bulfinche's contract, not one of Hell's. Traditionally signed in the beverage of choice. And for me, I pour me lifeblood into making the stuff, so tis the same difference."

"Looks like I signed in the right stuff after all," said Ramos, licking his finger clean.

Father Mike and Toni witnessed it, he in a Tom Collins, she in peach schnapps.

"Let the game begin," Ramos said grinning. The puck was dropped onto center 'ice' and each hit their paddles together the first of three times. "I must warn you," Ramos said as they hit the second time. "I was champion of my circle at this game." They hit the third time.

"Really?" asked Paddy, feigning awe. As Ramos looked up, he slammed the puck into Ramos' goal for the first point of the match. "I am so impressed," Paddy laughed. Fuming, Ramos returned the puck to center ice for the next face off. It went a little better for him and after a minute he scored his first goal.

"Yes!" he shouted in triumph.

The game continued, our attention torn between it and Toni's pre-birth contractions and grunts. Paddy turned to me and shouted, "Call Hermes on his cellular. If he doesn't answer, page him on his beeper. Tell him to get his butt back here and help with this birth." Distracted, Paddy lost a point.

"Paddy, concentrate on your game. I have done this before, you know," Demeter said indignantly.

"Regardless, you should have some assistance," he said.

"Like a man knows anything about childbirth," she shot back.

By this time I had made the call and Hermes had walked in. "Sorry it took me so long. Had some last minute shopping to, do and the only place open was in Tokyo. Hope everybody likes the sushi sampler," Hermes quipped, in gray trenchcoat, baseball cap and red, winged high tops. Sizing up the situation, Hermes quipped, "Toni, looks like you had a busy day waiting tables, attacked by demons and now having your baby. Opening your presents tomorrow is really going to be anticlimactic."

She answered with a grunt. Fred was holding her hand, trying to take her pain away by force of will alone.

"Paddy, the baby is coming. We need a sterile surface," Demeter said. "There is only one here. Can we use the bar?"

"What!?" said Paddy looking up, losing another point. Paddy treated his bar top better than a surgeon treats an operating table. It was immaculate, his pride and joy. He would not let a single shoe ever even touch its surface. He was torn, but looking at Toni he knew there was only one answer. "Go ahead."

Hercules and Heimdal lifted Toni up onto the bar. Fred coached her in breathing while Demeter did the hands–on work, Hermes ready to assist her.

The score was six to five, Ramos. Point game. The last volley lasted at least fifteen minutes. It looked as if it would last all night. Then Demeter whispered loudly "It's a breach!" Paddy was distracted again, and Ramos got his game point. Paddy ran over to see what he could do to help. Other than lend moral support, there was not much.

Heimdal, in his brown fur overcoat, took him aside, and said, "Paddy, that was a horrible game. I have seen you play better with your eyes closed."

"It wasn't a very important game," he replied with a smile.

"Oh yes, it was. Now Hell has a new foothold on the mortal realm. Fools will walk in here following a damn rainbow and find damnation instead of salvation."

Then a baby's cries were heard. "It's a girl!" Demeter shouted as Hermes cut the umbilical cord. They cleaned and wrapped up the girl, handing her to her proud, beaming mamma.

"That's nice," said Ramos. "Now all of you get out of my bar."

Everyone else had been so engrossed in the birth, that they hadn't noticed the result of the match.

"You lost?" asked Lucas, in shock and dismay that was matched by everyone else in the bar.

"I was watching, and if I didn't know better, I'd have to say Paddy threw the match," said Heimdal.

"Actually, I did. Will make what I have to do in a minute even more fun," said Paddy smiling. Everyone else was dumbfounded.

"Speaking of which, if you will kindly turn over all deeds and papers for Bulfinche's to me, you all can be on your way," Ramos said.

"Never!" shouted Hercules. "We won't let that happen."

"Relax, Herc. I have everything under control. Trust me," promised Paddy. Uneasy, Herc listened and backed off. Turning to Ramos, Paddy asked, "You would turn a newborn and her mother out onto the cold streets?"

"Absolutely. Unless, of course, she wishes to donate her daughter to the cause."

"But we agreed Hell lost all claim," Paddy reminded him, annoyed.

"True, but it said nothing about rejecting a volunteer."

"I am glad you said that. Relieves any guilt I may be having in a few minutes."

"Enough of this. The papers please."

Paddy walked behind the bar top and took something out, then returned to the floor in front of Ramos. "Which would you prefer? The bar of soap or the bar of chocolate?"

"Neither. The agreement was for Bulfinche's."

"Now the agreement said I would give you any bar I presently owned if I lost. These are them."

"You own Bulfinche's."

"Not presently. You see, before I drew up that agreement, I sold Bulfinche's Pub to Murphy over there for the sum of one dollar U.S.," Paddy said with a wry smile. I waved and held up the napkin with our contract. "Of course, if you feel badly about it, you can have both. Never let it be said Padriac Moran was not fair."

"You tricked me!" Ramos shouted.

"Ye can look at it that way. No lies were said. The wager stands."

"I will destroy you all!" Ramos shouted yet again.

"Some people get hold of one good line and run it into the ground," I said. "Sure, it was terrifying the first time. The second time I got weak in the knees. But now? I'm just not impressed. Try a new one."

"I will destroy you," he shouted again. Some people just don't learn from good advice.

"No, I am afraid not," said Paddy. "The wager ye signed specifically states ye cannot be harming any of Toni's loved ones which includes everyone in this bar. Wouldn't ye agree Toni, honey?"

"Absolutely," she said, joyful and defiant.

"Fine. But I still have my freedom," Ramos bragged.

"Again, I don't know about that. The wager settles things between you, Toni and me. It seems to me there are plenty of folks here who still have a score to settle with ye, Ramos. Considering I gave all of them full dispensation before I sold the place and gave you none, they are in an excellent position to get good settlements, wouldn't ye say?"

Ramos bolted for the front door but Hercules blocked his way. A mad dash to the parking lot door was cut short by Heimdal's presence. Hermes blocked the door to the living quarters. Lucas, Rumbles, Demeter and Persephone flanked and protected Toni and her daughter. Lucas had transformed into a snarling wolf. Judah and Rebecca, knife in hand, were advancing on him. He ran to me, begging.

"Murphy, please grant me dispensation and I will give you anything your heart desires." Ramos begged on demon knees.

"I asked you to leave once. You should have done it then. Too late now. And you shouldn't have defiled Elsie's memory by daring to even mention her," I said rubbing my bruised and purple neck.

"I can give you the world."

"You can go to Hell," I said.

"Not yet. But soon," said Father Mike, moving toward the demon.

"C'mon, Father Ryann. Remember the good times, the laughs. You don't want to throw all that away, do you?"

"Yes," he replied. "Without reservation."

"Have mercy. Do you know what they will do to me after a failure of this magnitude?"

"I have some idea," said Mike.

"I know," said Paddy.

"Surely they will have mercy on Lucifer's second in command, his left hand?" Mike mocked.

"I may have exaggerated a bit. That was what I was going to be if I pulled this off. I was still high up, but not even Lucifer can screw up with impunity."

"Pity. I bind you to this spot in the name of the Father, Son, and Holy Spirit. I cast thee out in the name of the Lord Jesus Christ. I expel you forever from the Earth in the name of my savior, Jesus Christ."

Ramos began to smoke and scream.

"NO!"

Father Mike finished, "I banish you to Hell for perpetuity in the name of my God, Jesus Christ." Ramos, wounds and all, was gone, hopefully forever.

The lot of us congratulated Toni on her Christmas baby, born one minute after midnight.

"What are you going to name her?" I asked.

"If it is all right with Paddy, I would like to name her Beatrice Gerald," she said.

Paddy beamed. Beatrice Gerald Bulfinche was his late wife's maiden name. "I would be honored; I am sure Bulfinche would be, too," said Paddy. He rarely ever had called his wife by anything other than Bulfinche, but her first and middle names still meant a great deal.

"What would her name have been if she was a boy?" I asked.

"Padriac," she said. Paddy smiled and kissed her and little Beatrice Gerald on the head before hugging them both.

In all the activity I had forgotten what I had planned as my main task for the evening. I walked over to the cookie plate.

"Hey, who ate Santa's cookie's and the reindeer's carrots?" I demanded.

"Don't look at me," said Fred. "With all the excitement I didn't have time."

"Murphy, I believe there is a note," said Dion, smiling.

I picked it up and read it aloud.

"Dear Murphy,

Thank you so much for the cookies. The only night of the year my wife lets me off my diet is tonight. The reindeers appreciated the carrots although for future reference they prefer apple slices. Tell Paddy he seemed a little busy and I did not want to interrupt since he seemed to have everything under control. Sorry to eat, give, and run but tonight is very busy for me.

Murph, you and the rest of the gang have been good adults and I left a little something for everyone under the tree. Tell Toni congratulations on her beautiful baby girl, Beatrice Gerald. There is a little something for each of them as well, even if she does not believe.

Enclosed is the cookie you promised Fred. Merry Christmas to all and to all a good night!

Love,
Santa"

"I missed him," I said, handing Fred the cookie.

"But he did not miss ye," said Paddy.

"Maybe there is something to this Santa stuff after all," said Toni. "Or maybe, after tonight, I am willing to believe in anything." She was referring as much to the new life in her hands as to the spectacle of demon magiks she had witnessed earlier.

Meanwhile, Fred had walked over and was searching beneath the tree for a present with his name on it. He found it and opened it, then ran over to me.

"Murphy, he brought it!" he whispered.

"Brought what?" asked Dion.

Fred showed him. Dion almost split his sides laughing. Paddy asked him what was so funny.

"Fred's gift from Santa. I am afraid our little satyr is growing up," Dion answered.

"What did he get?" Paddy asked.

"A mistletoe belt buckle!" Dion screamed uproariously. Paddy and the rest of us joined him. Fred looked a little embarrassed at all the attention, and looked meekly at Toni. Toni waved him over and took it from his hand.

"Thank you for protecting me from Ramos," Toni said.

"It was nothing," he replied shyly.

"No, it wasn't," Toni said, lifting the buckle above Fred's head and kissing him smack on the lips. His eyes went wide. "One more thing."

"Yes?"

"I better not ever see you wear this thing in front of the baby. Don't want her getting bad ideas in her head."

"Yes, ma'am."

"I also want to thank you, Murphy, Paddy, Mike, and everyone. Without you, I don't know what I would have done."

"Tis what family is for," said Paddy. "Now Murphy, here is your dollar back. If you will return the bar to me, we can begin preparations for the party. Everyone else should be arriving soon."

"Actually, Paddy, it is going to cost you a little more than that to get the bar back," I informed him.

"Murphy! I can't believe you would do such as thing. Out of everyone, I trusted you," Paddy said, dismayed.

"He's just following the example you set for him, Paddy," grinned Dion.

"How much is this going to cost me?"

Rubbing my hands together I went "Hmm?", making him sweat it out before I named my price. "Another dollar," I said. Shaking his head and smiling, Paddy gave me the second dollar and I gave him the napkin.

"Remember, you told me never to make an investment unless I could at least double my money."

"Well, you can start working on your next dollar by helping Fred clean the demon ichor off the floor. Oh and Murphy, Merry Christmas."

"Merry Christmas, boss. We have anything like this planned for New Year's Eve?"

"No," said Paddy.

Dion added, "Just consider it a warm–up for Saint Patrick's Day, when the rest of Paddy's relatives show up."

Fred and I looked at each other and groaned.

BE NOT PROUD

In the distance, I could hear the clink of glasses, as toasts to my memory were raised above the coffin I was laid out in.

"It's amazing; Murphy looks so lifelike." The voice belonged to Paddy Moran. Even if I did not recognize the brogue, I would know it was him. The boss would never be mistaken for a giant and the voice came from a low altitude, parallel to the casket in which I lay.

"You think so?" asked Dionysus.

"Nah. With a face like that, we should have went with a closed—coffin service," said Edgar Tonic. He was taking a break from selling hot dogs on the corner outside.

"No way. Then we would have to punch holes in the lid," said Lucas. "I want my coffin back intact." Lucas was a blood junkie, a vampyre. He sleeps in a bed but keeps the coffin for special occasions. He never offered what they were, so I never asked.

Even as they spoke, I found it hard to focus on their words. I drifted off. And there my problems began. Again.

I was alone. Not alone in the world, but in my heart. Once I was half of the most special thing in the universe. Now that is gone and the universe is but a shadow of its former self. And me, I was once part of something so fantastic that nothing else mattered. Now I am part of a whole that will never be again and I hurt. Bad. Not always. I smile and laugh. I'm even happy sometimes, but then I remember.

The worst time is what used to be the greatest, what made the day worth living. Not that everyone would call what I am doing now living. That time is the night, that special, quiet part in the darkness when, in my heart, I know I am the only one awake in the entire world. It's hard to sleep with that kind of pressure hanging over me. Tossing and turning, my heart pounds in the silence, overwhelming tranquillity. It pumps furiously, undaunted, despite being broken beyond repair. Finally, I do doze. Maybe a minute, maybe an hour. I am privy to paradise, a land where more than memory lives and I hold love. In my arms, in my heart, and in my dreams my love lives, forever immortal. Undying and undaunted by time and space. All is well, everything is how it should be.

Cherishing each second, I do not notice the exit of my spirit, drifting back to the land of the living, wandering to the one place she cannot follow. Half asleep, one foot still in the dream world, I forget. My heart knows joy, and her sisters, delight and ecstasy. Elsie's beautiful face is clear. Her smile lights up the world, but I do not have to even shield my eyes. Like a turquoise wave from the deepest ocean, I am engulfed, willingly, in her blue eyes. Paradise does not get any closer. It is as close to Heaven as I have ever been. As I reach out a hand to touch my Elsie, my foot slips on a cosmic banana peel called reality, and I come crashing and falling to Earth. In dreams, my wife yet lives and my pain is dead. In actuality, Elsie has gone but pain is alive, well, and living in my heart.

The hurt is supposed to stop. The loss is presumed to lessen. That's what "They" say. The famous, yet anonymous, "They" are wrong yet again.

Elsie was my everything. She took everything about me and made it better. I was able to return the favor. Together we were one, two hearts made whole by love. Without her, I do not even feel like half a person. The damn leukemia took her from me. It did not care that she fought it with all that she had. With all we had. Death does not care how valiant you are. It plays tricks on your mind, games with your heart. Lets you think you are winning for a time and you forget time is finite. Death does not. It yanks the rug out from under you and separates you from everything you ever cared about. Sometimes it seems the only way to get it back is to cross over from life to the beyond yourself. The coward's escape, the retreat of the broken—hearted. That was what tonight was about.

Death claimed my love. Stole her from me. Elsie went quietly into that long dark night. I was the one storming and raging. Death's sting went straight to my heart. Bells may have rang when we met, but they tolled when we parted.

After Elsie's death, I was a lost soul. Eventually I was found and claimed by friends.

I told these same friends how I was feeling, my mourning sickness if you will. They threw me a wake. Yes, I am quite aware that I have some strange friends, but I would not trade them for anything. Well, almost anything.

The wake was of the old fashioned Irish variety and was thrown at Bulfinche's Pub. Normally, I work behind the bar. Today I was on the slab, eyes closed and arms crossed over my chest. Now stuck in reality the voices of the mourners became clearer and I again could hear what they said as two more approached my resting place.

"Is this where we pay our respects?" asked Mista. Mista was six—foot—four and stout of build. Braided blond hair rained down in torrents to her waist. Some would call her fat, but it would not be accurate. Mista was muscle, solid and strong. A plus in her profession, an interesting one at that. Mista is a handmaiden of Woton. A Valkyrie. The head Valkyrie,. actually. With her was Heimdal. The two of them are an item. Not the same type item that you need ten or less of at the supermarket express lane, but they can still be seen checking each other out at fairly regular intervals. At least they don't have to wait on long lines.

Heimdal is the guardian of the Rainbow Bridge that connects Asgard to Earth. Used to be a job with no rest, not even a coffee break. Then Thor screwed up and his dad, Woton, decided to punish him. Made him take watch duty for the bridge. Heimdal found himself with lots of free time and ended up working for the boss for a few decades. Eventually, he had to return to his duty, but since he installed the video surveillance and security systems, he has had more free time.

"No. I think we pay our respects in the jar marked 'tips' at the foot of the coffin," said Heimdal. Hey, it seemed like a good idea at the time, but most folks don't seem to bring lots of cash to a wake. Poor planner that I am, I forgot to set up to accept credit cards.

"What I want to know is: when do we get to bury him?" asked Hermes. I could hear him banging his shovels together in anticipation.

"Now, now, you know Murph requested cremation," reminded Demeter, our chef supreme. "I have the oven warming up now." I had hoped it was for a send—off meal.

I guess if she did not cook me all the way, this whole thing would turn out to be a half baked idea.

Truthfully, I did say they were welcome to roast me, but I didn't mean it in the literal sense.

"Consuming fire; reminds me of home," moaned a wistful voice. It belonged to a vision of physical beauty named Ryth that made supermodels feel ugly.

At first, Ryth had worked for the boss waitressing. These days she runs her own 1-900 service. Makes a bundle and is investing much of it in a virtual reality version of procreation, the ultimate in safe sex. Won't have to even worry about computer viruses. Mathew has had less success in finding a paying job and still works here washing dishes. He is less than thrilled with his wife's business, but he trusts and loves her completely. No more need be said.

"I think the 'Yesterday was the last day of the rest of my life' pin was a nice touch," said Hercules. Herc watches the door. Occasionally, it watches him back. They can spend hours before one of them breaks down.

"Father Mike, do you think you should say a few words over the deceased?" asked Madame Rose., gypsy of the old school. Dresses the part, even though her psychic powers had made her and Paddy wealthy beyond imagining.

"I suppose I should say something profound and meaningful," said Father Mike Ryann. "Something that reflects the spirit and the life of the man we have all come here to honor." Clearing his throat, he continued. "Dearly beloved, four score and seven years ago, in a place far, far away lived three bears who were going to grandma's house, boldly going where no bear had gone before. Ipso facto and in conclusion, ashes to ashes, dust to dust, earth to Murphy. May God have mercy on your soul."

"That was beautiful," said Lucas, pretending to wipe a tear from his eye. "It is almost like he is still with us."

"I am still with you, you twit," I said from my place of honor inside the coffin.

"I can even hear his voice," said Lucas. "I miss him so. I can't bear to see him like this." With faked sobs, Lucas closed the casket's lid with me still inside.

"Let me out!" I yelled, banging on the inside of the coffin. Some first timers were watching the scene with amusement.

"I can't believe he has passed on," Lucas sobbed.

"Could be worse. He could have passed gas," suggested Heimdal.

"True, so true," said Dion. "Let us be thankful for the little things and treasure every moment we had with him. And all the moments to come that we will have without him."

"Here, here," said Paddy, raising his glass.

"Remember the way he would pour our drinks, always with a witty comment?" said Ismael Macob.

"That was so annoying," said Mista.

"True. So true," said Mosie, as the trio of them broke into a sobbing fit, blowing their noses on each others' sleeves.

A middle aged gentleman, with a shiny, hairless head and round spectacles had strolled in the place and over to the bar. I was still pounding away from the inside.

Paddy and Lucas were sitting atop the coffin as I hit the lid and raised it up a fraction of an inch.

"I'm sorry. Am I interrupting something?" asked the newcomer.

"No, not at all. Just a good, old fashioned Irish wake," said Paddy. I hit the lid again from the inside, lifting it a good half inch.

"Looks like he almost got out that time," observed Dion. "Can't handle the job, wee one?"

"Perhaps if I were cursed with ye girth, humongous swill maker, I wouldn't have any problem. Then again, the coffin would probably collapse under the strain, actually killing poor Murph."

Rubbing his wine belly, Dion laughed. "I certainly can't be held responsible for shoddy workmanship."

I tried banging, unsure if I could even be heard over the bickering pair.

The newcomer heard and opened his eyes wide. "My word, is the fellow still alive?"

"Technically, no. But today, for all intents and purposes, yes," answered Hercules.

"I'm not dead yet!" I yelled from within. Using one of my favorite movie quotes I screamed ,"I'm getting better!"

"Hush, Murphy," said Paddy. "Ye are frightening a customer."

"Sorry," I said, quieting down.

"Aren't you jumping the gun a bit?" the customer asked.

"Why wait until the last minute?" asked Madame Rose.

"I suppose so," he said solemnly.

"What is your name, friend, and what are you drinking?" asked Dion. "First one is on the house. Tradition."

"Second one is on the deceased," said Hermes. "He seems to have left his wallet in the land of the living." I hate that. Hermes has been stealing my wallet since the day I met him. One day, I thought I had successfully turned the tables and done the same to him. What I got was my own billfold back. I, of course, hadn't even noticed it was gone.

"Tom Finkas and bourbon and water, hold the water."

"Coming up. Let me introduce you to the bunch," Dion made the introductions all round, saving me for last. "The gent in the pine box is Murphy."

"Charmed," I said from the bowels of darkness. Well, maybe the pancreas.

"Likewise," Tom said. "I have heard of a Murphy bed, but never a Murphy coffin. Very convenient. Keep the dead around for the wake, when they start to stink up the place, put them up in the wall. A 'Tell Tale Heart' kind of thing. If you miss them, roll them out for a couple minutes. Interesting concept." Turning to Dion, he asked, "What did he do to get you mad enough to do this to him while he was still breathing?"

"Mad? It is nothing of the sort," said Dion.

"Yes, we are trying to make him feel better," said Lucas.

"He misses his dearly departed missu,s so we threw him a wake," said Heimdal.

"Oh."

"Are you going to let me out?" I asked.

"Nope," said Lucas.

"Hey, I just found the night light. Is there a bathroom?"

"Why?" asked Lucas.

"I gotta go."

"Well ye ain't coming out yet, Murphy me boy," said Paddy.

"Fine by me, but nature is calling loudly. Yodeling my name, in fact. I find it so hard to resist a woman yodeling. I won't be able to hold out much longer. It would be such a shame to destroy the satin cushions. Don't worry, Lucas. I know a great fumigator. Should be able to get out most of the stench."

"Maybe we should reconsider," said Lucas, turning to Paddy, worried about his casket.

"Do it fast. It is so small in here it is like holding a sea shell up to each ear. I can hear the roar of the ocean, and the thought of all that water isn't helping matters."

Lucas practically pushed Paddy off and threw open the upper and lower lids. "Out!" he screamed.

"Well, if you put it that way I will just take my tombstone and go home," I said, climbing out and slowly taking a seat on a barstool.

"Don't you have to go somewhere?" asked an annoyed Lucas.

"Nah. I can wait awhile yet," I said with a smile. Turning toward Hermes I demanded, "Hand it over." Reluctantly he complied, placing my worn wallet into my outstretched hand. "And the credit card. The cash too, please."

"Seems kind of strange, walking in on a wake like this," said Tom.

"Why's that, Tom?" I asked.

"I almost had one of my own. But the rumors of my death, while true, were shortlived. Or rather short deceased. I went in for cardiac bypass surgery, and for four minutes on the operating table, I was clinically dead. I was a ghost. Floated above my body for a bit, watching the doctors trying to save me. I was so detached it was like the person on the table was someone else. Music gently exploded above me and I looked up into the famous white light. I knew I was supposed to head toward it. Being dead, I had nothing better to do with my afternoon, so I headed up. Would not have been able to resist it if I wanted to. As I flew, my life played out before my eyes. Good show, actually. Saw some good bits I had all but forgotten about, some bad I had tried to. I had almost reached the source of the radiance, overwhelmed by feelings of peace and joy. I was ready to enter it willingly when it shut off. Just like a light switch. Screaming in pain, I lapsed into darkness and woke into life. What a letdown. The doctor could not understand why I was upset. Of course, everyone passed off the experience as a dream. Each day that passes, I wonder a little bit more if they were right."

"They were not," said Hermes. "There are many paths into the afterlife. The light is but one of the more pleasant, and presently the most popular myth, thereby the busiest."

"How do you know?" Tom asked.

"Part of my duties as Psychopompos."

"You are a pompous psycho?" asked Tom, trying not to stare.

"That is one way of describing him," I said.

Hermes smiled and told me to shut up. "No. I guide the faithful dead to the underworld. Hasn't been much call for it in recent centuries. The numbers of believers have dwindled greatly."

"Tell me about it," said Mista. "A few measly centuries ago I would be kept busy for weeks escorting the souls of those believers who were slain in battle or died as heroes to Valhalla. Now, if I make one run in a blue moon, it's a lot."

"Who are you people?" Tom asked, with the look of someone who believes himself to be the only sane person in a room of lunatics. We get that a lot, at least until they convert to our side. Tom came over quickly. Explanations were made and Tom took them in stride. Seemed to have more trouble believing that everyone got the first drink free than affirming that a leprechaun owned the place.

Looking at Hermes and Mista, Tom asked "So you mean you two can bring people over to the land of the dead?"

"Yes," said Hermes. "Provided they are believers."

"Why believers?"

"What you believe happens to you when you die has a lot to do with what happens to you," said Mista.

"You mean if I believe I am going to heaven I will go to heaven?"

"Maybe. But which heaven? Jewish? Christian? Which sect? How about Muslim? They have seven," said Mista.

"Actually they are all just different facets of the same place," said Mathew, a twinge of homesickness in his angelic voice.

"How many afterlives are there?" asked Tom.

"The number is potentially infinite," said Hermes.

"So whatever I believe is going to be the end result."

"No. The afterlife you choose has the right to judge you and decide which aspect you belong in. Some leave it to you. Some use persuasion."

"So Hitler would not go to heaven just because he believed that was where he was bound."

"Exactly."

"What about atheists?"

"Never met a dead one. They all believe something, somewhere, even if it is oblivion. And no aspect is forever. Souls can switch over."

"Not where I come from," said Ryth. "Heaven and Hell don't allow visitors. The Pit is forever."

"Actually, lass, ye are mistaken," said Paddy. His parents and her people were from the same place before they subdivided. "Hell can lead to Heaven as well as the reverse. It is a secret the masters of each place wish hidden."

"No, it's impossible," Ryth insisted.

"Really? They how do ye explain yours and Mathew's presence here?" asked Paddy with a knowing smile. Seraphim and Succubus fell into silent contemplation on that.

Hermes took up where they left off. "Egyptian Pharaohs were buried with their slaves, wives, and goods. Some of the underlings got bored with the whole setup and relocated to Hades. They like it much better there," said Hermes.

"Can't understand why," said Demeter. There was bad blood between her and Pluto, the ruler of Hades. Her daughter, Persephone, had eloped with Pluto, at his insistence. Demeter was not invited to the ceremony and has never forgiven her son-in-law. Caused quite a fuss over it, so much that her daughter spends parts of the summer with her Mom just to keep peace.

"Some even have left Valhalla, to go down into Hel to visit with loved ones. Still others get back on the merry—go—round of life for another try," said Mista.

"So anybody who believes can go with you?" asked Tom.

"There are a few more details. Being dead helps," said Hermes.

"Usually," agreed Mista.

"But exceptions have been made," said Herc, speaking from experience.

"True," said Mista.

"Wait a second," I said. "You mean you guys can take a living person over to the realm of the dead?"

"Sometimes," said Hermes, unwilling to commit himself to an answer. He could see the spark in my eyes.

"And the different realms are accessible from each other?" I questioned.

"Not always directly, but yes," said Mista.

"Then you can take me over. I can see Elsie again."

"Think about it a minute first, Murph," said Paddy. "Could ye find someone here in Manhattan if ye did not know exactly where they were and had no address?"

"Probably not," I admitted.

"The realms of the dead make Manhattan look like a fishbowl. A needle in a haystack would be simple to find by way of comparison. Do you know exactly what Elsie believed?"

"She was a good Catholic."

"That she was," said Father Mike. "But not all Catholics believe the same thing. Not to mention she spent a lot of time here at Bulfinche's. She met many people who could be considered divinities, each living proof of their afterlife. She could be in any of them, if knowledge was more powerful than her belief."

"Then I'll check them all," I vowed.

"That would take several lifetimes," said Demeter. "Besides, Elsie never met most of the various pantheons. Check the few you have access to here. Hades, Valhalla, Heaven, Hell and the Sidhe." The Sidhe, called Faerie by some, is the realm that Paddy's folk carved for themselves when they were cast out of Heaven for the crime of being innocent bystanders.

"Would you guys do that for me?" I asked.

"You have the heart of a hero. I could bring you on a tour of Valhalla," said Mista.

"Though it risk destruction if I am caught, I will show you Heaven's gate," said Mathew. He talks very properly. Not his fault. Upbringing.

"I can't ask you two to do that," I said. "If either Heaven or Hell catches you..."

Ryth interrupted, "Murphy, we know the risks. We also know love. It is worth the risk."

"What she said," echoed Mathew.

"Thanks guys," I said.

"I will check with some of the family. See what I can find out," said Paddy.

"Hermes?" I asked.

"Murph, you need not ask. You're one of us. If you truly want to go, I'll take you."

"Thanks guys. I can't believe it. I'm going to get a chance to see Elsie again."

"Murph, remember the odds are against you. Don't get your hopes up," cautioned Dion.

"Or I will get my heart caught with its metaphysical drawers down? Don't worry about me; I will find her. Will I be able to bring her back with me?"

Dion and Paddy exchanged worried glances.

"No. That is beyond hope," said Paddy, sadly.

"We'll see," I said. Together Elsie and I took on the world. Now we would get our chance at the afterworld. "How do we begin?"

"If I might make a suggestion," said Madame Rose. "A seance may help us locate her."

"A seance?" asked Demeter. "Not quite as scientific as reading entrails, but it couldn't hurt."

"Okay, but we need your dispensation, Paddy," said Madame Rose.

"Freely given."

"Now if those who knew her would join hands around the table."

"Doesn't it have to be dark and lit with candles?" I asked.

"That is only for the rubes." Rose spent a little time working a carnival. "What we are going to do is focus our psychic energies and love for her, to use them as a beacon to call Elsie to us."

"Will this work?" I asked.

"Probably not. Contact works best with a haunting or the recent dead. Still, we lose nothing by trying."

Try we did, those of us who knew and loved Elsie joined hands and concentrated on her. I waited for something spectacular to happen: furniture flying, pyrotechnics, possession. Nothing did. For a moment I thought I felt her presence as I looked at her painting, "Rainbow's End", but I chalked it up to my overactive imagination.

"Sorry, Murphy," apologized Madame Rose.

"Nothing to be sorry for, Rose. You tried. Thanks," I said. "How do we start my love quest?"

"Simple. We go down to the basement," Paddy said. Actually it was the basement of the parking garage, several levels down. While Paddy turned off all the alarms, Demeter pulled me aside into her kitchen and handed me a belt pack. Whispering into my ear she asked a favor. Chuckling, I promised to consider it. Pluto had never been kind to me during any of his visits to the bar.

I said farewell to the gang.

"I shall walk in the valley of death and I shall fear no evil," offered Father Mike.

"Actually, I was planning on doing the Limbo instead of walking."

"Perhaps even in Limbo."

"One never knows."

"Perhaps I should give you last rites, just in case," suggested Mike.

"That's not a bad idea."

After hearing my confession and giving me the rites, Mike chided me. "You really should go to confession at times other than when you are afraid of dying." He was right. The last time I went was just before we thought The Apocalypse was going to start. The time previous to that had been years.

I did not walk down the parking ramp alone. With me were Paddy, Hermes, Ryth, and Mathew. Mista would wait until we got back. When we got to the lower level, Cerberus was waiting. Normally the hound of Hades is a ferocious guard dog, letting no one pass. As we first approached he began to growl, with all three mouths. The sound was deep and dark, the type of growl that turns a brave man to jelly. At the sight of Paddy the growls transformed to excited, happy yips. Ever since the old man won him in that card game, Paddy has taken a shine to one of the deadliest beasts in creation, and calls him "pup". Makes sense. Cerberus acts like an overgrown puppy around Paddy. The boss comes down as often as possible to play with and feed all three heads of the dog. Pluto never fed him, because he felt that food would cause Cerberus to lose his edge.

Paddy won't stand for cruelty to people or animals, and got the pup on a regular feeding schedule. Also plays his blues harp for the mutt. Cerberus loves music, and the boss really wails on the harmonica. For the first time in his existence, the hell hound had a friend. Cerberus is incredibly loyal and affectionate. Since there are times when I am drafted to push the wheelbarrow filled with the carcasses that make up the hell hound's repast, I have gotten on pretty good terms with the pup. So good that once he even let me by to borrow the old man's vintage car for an emergency rescue attempt. Now we had to convince him to let the lot of us by into the afterlife. It had been done before. Music, drugged food, sweets, brute force have all worked. Paddy now was taking out his blues harp.

"Hey there, pup. How's me favorite furball doing today?" asked Paddy. His response was three huge dog tongues licking him simultaneously. Paddy laughed and gave each of the necks a hug and planted a kiss on each head. Hermes cringed. Still views Cerberus as a monster. He can get by with no problems because of his duty as guide to the dead, but he used to enjoy trying to outsmart the pup. No offense to Cerberus, but three heads does not necessarily triple his intelligence. He is much smarter than the average dog but that still doesn't bring him up to human levels. "Got a favor to ask of ye, pup. Murphy here is looking for his wife Elsie. She is somewhere on the other side. Will ye let him pass, there and back?"

All three of Cerberus' heads tilted to the side as if they could not believe what they were hearing.

"Tis for love," Paddy explained. Cerberus nodded three heads sagely.

"Please, Cerberus," I pleaded, coming over to pet each of his necks. Cerberus lay down on the ground, closed all six eyes and made a noise like snoring.

"I think the pup is trying to say he will look the other way. Get moving," Paddy ordered. The four of us obeyed. As we progressed from cement parking garage to dimly lit caverns, the sounds of a twelve bar blues progression could be heard rising up behind us, and three very badly out of key canine voices joining whole—heartedly into the song. Poor Cerberus: loves music, but can't make any himselves.

"We shall go to Hades first," said Hermes, "after a riverboat cruise across the Styx."

We climbed down a manhole cover into a sewer pipe and a drainage opening and came to the shore of that very riverbank. Where we climbed out was all cement and molded. Most of the rest of the bank looked more like a natural cavern. It was bright enough to see, but I couldn't make out a light source. The water itself was dark and murky, as if holding the woes of all those who had passed over it within its currents. The sewer pipe we climbed out of fed into it. We were smelling great, if you like sewage.

"Let me do the talking when the ferryman comes," said Hermes. Ryth and Mathew nodded silently. Crossing the Styx was the way into Hades. It was also a back door into Hell, one almost forgotten and the plan, therefore, had the greatest safety margin for Ryth. Any inkling of her identity would endanger her. The ferryman, by his very nature, could be bought, so we would give him no information to sell.

"Where is Charon?" asked Ryth, hoping her makeup and disguise, combined with Demeter's amulet, would hold up.

"I don't know. Usually he is cruising the river. Hates going out where he might see people. I don't see him or his rig anywhere," said Hermes.

"Perhaps that sign could explain his whereabouts," I said, pointing to a boat moored on our side of the river. It said "Gone fishing. Be back in ten years."

Hermes was not amused and took to the air. The cavern seemed only a few hundred feet high, but as Hermes soared above us, he appeared no closer to the top than we did. He shouted at the top of his lungs, "Charon! Show yourself, boatman and tend to your duty." The cavern echoed for miles, resonating amazingly.

"All right, all right already," said a man of medium height and build as he walked toward us with a fishing pole over his shoulder. Actually it was more of a stick with a piece of string. "Don't get your undergarments in an uproar."

When he saw the three of us, escorted by Hermes, he stiffened up. He threw the pole aside and threw the hood of the black robe he wore over his pale, white, sunken, and hairless head. It looked as close to a skull as a head could and still have flesh upon it.

"Psychopompos! I am sorry. I was not expecting you. Nor so many faithful dead," Charon said, his voice having dropped an octave and taken on a gravelly tone.

"Obviously, or you would not have neglected your post," Hermes scolded.

"But very few dead, faithful or otherwise, cross the Styx any more. Most use the tunnel of light."

I had discussed with Paddy going that way as well. He said it was possible. By hypnotizing me into believing I had a near death experience, I could travel the same way Tom did, but the risks were greater. The light's siren song might actually claim me, and then odds against me coming back were minimal. My near death would become real. Even if I fought my way back within seconds, I would forget most of what actually happened, which defeated the purpose of the trip. On top of that, nobody else could go with me.

"Regardless you should be ready, at all times," lectured Hermes.

"I am sorry," Charon said. In a whisper, he asked, "You won't tell Pluto, will you?"

"We shall see," Hermes said. Charon blanched, becoming even whiter if possible. "Unless, of course, you are willing to bargain."

"Yes?"

"Round trip fares for the trio."

Actually I was the only one who really needed it. The rest could fly back, but that would put Mathew and Ryth at risk.

"Round trip? Why?" he asked suspiciously.

"They go in search of a loved one. And this one," Hermes said pointing to me, "is a writer."

"Oh joy. Yet another Dante wannabe."

"Listen you..." I started, but Hermes had waved me to silence. Charon was slowly taking on an air of power. This was his place, not mine.

"Do we have a deal?" Hermes asked.

"Yes. Three two-for-one fares," Charon said, unhappy but accepting.

"What is the cost of the trip?" I asked.

"In what currency?"

"U.S."

"Five thousand each," he said with a smile.

"That's highway robbery!" I shouted.

"I'm the only game in town."

"For that price I'd swim across first."

"Be my guest," said Charon, bowing and waving me on with his outstretched arm.

"Don't," ordered Hermes.

"Why?" I asked, remembering the legends of Achilles and the like, who got dipped in the Styx only to gain invulnerability or another power.

"Mortals die unless they are the favored of the gods. You may qualify, but none of us have made any preparations. You won't need our help to find your wife then," Hermes said. I backed away from the riverside.

Charon smiled and held out his greedy palm and said, "So you have no choice but to meet my price or..."

"Or what?" I asked.

Picking up his rowing pole and brandishing it as a weapon, he threatened, "Or you might go for that swim anyway."

"Charon, stop," Hermes demanded. "These visitors are under my protection. Harm one at your own peril."

Bowing his head, Charon lowered his staff.

I wanted to yell at Charon, tell him he was being unreasonable, but would it have any effect? Or would it merely raise the price? Which was truly a bargain, once I thought about it. Fifteen thousand for a round trip for three into the afterlife. Two weeks in Australia would cost more, at least at peak fares.

There were other options. Hermes had been able to threaten with impunity. I on the other hand... had an idea. Working for Padriac Moran, some of the boss has rubbed off on me and stuck, even after showering. Everything was negotiable and the best way to negotiate was to have something on your opponent. Which I did.

"I guess you are right, Charon. I have no choice here. Unfortunately, I don't have that kind of cash with me, so I guess I'll be going. I'll have to discuss with Pluto the rates he sets for tolls." I said, piquing his interest.

"How will you do that if you cannot get into Hades?" Charon laughed.

"I'll just wait until his missus comes up to visit her Mom. He always stops by," I said. Charon stopped acting so arrogant. Pity. The performance was up to Academy Award standards.

"You know Pluto?" he asked, with a twinge of respect crawling into his tone, despite his best efforts to maintain his superiority.

"Oh sure. I work with his mother-in-law. Next time I see him, I will mention the problems we had. I'll also suggest that if he wants to give you a gift, that he get a fishing rod with a reel, some lures, the works."

"I see," he said, solemnly, weighing his options.

"Take it easy. So long," I said, trying to tip the scales, as I walked back toward the drainage pipe.

"Wait," said Charon, uncomfortable at the shift of bargaining positions.

"Yes?" I answered.

"I suppose I might be able to come down in price a bit. I forgot that today we were having a sale."

"How much?"

"One thousand per head."

"Ten dollars."

"Seven fifty."

"Twenty five."

"Five hundred."

"Fifty."

"Three hundred."

"One."

"One fifty."

One other thing I learned from Paddy is to be fair. I could probably get the trip for a quarter each, but he was only doing his job. "Deal, with one stipulation: I have the option to add on more passengers for the return trip at the same price."

"Your wife?"

"Hopefully."

"Agreed," Charon said.

"Great. You take credit cards?" He did. I couldn't wait to see what this charge showed up as. The five of us got underway. Charon, now silent, was pushing us along with his pole when I noticed a wooden crate covering something on the stern of the boat. I saw a trace of motor oil.

"Charon, since we are getting the discount rate, you don't have to give us the full service treatment."

Charon raised what were probably his eyebrows.

Nodding toward the crate I said, "You can use the motor if you like."

Charon smiled, nodded and lifted the crate up, revealing a four–hundred—and–fifty horsepower outboard motor, chrome shining brightly. He sat down next to it, hit the electric starter, and the engine roared to life. We started to speed along the water, skimming like a stone, wind blowing though our hair. Charon pulled down his hood and pulled out a yachting captain's cap.

Turning to me, he asked, "Do you mind?"

"Not at all, Oh captain, My captain," I said. Smiling, he put the cap on and proudly navigated the rest of the way. I tried to ignore the dark shapes the water in our wake made. We were let off on the distant bank.

"I expect you to be alert when we come back," Hermes demanded.

"Of course."

"Thanks for the lift, captain," I said, saluting the ferryman. He returned the gesture.

"My pleasure. I hope you find your wife."

"Me too."

"The underworld awaits," Hermes said.

"We'll wait here," informed Ryth.

"Good luck," offered Mathew.

"Ditto," said Ryth, she and Mathew holding hands as they took shelter on a slope.

We walked on, passing no end of people. A man pushing a boulder up a hil,l only to have it roll back down. A man standing in sweet, cool water with vines of grapes and other fruit above him. When he tried to move toward one or the other, it would move out of his reach. Another man sat on a couch, staring at a television, showing nothing but infomercials, unable to find the remote and unwilling to walk the ten feet to change the channel. Poor guy never even realized he was dead–thought he was just on extended vacation. To each of them I gave half a cupcake or cookie from the pack Demeter had given me. Tantalus, the gentleman in the water with the grapes, was the most appreciative. I gave out the goodies to every soul we met along the way, asking each if they had seen Elsie. None had. Only a few were being punished or pleasured. For the most part the place was dead–literally and figuratively. Boredom not only reigned, it poured. We were mobbed just because of our novelty. I had the impression that we would be the source of gossip for months. We continued on our way, not stopping in one place too long, taking the short road. For a while, harpies flew overhead, but kept their distance, eventually moving on.

The path had opened onto a huge cavern with a pair of thrones on the far end, each at least three stories high. Atop them, larger than life, sat Pluto and Persephone, each large enough to make King Kong seem the same height as Paddy. It was disconcerting. I had gotten so used to meeting divinities in Bulfinche's, where their powers are null and void, that I was taken aback by gods who actually acted the part.

Hermes announced us. "We seek an audience with Lord Pluto and Lady Persephone."

"Who stands before the Lord of Hades and his queen?" Pluto demanded. Before Hermes or I could say a word, another voice answered.

"Honey, can't you see it is Hermes and Murphy?" said Persephone. She knew who Ryth and Mathew were, and could be trusted to keep quiet. Pluto was another matter, which explains why we had come alone. Whispering, Persephone suggested he wear his glasses.

"What is the purpose of your visit?" Pluto asked, in a booming voice. The acoustics were not as good as the cavern by the Styx, but still impressive.

"Pluto, these are friends of ours. And Mother's," Pluto cringed at Demeter's mention. "We don't need to stand on ceremony. What do you need, Murphy?"

"Your mother sends her love and these," I said handing her the remainder of the sweets. Bending forward she lifted it using only two fingers, each of which was larger than me.

Enlarging and opening the packet, Persephone laughed. "If I eat of food from her realm I will not be bound here any longer?"

"That was the general idea," I answered honestly.

"You dare enter our realm and try to spirit our wife away?" Pluto boomed. I was knocked to my knees by the shear force of his tone.

"Come on, husband. You of all people know how persuasive Mother can be. You have trouble dealing with her. Have pity on Murphy. He is only mortal, after all," Persephone said. She did not feel any differently toward me because I wasn't divine, but she knew her husband did, and that prejudice was being manipulated to my advantage. I decided to keep silent about the rest of the food I had handed out. Each morsel had been cut in half, which granted Demeter the right to claim any of those who ate for half a year, if she chose. She probably would not, but she liked the idea of having something over her son-in-law. (Well, maybe she might take a couple–just for awhile.)

"Very well," Pluto said. "What do you want of us?" By "us" he meant "I". Talks about himself in the third person a lot. Gets annoying, but now was not the time to mention it.

"I come on a quest—" The gods have a soft spot for quests. Pluto sat up with interest. "–to find the second half of my soul."

"We were not aware your soul had been severed," said Pluto, curiosity growing, watered by my words.

"I assure you it was, by the death of my wife, Elsie," I said. Pluto threw up his hands in disgust. Not what he was hoping for at all. Persephone, on the other hand, became more interested. Stepping down from her throne she reduced her height to human proportions and offered me her hand.

"I knew Elsie. She was very special," she told me. I nodded my agreement. "What do you want of us?" By us she meant her and her husband. She didn't put on airs.

"I have recently been informed that belief may affect the path the afterlife takes for an individual. Since Elsie knew you and the others, she knew Hades existed. Therefore, I thought that her soul may have come here when she died."

"Oh Murphy. I am so sorry, but Elsie didn't come here. Did she husband?"

Pluto grumbled something.

"What was that husband?"

"We said, no, she did not," Pluto said softly. He seemed hurt and embarrassed to admit it. His realm was not exactly high traffic any more, and it hurt his pride. No man likes to look like a failure. Especially in front of his wife. Strangely, Persephone did not see him that way.

"I can ask around some of the other realms and see if they know anything. I will call mother with whatever I find out. And tell her I am here willingly and that I love my husband." With that, Pluto grew a smile about the size of a bus, and Persephone enlarged to her previous proportions, stopping to give her husband a kiss before returning to her throne, taking Pluto's hand with her.

"Thank you for your help, Persephone and you, Lord Pluto." Usually I don't use titles much. It just seemed like a good idea at the time.

"Good luck Murphy. See you both soon," said Persephone.

"Thanks. See you later."

Hermes said his good-byes and we went back the way we came. Eventually we got back to where Ryth and Mathew were laying in wait. Literally. Newlyweds.

Hermes cleared his throat discreetly. They took no notice. He did it louder. Still nothing. He started to yodel and finally Ryth looked our way. She informed Mathew of our proximity, and they broke their embrace, gathered up and donned their clothes.

"Any luck?" Mathew asked, slightly flushed.

"Not as lucky as you two got. We didn't find her. Where do we go next?" I said.

"Hell would be the logical choice. It is close by. All we need to do is get in, find a computer terminal, access the personnel files and get back out. All without being noticed," said Ryth. I did not really think Elsie was in Hell, she was too good a person, but she could have been taken against her will and her deeds. It happens sometimes. I didn't know what I was getting myself into, but I knew one thing: if Elsie was there, she wouldn't be there for long.

"Need any help?" asked Hermes.

"No. The more of us, the greater chance of us being noticed. Ready Murphy?" Ryth asked.

"Ready as I'm likely to get."

"I would go with you but..." Mathew said.

"I know. We are going where angels fear to tread," I said.

This entrance to Hell was simple and not at all forbidding. Makes sense. Who is willingly going to enter a lava pit? It was a three by three portal that looked like a doggie door. Apparently, if we walked down a ways, there was a larger entrance, unlabeled and camouflaged. One moment all would be well, and one step later, a demonic greeting committee would surround the unsuspecting soul.

"Where is the 'Abandon all hope' sign?" I asked, as Ryth lifted up the tiny door.

"Main gate."

"You mean it is for real?"

"Sure, only it is computerized now. The words change and giant television screens show highlights of the torments that await."

"Sounds pleasant."

"It is anything but for the damned. The demon population has been bred to enjoy their work," Ryth said, pushing me into the crawl space. My nose tried to jump off my face, overwhelmed by the foulest odor it had ever encountered. The crawlspace was filled with raw sewage. Sewage pipes seemed to be a theme today. I'm sure that meant something.

Following me in, she removed one of her stiletto heeled shoes and used it to prop open our exit. Seeing the question in my expression she said, "Just in case. This place is easy to get in. More of a problem to get out."

"Goody."

"We can still get out now."

"No. I need to know."

Ryth explained the plan. With the benefit of makeup, I would be made up to look like a low–level demon, Hell's version of the faceless middle class. She would be the human object of my special affections, demon style. Neither of us knew if I had the stomach for it. Ryth tried to assure me that, on some levels, she was a masochist and would enjoy it. She stripped to the skin. I could barely stop staring.

"In other words," I said. "If someone asked you why you hang around that sadist, you'll say 'beats me.'"

Despite herself, Ryth giggled. "Do you ever stop with the jokes?"

"Not yet. Helps keep me from screaming." And distract me from Ryth's nakedness.

"Good, that is my job, 'Master'. Use this," she said handing me a barbed whip.

"Ryth..."

"Shut up. The barbs are foam rubber. Maximum effect, minimal damage. Borrowed from Dion. A memento from an admirer." She locked a collar and leash around her neck and handed me the reins. She walked ahead of me on all fours, naked. Her clothes were back in the tunnel. Most of the humans were not permitted clothes. Demoralized them even more than torment, in some cases. "Let's go," Ryth said. We wandered in but my eyes refused to do the same, locked on the vision beneath me. Ryth noticed.

"Stop looking at me that way," she whispered.

"Sorry," I said, turning my face away.

"Don't be. I'm flattered. But as my personal tormentor, you must show nothing but disdain for me. Hit me."

I used the whip. The whole thing was foam rubber and it wouldn't hurt a fly, but it looked real enough. By Ryth's screams, no one would believe it. In fact, I got some applause from a passing demon overlord. I bowed and groveled my thanks.

"Keep up the good work," she said, as she rode by in a chariot pulled by a team of twelve men. To emphasize her point she used a cat–o'–nine—tails to prod along her team. Her aim was for their genitals. Bits and pieces were torn away. It took all my self control not to cross my legs in empathy. Alongside her, a male demon was trying to keep pace with a female team of his own, using a ten foot pole and torch to burn off skin in tender areas and along faces. The pair were drag racing, and I applauded their actions. I was angry and nauseated, all at once, but I knew I could do nothing. I cursed and hated myself for it, but what else could I do? To try to help would have endangered myself and Ryth, not to mention Mathew and Hermes on the outside. At least that is how I rationalized it. I hoped it would help when the nightmares started.

Ryth could see my torment. "You did the right thing. Murphy," I remained silent. "If it is any consolation, those damned were rapists."

"Even the women?"

"Of course. Rape is not just a physical act. It is spiritual and emotional. That was light duty for them. Still had their privates attached. Besides, everything will grow back."

I realized that was what Ryth was supposed to be disguised as. A rapist. I tried not to think about it. We moved down and away, then, at Ryth's cue, I began to whip her mercilessly. She begged for mercy. I laughed and dragged her into the nearest building, supposedly to have my way with her. Her screaming increased in volume but she was up and running, me right behind her. There was a terminal in this building and we found it.

Ryth accessed it, screaming in torment all the while, reminding me with hand signals to continue my maniacal laughter and the whip noises.

Between screams, we whispered.

"You know the password?"

"They don't use them. Fear works better. If they catch us, they will slice each hand off, one joint at a time, then wait for them to grow back and start again."

"Oh." My laughter was a bit strained for the next few seconds. Then I made the mistake of looking on the view screens scattered around the room. Physical torments beyond my meager imagining were displayed, wounds healing before being reopened. Then there were some more subtle. True masochists begging to be punished, instead being waited on hand and foot. People locked in a room with someone droning on incessantly for days about subjects not worth a second's contemplation. A line at the DMV that sent you to the back each time you got to the front because you had the wrong paperwork. They never gave anyone the right paperwork, of course. Parents were forced to relive lifelike images of their children dying, again and again. Others watching scenes from their life where they screwed up, knowing better, on a constant loop. Some were trying to escape, only to end up where they began. Some punishments seemed to fit the crime while others were grossly unjust. Despite my morbid fascination, I had to turn away.

"Done. Took me awhile because I didn't want them to be able to trace the inquiry, in case she was here. She isn't."

"Thank Go..." I started to say before Ryth's hand clamped over my mouth.

"Never say that name–in any form–here. The big boys would be on us in a second."

I nodded understandingly.

"How'd you do it?"

"Manually scanned all newly damned for the six months prior and after her death."

"How many was that?'

"You don't want to know. Now, there's a chance I can access Heaven's mainframe from here, but a greater chance of us being caught."

"Forget it. Let's get out of here."

Backtracking to the tunnel, we found we had a problem. A damned male rapist was being forced to clean the sewage the same way he tormented his victims. With his tongue. He had found Ryth's clothes and brought it to his demon master's attention, who passed it on down the line.

"They are on to us," I said.

"Not yet. Follow my lead."

First we joined in the search mob, screaming for our own blood. As we spilt into smaller search groups, Ryth guided us toward specific ones.

"Where are we headed?" I asked.

"The back door I told you about."

"But you said there were packs of demons there."

"True, but they're expecting incoming only. Outgoing rarely head that way. We will have the element of surprise."

Staying with the group was a slow progress. We were almost to the back door. Maybe a thousand feet, when I heard a familiar voice.

"Ryth? Murphy!?!"

The voice came from beneath knee level, from a head buried and enveloped by acid dripping insects. Most of the hair was burned away and one eye was missing, but I still knew the face of the demon who had almost killed Fred and myself in an attempt to abduct Toni's unborn child last Christmas Eve. He failed. Nice to know our good deed did not let him go unpunished.

"Ramos!" I whispered.

Ramos was shouting, perhaps in hope of redemption from the damned. "Over here! They are over he....urp," I cut off his words by kicking a baseball sized chunk of flesh into his mouth. I think it used to be on the end of Ramos' leg. Yes, I put his foot in his mouth. We ran, as if giving chase, toward the gate.

"Did he give us away?" I asked, afraid to turn and look back. I could imagine Ramos chewing through his own flesh to blow the whistle again.

"Well, I think that herd of demons charging at us should answer that," said Ryth, standing upright and ripping the collar from her throat. "Run for the back gate."

No need to tell me twice. Heck, I was moving before she finished saying it the first time.

A thousand feet can be an infinite distance, and I never was a track star. Ryth was five feet ahead of me, running all out. We were both losing. Crimson, bat—shaped wings sprouted from Ryth's back, flapping. She achieved lift off. Instead of flying toward the exit she did a reverse loop in the air, lifting me up on her back. Our hope was still five hundred feet away. We were making better time, but so were the demons chasing us. As we approached the packs of demons laying in wait they turned, destroying our "element" of surprise. Half-life's too short so it disappears too easily. Explains why it's not listed on the periodic table.

"Been nice knowing you, Murphy," said Ryth.

"It ain't over yet. Watch this," I said, standing upright on Ryth's back surfboard style, holding her long hair in my hands like reins. Ryth, by virtue–or perhaps sin–of her wings, was marked as one of the higher–ranked demons. I in turn was commanding her. Or so it appeared, which ranked me above her. In short, I was an overlord as far as they were concerned.

"You scum, refuse, lowly, poor excuse for demons! How dare you not bow when I approach," I ranted.

"Do we know you?" asked a pudgy, purple, wart–covered demon.

I signaled Ryth to dive bomb the inquisitive one, knocking him through the slightly glowing portal.

"Any other questions? Or shall I feast on more of your kidneys this evening?" I raved with a scowl. There were none. "Behind me race human damned, impersonating demons! Do not let their disguises fool you. They must be stopped or your pitiful existence will be transformed to prey for my pet here," I said, indicating Ryth, who transformed her mouth into a gaping monstrosity and her claws into two foot blades. For the first time I was distracted from her nudity.

We were obeyed without question. The pack engaged our pursuers in the nick of time. Ryth and I flew out of the gate and back into the caverns, past the unconscious demon Ryth had dive bombed. Hermes and Mathew saw us coming and sprang up.

"The gig is up!" I shouted. "Get out of here! All hell is about to break loose!" I was probably one of the few people who could say that and really mean it. The pair became airborne as we headed toward the Styx. We encountered some turbulence. Stupidly, I was still standing, and I tumbled off Ryth, down onto a field. I had the wind knocked out of me, but was otherwise unhurt. My three companions started back for me, which was good; the demons chose that moment to crash through the gate, which was bad. Hermes could see me, while the demons could not. This meant we could talk in relative privacy. Not talk exactly. Because Judah Maccabee is mute, the lot of us have learned sign language to better understand him.

I signed, "Go on without me!"

Hermes signed, "No!"

"No sense in both us getting caught. I will hide, try to head back into Hades. The demons won't follow me there."

"No!" Hermes signed again, but six airborne demons reached and attacked him. The attack was unsuccessful that time, but with him carrying me he would not outrun them as easily, if at all. Hermes realized that and retreated over the Styx, but not before signing "I will be back, with reinforcements." I could see Mathew literally dragging Ryth through the air, with her struggling to come back for me. Hermes added his efforts to Mathew and the trio were gone from my sight, a flock of flying demons in hot pursuit.

They would be back. Could I stay hidden that long? Or risk endangering my friends? Not that I had any choice in the matter. I had friends to die for and who would return the favor. They would follow me straight into Hell itself if need be. It would be better for all involved if I got away somehow. Problem was, the demon ground troops were searching. I could hear Charon's engine revving up and bolting away. Hades was a long way off and I was caught between the devil and the deep blue sea. All right, a bunch of demons and a murky black river. It still didn't make it any easier. Slowly I inched my way over the hills, foot by agonizing foot. Finally, I paused, thinking myself safe, when I heard the yells. Someone had spotted me. Stealth was no longer an option, so I got up and ran. Demons with four and six legs ran faster, and they were closing up the gap quickly. I ran for all I was worth, and would have mortgaged my soul for more speed. The metaphysical banks were closed and my legs were getting tired. I was traveling so fast that I wasn't bothering to look where I was going. It cost me. I fell in a gap between hills. The growls of my pursuers were getting louder. This was it, I thought.

I started to hear voices calling my name.

"Murphy."

I knew the voice, but in my panic, I couldn't place it. I looked around for the source and saw a white mist burrowing out from a hole in the hill.

A delicate, soft hand appeared in the mist. A red maw appeared over the top of the hill.

"Murphy, quick! Take my hand!" said the soft voice in the mist. I reached for the hand, and as it pulled me into the mist, I felt demon jaws close and miss me by the skin of their own teeth.

As my vision started to clear, I looked around. I was in a well lit but not incredibly bright place. It still took a minute for my eyes to adjust from the darkness of the caverns. A blurry figure was standing over me.

"Elsie?" I asked.

"No, silly. It's me. Peter."

"Peter!?" I said, grabbing the little imp and hugging him. He was amazingly solid. Jack, his killer was no more. We made sure of that, but I was also sure that nothing could bring him back. Until now. "But you're dead... how?"

"It's a long story, one I can't tell you all of right now. Are you okay?"

"Yes, thanks to you saving me. Thanks."

"It was nothing."

"It certainly was. Do you know why I'm here?"

"Yes. The pretty lady told me."

"Elsie?"

"No. This lady was... a friend of Paddy's. She's been taking care of me. She told me you were looking for your wife. She couldn't come because you and her never met, but I could. We don't know where she is but we can help you look. I will be your Guide. And to think you guys wouldn't even let me cross the street by myself."

I chuckled at the joke.

I looked around and noticed we were not alone. Dozens, perhaps hundreds, of people were milling around aimlessly in a large chamber.

"Where are we now, and who are all those people?" I asked.

"We're in Limbo, but no one here even has a broomstick to play it with," Limbo was one of Peter's favorite games. "The people are folks not sure of what they believe or are waiting for loved ones to join them. Some just don't care, so they stay here for lack of anything better to do," Peter said, looking around and failing to understand that mentality. He was not alone. "Where would you like to go first?" he asked.

"Where Elsie must be. Heaven."

"Okay, but..."

"But what?"

"It will be easier to show you," Peter said, as mist began to surround us and shift and change. The mists grew and a bright light emerged.

"Is this the tunnel?"

"No. The end of it. One of them anyway."

"Is it Heaven?"

"The outer slopes. Up ahead is the gate."

"Let's go."

"Not a good idea, Murphy."

"Why not?"

"First off, you aren't dead. They will know that, and they are sticklers for rules. Second, if they decide to let you in, you will not want to come out again. If Elsie isn't inside, you will never see her again. Third, they are not happy with any of you for stopping their Apocalypse. Or for hiding Mathew."

"Oh."

"But I'm dead. And a Guide. That carries a little weight. They have to let me in and back out again. Eventually anyway. I will go ask. Please wait here."

Peter walked over to the gate and started asking questions. I looked down at my feet and wondered how the mist was holding me up. As I did I started to sink. I chased those thoughts from my mind, trying to think only happy thoughts. I was on solid air again. I squinted and strained to see past the gate and the mist to no avail. Peter came back with a sad look on his face.

"They said it was classified and wouldn't tell me. I think that means they didn't know, which means she isn't there. We better go."

I looked back at Heaven's Gate and realized that this was literally the closest I had ever gotten to Heaven. Know what? It did not even begin to compare with the time spent with Elsie. I smiled despite myself.

"Where to next?" I asked.

"Purgatory. Just remember that Purgatory is different for everyone," Peter advised. The mist shifted again and we were standing on a city sidewalk. A New York City sidewalk.

"We're on Earth," I brilliantly observed.

"That is Purgatory for some people. Some are ghosts. Some are reincarnated as people or animals. The better they do in life, the better they do in the next, until eventually they reach Heaven."

"Hinduism?"

"Among others. Purgatory can be many places and is different for everyone. Most you wouldn't have heard of because they so are personal. Others you know," Peter said, as the mists began to swirl again, but this time they did not fade. They felt hot, like steam, and there were big, oblong, white and tan clouds that looked almost solid.

Again in a strange place, I heard someone call my name. It was great to be popular.

"Murphy? What are you doing here? You just left for Hades," asked Tommy, dressed in his 1920's style gangster suit, white tie and matching spats.

"Tommy? Where are we?" I asked.

"The bunwarmer in Edgar's cart. Business is business, after all. Decided to wait it out at home. And who is we?"

"We is me," came the voice at my side.

"Peter!" Tommy yelled and gave him a hug, same as I did. "Did they make you a Jinn?"

"No silly. I am a Guide. I was showing Murphy the afterlife, and we were up to Purgatory."

"I see. But Elsie didn't abuse power, so she wouldn't have been made a Jinn."

"True, but I can only show what I know. I'm still new at this," Peter answered. "We have to go."

"Wait. Let me get Paddy and the rest of the gang so they can say hi," Tommy suggested.

"Can't do it. I wish I could."

"Too bad you didn't hold my bottle, or I could make that wish come true."

"It is better that you aren't a slave anymore," Peter said.

"Absolutely. Can you at least harass Edgar before you go? You never met him, Peter. He is a little gruff, but he is really an okay guy."

"I guess Murphy could. I can only talk to people who are dead or knew me when I was alive."

"Hey Edgar!" Tommy shouted.

"What?" came a whisper from beyond.

"Murphy's in here with me."

"Sure he is. I'm working out here."

"Don't strain yourself," I said.

"Murphy?" he asked. My name was becoming a cosmic catch phrase.

"Yep."

"How did you...Good day, ma'am. What can I get for you?"

"Edgar's hot dogs use horse meat and rat part fillers!" I shouted and started neighing and squeaking. Tommy and Peter joined me.

"They do not!" Edgar shouted at his bun warmer. Turning to his customer he said, "Sorry, installed a two—way radio so I can keep in touch with my boys. Now I can't turn the thing off, and they like to play practical jokes." I gathered the woman walked away. "See what you did!"

"Sorry Edgar," I said. "I'll pay for her order, but I need you to do me a favor. Hermes, Mathew, and Ryth are going to be coming back up soon and they are probably going to try to mount a rescue party for me. Tell them not to, that I am safe, okay?"

"Got it covered, Murphy. You owe me five fifty."

"Ask Hermes for it. He probably has my wallet anyway."

"We really have to go," Peter said. "I don't want to get in trouble."

"Okay. See you later, Tommy."

"Bye, Murphy. Bye, Peter. You be good, okay? Stop by anytime," Tommy said, grabbing another hug.

"I will if I can. Bye, bye Tommy."

The steam became mist again and we were back on the street. This time we were outside Bulfinche's. No one else could see us.

"That's all I can show you, Murphy."

"But we didn't find Elsie."

"I know. I'm sorry, but like I said, I am still new at this. Maybe after a couple more years, I will be able to find people every time."

"Thanks for trying. And thanks again for saving my life. You will make a great Guide."

Peter beamed at the praise.

"I miss you, you know," I told him. "We all do. We all love you very much."

"I love all of you, too. Tell everybody that, especially Paddy, Roy, and Rebecca. They need to hear it the most. Tell them I'm fine and Paddy's lady is taking good care of me. Tell Paddy she still loves him very much, and not to miss her so much. Part of her will always be with him. Same as part of Elsie will always be with you, Murphy. Got to go. The Lady is calling."

I hugged the kid, tears welling up in my eyes. The mists were swirling in his eyes, too, then around the pair of us.

"Bye, Murphy," he said as the mists took him away. I saw the outline of a woman take his hand and wave to me. Being polite I waved back as they both vanished. The mist swirled one last time and returned me fully to the land of the living.

I went back inside the bar though the front door.

"Murphy!" shouted everyone. Like I said, it must be some sort of universal "Say Murphy's Name Day".

Ryth ran over and hugged me. She was wearing Hermes' gray trenchcoat. It looked better on her than it ever did on him.

"How did you get out of there?" Ryth asked.

I walked over to our wall of photos and took down a very special one. It was Peter dressed as a clown, a cherry tomato for a nose and a head of lettuce for hair. It was the day he helped save Roy G. Biv from a life of self–pity and gave him the inspiration to continue being a clown, despite his paraplegia and being confined to a wheelchair.

"I got out with a little help from my friend," I said, still crying. I told everyone what happened and gave them Peter's love. Then I bought the house a round and we toasted Peter. After awhile, I stopped weeping and told Paddy the rest of his message.

"Peter also said to tell you that your lady was taking good care of him, and that she said to tell you she still loves you very much and part of her will always be with you."

"Did he say her name?"

"No," I said. We both got very quiet, until I changed the subject. "How'd you guys get out?"

"It was a close call," said Hermes. "We made it back to the garage, but the demons were breathing down our necks. They had not brushed in decades. Luckily, Paddy sicced Cerberus on them. They turned tail and flew for all they were worth. Then Paddy closed down that aspect for awhile, at least until they're all back in Hell. The only reason they were able to follow us is because they were chasing you two. Gave them the right."

"Sorry about that."

"You have nothing to be sorry for. I am truly sorry we had to leave you. Paddy was ready to open the aspect up and charge into Hell riding Cerberus bareback. Hercules was handing out rocket launchers. Luckily, Edgar got your message to us first."

"Thanks Herc, Boss, everyone."

"'Tis nothing ye would not have done for me," Paddy said.

"Head into Hell, sure. Ride Cerberus bareback, I don't know."

"It is good to have ye home, regardless."

"Ready for Heaven?" Mathew asked.

"Been there, done that," I said, explaining my tour.

"You still interesting in checking out Valhalla?" asked Mista.

"Sure," I answered. I should have been thrilled with the prospect of exploring a new realm, one that very few people have ever seen. It was an honor and a privilege. Instead, I was despairing. Elsie would probably not be there either.

Mista had two modes of transportation these days. A winged horse named Grinmswan has been with her for thousands of years. She also rides a motorcycle customized by Vulcan. It looks very similar to a Harley Davidson, but has a few more features, including a side car, which was where I rode. Handing me a plain helmet she put on her own. It was of course, solid metal with carved wings on the side. We pulled out onto the street and accelerated quickly. A light ahead of us switched to red, but instead of stopping we went into the wild gray—and–blue yonder. The colors of the sky warped into all ends of the spectrum simultaneously. Mista, as a Valkyrie, was not restricted to use of the Rainbow Bridge to cross over. Before long, we were back on solid ground again, speeding along a dirt road. Ahead a castle, Gladsheim by name, loomed in the distance. This was a fortress the US Marines would think twice about storming, even with modern–day weapons. We pulled into the main gate, which Mista opened with a remote.

We were greeted by a dozen women, decked out in leather, armor, and chain mail. I could have been in the Village except for the lack of body piercing.

"Hail Mista!" they shouted.

"Hail Sword Sisters!" she shot back.

"What do you bring with you?" one asked. Guess she did not know of the holiday and the requirement to say my name upon meeting me. Hope the powers that be took it easy on her.

"This is a noble hero, Murphy."

"You talking about me?" I asked.

"Of course."

"He is not dead," observed another.

"No, he is not. He is on a quest," Mista informed them. All nodded. A quest was a quest. "For his lost love."

"By what right does he claim entrance to Valhalla? What warrior deeds has he done? What makes him a hero?"

Uh-oh, I thought. They're on to me. Mista was not stumped for a minute.

"Why just today he invaded the realm of Hell, armed with only his heart. He faced off against demons and willingly sacrificed himself to save his comrades in arms. Then he escaped, unharmed."

"Well done, Murphy," a Valkyrie cheered.

"Thanks," I said, amazed at the way she arranged the details. Must be taking lessons from Herc.

I was escorted into the great hall, and was greeted by the biggest bar fight in recorded history. Thousands of warriors, from dozens of ages and times were crossing swords and machine guns in an eternal battle. Actually, it stopped each day at sunset so as not to ruin dinner. As it was not yet time for the sun to lay down for the evening, the fighting was still going on, but the ranks had been thinned out a bit. Hundreds lay unmoving on the ground. The floor around them was covered in a thick film of blood that ran down drains built for that express purpose. All involved were having the time of their deaths. Many, with holes though their chests, missing limbs and occasionally holding a head under their arm, were munching at the buffet table. Rather friendly, all things considered. Though not truly alive, the warriors could be wounded, but not killed, so they ran the contest on the honor system. One mortal wound and you have to remove yourself from the battlefield. Before the evening meal was served, all wounds magically healed, and the last warrior standing was declared the winner. Next morning the fun started anew.

I knew instantly Elsie could not be here. Still, Mista checked the records, since Elsie's fight against her leukemia qualified her as a warrior that died in battle. I was right. She even checked with Hel, the ruler of the Asgardian underworld, with no success.

The warriors and their decapitated heads asked me to dine with them. I politely refused, knowing enough to turn down food in a magic realm, lest I have to stay. The good-byes were brief.

We rode back to Bulfinche's in silence.

Persephone had called and none of the underworlds she had friendly relations with had Elsie. Shanna, a young, pretty banshee and the boss's cousin, stopped by to say she had checked the Sidhe, but no Elsie. Shanna offered to bring me with her to search, but I knew what the end result would be, and my heart just was not in it.

I didn't work that night. I just sat around, staring out the window. I was given my space. Closing time came around without my even noticing. The boss came over.

"Ye will be okay, Murphy. The pain will always be with ye, but it dulls with time."

"Thanks, Paddy. I just need to be alone."

"As if ye could ever be alone in Bulfinche's," Paddy said, putting his hand on my shoulder. I smiled back. He had been where I was, where we both would be again.

As the door behind the bar that leads to our living quarters swung closed behind Paddy, the street door swung wide. We keep the front door unlocked.

The man who had opened it came in. He was tall, muscular and good looking. He wore black jeans and a black turtleneck sweater. I would swear I never saw him before but something about him was disturbingly familiar.

"We're closed," I said. Did not matter. If he wanted a drink, I would get him one. We don't worry about little things like laws regarding when alcohol should be served.

"I KNOW," he said. His voice was deep and rich with a trace of sadness lining the edges. "I CAME TO SEE YOU, JOHN MURPHY."

"And you are?"

"I THINK YOU ALREADY KNOW THAT."

Oh crap, was all I could think, but what I did was another matter entirely. I walked up to him, looked him straight in the eyes, and burst out in hysterics.

"WHAT DID YOU DO THAT FOR?" he asked.

"I always wanted to say I stared Death in the face and laughed," I answered. He cracked the smallest hint of a smile. Any good detective with a magnifying glass would have been able to find it in less than an hour.

"NOT BAD," he said. "ARE YOU WONDERING WHY I HAVE COME HERE?"

"Thirsty?"

"ACTUALLY, I COULD REALLY GO FOR A ZOMBIE," he said. I started to comment but he cut me off. "THAT WAS NOT A STRAIGHT LINE."

"Could have fooled me," I said, making his order, then handing him the drink. He took a pair of old looking coins out of his pocket. I didn't need to ask where he got them. One looked as if it still had an eyelash stuck to it.

"Put your money away," I said.

"BUT IT IS NOT MY FIRST VISIT TO BULFINCHE'S."

"I know," I said. We had our share of death. "Last time I saw you, you had a black trenchcoat with a hood and were with the other three horsemen."

"THE DRINK SHOULD NOT BE FREE."

"It's not. I'm buying," I said. Death lifted his hand as if to protest. "Don't argue with me. I'm not in the mood."

"THANK YOU," Death said graciously.

"You're welcome. Why the outfit change? Grim Reaper casual wear?"

"NO. I APPEAR TO EACH PERSON AS THEY ENVISION ME. TO SOME I APPEAR SKELETAL WITH A SICKLE. TO OTHERS I AM A FRIEND, A RELEASE, OR THE GREAT ENEMY. TO SOME A BEAUTIFUL WOMAN OR A BIRD OF DARKNESS. AN ANGEL WITH HUGE BEATING WINGS. I TOOK YOUR WIFE FROM YOU, THEREFORE YOU SEE ME THROUGH THE EYES OF A JEALOUS LOVER."

"How is she?"

"WELL."

"I want to see her."

"THAT IS WHY I AM HERE. IN ONE DAY, YOU HAVE CROSSED OVER INTO NO LESS THAN SIX OF MY REALMS. A VERY IMPRESSIVE ACCOMPLISHMENT. ONE PROBLEM. IT IS NOT PERMITTED. YOU MUST STOP YOUR SEARCH."

"Maybe for a few days, until I get over my blue funk."

"YOU MUST STOP FOREVER. YOU TAMPER WITH THE FABRIC OF REALITY."

"Just when you thought those tamper–proof caps were doing their job."

"IT IS NO LAUGHING MATTER."

"For me, I gotta laugh or cry. I have no desire to drown myself in my own tears. If I started crying, I would never stop. Besides, Paddy would make me clean up the mess." Speaking of short people, I heard the door behind the bar squeak open, despite being well oiled. "Or you can simply point the way. Then I will only cross over once more."

"AND YOUR FINAL TIME," Death said, letting the phrase hang in the air like a lead balloon.

"Are you threatening me?" I demanded, unsure of what to do if he said yes.

Death hesitated before answering. "NO."

"Good. Then draw me a map and I will be on my way."

"I CANNOT. I AM BOUND BY RULES EVEN I CANNOT BREAK. I WOULD HELP YOU IF I COULD."

"Honest?"

"YES."

"There is an interesting property about this bar. Powers, curses, bindings are all null and void here. Of course, some universal laws are beyond its control, like the act of dying, but as far as breaking a few rules goes, it should be no problem."

"I COULD ARRANGE A MEETING IN THE TUNNEL OF LIGHT, IF I WERE PERMITTED," Death said, looking over my shoulder. I could almost hear Paddy nodding 'yes'. "AND IF YOU SWORE ON THAT WHICH IS MOST SACRED TO YOU, YOUR LOVE, THAT YOU WOULD RETURN."

"You would let me return?" I asked, surprised.

"YES. IT IS NOT YOUR TIME. YOU MUST RETURN OR..." Death trailed off.

"Let's do it," I said.

For a moment Death shifted and suddenly was holding his scythe. The next instant it was slicing through my heart. Comparatively, the pain was nothing. For a moment I floated above the bar. Paddy had stepped out of the shadows and caught me before I hit the floor. He cradled me, placing a dishrag behind my head.

"Ye better be bringing the boy back, Thanatos, or there will be trouble," he told Death.

Sipping his zombie, Death replied. "I GAVE MY WORD AND AM BOUND BY IT. THAT YOU KNOW."

"Yes," Paddy said, wanting to speak but holding back his tongue. It was an epic struggle when Death decided to tag team with the tongue against Paddy.

"GO AHEAD. ASK."

"The lady Peter mentioned, it was Bulfinche, wasn't it?"

"YOU ALREADY KNOW THE ANSWER."

"If I already knew the answer, do ye think I would be wasting my time asking the question?"

"YES. IT WAS SHE."

"So she is a Guide."

"MORE THAN THAT," Death answered. Paddy nodded and walked away, turning his back on the good–looking gentleman aspect of Death. "WHY DO YOU HATE ME SO, PADRIAC MORAN?"

"Why? Because you take away these mortals in the blink of an eye. They barely have time to shine before you cut them down."

"BUT THEY DO SHINE. BRIGHTLY. AND IT IS MY DUTY."

"And it is my duty to stand against ye."

"I DO NOT MAKE THESE DECISIONS BY MYSELF," Death justified. "I AM NOT ALWAYS A MONSTER. SOMETIMES I AM VIEWED AS A FRIEND, AN END TO PAIN."

"Sounds like justifying to me."

"PERHAPS. BUT YOU HAVE THE POWER NOW TO MAKE MORTALS LIVE, PERHAPS FOREVER, ALL BECAUSE OF YOUR LOVE FOR BEATRICE GERALD BULFINCHE MORAN."

"Only a few and probably not forever. Now I am put in the position to choose who I grant the gift and who I let ye claim. But all of it too late to do her any good. Couldn't ye have given her an hour more? Even five minutes might have been enough."

"NO."

At about that point I stopped following the conversation. Music sang from above me. I recognized the song. It was "Story Book Love" from *The Princess Bride*. It was our song. The song was accompanied by the most incredible light show. A beam of pure light shone down. It was not exactly white, more like every color ever rolled into one.

It was my cue, and I headed into the breach.

I saw my life play out. Amazing, but I barely remember it now. Then it was all so clear, especially the parts with Elsie in it. I floated and sped down a tunnel, toward the source of light. Almost to the end, I prepared to go in, but something more beautiful made me veer off.

"Elsie!" I laughed, cried, and wept.

"John!"

"I missed you so much. I love you so much. I..."

"Shh. We don't need to talk."

And we did not. We grabbed onto each other and held on for dear death. All creation was caught up in that moment. I knew everything she was feeling, every thought she had, and she knew mine, all that had happened to me since her death. Our pain, remaining in each other's soul, was shattered and destroyed by our embrace. Our love burned a new light in the tunnel of death. We stayed that way forever. The rest of what happened is too private to tell, but imagine paradise and cube it.

Forever is not as long as it used to be. The tunnel's light started to blink like the overheads at the end of a Broadway intermission.

"It is time, John. We have to go."

"I don't want to."

"Neither do I, but we both gave our word. We will be together again. Until then, we will never truly be fully apart."

The light began blinking faster.

"I love you, Elsie."

"I love you, John."

"Goodbye, sweetie."

"No, guy, not goodbye. Until later."

"Later."

The light shut off and I went plummeting, a shooting star through the cosmos. I woke up where I had started. At Bulfinche's.

I was weak, nauseous and couldn't stand on my own. I had never felt better in my life.

"I saw her, Paddy. I held her. I got into Heaven," I blathered, a big goofy smile spread across my mug. I was more intoxicated than I had ever been, drunk on love. Best part is, no hangover.

"I know," said Paddy, with a sad smile. He was happy for me, but also jealous in a way.

Paddy hefted me up on his short shoulder like I was a rag doll and made for the upstairs door.

"MORAN."

"Yes?"

"I COULD DO THE SAME FOR YOU."

Paddy stopped short and almost dropped me. He was caught fast in a quandary.

"No. I cannot. Someday we will meet on less friendly terms. I can't afford to be indebted to ye."

"I SEE," said Death, genuinely disappointed. "I WAS NOT OFFERING TO PUT YOU IN MY DEBT. IT WAS AN OFFER OF...."

"Friendship?" asked Paddy.

"YES. MINE IS A LONELY PATH. EVEN GODS HATE ME, FOR MY

POWER SURPASSES THEIRS. WHEN LAST I CAME FOR THE APOCALYPSE I SHOULD HAVE BEEN UPSET THAT I WAS CHEATED OF MY MOMENT IN THE SUN, OF MY GREATEST PRIZE."

"Two thirds of the worlds population. Billions and billions," I muttered from my perch.

"Hush, Murphy," Paddy said to me. Turning to Death he said, "But?"

"BUT I HAD A GOOD TIME. I FELT AT HOME. EVEN WITH THE SATYR BEATING ME AT CHESS."

"His name is Fred. So you wish a place to rest from your journeys?"

"YES."

"We might be able to help ye with that. Provided you agree to some ground rules."

"WHICH WOULD BE?"

"We could form them tomorrow during business hours. It is permissible for you to trade for a kindness done to you?"

"IF I SO CHOOSE. BUT IF YOU ARE KIND TO ME JUST FOR THAT PURPOSE..."

"Not me. But the folks here are good to almost everyone. Could work to their favor, wouldn't ye say?"

"PERHAPS."

"Excellent."

"CAN YOU FORGIVE THE PERSON WHO YOU BLAME FOR YOUR WIFE'S DEMISE?"

"Perhaps, if I had good reason."

"FAIR ENOUGH."

"Come in this aspect so as not to let all know your identity. Agreed?"

"AGREED. SEE YOU TOMORROW."

"Yesterday, I would have taken that as a threat. Today I find myself almost looking forward to the prospect of Death darkening my door."

Death left, and Paddy opened the door to take me up to my room. Hanging over his shoulder, I lifted my head up so I could see Elsie's painting, "Rainbow's End": her rendition of Bulfinche's and all within. Not for the first time, I thought I saw her smiling face shining down on me from the heart of the rainbow. For a moment, before the memory fled, I knew where in the afterlife she was. And I smiled back.

BULFINCHE'S MIXOLOGY

The place was packed. The fire inspector's legal requirements for maximum occupancy were exceeded twofold, but we still had room to maneuver. I don't think it is possible to fill Bulfinche's Pub to capacity. It seems to expand to the amount of people it holds. Inside, everyone feels comfortable and cozy, whether there be two or two thousand patrons. Not that we needed an excuse, but there was a reason for the crowd. The Day had rolled around again like clockwork. Same time every year. Days are funny that way; put them on a calendar and no matter what you do to try to stop them, it's never enough. I thought about trying to run away and hide for The Day, but truth be told, I enjoy it. Despite all the extra work and hours I have to put in getting everything ready, it's the biggest party anywhen.

The Day is a tradition at Bulfinche's and, like many of our other traditions, is observed without fail. This year it started out normally enough, but that is often the case. Of course, my version of what's normal may differ significantly from the average, but what else could be expected from a barkeep at Bulfinche's Pub? Consider who I work for and that our patrons tend to make the staff look normal by comparison, and at no time more so than on The Day.

The Day has a long history, far longer than anyone here can remember. That predates recorded history. Strangely enough, most of The Day happens at night, as the days do grow shorter during the late autumn. It is a beautiful time of year, even here in Manhattan. You can see parents taking their kids out to watch the smog change colors over the skyline at sunset. Or, for true nature buffs, there are always the street trees planted in three–foot–square breaks in the sidewalk. Central Park has a beauty all its own, but tourists are put off by its reputation. Still, it is a must see. Here at Bulfinche's we are lucky beyond compare because Demeter, Greek goddess and cook supreme, keeps her atrium up in the penthouse. Not a true penthouse, more like half of our roof that was made into a glasshouse where all things green and beautiful grow year—round. The wonders within would keep a rain forest botanist busy for three lifetimes. She also grows all her own herbs, as well as most of her own fruits and vegetables. Demeter only allows the staff and special patrons, mostly our regulars, to partake of its majesty. The rest have to make do with looking in the window of the flower shop down the street.

On The Day, the atrium was off limits to all unless given special leave by its mistress. Foster, an intelligent plant elemental, worshiped by some dust heads back in the seventies, spends most of his time up there. He had almost been killed when his devotees found out that smoking his leaves brought on a special form of enlightenment. Luckily, after some self pollination, a plant's version of masturbation, only with the intent of becoming pregnant, he was able to send his seeds off. One landed in Demeter's hot house, and he was able to transfer his mind to it in safety. The others scattered around the world and each plant is a possible home for him.

The Day has myriad names in multitudinous cultures. It is the single best time for the Otherworlds to open wide to the mortal plane. It is a time when even the dead, mortal and not, could walk the earth again. To the Gentry, the boss' people, it is known as Samhain Eve. Americans in the twentieth century know it as Halloween. We just refer to it as The Day.

Bulfinche's is a foci, a nexus of belief. Just by existing, it acts as both a doorway and a magnet for parts of reality which have slipped away over the years. In the days of yore there were as many different beliefs as there were tribes, and each belief fostered a different part of reality. I have never gotten a satisfactory answer as to whether gods foster belief or belief creates the gods. It seems in most cases that belief at least strengthens a god, increasing his or her power. That is the purpose of most rituals. To increase belief, magnify it and channel it to the object of its attention.

As Empires grew and cultures were acclimated, old beliefs died out as new ones took their place. Unable to compete, many less powerful deities died off or left Earth for the Otherworlds. Some took on mortal aspects and acclimated themselves into human culture, passing for normal folk. It has gotten worse for most deities in the last hundred or so years. Even more devastating than the spreading of Christianity and Islam to the divine was the media. With the advent of television, movies, and mass communication, the beliefs of the world were becoming more uniform as to what reality was than during any time in history. Reality bends to belief, and in fact embodies the old saying, "What people believe is true is more important than what is." Even the Roman Empire tended to adopt, not eradicate beliefs. With media censorship, however unofficial, and political correctness, the beliefs of the world on reality are closer to each other than ever before, leaving the fringe beliefs little room to exist outside the pages of tabloids and science fiction or fantasy venues. These days, most deities are not looking for worship. They just need someone to believe in them in order to survive. Don't we all?

Goddesses and gods these days are hiring publicists, authors, video game programmers, and screen writers to immortalize them. A member of the Greco-Roman pantheon, who shall remain nameless, actually commissioned Thomas Bulfinch, no relation to the bar, to do his Mythology books. Members of other pantheons got in on the act giving him more tales than he could possibly use. I don't think they actually told him who they were, passing themselves off instead as scholars of myths and legends. Thor pulled off quite a coup, back in the sixties, when he got his very own comic book. Unfortunately, due to a coloring error, he was featured with blond, instead of red, hair. Proud, he refuses to dye his hair and is unable to take full advantage of the situation. Hercules has had several books, TV shows and movies made about him, most of them bad, to his dismay. He himself wrote one of them and tried out for another. The script was altered so much that the only resemblance between the finished product and the original was the same spelling of his name. The producer of the film he auditioned for told him he was not right for the part; nobody would believe someone with all those muscles. That film did not gross back its production costs.

Lucas Wilson, vampyre by nature, programmer and hacker by trade, has been supporting himself creating some of the above—named video games– showing warrior gods, goddesses, and heroes doing battle in an organized tournament. Based it on his own experiences while on a road trip with Hercules and some of our regulars. I myself have even been approached to do a series of stories or a novel by several deities. In the category of deity, I lump all people of legendary status, whether they were considered a god or not. Most do not appeal to me, so I politely refuse.

Robigus keeps trying. Haven't heard of him? Not surprising as he is one of the deities who could not enter the mortal plane without help from a place like Bulfinche's. He is a member of the Roman pantheon who comes to Earth on two occasions a year: the first is The Day; the second is his feast day, April 25. Still wondering why you've never heard of him? The answer is simple, really. Robigus is the Roman god of mildew. Yes, mildew. That is what he rules over. He has been so persistent that, while I refuse to do a complete story around him, I will mention his name if for no other reason than to get him off of my back. That and he, with the boss' dispensation, cleaned the green stuff off of my bathroom tile and shower curtain. He promised it would not return, and so far it has not. I do not even have ring around the tub. I have mentioned this to Paddy, and suggested he finance a bathroom cleaner developed by and named for Robigus. Robigus had tried unsuccessfully for years to become the trademark of a dozen mildew cleaners. Maybe one of his own might work. Look what being a trademark did for Hermes. Despite the belief it inspires, Hermes hates it. Whenever someone wants to get his goat, they send him a pick—me—up bouquet.

The belief syndrome is one of the reasons Paddy Moran, my boss, gives me his blessing to write these stories. They might foster belief, allowing people of myth and legends to remain in existence a little bit longer. Folks not strong enough to manifest on their own can draw on our strength all year round. On The Day, the foci's power is magnified manyfold, which explains how folks like Robigus arrive.

Our regulars arrive under their own power, for the most part. Some arrive with a little help. Paddy had opened wide the fire hydrant in front of the pub just as the sun was setting. He had done the same at sunrise. A bridge as insubstantial as a dream, brilliant as a rainbow appeared in the mist, discharging two passengers. The remainder of the Norse contingency had arrived. Paddy waved to the shadowy figure who stood at the top of the rainbow bridge. Two ravens perched upon his shoulders. The one-eyed gentleman waved back. He had decided not to attend this year's festivities for reasons of his own. Still, his presence would be felt as one of the ravens flew down and perched itself upon the trickster's shoulder, to guard Loki from causing too much trouble on his annual night of freedom. Heimdal escorted him inside the doors without incident, before exchanging embraces with the senior staff. That would be Paddy, Dion, Hercules, Hermes, and Demeter.

During Prohibition, Thor had screwed up and as punishment was sent to relieve Heimdal at his post of guarding the Rainbow Bridge. A difficult task, considering he was too heavy to be allowed to stand atop it. This freed up Heimdal's schedule for well over a few decades. He headed down the Rainbow Bridge to Midgard, Norse slang for Earth, and landed right at Bulfinche's door.

Heimdal had lived and worked here for a few decades, and helped the gang bootleg booze and make a fortune. In short, he was family. Loki was tolerated because Paddy owed Woton a favor and because of Loki's own actions. Their reunion with Heimdal was robust, joyous, and thunderous.

The doors prevent sound outside from coming in, but allow noise to exit, so we were full up with people who had never been in Bulfinche's before. People know a great party when they hear it. Most were shocked at another of our traditions getting the first drink free. After that, it's whatever the market will bear. Usually it is kept reasonable. Tip good, behave yourself, and the prices will be excellent. Otherwise, you may regret your actions.

This evening, for instance, two gentlemen (I use the term loosely) found out our first drink policy and ordered bottom shelf for themselves and top shelf for their dates, who were dressed as belly dancers. Bottom shelf is where Paddy keeps our best stuff, so he can reach it easier. Top shelf is where the more economical libations are kept. A switch from the norm. Unless you are a regular, ordering bottom shelf here is a mistake you may regret for the rest of your life. Our top shelf, even the stuff we mop up from the floor, is better than the stuff you will get anywhere else in the world, or most of the Otherworlds. Dionysus does most of the fermenting and imbibitions, save the whiskey and beer which are Paddy's domain. To say Dion deserves the title god of wine is an understatement. It barely touches the surface of his skills.

The bottom shelf is almost his very best. The very best is saved for extremely special occasions, which I, fortunately, have not been privy to. It ruins the palate for anything less, which is everything else. Compare it to someone having eaten prime rib all their life, then being forced to eat cow manure forever, only more extreme. We tried to warn them, but they would not listen. All they knew is they were getting something expensive for free. They did not know how costly. When they ordered their second round they found out, not only could they not afford to pay cash, but it even maxed out their plastic. Instead of talking the situation over like reasonable people and trying to reach a solution, they headed outside, smiling and whispering in conspiring tones. The pair paid two guys one hundred dollars each to trade costumes. They had been pirates, upon their return they were gorillas. Disguising their voices, they ordered two more of the same. They walked away from the bar, not expecting to pay. Dion was not amused.

"Gentlemen, I believe you still owe for those drinks."

"But I thought the first drink was free," said one of the apes.

"It is," answered Dion.

"Well this is our first drink."

"Only since the last one, me buccaneers," I added. We bartenders here tend to develop a second sight, and an amazing communal memory of who has been served here before. Ever. It is the only paranormal ability I seem to possess, other than making bad jokes. "The freebie is a one—time offer only good for the first visit. No return trips."

The apes turned to look at each other dismayed and confused. They had considered their plan foolproof. We were no fools. Paddy came over and towered under the participants. For a time, they wisely cowered away.

"Problem?" he asked.

"The gorilla brothers have ordered drinks and now refuse to pay for them," said Dion. Paddy frowned at the news. He takes money matters very seriously, especially when it is his money.

"They switched their pirate costumes and came in again, expecting to deceive us into believing their second was their first trip to the bar," I added. Paddy's frown deepened. He takes honor and deceit very seriously. He can forgive duplicity if it is for a good or fun cause. If he could not I would not be here. But to try to take advantage of his generosity for nothing but a free drink was unforgivable.

"It is a problem very easily solved. Simply pay for the drinks," Paddy suggested.

"Why? We've never been here before so we shouldn't have to pay."

"How did you know the drinks were free if you've never been here before?" Dion asked.

That stumped them. "Some guys told us outside."

We all laughed at that one. Dion answered them. "Except you two, there isn't anyone who has left this party since it started at sunrise and I doubt anyone else will before the next sunrise. Except you two."

"But we can't afford that."

"Not without selling our cars."

"That's okay, boys," Paddy said with a smile. "You can sign the cars over to me and we'll call it even."

"But they are both Porsches."

"I know I am getting the short end of the stick, but I am willing to come down in price just to be neighborly." Actually, Paddy would have accepted the cars if they were Yugos. He was trying to teach these boys a lesson.

"Fine. Just keep the drinks. We'll just leave. And we're never coming back here again."

"You have that right," said Dion. "But first we have to take care of a few things." With that he jumped over the bar, one hand on the counter, his legs and wine belly coming over sideways. I am unable to clear the bar without touching it with my feet, a definite no-no, so I walked around the short way. At our approach they backed away.

"Hey you can't do this. I'll call a cop."

"Go ahead. There are half a dozen over by the donuts, dressed up like gangsters, and Jasmine is dressed like a moll. But before you do, you should realize that the drinks you stole were expensive enough to make your crime a felony. Not less than a year in jail," Paddy said. They stopped complaining and ran for the door.

They were blocked by a four–foot–eight inch busboy named Fred. For the evening, he had made no effort to hide the three–inch horns that protruded from each side of his forehead. Not that there was anything wrong with horns when you are a satyr. They were even polished for the occasion. Fred had even lost his pants, although he still wore a white button shirt with a bow tie. His father, Pan, was due to show any minute.

Normally Hercules bounces and covers the door, but presently he was otherwise occupied arm wrestling with Samson. Thor had dibs on the winner. Same story every year, they have to see who is the strongest. Since curses and powers are null and void once inside, it is mainly a question of heart. Demeter beat the exhausted winner of the three two years ago, then Rebecca beat her, so they don't let either of the ladies play anymore. Their egos couldn't take it. The two gorillas had enough ego between them to discount Fred because of his diminutive height. They learned the error of their ways when Fred plowed under them, knocking them onto their posteriors. With those cloven feet, Fred can really travel at amazing speed. Nothing in Hermes' class, but well beyond that of an ordinary sprinter. More akin to an aging racehorse. Before they could rise again, Dion and I were on them.

"Did you slip on a peel?"

"Must be making you bananas."

"Hey Kong, is it good to be King?"

"Wave 'bi' to the planes."

"As Johnny Weissmuller used to say, 'Cheetah's never win.'"

Paddy was moaning loudly and could not take much more. "The next one to pun is out of a job," he said jokingly.

"I'll be a monkey's uncle," said Dion.

"That explains Fred," said Paddy. Pan was Dion's brother in name and spirit.

"Hey!" screamed Fred indignantly. Dion and Paddy chuckled. But now it was time to enforce a rarely needed policy I learned about my first day on the job.

"Time to evolve boys," I said, as the four of us began to strip off the ape suits and everything else until the pair was wearing no more than looks of terror on their faces. Their dates turned and recognized them.

"I guess the King Kong puns were out of place," said Dion.

"But the Cheetah ones were right on target," I shot back. The belly dancers giggled. Paddy called to Ismael Macob who, dressed as a mummy, burst out the side door to the private multi-level parking garage. He knew the drill. Before we completed opening the front door, his cab was out in front. We threw the pair in the back seat, and Ismael was doing sixty before the door shut. New York cabbies normally negotiate traffic with the skill and daring of jet pilots and the grace of a wounded hippopotamus. Ismael was top notch, which made both his passengers and pedestrians nervous, but like the man says, if you don't like the way he drives, stay off the sidewalk.

The pair would find themselves starkers on the streets of the South Bronx inside of fifteen minutes with Ismael at the wheel. After a suitable period of terror the pair would safely find their way home. They were stupid, not evil, so Paddy would make sure they survived physically unharmed. He just wanted to teach them a lesson they'd never forget.

Their dates had not gotten upset or made any move to go with them. Hercules and Samson were hitting on the belly dancers as we came back inside. The women were barely this side of drooling. Samson had his long black hair tied back in a pony tail and dark sunglasses covered his eyes. He carried a blind man's walking stick, but rarely seemed to actually need it. Judging by the expression on his face, he knew exactly how the young women looked. The veiled woman nearest to him was admiring his ponytail and Samson was making small talk with her while he sipped his ginger ale.

"What do you do for a living?" asked the costumed dancer.

"I've been... retired for many years now, but I had been a freedom fighter working to liberate my people."

"Like in South America?" she asked.

"Something like that," he answered with a smile. Loki, raven still perched atop his shoulder, had walked up behind Samson. As a joke he threw a coin in Samson's cup, as someone might do to a blind beggar on the subway. Samson's walking cane shot out from beneath the table and between Loki's legs. The trickster plummeted down, his chin landing atop the glass he was carrying and shattering it in the process. Fred was already cleaning it up before Loki had regained his footing.

"Sam, looks like you killed that drink with the jawbone of an ass," laughed Hercules.

"Old hat, really," chuckled Samson back. The raven, unamused, was pecking at Loki's ears as he fled across the room. The quality of his mischief has diminished over the centuries. Having a snake drip acidic venom continuously on your face for over a thousand years makes it hard to plot and scheme. For the first couple centuries his wife, Signe, stayed with him, using a large bowl to catch the venom and dump a good chunk harmlessly aside. Loki never did anything but complain and abuse her, so eventually she left him and found happiness with someone who appreciated her. According to the rumors, it was with a mortal, no less. Loki has mellowed considerably since. While running to avoid the raven, he kept an eye out for Heimdal more so than Thor. Heimdal is fated to kill Loki at Ragnarok. This gives Heimdal a great psychological advantage when dealing with the trickster and explains why Woton chose him, not Thor, to retrieve Loki from his punishment. As to why he gets one day off each year, let's say it was for good behavior and leave that story for another day.

Still, it must be difficult for the lot of them to know exactly how and by whom they would die, just not when, and be helpless to stop it. For the most part, they just put it out of their minds.

Mosie is not much better off. Sober, he knows all. Drunk, his usual state, he knows more than most. He knows how and when all his loved ones will die, not to mention the method of his own demise. Being blind drunk helps numb the knowledge.

Meanwhile, Samson had no such worries. He had already met his end once and was more concerned with matters of the heart and other organs.

"What do you do for a living, Kathy?" he asked the young lady.

"I'm a hair stylist."

"A hair stylist?" asked Samson in genuine horror.

"I'd love to trim your pony tail," she offered. In response Samson fainted dead away. Roaring with laughter, Hercules lifted and lugged him over to the bar, where Dion revived him.

Meanwhile, I was refilling Prometheus' club soda. He steered away from hard liquor of any sort. Said his body could not take it. Liver trouble. Strangely enough, he and Loki were drinking together. Prometheus is the nicest guy you will ever meet. The type to give you the shirt off his back. Loki, in contrast, would convince you the only way to save your life would be to give him every piece of clothing you owned, then refuse to take it from your begging and pleading hands. Loki is a master of practical jokes, even by the admission of Hermes and Paddy, who are grandmasters themselves; Hermes by temperament, Paddy by upbringing. Leprechauns are notorious for practical jokes. If you don't believe me, stop by any Saint Patrick's Day but make sure your life and medical insurance is paid up.

Loki and Prometheus seemed to share a bond that made them closer than brothers, even if their temperaments were at opposite ends of the spectrum. Spending millennia being tortured at the whim of the all-father of a pantheon gives them something in common that no one else can truly understand. They spoke in quiet tones while listening to the band.

What a band it was. Shanna and Lori were the lead singers, a banshee and siren respectively. Lori's voice was a thing of absolute beauty, musical crystal, if you will. A song, and you fell hopelessly in love with her. How many men can say they heard not only the siren's song, but her whole set? Shanna, the boss' cousin, sang with the sadness of the ages carried on each of her words, normally shrill and reserved for the nearly departed. She, you wanted to wrap your arms around, comfort, and protect, as her voice touched that inner sanctum of the soul we all keep sorrow and heartache boarded up in, lest we give up on life. Outside, each lady's voice meant death. Here, their song blended divinely, no different from that of two extremely talented mortals.

As for the rest of the band, there was Gabriel on trumpet. Jericho was also in the horn section. He really brought the house down. Heimdal also sat in on sax. Hermes would join in every so often on any of a dozen instruments.

At one table sat Joseph, the formerly Wandering Jew. For the past several months he had been able to rest here after two millennia on the hoof. Now I guess he should be called the stationary Jew. Joseph was swapping stories with Father Mike Ryann and a gentleman who had an albatross necklace lying on the table beside him. Rope burns marked his neck where he had wore the avian jewelry. None of the stories even touched on sea cruises. Ismael had returned and was buying the round. Pineapple juice for him, beer for his companions.

Three older but lovely ladies at the next table beckoned to me. As our waitress, Toni, was busy taking orders elsewhere, I went over. They seemed to be arguing who was the hottest, most beautiful one. As I arrived to take their order, I found out drinks were not what they had in mind.

"What is your name, handsome?" one asked.

"Murphy. Murph to my friends and customers."

"I hope we can become good friends, Murph," purred one of the three. The more matronly of the trio harrupmhed at the implied offer.

"Murph, we would like you to settle a bet for us. Which of us do you think..."

Before she could complete the question and I could answer, Hercules arrived. Herc put his hand, gently but firmly, on my shoulder and led me away saying, "Sorry ladies, Murphy has a previous engagement. Besides, didn't you all learn your lesson the first time?"

Indignantly, they turned their delightful noses up at his suggestion.

"Stay away from them, Murph. When they get together it is bad news. Especially my stepmother."

"Thanks, Herc," I said, having finally figured out who the trio were. I made my way back toward the bar, but I did not get far. The hands of Hermes pulled me atop a table to join him, Ra and Father Mike in an Irish jig. On the table to our right, a group of sailors were dancing with Demeter and her daughter, Persephone. Persephone's husband, Pluto, was sitting across the room, glum and pouting because Paddy again had refused to let him cater. His realm hadn't had many new arrivals in quite some time and anyone who ate his fare would be obligated to go to Hades. He had spent most of the day moaning with Hel who had been having similar problems. The other death deities steered clear of the pair, finding them too depressing. Death himself, tonight going by the name John Thanatos, was doing his best to avoid them. He was at a party and did not want to discuss business.

On the table behind them, Paddy and Rebecca were doing the tango. Rebecca was leading. One might think Paddy would be worried by all this dancing atop tables, but he wasn't. He had the tables made special for that purpose. Claims they could hold a dancing elephant, which technically they were if one looked at the trunked and tusked form of Ganesh break–dancing atop another.

When the day began, it was bright and sunny, but as we danced atop the furniture, the outside became the tiredest of clichés–a dark and stormy night. Fred came in from outside and cut in on Rebecca with Paddy.

"Boss, we have a situation outside," Fred told Paddy, do-si-doing. It was then that Paddy noticed the torrents of rain pounding the night streets faster than the sewer drains could carry them away.

"What's going on?" Paddy asked.

"Battle of the stormers. Thor got to boasting about his control of the weather. Lucas called him on it. They stepped outside, across the street." Outside of Bulfinche's influence. "Lucas went first and caused a respectable squall. Thor called down a thunder and lightning storm which dwarfed Lucas' attempt. Then Tarnis got in on the fun, adding to the gale. Coco Joe increased the tempest. Next Perkunuoes and Marduk joined in, adding hail. Finally the father and son team of Veric and Dyaus tag–teamed the others, who in turn joined forces against them."

"Oboy," said Paddy.

Meanwhile, I had turned on the weather channel. There was an emergency broadcast system warning, describing the sudden appearance of two hurricane fronts over the East River and the east side of Manhattan. Tornadoes were traveling down Park, Lexington, and Third avenues. Ball lightning was taunting the giant TV in Time's Square. Amazingly, no damage had occurred yet, at least outside. I relayed the info to the boss.

Ismael Macob joined the onlookers who had wandered outside to watch the match. Drenched from head to toe, he waltzed in the door, literally, with Bubastis, of the Egyptian gang. She was leading. Her feline head purred with delight. Originally Ismael, being a devout Muslim, had some difficulty accepting the gods of his ancestors, but he seems to have gotten over that. Ismael's wife, Mona, followed him in, merenguing with Anubis, Bubastis' jackal–headed uncle. The four joined the group of us around the TV. Considering the physical aspects of the Macobs' dancing partners, I could not resist the obvious pun.

"Raining cats and dogs out there, huh?"

"Yes, I almost stepped in a poodle on the way over here," answered Anubis with a mongrel smile. Bubastis purred with laughter, preening herself clean with her tongue. An oddly sensual experience to watch. Noticing my interest, she slinked over my way and asked me to scratch behind her ears. I happily obliged and tried to remember where Paddy kept the catnip.

"It could be worse," said Ismael, barely able to contain himself.

"How?" asked Fred, not knowing any better.

"It could be hailing taxi's," answered Ismael, unable to suppress a grin. Paddy threw his soaking form back out into the rain, aided by Mona.

The singers had taken a break and Kali had gotten up on stage to fill the gap. Problem was, all she wanted to sing was "I Want To Hold Your Hand."

Meanwhile, Lori had gone over to one of the boys from the fleet, and was successfully flirting with him. I only heard the siren's opening line.

"New in town, sailor?"

Dion, observing the scene, turned to me and proclaimed, "Lori is only a sailor's daughter but all the seamen know her."

Paddy heard the line and grabbed Dion and threw him out after Ismael.

Shortly, a poker game got started in the corner between Paddy, Hermes, Loki, Rebecca, Mosie, Nero Domitian, and the Coyote. No one else had the nerve to sit in, although with all the cheating going on, it was pretty evenly matched. I counted no less than twelve aces in the deck. By house rules, cheating is fair, so long as you don't get caught.

Mista, the Valkyrie, had come over by me to watch the game.

"Believe it or not, Thor and Loki used to team up to play bridge together. A killer team. They cheated, of course. They were able to communicate what they had wordlessly," Mista let me know.

"How did they do that?" I asked.

"Haven't you ever heard of Norse code?" was her reply. Paddy, who had been in hearing distance, got up from the game, grabbed hold of Mista and threw her, armor and all, out into the rain. It had got so that being wet was a badge of honor for bad puns this evening. I was disappointed; I was still dry.

Pan had arrived while I was not looking. Dion and Fred were taking turns embracing him. They introduced me and I shook hands. Pan felt this was a rude greeting and hugged me instead. I just wished he had not put his tongue in my ear.

Fred introduced Toni, who he had a killer crush on. Pan kissed her full on the lips, which was further than Fred had gotten. When she went over to refill the glasses of the poker players, Pan asked his son a question.

"So have you bedded her yet?"

"No, not yet, Father."

"Why not?"

"Because Toni is special. I want our first time to be just as special."

"Anytime is special."

"No. I care about her. I think I love her," Fred said, grimacing at the backlash he expected. It never came.

"Nothing wrong with that," said Pan.

"There isn't?" asked Fred, pleasantly shocked.

"Of course not. I love all the women I am with. I have no problem with that. It is remembering their names that gives me trouble."

"Never mind," Fred said, wandering off to find something to clean up, his head bowed low.

Dion walked over to Pan. "He's a good kid. He just takes after his mother more."

"That he does," said Pan, shaking his head sadly. Paddy, having folded to his old friend the Coyote's bluff, came by to say hi.

"Welcome, Pan."

"Hey, yourself Moran. Don't you have any decent music around here?" he asked. Kali was still singing. Hermes had disconnected the speakers but she only shrieked louder.

"The band is on break now, but if ye think ye can do better ye are welcome to try."

"If I think I can do better? Surely you jest, Gentry. I can outplay anyone in the house."

Paddy chuckled. "Can ye now?"

"You laugh? Who do you think is better than me?"

"Me," said Paddy, smiling.

"You? Faerie folk can't play without benefit of magik."

"I can."

"Is that a challenge?"

"I guess it is."

"Where? When?"

"The stage. Now."

"The stakes?" asked Pan.

"Have to be something appropriate, valuable," said Paddy.

"Money?"

"No," Paddy was cheap for principle's sake. Pan did not have near enough money to interest the boss.

"I got it. Your blues harp against my pipes."

Paddy hesitated for a moment. The harmonica had been a gift from his late wife, Bulfinche.

During that moment, Fred spoke up.

"But Father, you promised me your pipes at my coming of age."

"Not to worry. You don't think I could lose to the likes of him, do you?" Pan asked. Fred didn't answer. He only looked hurt.

That got Paddy riled and made his decision. "Very well, son of a goat and a lonely shepherd. I accept ye terms. Two songs each, the audience decides the winner."

"Deal. You can even go first," Pan said, waving him on toward the stage.

Dion went up to the front saying, "Clear the stage!"

"But I'm not finished yet," Kali said, as Dion lifted her up and carried her off the stage.

"Always leave them wanting more," said Dion. A grateful crowd gave him a standing ovation. Kali, thinking the applause was for her, started blowing kisses with each of her four hands to the crowd. Depositing her in a chair, Dion returned to the stage.

"Folks, we have a treat for you. A contest of champions, a battle of song here on our stage between two minuscule giants. In this corner weighing one hundred and forty pounds, your host, Padriac Moran. In the far corner, weighing in at two ten, the challenger, Pan," Each took their bows, almost refusing to give them back. "You, our audience will decide who is the better musician based on whatever you like. And without further adieu, here is Paddy."

The boss took the stage and the microphone.

"Good evening to one and all. Glad ye all could join with us on this day of celebration. Now let's raise the roof a bit and have some fun."

Paddy put the harp to his lips and music poured out like sweetest honey. He started out with some rock riffs and seamlessly moved into an Irish jig. The jig transformed into a hootenanny. People got up from their seats and began dancing. Finally the song was done and the applause was tremendous.

The spotlight was handed from Leprechaun to Satyr.

"Beat that," challenged Paddy.

"I shall," promised Pan.

Pan did not bother with the microphone and only said one line before he started.

"Let's get naked and party!"

The notes from his pipes came fast and furious, covering dozens of musical styles, yet was something completely different. The music reached into something primal in the listeners and pulled it to the surface. The music lifted and carried us away. Again the crowd danced, with more energy and passion than they had the first time. At some point it ended, but the crowd kept moving for several minutes. When it stopped, the applause was booming, drowning out the thunder from the stormer contest outside.

Now I love the boss and would do anything for him, but I can't say he played better than Pan. In his defense, he had only been playing a little over a hundred years, while Pan had been piping for thousands. One look at the boss's face and I could tell that didn't matter. He knew who had played better.

"I'm doomed Murphy. I am going to lose the harp," said Paddy. "Pan is a hundred times better than me. I can't beat him."

"You're right," I said. "You can't beat him at his own game."

"Thanks for the comfort and encouragement."

"I didn't say you couldn't beat him. You just have to switch games."

Paddy raised a single eyebrow. "What do ye mean?"

"You have no hope of playing happy songs better than Pan. I doubt many people could. I'm surprised you even tried. Upbeat music is not your strong suit. The blues are where you shine. Your music converts your pain over into something beautiful. Recycling on a metaphysical level. People know pain. You can hit them where it counts. In the heart. I suggest you either play the blues or just hand him the harp now."

"When did ye get so wise?"

"Part of being a bartender."

"You are good at ye job."

"Mind telling my boss that?" I asked. "Maybe he'll give me a raise."

"I wouldn't count on it," Paddy grinned. With a determined pose, he walked toward the stage as Pan climbed down.

"Are you that much of a glutton for punishment? You have no hope," Pan mocked, his arm around Jasmine. Pan liked his women big and Jasmine was six foot four with flaming red hair. Unfortunately, Jasmine didn't swing that way and he used a martial arts flip on the satyr. Unfazed, Pan jumped up, kissed Jas on the mouth, then ran off to the other side of the stage.

"Really? Have ye not read the sign over the door on yer way in?" asked Paddy.

"Why? It is in gibberish," said Pan.

"No. It is in Gaelic. It means 'Hope and Happiness Never Die.'" Paddy said. Picking up a salt shaker he handed it to the satyr.

"What's this for?" Pan asked.

"To make eating yer words a bit easier on ye," said Paddy, a devious grin on his face.

Quietly he climbed the steps and again took the mike.

"This song is titled "Gone but not Forgotten" and is dedicated to the love of me life, my dear wife, Bulfinche," said Paddy.

He began, slowly. A wail that Shanna could never hope to match in all her Bansheeing days. The wail flowed into a warble. The song, written by Paddy after Bulfinche's death, had lyrics, but they were not needed. The music told of their love and their life together. The highs and the lows, the devotion and the affection they had together. Their fire and passion. The music made it all real, made the listener a part of the flame. We lived her life though Paddy's eyes and notes. Then the music took a sad turn. We could sense Paddy's frantic search and struggle to save her from her own mortality. The music lifted us as he succeeds, only to be too late. The music stopped and we knew. The pause was a moment of silence. Bulfinche had died. Again. Her new life had lasted but minutes, but each listener mourned her passing no less because of the brevity. Not one eye in the house was dry. People were weeping openly. The Coyote and Ted Brand, the werewolf, howled their pain. Paddy stood silent and alone on the stage.

Again putting his harp to his lips he played, this time of his loss and pain. Of having his heart cut away. Of the great emptiness that can never be made full again. The music, like Paddy's love, kept her memory alive. The song ended hopefully, singing of Paddy's courage to go on, as Bulfinche would have demanded of him. Done, he collapsed exhausted onto a stool. The place was silent. Not one person dared break the silence or sully it with applause.

Pan, silent, walked up to the stage and placed his pipes at Paddy's feet, admitting defeat without even playing his second song. He poured the entire contents of the salt shaker on his tongue and swallowed. Fred watched the entire transaction and his sadness deepened as his saw his birthright given away.

I looked over to the corner where John Thanatos sat. As I mentioned earlier, John is actually the Grim Reaper. John and Paddy had worked out the details of their deal, so he was allowed to visit the bar in mortal form. He had sat spellbound through the entire song. Tears rolled down his cheek. He looked the same, but his eyes were different. For the first time in his existence he realized, and vicariously felt, the pain he inflicted when he took the life of someone who was loved. The music had changed him more than any other listener. I doubted he would ever be able to look at his job the same way again.

The silence was overwhelming. Dion raised up his glass in a simple yet eloquent toast. "To Bulfinche!"

As one we answered him. "To Bulfinche!"

The celebration resumed its previous momentum.

I brought drinks to a table where Vulcan, his walking cane by his side, was sitting and drinking with two other men. Vulcan looked about sixty, with a bushy head and beard of dusty gray hair. His drinking companions were Pluto and Mars. Mars and Vulcan go back a long way, none of it good. They have competed over a woman, which in the end neither man won the heart of. Mars, a big burly guy, is an arms dealer, but Vulcan, a master weapons maker, just for spite tends to sell higher quality, lower priced, less lethal weapons to Mars' competition. Pluto just likes to argue. Presently they were discussing glory days and who was the most important of the three. Vulcan was being tag–teamed.

"Our temples dwarfed yours. Even Janus will admit that," boasted Pluto.

"Leave that two faced Janus out of this," said Mars. "Your temples were barely shacks compared to ours."

"Perhaps, but a shrine still exists to me. Can either of you say the same?" asked Vulcan.

"A shrine? I would hardly call a statue in Birmingham, Alabama, a shrine. Besides, each of us has a planet named after us," bragged Mars. "Mine of course being the most written about."

"The days of Martians are past. Plutonians never even made the bestseller list. My planet, however, is mentioned frequently in books that make the bestseller list and on TV shows watched again and again by millions."

"There is no planet named after you," informed Pluto.

"Really?" asked Vulcan, standing up and taking hold of his cane. "I beg to differ. Let me help your memory with this parting blessing," said Vulcan, as he lifted his hand up and parted his middle and ring fingers in a familiar hand gesture. "Live long and prosper." Pluto and Mars frowned. Vulcan smiled and walked away to consult with Roy G. Biv about souping up his wheelchair.

Meanwhile, Samson was standing with the three ladies who made Trojan a household name. They asked him to decide the same question they had asked me earlier. He informed them, since he was unable to see, he would have to use other, more tactile methods, to determine their beauty. They agreed and presently he was enjoying letting his hands lead the way over hills and valleys.

A group dressed up like aliens, medieval lords, ladies, and starfleet personnel came in, ordered drinks and looked around. One of them called me over.

"This is great. No fireplace, right?" she asked.

"Nope. Don't break any glasses either or you're buying them, then cleaning them up."

"We love bars. That's what we do, look for them. We've searched out in Suffolk County along 25A for years. We've gone overseas and walked along the Thames, listening for the sound of newspaper presses for days, finding nothing. Then today, the freak weather starts, and we follow the rainbow here."

"Congratulations," I said.

"You wouldn't happen to have the addresses of any other famous bars, would you?" she asked, running off the names of more than a half dozen more, some not even accessible from this time, planet or reality.

"Sorry, can't help you there," I said.

"No problem. Half the fun is in the searching. We'll start back up again on the weekend."

In the corner, Gabriel and Mathew were trying to answer an age old philosophical question by doing a jig on a bowling pin. Of course, they both kept falling off, so perhaps we will never know how many angels can dance on the head of the pin.

Gabe was a bit of a rebel and Mathew's mentor, not to mention a New Yorker. Of the heaven born, he alone could be trusted not to turn Mathew and Ryth in.

Dr. Russ Idolatrous, our resident shrink, was buying Hermes a drink and offering to help him beat his kleptomania. The stormers had called it a night, despite it being more of a morning, and I still hadn't been thrown into the rain for a bad pun. No winner was determined in the weather-off. They had ended actually teaming up, and the result was two feet of snow just on the street in front of the bar. A snowball fight had broken out and nobody was trying to fix it. Judah Maccabee, who's at least seven—feet–tall, had rolled a three foot snow ball and dropped it over Fred's head, effectively burying him. The kid barely noticed it, he was so upset. Even the sight of Toni smiling failed to turn his head.

Paddy set out to change Fred's mood. "Fred, come here," said Paddy.

"Yes?" asked Fred.

"You have been doing a great job here. So good, in fact, that ye deserve a bonus."

"Money?" asked Fred.

"I would not insult ye with money," said Paddy.

"Feel free to insult me. As large an insult as you like. Six, seven zeros. Don't worry. I can take it," I said.

"Shut up, Murphy," ordered Paddy. "No, Fred. I have something I think ye might like much better. I seem to have come into these pipes and I have no use for them," Paddy lied. He gathers artifacts. Pan's pipes would have been a prized addition to his collection. But Fred was family.

"My father's pipes? I don't know what to say," Fred blathered.

"Try thank you," suggested Paddy.

"Thanks, boss," Fred said, hugging the old man.

"Enough of that. Try playing," suggested Paddy. Fred did. The horrible sounds that came out made me wonder if it was the same instrument.

"Perhaps ye should practice some more," Paddy said. Fred lifted the pipes as if to play. "But not here. Somewhere far away, and preferably soundproof." Fred ran over to Toni, grabbed her hand and pulled her over to the door that leads to the parking garage. "Stay away from Cerberus, ye hear. Ye will scare the poor pups with those sounds."

Pan had seen the whole exchange.

"Moran, I want to thank you for what you did for my boy. I did promise him the pipes. I was just certain I would win."

"Say no more. Bulfinche's takes care of its own," said Paddy.

"I really haven't been much of a father to the boy," said Pan.

"It is never too late to start," said Paddy.

"But how?" asked Pan.

"Be understanding of his feelings toward Toni. She may be your daughter-in-law some day," said Paddy.

"A child of mine marrying? The shame of it."

"Don't knock it till you try it."

"Not for me," said Pan as shrieking pipe sounds came from the garage.

"Ye could also give the boy lessons on those pipes. I would consider it a personal favor," said Paddy.

"I will see what I can do," offered Pan, heading toward the garage.

"Paddy, Pan was right. That was a great thing you did for Fred," I said.

"Thanks, Murphy," said Paddy.

"I mean, how many people can say they made someone's pipe dreams come true?" I said.

Paddy merely looked at me, shook his head, and walked away.

I turned and saw Madeline Raymond, Hermes' lady friend, talking to the Coyote. She was up to her old tricks and was trying to set him up with her neighbor's French poodle.

My attention was drawn away from their conversation by the sensation of running water over my head. Paddy had poured a pitcher of ice water, mixed from the snow outside, over me.

"Thank you," I said. "I was beginning to develop a complex."

"You're welcome. Now clean up this spill," Paddy ordered.

"Okay, Paddy," I said.

A table in the corner was playing spin the bottle with Tommy inside. It was not his bottle. I've heard of drinks stirred and shaken, but this was a new one. Spinning Jinn. Three of the ladies playing were in Demeter's sewing club. Very famous ladies. Go by a bunch of names: The Fates; The Norns; The Weird Sisters; The Manhattan

Sewing Club. The youngest and prettiest, who these days goes by the name of Sue, spun the bottle too hard and it flew off the table and landed at my feet. I picked it and Tommy up and brought it back to the table.

"Tommy," I said looking into the neck of the bottle. "If I put seltzer in this bottle sluggishly would that make you a slow jinn fizz?"

"No, but it might cause me to start singing 'Tiny Bubbles'," Tommy said.

"Or it might cause me to start quoting old Bill," said the oldest of the Fates, who calls herself Maggie. Usually collect. Worries her friends. Maggie looked about a hundred and five and forgot to put her teeth in today. A large mole complete with four hairs growing out of it adorned her left check. She squinted one eye when she talked. "Bubble, bubble, toil and trouble, tea boils and seltzer bubbles." Maggie took the bottle from my hands and spun it round. It stopped and was pointed straight at me.

"C'mon and give me a kiss, honey," she cackled.

"Really, it's all right," I said, trying to back away gracefully. The third Weird Sister, Joan, who looked around fifty and was not unattractive, blocked my retreat.

"Good then. Get on with it," Maggie demanded.

"But..." I stuttered.

"Pucker up!" shouted Edgar Tonic, who was also playing the game.

"You are tempting Fate," warned Maggie.

"I can close a button on my shirt if I am being too provocative," I offered. It was declined. Maggie wrapped her arms around my neck and pulled me in. I tried for the cheek.

"No, Murphy. Full on the lips."

"I guess I might as well resign myself to my Fate," I said, completing the kiss. It was quick and painless and dark with my eyes closed the whole while.

Maggie let go of my neck. "Your Fate? Don't go rushing things now Murphy. One kiss doesn't mean you own me. I am my own woman."

"I'll try and remember that, Maggie. I have to get back to work now," I said.

"But Murphy, it is your turn," purred Bubastis, who was also playing the game. She started to clean her shoulder fur with her catlike tongue.

Maggie whispered in my ear. "If you spin, I promise it will land on the cat lady."

"If you don't want the pussy cat, Murphy, I'll take her," came a voice at my feet. It was Coyote.

"In your dreams, fleabag," shot back Bubastis, who had heard every word.

"Anytime," offered Coyote. Bubastis hissed, Coyote growled. I walked back to the bar.

Prometheus was sitting on a stool talking to Father Mike.

"You ever regret doing it?" Mike asked.

Prometheus looked around at the glorious chaos before answering. "No. Although sometimes I wonder. I was talking to Madeline before, and told her I had just ended a relationship."

I could not resist. "The temptation of Prometheus on the rebound was too much for the matchmaker," I said. The now familiar sensation of snowy water pouring down was upon me again.

"Ignore Murphy, Prometheus," said Paddy. "The rest of us do."

"Actually he was right. She wanted to fix me up."

"Consider yourself lucky," said the Coyote, hopping on a stool and putting his paws on the bar, lapping up whiskey from a bowl. "The first question she asked me was if I was fixed. I'm not even broke."

Thor meanwhile had joined in with the band for the song "It's Hammer Time."

"Women. Bah! Who needs them?" spat Loki into his beer. It was obvious he did. He missed his wife. Hated himself for overestimating Signe's understanding and endurance. Also, his night was about over, and it was almost time for him to go back to his punishment; he would not go gracefully. The raven had stopped no less than four escape attempts. There would be more by the time the sun rose and the Rainbow Bridge was again summoned by the opening of the fire hydrant.

"Prometheus, what did you ever get out of your gift?" I asked, knowing the punishment he endured before Herc freed him.

"The satisfaction of knowing that I did the right thing," he answered.

"Ha. Some comfort there," scoffed Loki.

"It is actually. Have you ever tried it?" asked Prometheus.

"Not in this lifetime," said Loki.

"Except once," added Paddy.

"Except once," agreed Loki.

"How did it feel?" asked Prometheus. Loki muttered something. Prometheus asked "What was that?"

"Good," he whispered, embarrassed by his own words. "I have to go to the bathroom," Loki said heading off to the back, the raven in close proximity.

I walked over to the pile of belongings we had taken off the monkey boys earlier and found what I was looking for. A gold plated flip top lighter. I brought it over to the bar and engraved a message on it with a fork. Done, I handed it to Prometheus.

"What's this?" he asked.

"Read it," I said.

It read:

Prometheus,

Thank you for the start. Hope we can forever keep the light burning brightly against the darkness.

Murphy-
Self–Appointed Representative of the Human Race.

"I will treasure it always," said Prometheus, grasping my hand. Loki came racing out of the bathroom, raven in hot pursuit.

"Let me borrow it long enough to fry a raven," he shouted, shielding his eyes from beak and claw.

"There are no windows in the bathroom large enough for him to get out," I said.

"True, but that wouldn't stop him from trying," said Paddy.

"Knowing the fascination you two leggers have with indoor plumbing, he probably tried to flush his way to freedom," said the Coyote.

Rumbles the clown had just beaten Mars at air hockey for the fourth game. Mars was not losing gracefully.

Tom Finkas, who came to us after a near death experience, sat down next to John Thanatos.

"I could swear we have met before," Tom said.

"WE HAVE," said John. "YOU JUST WERE NOT READY."

"You a cabbie like Ismael or something?"

"NO. DO NOT WORRY. YOU WILL REMEMBER EVENTUALLY. IN THE MEANTIME, LET ME BUY YOU A DRINK," John said, pulling out a pair of old coins.

"Wow," said Tom. "Those coins look ancient. You a collector?"

"YES, BUT NOT OF COINS."

"Where did you get them?"

"GIFTS FROM CLIENTS."

"What business are you in?"

"I HELP PEOPLE MOVE ON."

"Moving business, huh? Much money in that?" asked Tom.

I arrived with their drinks. Fuzzy navel for Tom, a zombie for John. "You might say he makes a killing," I said. John gave me a dirty look.

"MURPHY EXAGGERATES, BUT IT IS A LIVING," John said, smiling. I think it was his attempt at a joke. It was not up to par with some of the others, but for him it was a huge effort, so I dumped some cold water on his head. Instead of being annoyed, Death actually smiled. He enjoyed being included in our living games. Tom looked at both of us strangely. I shrugged my shoulders and moved on, having gotten picked up by a conga line headed by Grace Devine and Hard Rider. Nero was sandwiched between them. Nellie, Shellie, Corny and Brian followed behind, thrilled to be up past their bedtimes.

The party went on till dawn, but then the crowds started to thin down from mobbed to merely crowded. Some folks, like Robigus, had no choice but to leave. Others, like Ismael and Edgar, had jobs to go to. Oddly, Rebecca had actually left to check on her streets, and she was returning as most people were leaving. She helped every morning to help set up our breakfast for the homeless and hungry. Father Mike and Demeter pulled themselves away to help her. Pan and Fred made peace, for now. The Norse trickster's escape attempts were all unsuccessful. Heimdal and the raven escorted Loki back to his place of imprisonment. I felt sorry for the guy. Bubastis wished me goodbye with a kiss, as did Maggie. A few dozen folks lingered. Demeter was still debating on whether or not to tell her son-in law that dozens of the denizens of his realm were obliged to her, having eaten of her food on my visit to Hades. Gabriel looked the other way as Mathew and Ryth left. The Day was still far from over.

The homeless, after having breakfast, joined the party. Shanna, Lori and the rest

of the band played on.
As did we all.

MURPHY'S ⊚ LORE:™

PATRICK THOMAS

ISBN 1-890096-07-5 $14.00 US

TALES FROM BULFINCHE'S PUB
Patrick Thomas

See how it all started with Murphy & the rest of the gang. The orignal collection is back with 4 all new stories about leprechaun Paddy Moran's bar at the end of the rainbow, where Dionysus pours the drinks and Hercules watches the door. The name of the place is Bulfinche's Pub. It is a second home to the legends of our day and a beacon to troubled souls, all lead there by the simple magic of the rainbow. One never knows what will come in the door next: Armageddon, or aterrified man with no socks. Whatever happens, two things are certain ope and Happiness never die, and the first drink is always on the house.

"A MASTEPIECE. THE MUST READ OF THE YEAR." -**MURPHY'S MOM**

"I COULDN'T PUT IT DOWN. Murphy glued it to my hand."-**ROY G.BIV**, *parapelgic clown, patron*

"WORTH ITS WEIGHT IN GOLD, at least in trade paperback." -**PADDY MORAN**, *Leprechaun. Owner & Proprietor of Bulfinche's Pub*

"DEVILISHLY CLEVER." -**MATHEW**, *Angel on the lam. Dishwasher.*

PRAISE FOR THE MUPRPHY'S LORE SERIES:
"AMUSING STUFF. WONDERFUL STUFF."   -*Andrew Andrews*, **TRUE REVIEW**
"I WAS THOROUGHLY ENCHANTED... AN OFF THE SCALE BOOK."
                                          -*Leann Arndt*, **THE BUZZ BOOK REVIEW**
"A DELICIOUS COCKTAIL OF HUMOR, FANTASY & HEART WITH A DASH OF SUSPENSE THAT YOU WON'T BE ABLE TO PUT DOWN."   -*Beth Hannan Rimmels*, **THE LONG ISLAND VOICE**
"WANT TO LEAVE YOUR LIFE BEHIND? THEN FOLLOW ME TO BULFINCHE'S PUB... THE CLIENTELE WILL NEVER CEASE TO AMAZE YOU."   -*Michael Laimo*, **PIRATE WRITINGS**
"HERE MAGIC IS THE NORM... MURPHY'S LORE OFFERS THE READER A LOOK AT THE WORLD BEYOND."   -*Alan Zimmerman*, **THE NEW YORK PRESS**
"OUTRAGEOUS..."   -**THE TIMES BEACON RECORD**

FOOL'S DAY
Patrick Thomas

Murphy & the gang are back. This time it's April Fool's Day, the annual contest to determine the best trickster. Most of the regulars have headed for the hills, in an attempt to avoid trouble. Trouble comes calling anyway, and it's up to a handful of tricksters to face off Faerie royalty Mab and Oberon, not to mention the US Air Force, before they start a war that unleashes deadly Nuclear Magic™ on an unsuspecting Earth.

"I LAUGHED, I CRIED, I FELT HUMAN AGAIN. Not that that's a compliment by any stretch of the imagination."
          -**COYOTE**, *Native American Tricker god*
"MORE FUN THAN A BARREL OF HUMANS. Even one going over Niagra Falls." -**SUN WUKONG**, *The Monkey King*

ISBN 1-890096-11-3 $14.00 US

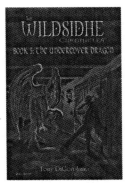
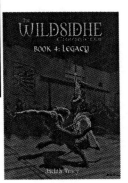
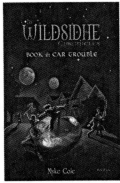

THE BEST OF
PIRATE WRITINGS
Tales Of Fantasy, Mystery & Science Fiction Vol. 1
Edited By Edward J. McFadden
Trade Paperback ISBN 1-89009604-0; US $12.95; 224 Pages
27 New Illustrations;
Limited Editions include:
100 Numbered Trade Paperbacks Signed By Editor $19.95 US
26 Lettered Hardcover Signed By Editor $75 US *ISBN 1-890096-06-7*

Christine Beckert - David Bischoff
Carroll Brown - Jack Cady
Jennifer B. Crow - Charles de Lint
Paul DiFilippo - Alan Dean Foster
Esther M. Friesner - Ed Gorman
Geoffrey A. Landis - Sharianne Lewitt
Ardath Mayhar - Edward J. McFadden III
- Bobbi Sinha-Morey - Leland Neville
Lyn Nichols - E. Jay O Connell
G.F. O Sullivan - Tom Piccirilli
Robert J. Randisi - Mike Resnick
Jessica Amanda Salmonson - A.J. Scott
Timothy S. Sedore - Eric Sonstroem
- Nancy Springer - Allen Steele - Sue Storm
and
Roger Zelazny
(One Of The Last Amber Stories)

PIRATE WRITINGS has been providing countless readers young and old, with cutting
edge & traditional fiction since the winter of 1992.
THE BEST OF PIRATE WRITINGS
is a premiere collection of the very best of the magazine s tales featuring the talents of
all the authors listed above.

Pirate Writings looks fabulous   quite an achievement ....
Dean R. Koontz

The contents [of *Pirate Writings*] are excellent.
Science Fiction Chronicle

"Sign on under the flag of McFadden's Jolly Roger now!"
Paul Di Filippo, **Asimov's**

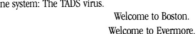